Roland Vernon was born in 1961 and educated at Eton, King's College Cambridge, and the Royal College of Music. Between the ages of sixteen and twenty-eight he spent about four months of every year in Greece, developing a close affinity with the country, its people and history. After a brief career as a professional singer, he settled in the countryside, dividing his time between writing and managing his own small rural business. He is the author of several biographical books about musicians, and, most recently, *Star in the East*, a biography of the philosopher Jiddu Krishnamurti. He lives in Somerset with his wife and three sons, and still visits Greece as regularly as his commitments allow.

A Dark Enchantment is the inaugural winner of the *Daily Mail* First Novel Award, an exciting partnership between the *Daily Mail* and Transworld Publishers to discover new British writing talent.

To find out more about the *Daily Mail* First Novel Award and how you can enter for next year's award visit www.dailymail.co.uk/books or www.booksattransworld.co.uk.

A DARK ENCHANTMENT

Roland Vernon

BLACK SWAN

TRANSWORLD PUBLISHERS
61-63 Uxbridge Road, London W5 5SA
A Random House Group Company
www.rbooks.co.uk

A DARK ENCHANTMENT
A BLACK SWAN BOOK: 9780552775007

First publication in Great Britain
Black Swan edition published 2008

A CIP catalogue record for this book
is available from the British Library.

Addresses for Random House Group Ltd companies outside the UK
can be found at: www.randomhouse.co.uk
The Random House Group Ltd Reg. No. 954009

The Random House Group Limited supports The Forest Stewardship Council
(FSC), the leading international forest certification organisation. All our titles
that are printed on Greenpeace approved FSC certified paper carry the FSC
logo. Our paper procurement policy can be found at
www.rbooks.co.uk/environment

Typeset in 10.5/12.5pt Giovanni Book by
Falcon Oast Graphic Art Ltd.

Printed in the UK by CPI Cox & Wyman, Reading, RG1 8EX.

2 4 6 8 10 9 7 5 3 1

This book is dedicated to my eldest,
my Freddie

Acknowledgements

I would like to thank those who assisted me in researching the background for this book, those who supported the project from its conception, and those who helped polish the manuscript. Foremost amongst these was Irene Noel-Baker, who did all the above and helped me with various linguistic conundra (including, after much deliberation, settling on the names Thasofolia and Pyroxenia). I also acknowledge, with much affection, the encouragement and help of her late mother, Barbro Noel-Baker, now mourned by all who knew her, who was herself a fine historian of nineteenth-century English philhellenes.

Several people contributed their time generously by reading the manuscript and suggesting amendments, most importantly, Cecilia Fattorini, Emma Craigie, Carol O'Brien, Fiona Massari, and my mother, Min Peake. Others contributed valuable ideas from a more professional perspective, most notably Andrew Lownie (and his several readers), but also Jim Cochrane and Natasha Fairweather. My former agent, Caroline Davidson, helped considerably by allowing me to consult her notes for first-time novelists, a document which, despite its crushing pessimism, helped me to avoid some of the main pitfalls!

My agent, Annabel Merullo, has been a rock of support and confidence, and certainly helped to rescue this book from the oblivion to which – at one point – I believed it was destined. And then came along Francesca Liversidge and her fellow judges of the *Daily Mail* First Novel Award, and all was well. I thank them all for choosing this novel for the prize, and also the whole team at Transworld Books for their friendly, dynamic approach. Thanks, too, to Ted Damamme, my father-in-law, who suggested submitting the manuscript for the Award.

And then there is darling Helen, whose belief in this novel never for a moment wavered, whose unconditional support lightened my gloomiest moments, whose optimism is worth a million prizes, and who makes every day for me a gala.

Main characters

Thomas Brooke (deceased)
m. Rebecca (deceased)

Mag Brooke   Edgar Brooke   Percival Brooke   Alithea Brooke
             m. Eliza (deceased)   (deceased)

Lydia Brooke   Daniel Brooke

Godwin Tudor – photographer, gentleman traveller
Sir Harold Tudor – statesman, Godwin's father

George Farkas – agricultural industrialist
Mrs Farkas – his wife

John Straker – English diplomat in Athens, and old school
friend of Godwin's

Sir Thomas Wishart – English Minister (Ambassador) in
Athens
Lady Wishart – his wife

Fortinbras Pierrepont – English engineer in Greece

Samuel Hill (deceased) – briefly Thomas Brooke's business
partner and co-owner of Thasofolia estate

Prince Leopold – member of a north German royal dynasty

Petros Cameron Solouzos – politician. Deputy (parliamentary representative) for the island of Pyroxenia

Elias Lambros – Edgar Brooke's estate foreman, and Mayor of Thasofolia village
Katina Lambros – his wife
Demetrios Lambros – chief brigand, nephew of Elias Lambros. Also Edgar's godson
Christos, Pandelis, Adonis, Petros, Theodoros – brigands, members of Demetrios' gang (latter two are brothers)

Barba Stamos – chief cook at Thasofolia
Panayiotis – Edgar Brooke's chief male servant, son of Barba Stamos
Maroula – chambermaid at Thasofolia, Panayiotis' sister, daughter of Barba Stamos

PART ONE

Chapter 1

The first-class passengers were affronted by the way the captain and chief steward had handled the situation that morning in Messina, and they exchanged their outrage in fiery terms with fellow ticket-holders. So fiery, in fact, that a detached observer might have said their high-pitched, animated voices betrayed a sense of excitement rather than anger. For all their annoyance they were alive now in a way they had not been at dinner the previous night, or, indeed, at any time since coming on board at Marseilles. It was perhaps because they sensed the Orient was now upon them.

Their complaint was that untold numbers of riff-raff had been let on at the Sicilian port, and as the steamer had already been complete with European passengers, the new arrivals ended up being herded, baggage, livestock and accompanying vermin, on to the only remaining open spaces, including the upper weather deck and the interior first-class deck. Benches and chairs were thrown aside in the hurry to lay down sheepskin rugs, cushions and quilts. Assorted Levantine journeymen – wizened elders and shriek-ing children, the bearded and the veiled – fought for a patch to roll out their belongings, and in no time the old French vessel's decks were teeming with cross-legged figures in coloured silks and turbans. Those in the know had paid coins to shoeless boys from the quayside who slipped aboard soon after the ship docked and were still busy scampering

13

around the deck, dodging each other to reserve the remaining deck space for a few pennies a plot.

The first-class ticket-holders complained that their promenade would be curtailed and that surely some mistake had been made; but the new passengers, deaf to such protestations, spread themselves out comfortably, clan encamped back to back against clan, babbling in multiple dialects, playing with strings of beads and singing songs. The men smoked cheroots and spat husks from their mouths, while their womenfolk broke bread and peeled garlic. A cross-beat of drummed rhythms, dislocated melodies and burbled voices pervaded the scene like a subdued carnival above the continuous rumble of the ship's engines. Those European passengers who had been at breakfast when the invasion occurred now noticed a pungent scent hanging in the morning air, smoky, spicy and unclean; it drifted down the decks past the polished brass window frames of the upper-class salons. The occasional gentleman would still venture out of these quarters, but most of the ladies confined themselves within, safe from unsavoury sights and smells or perhaps worse by night. After their initial outrage had subsided, they whispered to each other breathlessly about it over their coffee, where one of them, a spinster from America, fell into a swoon at the talk of dusky cut-throats and slave-snatchers, and had to be carried back to her cabin in the ladies' section.

The wind had vanished and it turned into an unusually hot day for early October; but by the evening, when the sun set over a glass-still Ionian Sea, the air outside began to nip. In the half-light they glided past a wooden fishing vessel which was rocked, but only gently, on ripples created by the passing steamer. Those who cared to look would have just made out the figure of a stooping fisherman illuminated by a candle in the boat's cabin, sitting down alone to his evening meal.

One passenger leaning against the ship's rail noticed the

little scene as he lifted his collar up around his neck and folded his arms in front to warm up. His rather aquiline nose had begun to redden in the chill. He wore neat and well-fitted clothes, fashionable but not flamboyantly so. He looked about thirty years old, a good age: young and athletic enough still to be called a fine young man, with all the handsomeness that description implied; fresh enough still to be innocent to wonders and novelties, and yet old enough not to allow his heart to leap at the first hint of beauty, not to swallow the world and its promise without first tasting and recognizing its constituents.

His name was Godwin Tudor and he had been on this spot for several hours, having picked his way across the deck-dwellers earlier in the day to find a place to observe the view. As he gazed at the passing waters fading in the gloom he was brought abruptly back to his senses by an awareness that he was not alone. A short and stocky young man had arrived beside him, wrapped in a fur-collared coat with a black hat pulled low. He had a fresh face with soft, almost blushing skin that seemed too young to sustain the thick dark moustache that hung beneath his nose. He introduced himself as George Farkas, an Englishman of Greek parentage returning to the land of his ancestors in order to fulfil a commission on behalf of his father, Theodore Farkas, of Liverpool, recently deceased. He spoke briskly above the background drone of the engines, a sound which Godwin felt as a distant tremor in the varnished wood of the ship's rail.

Mr Farkas explained that his family had left their village in northern Greece sixty years before; they had settled in Liverpool, taken jobs at a mill, and from humble beginnings had risen meteorically. He was now the proud head of a farm machinery empire, building traction engines, hay-loaders, potato-spinners. 'And we are planning to take the machines out into the field, to plough and harvest. You may have heard of us. Farquharson. Appointed to the Crown Estates,

15

the Duchies of Devonshire, Cornwall, and the Cooperative Association of Norfolk Grain Producers, to name a few.'

'Of course,' said Godwin with a genuine smile. 'Your machinery is the envy of every farm in the land.'

'You are really much too kind, and that is an exaggeration,' replied the young man, looking out at the dark seascape with a satisfied smile, as if he were surveying his own estate, boundless in size and yield. 'But did you know that half a century ago we were not Farquharson, but Farkas and Son. And we were not the only ones. There are others like us, who found fortune beyond the shores of their enslaved homeland. I tell you, now that Greece is free from the Turkish yoke there will soon be no nation on earth to compete with her. We are a people who not only take opportunities, we make 'em. And we have our ports, our wonderful climate, our position at the navel of the earth between East and West. What a people we will become!'

'You come back often then?' Godwin asked.

Farkas looked ruffled by the question. 'No, actually this is my first visit. But I feel as if I have known the country all my life. The pine and the cypress, the olives shimmering silver in the Aegean breeze against a background of vines and figs, crowned by an azure eternity.' He raised a gloved hand to the black night sky.

'You're a poet as well.'

'I only dabble,' said Farkas shaking his head modestly. 'Yes, this is my first visit, the first of many. I come with three hundred thousand drachmas to build a museum to the memory of my father. Have you any idea how many pounds that is? Ten thousand!'

'What sort of museum?'

'Antiquities, of course. What else?'

'It merely occurred to me that many others have spent fortunes housing relics from Greece's past, but with your expertise you could lend great service to the Greece of today. Perhaps in the area of agriculture.'

Farkas received the comment with a cold stare. 'Sir, we may be men of commerce, but we are also men of culture. Greece did not acquire her rank as the foremost nation of the ancient world merely through the sweat of her labourers and the blood of her foot soldiers. Thankfully, there were men then, as there are men today, set upon a higher goal. Good evening, sir.' He was clearly piqued as he put a finger to his hat and began to weave his way back through the seated groups on the deck, his leaden coat brushing their coloured velvets and silks as he passed. The indelicate footwork he was obliged to undertake, in order to keep his balance, made him curse more than once.

Godwin could not sleep that night and eventually gave up the struggle, turning instead to write his journal. The berth was barely wide enough for him to turn. There was very little other room in his cabin – a seven foot windowless cube – and any spare space was taken up with his photographic equipment; he had insisted on keeping these cases with him rather than store them in the hold, because of their fragility, especially the chemical bottles and sixty-four precious plates. His only company as he lay too cramped to move was the noise of the ship's four engine cylinders and the throb of the monstrous flywheel that cut through the decks from top to bottom at the centre of the vessel; he could distantly hear the restless movement of the chain-links, the hiss of steam valves and the churn of the propeller shaft buried deep below, which sent a shudder down the hull from end to end, through iron and steel, through every joist, dowel, bolt and pane of glass.

Then, close to dawn he was aware of another sound which he did not instantly hear as a human voice, but soon recognized for what it was. He had not heard it before, but had read others' accounts of its extraordinary haunting quality, the very music of exoticism. He leapt from bed, snatched his coat and notebook, and hurried up to the fore weather deck to see and record for himself. He was halted by what he saw when he arrived. The bed rolls and covers had been packed away, and the entire deck, edge to edge, was full of men on their knees, in neat rows, bending forwards on individual mats, lowering their heads towards the bow of the ship. An imam stood on a raised step near the prow and was chanting verses from a book that he held; it was a powerful nose-resonant sound, piercing and twisting through the dawn air like a virtuoso clarinet.

A dull mist hung, rain began to spit and the clouds looked threatening. The lightest part of the sky was directly behind the singing cleric, eastwards, where the clouds had broken, allowing a clear patch for the pre-dawn glow. It was the direction the men on deck were sending their prayers, the same way Godwin now was looking, the way they were all heading. Against the distant area of cloudless sky, a thin blue headland came into view, the coast of Messene, their first view of Greece.

Godwin remained until the ritual's end, watching the headland grow in colour and shape, before it slid majestic-ally around to the port side as the great steamer turned south, its first change of direction since the previous evening. By this time the men had dispersed and the little settlements on the deck had been deftly rearranged for the day ahead.

The weather now closed in and it began to rain heavily. They sailed near enough to the western seaboard of Greece for Godwin to be able to pick out the shapes of far-off bushes and rocks, and to see the occasional cluster of hillside houses beneath dark low cloud. It was a barren wilderness of a landscape, a god-forsaken place, its shores unwelcoming, its hillsides defying habitation.

Rounding Cape Malea in the early afternoon, the steamer turned once more, and now faced due north for the final leg of the journey, the approach to Piraeus, port of Athens. By the time they passed the island of Hydra, night had closed in. Rain now lashed at the windows, blowing horizontal in heavy gusts. The ship lurched from side to side with a forward and back roll, in an unending cycle, the ship's rail shuddered and a sour fragrance of vomit hung in the air. Progress had slowed.

The lights of Piraeus all at once appeared through the impenetrable darkness ahead as they turned into the mouth of the harbour, and Godwin could no longer resist the temptation to go out on deck and watch their arrival. He had pictured Greece so often in his reading and had imagined sailing into this port, with its famously narrow entrance and basin-like interior, but nothing that he had ever read or imagined prepared him for this. Piraeus could not have contrived to be less hospitable. It was eleven o'clock, the rain had settled in for the night and joined with an unruly wind that whipped in from the sea, circling on itself as it hit the shore to blow back from the opposite direction. Hats were tossed off heads, thin soles slipped on the damp deck; ropes, rigging and shackles near and far lashed rhythmically against a forest of swaying ships' masts. The awesome outline of one or two men-of-war could be seen in the deeper water.

It was not the first storm Godwin had weathered on his journey to reach this point. The most fearsome had been the fury of his father. Sir Harold Tudor was a distinguished retired politician with puritan taste and frugal ways, who considered frivolities such as humour and expressions of sentiment to be constituents of an unmasculine temperament. Poetry – excepting that in the English Hymnal – belonged either in the nursery or a woman's boudoir; and notions such as self-fulfilment or career happiness were the very terminology of sin, stuff that an adult should leave behind in childhood, along with toy swords and masturbation, to be replaced by the higher ideal of service. He was deaf to Godwin's protestations about the wonder of travel and the marvels of the Levant, but that came as no great surprise. Sir Harold had been deaf to much of what his son

19

had said throughout his lonely upbringing; and especially since Godwin's inexplicable childhood illness. A succession of doctors – the finest in the land – had reported back to Sir Harold, scratching their learned brows apologetically, and conceding that there was no known scientific cure for 'voices in the head'. Perhaps the boy should be sent to a Mesmerist? And as for the child's long weeks of apparent inertia and inability even to communicate: Sir Harold viewed it all with the deepest suspicion, interpreting it either as a tremendous piece of deception, or, if genuine, as a sort of divine reprimand placed upon himself for having spawned so useless a son. Which was very different from the way he regarded his elder child, Henry, the golden boy who could do no wrong, who had won military glory in India, produced five grandsons, and who now held the parliamentary seat for Salisbury. The sallow-cheeked Godwin had never been able to compete. When, as a teenager, he had recovered from his long illness, equally inexplicably, it served only to reinforce his father's conviction that the whole thing had been concocted.

Sir Harold declared his opposition to Godwin's foreign tour at a formal meeting in his study; and for the duration of the quiet, controlled interview, his outstretched palm was sealed to the surface of his desk in a gesture of indisputable finality. Young men who travelled and who dallied in the so-called gentlemanly pursuit of knowledge, he said, were nothing more than wastrels and burdens to their families. But Godwin had resolved to achieve his end, and devised a plan to justify the trip in his father's eyes. He would pen a pictorial encyclopaedia for schoolchildren, and illustrate it with his own photographs, on the subject of Greek antiquities. It would be the start of great things, he explained, his chance to make good the wasted years. He vowed that the venture would bear fruit and influence, for the good of a whole generation of young gentlemen. The point had been made, and had received a surprising endorsement from his otherwise matrimonially obedient mother. Godwin thereby retained a thread of credibility and was reluctantly allowed to go. But that stormy night in Piraeus, as the steamer's anchor chain rumbled into the black water of the harbour, he felt a chill. He had not anticipated that Greece would be at all like this.

A swarm of rowing boats, with flaming torches in the prow of each, had already begun to cross from the dock, and soon the ship was invaded by guides, porters and hotel touts, energetically recommending themselves and their establishments in a burble of broken French and English. Most of the travellers were too tired and disheartened by the weather to put up much resistance, and allowed themselves to be herded into small groups for the rowing boats. Godwin found one canvasser who declared himself to be commissionaire from the Hotel d'Angleterre in Constitution Square, the very hotel to which he was bound. The man sported an extravagant moustache and was dressed in the customary Greek style, with a thickly pleated white kilt, or *fustanella*, together with woollen stockings and an embroidered jacket. He led Godwin, along with a group of other travellers, to a waiting boat, while near to them a pair of sheep were being slung like medicine balls over the rail and into the hull of a gaudily painted caïque alongside. There they lay on their backs motionless with fear and confusion as they were lassoed tight around the neck. Other items of cargo were piled in from the ship around them – barrels, timber cases and large wicker baskets.

The rain had not let up, but the commissionaire talked incessantly as they crossed over to the customs dock, welcoming them to the most beautiful country in the world, which he would be happy to show them, either by the hour around Athens, or by the day, taking them into the reaches of Attica; every desire could be accommodated. In the meantime they should relax, make themselves 'comme si vous étiez chez vous' in his boat, while he managed the arrival protocol on their behalf.

21

One boat overtook them on the inside and pulled into the dock a few yards in front. Godwin saw the uniformed customs officers step aside and move themselves further down, vacating the area for a smartly dressed reception committee hovering nearby. He then saw Farkas emerge from the boat and climb on to the quay, followed by a young woman, a tiny creature with white skin and round cheeks, like a porcelain doll. The waiting group of portly men now formed a semicircle, and each shook Farkas heartily by the hand while umbrellas were held out to protect him and his wife from the rain. The short formalities complete, they climbed into a collection of what looked like state carriages and drove off into the night.

The guides and touts who had been so predatory on the ship's deck now acted as bodyguards to shield their disembarking passengers from the hordes who waited on the dock. Those passengers who had stuck out and come ashore independently were now swamped by a crowd of opportunists, shoeshines, water-sellers, mule-drivers, beggars and an army of hoteliers' boys. Tempers were short all round, and disappointed touts did not hide their anger, but cursed openly at passengers and spat at the ground by their feet.

It was at this point that Godwin realized he could not account for one of his photographic cases. The hotel commissionaire railed at the porter responsible in the most violent terms and seemed about to strike him, but Godwin intervened, shouting above the growing hubbub that the others should go on into Athens and that he would follow as soon as he had retrieved his case. He then began to fight his way back towards the quay against the tide of people, the wind and the rain, holding firmly on to his hat.

After searching fruitlessly for a while, he decided to retreat into one of several taverns set back from the sea-front, thinking that he would be able to make himself understood to the dockside officials once the rush of disembarkation was over. Relieved to be sheltered from the squall, he took off his wet coat and hat, and was surprised to hear a voice calling him from across the room.

'Mr Tudor, come over and join us.' One of his travelling companions from the steamer was there, a middle-aged Dane called Pedersen who had several times on the journey boasted his familiarity with Greece and the Greeks. Godwin had not particularly taken to him or his complacent assuredness; he was the sort of man who prided himself on being a citizen of the world, the possessor of privileged insights, one who liked to let it be known that he had travelled much, mixing freely with all types of men and cultures, and was therefore qualified to sit in judgement over them.

He was standing with a group of swarthy and moustached men, and they were huddled around a pan of charcoal for warmth, grinning at some piece of shared humour. 'Come and see what we have here,' Pedersen said, and then rattled out a few sentences in Greek to a small elderly man who stood near to him guarding something between his feet. Godwin could now see that the group had gathered there to see what this man had in his possession, and they were all looking to the floor for him to reveal it. Godwin approached, wondering what it could be, so small and low to the ground, that had them all so enthralled. The men were dressed roughly, like country labourers, a few of them in dirty *fustanellas*, and carrying rifles, as though they had returned from a day's hunting. The small man at the centre did not say a word, but stood back to disclose his prize with a blank expression.

'George is very proud of himself,' Pedersen said, nodding in the little old man's direction, 'because today he has not only done a great service for his country, but more importantly he has ensured that he and his family will not starve for the next quarter of a century. Just see what a treasure he has procured for himself.'

The man took something spherical out of a colourful woollen saddle-bag on the floor, and Godwin wondered if it might be some kind of ball, a sporting trophy, perhaps. It was wrapped in cloths which the man now peeled off, not without a slight flourish, and held out his prize for everyone to see. His fist was clenched tight around some silvery hair.

Godwin was not prepared for the sight. It was a man's head, staring sightlessly from between half-closed eyelids, its beard tangled beneath an open mouth, out of which hung a dusty tongue. It was a broad face, with deeply graven lines and dark skin, almost noble, a face that had seen much life, that had loved and loathed its full share. The little crowd let out a cheer of approval, and everyone smiled. One onlooker squeezed its lifeless cheek as if it was a baby. Pedersen sipped his drink and looked at Godwin.

'My God.' Godwin stared at it. 'Oh my God.'

'Mr Tudor, meet Christos Drakos,' said Pedersen gesturing to the head. The skin of its neck had been cut coarsely and dangled down in torn strips, congealed with blood. 'Mr Drakos here was a famous outlaw about twenty years ago, and there has been a very high price on his head – this head – for a long time. He was a legendary personage, and quite ruthless, a thief, a bully and a murderer. Of course, he's been in retirement for a while. Rumour had it he was suffering from a slow disease of the mind. Quite harmless and pathetic, really. He met a girl, had a child and has been keeping bees on Mount Hymettus for years. Under an assumed identity. This nice fellow was his friend, until he discovered the truth, a week or so ago, and then all he could think about was the prize money. He got him at the well, as the old bandit went for his drink.'

Suddenly, the door of the tavern burst open and a group of armed policemen came in. The officer in charge quickly dispersed the group of onlookers and began asking questions of the small man in possession of the head. He held it close to him now as a schoolboy guards a precious toy from rival children, but the chief officer grabbed it from him with both hands and held it up by the ears to examine it closely in a better light. He strained towards it aggressively, but seemed almost overpowered by the calm expressionlessness of the dead man's face.

A policeman appeared in front of Godwin and barked in his face for not having moved back, so that Pedersen had to take his arm and lead him away. He accompanied him outside to help find the missing luggage. Pedersen's easy command of Greek reduced the task to a couple of enquiries and they found the wooden chest in a warehouse not far from where they had stepped ashore. It was covered with an old rug and tucked away beneath a customs officer's desk. The official on duty looked embarrassed, shrugged his shoulders and scratched the back of his neck, claiming complete ignorance. One of the officers had found the box abandoned on the quay earlier, he said. When Godwin opened it he found that its precious contents of collodion glass plates were miraculously still unbroken.

It was by now after two o'clock, and the bustle of Piraeus had begun to subside. 'There is much in this country to repel the visitor,' Pedersen said as he took his leave of Godwin, shaking his hand. 'Especially the Greeks. Take my advice, my friend, and forget any romantic notions you may have of Alexander, Achilles and the like. Modern Greeks are a monstrous race. Don't trust them. The most honest man in Athens would be a man of exceedingly doubtful reputation in London or Paris, shunned by respectable society. He makes a virtue of deceit. He is idle, insolent, undisciplined and never to be relied upon. But don't be put off,' he concluded: 'you will find passions here you never knew you possessed.' He patted the Englishman condescendingly on the back, waved and disappeared into the night.

Godwin had left it late and now had to pay well over the odds for a carriage and driver to take him the few miles into town. The journey was uncomfortable, the bench was not upholstered, and he could hear the wheels splash through an endless succession of puddles; the occasional splatter of mud would come through the window which had long since lost its glass. By three o'clock they had entered paved streets on the western fringe of the city, lined on either side with elegant new buildings, and shortly after came to a large open area, planted with young fruit trees. This was Constitution Square, home to the royal palace at its upper end, and Godwin's hotel at its lower.

Chapter 2

It was the first clear dawn since Godwin had come to Athens, eight days earlier, and he was well placed to observe it. He stood in one of the uppermost alleys that clung to the Acropolis' flank, and watched as the sun broke above the bleak outline of Mount Pentelicus, twelve miles to the east. All at once, the vast and barren plain of Athens, stretching all the way from the encircling mountains to the sea, was flooded with golden light, clear and evenly spread. In summer, the force of the sun in that shadeless wasteland was such that it sucked the life from plants and turned the soil to sand; but by the late autumn, especially after a week of cloud and rain, its warmth was a welcome respite. Godwin longed to disappear into the dreamy haze of that distant landscape.

How far it all seemed from the manor house in Surrey that he called home; that large and symmetrical Elizabethan warren with its ornamented ceilings and black oak timbers, where his parents' stately lives at one end of the immense windowed gallery were insulated in every sense from the world he and his brother inhabited as children at the other. Even here, alone, with Attica spread before him, he felt his stomach move at the thought of the corridor outside his father's study, that portal to the seat of ultimate, un-assailable authority in his life. He remembered the faint odour of beeswax, the noiseless hinges of the door as it opened to summon him across the threshold, and the per-fectly engineered click of the handle as it closed behind him. Everything about that room announced the character of the man who occupied it. Purpose and utility hung in the air like a scent, a masculine scent – stripped of sweetness but strong in dignity. The furniture was polished mahogany with castors that gleamed like gold in the morning light. There were no ornaments, no decoration and no art; the walls were empty except for row upon row of gilt-tooled books, and three large maps: of the constituency, the nation, and the world.

Godwin blinked as he shook aside the memory and looked down at Athens before him. He could see that the city was expanding. The tiny original hovels that snuggled into the shadow of the Acropolis were giving way to broad avenues and impressive new residences. Building work was everywhere and defined the daytime atmosphere in the city; clouds of marble dust billowed from hand-powered stone saws, picks and hammers vied with each other in syncopated cross-rhythms, sites were being cleared of scrub, men in suits and top hats measured out quadrangles on the ground with lengths of string, and cartloads of cut stone rumbled daily in convoys from the quarries of Pentelicus. The city was fast modernizing, and Godwin was captivated by the urgency of the transformation. This was a people reborn and hungry for prosperity.

Within a few days he had jettisoned his plan to make a photographic record of antiquities, seduced instead by the immediacy and peculiar juxtapositions of the modern city. The ruins failed to surprise or particularly inspire him. He had already been up to the Acropolis twice, and his findings echoed everything he had read and re-read in many other accounts. He felt that he was the voluntary participant in an overcooked intellectual cliché, and was repelled by the guides who dulled everything with their platitudes and horse-fly persistence. In any case, it was not the hallowed marble hulks dotted here and there around the city that impressed him, but the life that continued in and around them. The ancient archway towering solitary out of the dust was less interesting than the old men with anxious faces who drew up simple wooden chairs in its shadow, and sat for hours over empty coffee cups, tossing strings of beads and staring at passing foreigners.

The defiance Godwin felt towards his distant father tasted like sweet triumph as he decided to cock a snook at the degrading tourist caste into which it was assumed he would contentedly merge; instead, he determined to explore the heart of this young country, observe its nascent culture and seek out its wildness. To this end, he resolved to follow up the two leads he had brought with him. First, there was the English Minister in Athens, Sir Thomas Wishart; Godwin had a letter of introduction. The British Legation was a short walk from his hotel and he had called by there earlier in the week to leave a carte-de-visite. Two days later a letter arrived for him at the hotel from the Minister's wife, Lady Wishart, inviting him to dine at the Legation the following week.

And then there was his old school acquaintance, John Straker, who lived in Athens as secretary at the Legation. Godwin had sent a message a few days ago warning Straker that he would like to call by this morning, and although he was a little surprised not to have had a reply, he decided to walk the distance to Straker's home anyway. It was not far, and would take him through the heart of the city's most colourful district.

The sun was now quite high in the sky as Godwin began to make his way through the bazaar quarter around the old mosque. Trading was already under way. A nut-seller had opened out a collapsible trestle in the street, his first opportunity for days, because of the rain, and was warming his hands in front of the cylindrical stove he had lit for the roasting pan. A passing donkey, laden to three times its own width with fruit baskets, helped itself to the mountain of hazelnuts, starting an exchange of noisy remonstrances between its driver and the nut-seller. A jingling bottle cart rolled on past, with metalled wheels that bounced over the cobbles, while old dogs lay asleep in safe nooks and shadows on the side, their scarred muzzles resting in the dirt after their adventures of the night. All manner of craftsmen and merchants were beginning to hang out their wares in front of narrow shops, using great rods to reach hooks above the ground. Gunsmiths, carpenters, rug weavers, a man peddling remedies, another telescopes. The diversity of stores juxtaposed in peculiar combination gave the impression of boundless abundance, and as Godwin picked his way down the alleys – an incongruous figure with his cane and English tweed shooting jacket – he felt invigorated with the novelty and curiosity of it all. It was as if anything might be found here, luxuries or necessities, animal or vegetable, alive, pickled or dried. A child was selling birds, a chained monkey danced to the prods of a dwarf's stick, an old shoeshine with cropped white hair and a face like Bismarck stooped to polish a young soldier's boots. All the while men with hanging trays at their waists meandered beneath the overhanging canopies, advertising their produce – olives, onions, trinkets, tobacco – in rasping nasal tones. And the smell of bread, that indispensable bedrock of nutrition in every Greek household, wafted here and there from the many bakers' shops.

Godwin arrived outside an impressive portico at the address he had written on a card, and was met by a man-servant who led him through a dark vestibule into a courtyard. It was paved with white marble around a pretty mosaic, centred on a circle of lemon trees and a fountain. All around were battalions of glazed pots, full of soil, which must have been beautiful and abundant at a different time of year, but the plants had been taken out or cut down to brown stalks for the winter. The servant who received him was a young man and still handsome, but had a tired pallor about him, like a fruit that had lost its moist bloom from being left too long untouched in its bowl, and needed replacing before the flies descended.

On asking whether Kyrios Straker was at home, Godwin received the reply, 'He sleeps.' It was surprising, given the time, and, determined not to be thwarted, Godwin said that he would wait until the gentleman was up. He felt sure that Straker would not be offended. They had known each other well enough as boys not to have to stand on ceremony to any great degree.

Straker had been a serious type at school, quietly reliable; not a rule-breaker, but a solid alibi for those who were; his blue-eyed, open-faced testimony, ingeniously inventive in its deceit, rescued his friends from many a tight scrape, defusing the housemaster's suspicions – a man who quite visibly melted whenever Straker opened his mouth. To the disappointment of his father, John Straker never showed much interest in the estates he was set to inherit, which were said to stretch uninterrupted from one coast of northern England to the other, and was happiest when walled up for hours in the classics library. After university his interests had turned to oriental studies, and he later joined the civil service in the hope of one day earning a post in the Middle East. Greece was the nearest he had yet come.

The house was fashionably Pompeian, with a colonnaded cloister surrounding the open courtyard, off which various rooms radiated, and out of one of them there now emerged a boy of about fourteen. He took no notice of Godwin, but walked straight across the mosaic towards the vestibule, looking at the ground and scratching his ear through the folds of a yellow silk turban. He did not exchange eye contact with the servant either, who opened the front door for him to leave and closed it straight after.

A few moments later Straker himself appeared from an adjacent door in the shadows. Godwin immediately got up, but Straker did not walk directly across to where he stood, preferring to take the long route, around three sides of the cloister, hands held behind his back, like a monk in thought. He was dressed in what looked like white linen pyjamas with gold thread beaded around the edges, and a full-length dressing-gown over the top.

Godwin was surprised at how much he had changed. He had lost his fresh-faced beauty, put on a lot of weight, and his hair was oiled back to his skull, down to a little curl at the neck, which gave him a rather rakish look. When he arrived in front of Godwin he looked up with a faint smile. The voice sounded the same, plaintive and produced in the front of his mouth, where the teeth protruded very slightly.

'Good to see you, Tudor. Is your father well?' he said, before turning to one side and sinking into a chair next to him. 'It's warm enough to sit outside for a bit, don't you think?' He then called out to the servant, who came running, suddenly animated by his master's voice, and knelt down on one knee beside him, holding Straker's hand as he listened to his instructions.

'Has he gone?' Straker asked softly.

'Yes, sir.'

'Did he say anything?'

'No, sir.'

Straker then waved his man away with a flip of the wrist and sat staring towards the other side of the courtyard. Godwin felt a prick of alarm at his friend's condition. There was an uncomfortable ambience in the house, like a disease that bided its time in the shadows, gnawing almost imperceptibly at its victims as it multiplied. He could sense it like an affliction that was noticeably hostile towards him for having come in fresh from the outside, fit and able as he was to observe its advancing decay.

'I was shooting last week, up at Lake Copais,' said Straker inconsequentially. 'Snipe.'

'How was it?' asked Godwin.

'Too many birds. Not really sport. Would you like a smoke? Abdul picked up some excellent Livadia tobacco on our way back. Did you know most of the tobacco that goes for Turkish in London is actually grown in Greece?'

'No, thank you, I don't take it.'

Godwin defused what threatened to be an awkward

silence by talking about his experience of Athens so far and his plans for the future. He noticed that Straker did not touch his coffee until it was nearly cold, then drank it all in one and proceeded to eat the sediment, scooping it out by the fingerful. Godwin had seen old Greek men in cafés do the same.

'Might I see you on Sunday night for dinner at the Legation?' Godwin concluded. 'Lady Wishart has invited me.'

'I will be there,' replied Straker, 'won't I, Abdul?' He yelled the last syllable in the direction of the kitchen, from which his servant now came running. 'Have you met my old friend Abdul?' he asked Godwin, taking hold of the servant's finger and swinging it.

'Of course. He met me at the door.'

'Abdul's from Cairo. I've had him ever since I travelled there after Oxford. We've never been apart. Would you like to go back to Cairo, Abdul?' he asked, turning to look at him. Abdul did not answer but looked at his master with a pained expression. 'It's all right, you can speak freely, old boy.' Abdul stared on and blinked in silence. 'Well, go if you want,' sang Straker in a sort of high-pitched falsetto, letting go of his hand and waving him away again. 'Problem is, you don't know what you want.'

Godwin got up to leave. 'Until Sunday, then,' he said.

At this, Straker's expression changed as if he was reminded of something, and he looked at Godwin quizzically. 'By the way, has anyone warned you?'

'About what?'

'I wonder how you'll get on. We don't dine there very often, if we can help it. Too bored with each other's company. Occasionally the Greeks like us to put something on, or we have to call them to heel for something, so Wishart goes through the old dinner routine. This one's for Edgar Brooke, who's on a visit. Has anyone warned you?'

It was the first time Godwin had heard the name. It did not mean anything to him, nor did it create much of an impression. Just two short words thrown out by the weary voice of John Straker in the courtyard of his Athens villa, that sunny morning of 11 October 1869. Edgar Brooke. Three little syllables punctuated with four mildly explosive consonants, that required a satisfying click of the tongue to enunciate. In time to come he would remember first hearing the name, and wonder that something so pivotal to his life should have arrived before him in so cursory a manner.

'Warned me of what?'

'About him. Brooke. The fellow coming to dinner. He's very –' Straker paused and skimmed the tip of his tongue across the front of those slightly buck teeth, '– very unusual. Doesn't come to Athens very often, especially since his wife died. I think she had him pegged, but now there's no one to keep him on the straight.'

'So he's not resident in Athens?' said Godwin.

'No. He owns an estate out on the island of Pyroxenia, bought by his father from the Turks before they abandoned the country. He was born in Greece, and that's half the problem. Doesn't really know where he is or what he's about. English, Greek, Greek, English. And living all the way out there, as well, he's rather cut off. Forgotten how to behave. You'll see. Strange place he runs out there. Strange family, all in all.'

Godwin was intrigued, but Straker volunteered no more on the subject and held out his hand from where he sat. Godwin shook it before being led by Abdul – who hurried from the kitchen with a tea towel over his arm – towards the outside door.

Chapter 3

The British Legation was housed in a spacious neo-classical mansion a few hundred yards away from Constitution Square and the Hotel d'Angleterre. Godwin was met at the entrance by a Maltese footman, and led straight upstairs towards a drawing room where some of the guests were already assembled. On his way up he heard masculine voices roar with laughter above the general conversation, the noise echoing off the marble walls in a distorted burble. The hall stairway was reminiscent of its equivalent in some of the grander institutions of Pall Mall or Whitehall, except it lacked the opulence. Where there might have been a bronze ornament there was terracotta, instead of oil portraits were line engravings, plain wood was substituted for gilt, and plant stands for statuary; and everywhere there hung a faint smell of cooking, like a school corridor that led down to the dining hall – the same pale brown meat and fat atmosphere, spreading from hidden vats of broth. Along with the smell came a distant spinning clang, the sound of pans dropped on flagstones, and the shriek of sweaty women exchanging jokes in the scullery.

Six people were assembled in the upstairs drawing room. At the door he was met by Sir Thomas and Lady Wishart, who introduced themselves cordially. Sir Thomas was a man of around fifty, short, dapper and rather fleshy, who spoke to Godwin for a full ten minutes without saying anything of substance. He made several references to Sir Harold and Lady Tudor, relating the times when their paths had crossed, his stories punctuated with appropriately deferential compliments. It dawned on Godwin that he had been invited to the Legation not for his own benefit, as a way of assisting or introducing him to Greece, but *ex officio* in relation to and representing his father. Nothing was said of his old acquaintanceship with Straker. In fact Godwin noticed that Straker was generally ignored, and Sir Thomas hardly exchanged a word with him all evening.

Lady Wishart was considerably younger than her husband, and might have been described as elegant, but for a fidgety, perplexed air that undermined the dignity she sought to affect. As a result, beauty eluded her, though its constituents were there.

Straker was standing near to a slender young English gentleman who was introduced to Godwin as Fortinbras Pierrepont, the agent of a British engineering firm that had great plans for Greece. He had a natural, bright-eyed enthusiasm and a firm handshake that Godwin found refreshing; he looked forward to talking to him later. Straker was holding a glass of water and wearing a suit and tie so that he did not appear as unconventional and therefore not quite so much changed as he had a few days earlier.

Godwin's interest was soon being drawn to a corner of the room where two men sat apart from the others, completely engrossed and clearly enjoying themselves. They were talking in Greek, fast and animated, the flow of conversation peppered with convulsions of laughter and spluttered giggles. They seemed entirely at ease, in contrast to the rest of the party, set apart in mood and manner in a way that was almost brazen. One of them, a dark-skinned man of about Godwin's age in a well-cut charcoal suit, leant forward to speak to his companion, gesticulating much with hand and head. The other sat back in his armchair, talking less but laughing more; when he did speak it was in faultless Greek, rattled at a pace and with the lilting inflections of one who does not need a moment's pause to translate his thoughts.

He was around fifty, stockily built, with unruly curling hair that was turning from fair to grey. His pale blue eyes were deeply set beneath bushy eyebrows, and he had leathery cheeks and a muscular jaw. He gave the impression of more than average strength and vigour, someone who was used to outdoor work and did not shrink from getting a job done by the labour of his own thick hands and shoulders when the need arose.

Godwin knew instantly that this must be Edgar Brooke, the maverick landowner from Pyroxenia, though these unfamiliar names and the fragments of description he had heard in advance did not mean a great deal now as he glanced across the room at him. There was something compellingly attractive in the way the man's eyes focused intently on his companion, the lightning speed of his responses and the dark grain of his voice when he spoke. Although Godwin could not understand a word that was being said, he detected an intelligence there which he would have liked to tap. He wanted to recommend himself, to be included in the intimate full-blooded exchange, so much so that he suddenly felt irrationally resentful of it. It was a rather poisonous and disconcerting sensation, which he sought to suppress. He looked at the older man, who had not as yet even registered Godwin's arrival in the room, and found himself searching for fault. He watched him take two glasses from the drinks waiter, one of which he drained in a single gulp, before sipping on the second. A secret ink-squirt of venom released itself into Godwin's thinking as he now found an easy way of explaining and condemning the man's ebullience. But still he continued to glance across, drawn by those deep-set blue eyes and the wide tanned face.

'That's the man I told you about.' Straker had arrived beside him. 'Look at the way he drinks. He doesn't get decent wine out where he lives, just the native poison, and so makes the most of the opportunity when he's in Athens. His father used to keep a good cellar, by all accounts, but a band of brigands sacked his place in the Forties and drank the lot. Barbarians. Brooke had an invalid sister who died of fear when she was made to watch the servants having their throats slit. Twelve years old.'

'How terrible.'

'Enough to make a sane man pack up and leave the place for ever.'

'Who's the man he's talking to?'

'That's Theodoros Dragoumis. Quite the rising star. Belongs to a well-known old family from Constantinople and has just been appointed ambassador to Paris. I'll introduce you.'

They stood in front of the seated pair without acknowledgement while Brooke and Dragoumis finished some part of their conversation. Dragoumis looked up with a slight frown at the distraction, but made the effort to get to his feet, and managed a courtly smile of recognition as Godwin was introduced, in French. Edgar Brooke looked to the other side of the room at something else. It was not rudeness, or even as pronounced as uninterest, but more wounding than either; it was simply non-attention to something or someone that was an irrelevance. When Godwin held out his hand, Brooke finally turned to observe him, but only for a moment, with a nod, and without rising. He then resumed his Greek patter with Dragoumis. Straker had wandered away and Godwin was left standing in front of them, excluded. He felt his resentment mount with a rush of blood to his face, and spoke without thinking.

'I am told, sir, that you have lands some way distant from Athens. May I ask what is your principal crop?' he said directly to Brooke, who now at last faced him full on, his pale blue eyes fixed still and expressionless. The reply came lightly voiced, in a cold tone, as if the question were a nuisance.

'Timber. Could you ask that waiter to come over here?' Godwin turned to look, but Brooke had already caught the eye of the waiter and gestured to him to bring the decanter across. There was a pause while Godwin turned back, thinking of something to add. He now regretted his reckless intrusion.

'And that brings a reasonable return?'

'Yes, thank you,' said Brooke, looking across the room as he sipped.

'Is most of your trade within Greece or exported?'

'Both.' His replies were airy, almost sung, distracted; but Godwin did not know how to terminate the conversation and so persisted.

'And is the profit in relation to land yield in any way comparable to that generated by estates in other parts of Europe?'

Brooke looked away and drained his drink. 'Well, it's not quite as simple as that.' There was another pause as the waiter refilled his glass, for which Brooke thanked him in Greek.

'Meaning?' said Godwin.

'Meaning what?' snapped Brooke.

'I meant . . . I was asking if . . .' He stumbled to a halt, but Brooke interrupted, preventing any further progress.

'If I'm wealthy? No. If I have much land? Yes. If I exploit the Greek peasantry? Ask them. If Greece is an appropriate destination for British investment and speculation? Come back when you know what you're talking about.' He muttered a few sentences to Dragoumis in Greek, who nodded back in silence, and then got up to walk away without a word to Godwin.

Dragoumis remained, and began to speak to Godwin in French, about his journey, what he had seen, and ultimately about his father once again. His manner was pleasant enough, but Godwin felt shocked by the encounter with Brooke and found himself answering in stilted sentences, his command of French suddenly impaired. To save more embarrassment he excused himself and wandered slowly back across the room to where Straker was talking to Fortinbras Pierrepont. He tried to reassure himself with silent vituperation against Brooke. The man was unpleasant, ungenerous and supremely self-satisfied. Godwin could see him on the other side of the room now. His clothes were deeply creased and clearly not the work of a European tailor – the cut was approximate in relation to the shape of his limbs, and the stitching crude. His brown shoes were old and scuffed, the leather cracked and the soles worn down thin at the edges. Brooke's attire spoke of a coarser life than that of Wishart, Straker or even the dapper young Greek statesman, Dragoumis.

Godwin was beside Straker again when the last guests arrived, an event preceded by the entry of a military servant in traditional Greek costume who marched into the room, swinging his arms like a wound-up toy soldier. All fell quiet as the Maltese butler announced the entry of Mr and Mrs Tsavelas, and in walked an elderly Greek couple; the man entered first, dressed in a *fustanella* complete with crimson waistcoat and jacket, wildly embroidered. He was a frail, bent figure, and his costume, presumably fitted in former days when he would have stood full and proud, now protruded stiffly around his shrunken frame, like the armoured shell of an exotic insect. His full white moustaches fell heavily and obscured his mouth completely, extending a further three inches beyond the width of his face. He entered leaning on a stick and concentrating hard, his eyes darting up and around nervously in between movements, in the way of old people whose confidence has been eroded by slow decay and the inexorable approach of the abyss. His wife, a stone-faced matron, followed behind. The pair radiated venerability, and their entrance was tailored for effect.

Sir Thomas ceremoniously put out an arm for the old man to take, and led him to a chair, after which conversation in the room resumed. Edgar Brooke raised his glass from across the room at Mr Tsavelas, and half shouted a greeting in Greek. The old man heard something but could not see clearly where it had come from and had to ask Sir Thomas what was going on. After being told, he lifted his arthritic wrist into the space in front and waved it once. Godwin caught the suspicion of a grimace cross his face as he did so, but whether it was from some hidden pain or the thought of Edgar Brooke it was impossible to tell.

Straker explained that Harilaos Tsavelas was a veteran from the war of independence, a warrior, or *pallikar*, one of the few left, and that he and some of the other heroes of the war had enjoyed long political careers as a result of their involvement in the struggle. The hot-headed exploits and daring raids of their youth had earned them and their families elevation to high social status in the new country. Nowadays, many of the ministries once dominated by these former soldiers were the fiefdoms of their sons, who carried the same names and thus represented to ordinary Greeks the continuance of a natural social establishment. But the new generation never donned the national costume in the way these few old men continued to do. Clean-shaven, multilingual gentlemen in slim-fitting dark suits were replacing broad-shouldered old *pallikars* in the corridors of government, and many of them laughed amongst themselves at the amateur political skills of their fathers.

It was clear at dinner that Brooke had already had much to drink, but its effect at this stage was merely increased euphoria and talkativeness. He directed his conversation during the meal entirely at old Mrs Tsavelas next to him, who spoke not a word of English, but listened, while she chewed, to his non-stop stream of Greek. He did not seem particularly aware or even concerned by her lack of participation, but continued, talking with his head turned slightly in her direction, at times frowning as he spoke, at times smiling, and always amplifying his words with a repertoire of vernacular gestures. Godwin observed him, wondering what he could possibly be saying to the old woman, whose thin lips were sealed tomb-like beneath an impenetrable façade. Straker leant over to Godwin.

'He talks just like a peasant. Plenty of country patois and a thick accent. As a boy he spent most of his life with goatherds' sons and had to be dragged kicking and screaming back to his governess in the manor house. Some people in Athens joke that they can't even understand his sort of Greek. This old witch will be happy, though. She's from farming stock. Just watch how he'll melt her.' Straker was right, and Godwin saw over the next half-hour how Mrs Tsavelas warmed to her neighbour, at first with fleeting smiles, then gradually allowing herself to be drawn into an engagement, and eventually entering wholeheartedly into his flow, travelling with him though a range of conversational climates so that every other dialogue around the table sounded laboured in comparison. By the time dessert was in front of her she barely noticed it for talking, and bore little resemblance to the pillar of silence who had just an hour before taken her place at the table.

Lady Wishart, at the end of the table, was talking to Dragoumis and Mr Tsavelas, and Godwin could hear that there was much reminiscing on the part of the old warrior. Lady Wishart listened wide-eyed like an alert schoolgirl. Battles were being relived in stumbling French prose and a failing voice; names that even Godwin knew to be legends tumbled in and out of the narrative, with Tsavelas himself at the hub, cutting his way through the midst of the slaughter, defying the odds, steering the fortunes of many from despair to glory. It was clearly a favourite topic for the old man, one he had revisited countless times through the decades, though there was a tiredness about him which made Godwin think that the stories had perhaps lost their shine or now seemed distant and irrelevant. Occasionally, the weight of years became too great and his heavy eyelids would close in confusion. If the pauses grew too long or the stories threatened to cave in on themselves, Dragoumis would lean over and help him with a discreet word, while Lady Wishart ignored the inconsistencies and elaborations.

Godwin heard only snatches from the stories, because Straker, on his other side, had launched into a weighty state-ment of his own, begun quite without prompt or warning and with such a serious voice that Godwin assumed at the start it must be some kind of dark joke. As before, Straker was drinking only water, and could not have contrasted more sharply with Edgar Brooke sitting opposite, whose bubbling euphoria threw everyone else's sobriety into relief.

'I may as well tell you, as I've got to tell someone, and you're the nearest I'm going to find to family in this god-forsaken place,' he began. Godwin turned to him with a half-smile, and Straker continued:

'I'm not going to stay the course here, you know. I'm not right for these people, and'– he struggled to find the words – 'some ghastly things have happened.' He took a mouthful of water. 'That boy, the other day – do you remember seeing the boy who left my house? I'm certain that you will have drawn conclusions from what you saw. Am I right?' He was inter-rupted at this point by the sound of a spoon tapped against a glass. It was Edgar Brooke, who had turned his attention away from Mrs Tsavelas and called the table to silence. He stood up, steadying himself with one hand on the back of his chair. A shadow of a frown glanced across Sir Thomas Wishart's face at the end of the table.

'May I ask you to drink the health of our distinguished visitor, Harilaos Tsavelas, and his beautiful wife, of course.' He lifted his glass and bowed to his neighbour. 'We all know the debt Greece owes to this outstanding hero.' He raised his eyes to the ceiling. 'The man who severed twenty Turkish heads with a single blow.' He made a slicing sound. 'The man who personally stormed all the great citadels of the Peloponnese, and was the first to plant the flag on their summits, Corinth, Argos, Mycenae, to name but a few.' Tsavelas was frowning but not understanding a great deal, and so depending for a translation on Dragoumis, who was looking extremely uncomfortable and floundering in his account. Mrs Tsavelas, not speaking English, had heard her name and was looking up at Brooke, nodding approvingly. He continued.

'After the war this Hercules of modern Greece quite appropriately rose to great wealth and fame' – he swayed on his legs and lowered his glass to the table. 'We have Mr Tsavelas to thank for steering Greece to the heights she now enjoys – a land of peace, harmony and prosperity.' He could not hold back a snigger, but recovered before concluding, 'Ladies and gentlemen, we sit in the presence of a great personage, a Hellenic legend.'

'Mr Brooke,' interrupted Wishart quietly, 'why not return to your seat?'

'But why? I want to drink the man's health. Look at him. Doesn't he look splendid in all that gold?'

'We have not yet toasted the Queen,' said Wishart.

'Oh, damn the Queen,' Brooke retorted, and sank back into his chair, more from failing stability than obedience. Wishart was up on his feet, glass in hand, taking over before the shock could spread.

'Ladies and gentlemen, Her Majesty the Queen.' Brooke stayed slumped in his chair while the rest of the company rose, including Tsavelas, who was helped by Dragoumis.

'Before you all sit down,' said Brooke as they swallowed in silence, 'let's change around. You!' he pointed at Godwin, 'what's your name?'

'Tudor. Godwin Tudor.'

'You come over here, Tudor Godwin Tudor. You've got an interesting face, and I've had enough of this old bat.'

'I will move,' said Dragoumis from the other side of Brooke, and swiftly exchanged places with Godwin, leaving Mrs Tsavelas none the wiser.

A heavy silence descended, which Sir Thomas dispelled by suggesting that the two ladies might now like to withdraw. Lady Wishart led the way for Mrs Tsavelas, leaving the seven gentlemen to their port and smoking.

Brooke had turned his attention to Godwin and was about to start talking when Sir Thomas cut across and brought the whole table's attention to himself. He began to talk of politics, emphasizing England's long-standing friendship with Greece, and tactically placing a warning about Russia's territorial ambitions in the Balkans. His style was public and amicable, though it was clear his words were meant for Dragoumis, on the understanding that he would report back to his government colleagues: Britain would not tolerate new ties between Greece and Russia.

As the little lecture progressed, Edgar Brooke smoked a cigarette, listening and sipping port, occasionally letting out a quiet grunt of a laugh.

Dragoumis had obviously been expecting Wishart's diatribe because he now replied with a formal statement of his own, as platitudinously polite and friendly as the English Minister's, though noncommittal on the matter of an alliance with Russia. He finished and there was a brief silence as it fell to a smiling Sir Thomas to collect his thoughts for an appropriate reply; but before he could speak, Edgar Brooke raised his chin and let out a single word, loud and clear, ripping through the diplomatic pause like a hot blade.

'Fart.'

'I beg your pardon?' said Sir Thomas.

'I said fart.'

'For God's sake control yourself,' said Sir Thomas.

'And sit here listening to fart?' Another sentence followed to reiterate the point, half to himself, inaudible muttered obscenities, before he spoke out once more at Sir Thomas. 'First you, with your pompous little speech. England! Greece's cherry-pie best friend. Then that whiskered dandy,' he flicked his hand towards Dragoumis, 'steaming on about honour and whatever.' His words were slurred and he held to the substance of what he wanted to say by the barest thread. 'Great nations. Glorious futures.' He drew on his cigarette and exhaled. 'What about the Greeks? Poor little mister

45

nobody average penniless Greek'—he swallowed a belch,—
'person. All the real little Greek persons. Because while you
talk fart, they are – ah, God, the shit of it all.' He lost his
thread now and fell once more into the slurred murmurs of
drunken anger before rallying again. 'This country's never
had any bloody honour. Not today, and certainly not in this
buffoon's day,' he finished, pointing his cigarette at Tsavelas.

'Your father, sir,' said Tsavelas, rallying, 'would never talk
like this.'

'My father! My father was too good for you or your
damned country. You and your friends did your damnedest
to ruin him, just as this man,' he nodded towards
Dragoumis, 'and his friends will soon try to ruin me.' Brooke
was sparing none in his tirade. 'My father was loved by his
people. Real people. People who understand the meaning of
honour. But you—' He pointed at the ancient statesman.
'Look at you! You're an inflated fart who can't remember
where he's come from. I know a peasant when I see one, and
I can smell goat shit no matter how much gold is piled on
top.' His pale blue eyes were staring directly at Tsavelas, and
as if to hammer home the insult he repeated the last
sentence loudly in Greek, so there could be no mistaking.

Tsavelas struggled to his feet. 'Are you, sir, saying that I am
bad bred?'

At this, Brooke fell into laughter and filled his port
glass. The air eased somewhat and Dragoumis persuaded
Tsavelas to return to his seat, saying there had been a
misunderstanding.

Young Fortinbras Pierrepont, the engineer, now spoke up.

'Mr Tudor, do you intend to travel further into Greece
during your stay? Perhaps you would like to call on me and
I could be of assistance in advising you where to go and what
to take.'

'That would be most kind,' replied Godwin. 'I should like
that very much.'

Edgar Brooke now looked across the table and narrowed

his eyes at Pierrepont, as if noticing him for the first time. 'I know you, don't I? Didn't you come out to us in the summer, if I'm not mistaken?'

'I did, sir. You kindly accommodated us on our way through to the north of Pyroxenia,' said Pierrepont, smiling through his blushes.

'Are you the one who's been writing to my daughter?' Brooke asked, his eyes narrowing further.

'Well, sir,' Pierrepont now went a purple shade of crimson, and Godwin could not help an innocent enjoyment of his discomfort; the young man clearly longed for the ground to open up beneath Stadion Street and for the entire Legation, if not Constitution Square or Athens itself, to disappear into the bowels of the earth, 'Miss Brooke was generous enough to give me reason to believe our friendship might be extended.'

Edgar Brooke smiled, approvingly. 'Good,' he said. 'You must come again. Soon.' Pierrepont looked up with relief and delight. But Brooke was not finished. 'And you must come as well.' He looked at Godwin. 'It will be good for her to sense the cocks fighting around her. She's of that age, now, and can't be cooped up without dying of frustration, living where she does. Sooner or later some young buck will get through and mount her, I don't doubt. Might be you.' He pointed his cigarette at Pierrepont and began to laugh again.

Dragoumis muttered a few words to Tsavelas, who nodded wearily and both of them rose to depart. Sir Thomas made to accompany them to the door, but was waved back by Dragoumis.

Now there remained just the five Englishmen. Straker had said very little for some time, and stayed silent now. Wishart, Pierrepont and Godwin continued to talk, mostly about politics, while Brooke drank more port and sank into his own world of hilarity and singsong mutterings. Occasionally he would catch some sentence from their conversation and repeat it to a tune before dissolving into hissing convulsions at the absurdity of it all. Godwin could see that he was blind drunk, but there was a sense of irony there still; the rest of them were trapped in a mire of hollow pomposity, while Brooke was enviably free of it.

At a pause in the conversation Brooke turned his swaying head to Godwin.

'So you'll come?'

'Come where?'

'To stay. In Pyroxenia. This week, if you can. Bring whatsisname.' He lifted a finger vaguely across the table.

Godwin was taken aback. 'I'm not sure, I . . .'

'Don't be such a shrinking violet. Come! It's . . . it's . . .'

'It certainly is the most heavenly spot on earth,' interjected Pierrepont brightly, but Brooke waved his comment away as he would a bloated house-fly, and leant closer to Godwin. His face swayed this way and that like an unmoored dinghy.

'You will not know beauty until you see my home.'

They sat face to face, just a few inches separating them, a clear moment in the plunging maelstrom of Brooke's descent. Godwin was under no illusions about his condition, but there was something there that held his attention for a moment, something in the sincerity of Brooke's last words, though they were uncertainly anchored, that cut through his absurd display as if to say, 'that's just my game; this is real'. For an instant Godwin was electrified.

Suddenly Straker was on his feet.

'Sir Thomas. Gentlemen. I must be on my way.'

'Someone waiting for you at home, Straker?' said Brooke, forgetting Godwin. 'How old is he this time? Old enough to fight back?'

'Brooke!' said Sir Thomas. 'If you cannot contain your remarks, I shall have to send for your carriage.' Straker had taken no notice, but walked silently from the table, the clap of his shoes on the polished wooden floor echoing round the room until he found the door at the far end. Sir Thomas was on his feet; Pierrepont and Godwin followed his lead.

'So this is the end, is it?' said Brooke. 'You fellows are all . . . all . . . fellows are a lot of . . . of . . .' But the words were lost in a jumble of sounds as Brooke negotiated himself up and out of his chair. A hand went quickly down on the table to steady himself, catching the edge of a saucer that spun dangerously close to the edge before being caught by Pierrepont. Brooke had not noticed; his attention was now drawn down to the top of his trousers, where he began to fumble with the buttons. Godwin watched, aghast.

'Really, Brooke, this can't carry on,' said Sir Thomas. 'Mr Brooke, please! Edgar!'

His remonstrances were in vain. Brooke had pulled his penis out of his trousers and was relieving himself with a contented sigh over the plates. The urine splashed and splattered merrily off the porcelain before it streamed on across the mahogany and tumbled in a steaming torrent over the edge to the rug below.

Of Lady Wishart there had been no further sign. Godwin presumed she had been tipped off by Dragoumis as he left.

Chapter 4

Godwin liked to climb the lower slopes of Mount Likavettos, behind his hotel, to watch the sunrise before breakfast. By the time he walked back, Constitution Square was barely recognizable as the same place he would pass through in the pre-dawn darkness. Then it was the bleak and silent fiefdom of a few stray dogs who eyed him dangerously; but after daylight broke across the roof tiles of the royal palace, the square would fill with men and women going about their morning activities in the sunshine, and the many cafés would do good business. There was a more affluent kind of citizen here than in the old town, the men dressed for the most part in tight-fitting European suits, and carrying gloves and canes. But Athens was a culture in transition, a hybrid of East and West, and many white turbans, fur caps and crimson fezzes were to be seen peppered amongst the bowler hats as pedestrians flitted beneath shop canopies or meandered between the young orange trees that were planted along the length of the boulevards.

Two days after the Legation dinner, Godwin returned from his morning walk to be accosted by the hotel commission-aire, scuttling across the lobby, and was handed two letters in an extravagantly baroque manner. If there was a message or piece of news waiting for Godwin, the commissionaire always took it upon himself to play the part of sole guardian and fixer, the indispensable agent of any contact Godwin might make in the city. The ingratiating smiles, as he backed away, quite clearly communicated his assumption that, with the delivery of each note, his as yet open account of final reward was expected to be advanced a notch.

The first of the two letters was from Edgar Brooke. It was written in a thin, neat hand, not entirely reminiscent, Godwin thought, of the man whose signature appeared at the bottom.

Mr Tudor
My man will arrive at your hotel on Friday, 21 October.
Please meet him, prepared for immediate departure, at five
o'clock in the morning. His name is Panayiotis. He will
bring horses and everything you need. Do not be late. Do
not take money or weapons with you as they might draw
you into situations of unnecessary unpleasantness on the
journey. If you are determined to bring money, place it
inside your pillow at night. I have arranged for Mr
Pierrepont also to come to your hotel. You may wish to
discuss your arrangements with him. A third member of
your party will be Dr Schillinger, an eminent Swiss
classicist, together with his student, and for their sake you
will have to endure a rather circuitous route. My man will
take you overland to the pass of Eleftherae, Plataea,
Thebes, across a section of Boeotia to the town of Páparis
and thence over the mountain to my home, Thasofolia.
Dr Schillinger is keen to experience these sites. My man
will arrange your accommodation for the two nights. Do
not pay him anything. You can settle any expenses
outstanding to me next month on your return to Athens,
with a circular note to my bank. Miss Brooke, my sister,
will expect your party in time for dinner at half-past seven
on Sunday evening.
Edgar Brooke

Godwin dropped the letter beside his journal on the desk and looked out of the window across the dazzlingly bright marble pavements of the square below. A carriage and a couple of affluent men in suits had stopped to allow a peasant with a sheepskin cloak to herd his inquisitive-looking animals across the avenue. This letter tickled Godwin's interest. The voice behind it was bullish and dictatorial and revealed an inherent assumption that the reader should unquestioningly bow to its decrees. There was a hint of his father in its tone, but there was something else as well, something more than mere presumptuous authority. It was a kind of recklessness, a join-me-or-be-damned quality, that lent its writer an irresistible magnetism in Godwin's eyes. Brooke clearly defied both convention and adversity to achieve his ends. Not only had he clearly recalled their meeting, through the haze of his stupor, but he had taken it upon himself to arrange everything in his determination for the visit to happen. Why so keen? wondered Godwin. Such enthusiasm was flattering. And it was tempting. Godwin had been looking for a way to escape Athens and encounter the heartland of Greece. This unusual Englishman in his distant homestead might be offering a possible route.

He now turned his attention to the second letter. It was from Fortinbras Pierrepont, who had received the same invitation from Brooke and wanted to liaise with Godwin for the journey. He suggested Godwin come to his house that same day, for tea, to discuss their arrangements. Accordingly, Godwin sent a reply and arrived at the address, a short carriage drive away on Eolus Street, at four o'clock.

The door opened before Godwin's gloved knuckles had the opportunity to rap on it, and the blond-haired Pierrepont was there, beaming and bright-eyed. He was possibly a little younger than Godwin, almost femininely pretty, and his face shone with perpetual good humour. His eyes opened wide when he mentioned the thrilling prospect of their departure to Pyroxenia, so that it did not occur to Godwin to contradict him.

Pierrepont had done quite a bit of travelling outside Athens, it transpired, surveying the route for a potential road connecting Athens to the north of Greece, perhaps even as far as Salonika. His company in London was keen to exploit Greece's lamentable lack of overland communication routes, and the government in Athens, eager to be recognized as modern and cosmopolitan, was giving the project every assistance. The previous June, Pierrepont had visited Thasofolia *en route* to Pelos, a town across the channel at the top of Pyroxenia, where he intended to complete the first stage of the road link from Athens northwards.

'In your wildest dreams you cannot imagine a more enchanted place,' he said. 'Though I doubt it's the same in winter as it was in late spring. I hear they can get a lot of snow and cannot leave the village for weeks at a time.'

'I still don't understand why Brooke should choose to settle so far from civilization,' said Godwin.

Pierrepont smiled. 'It was his father, Thomas Brooke. He bought the land from a Turk at the end of the war, some time in the Thirties. Turkish landowners were getting out as fast as they could, and were grateful for any money. He was very lucky, really. A marvellous time to buy, terrific bargain.

'Thomas Brooke had come to Greece during the war, in the wake of Byron and a few other deranged idealists. Edgar was born in Athens and remained there with his mother while Thomas went back to England to find a business partner. When he returned, they all went out to Thasofolia and began to get the place moving. There were no end of problems: the government, the climate, the workers, infernal livestock, disease. Then there was the brigand attack, when they stole everything, murdered the servants, and Thomas' daughter died of shock. Poor fellow. He meant well but it broke him down in the end. After the death of his wife, in the late Forties, he finally gave up and went back to England. Edgar was left in charge. He can only have been in his early twenties.'

'And Edgar Brooke now manages to maintain a proper British household in such a remote place?'

'Most proper, and, yes, I'd say it was British in its way. But built out of local materials, and not at all like an English house. They dress like us, eat off silver and porcelain, all that sort of thing – fine portraits on the wall, standing clocks. But it's not the same. It's most unusual. You'll see.'

'And the family?'

'There's Brooke's elder sister, Miss Brooke. Very hardy, with cropped hair and something of a cropped tongue. Doesn't say much, but when she does it's to the point. Rather frightening. Then there's the son, Daniel. Marvellous young fellow, about twenty. Lively, sporting and friendly. And Brooke's daughter, Miss Lydia Brooke, of course. Lydia.' He paused.

'And this Lydia holds some special place in your heart?' asked Godwin with a conspiratorial smile.

'Of course not,' Pierrepont replied, his bonhomie fractionally cracked. 'She's only a girl of around sixteen years.'

'I had no idea.'

'No matter. You would never think she was so young. Her letters are extraordinary. Brooke educated both his children almost without help.'

'Letters?' said Godwin.

'Yes, we have exchanged a few. I'm sure she regards me as a kind uncle. Someone rather different from the people she meets in the village.'

Their discussion then turned to the practical arrangements for the trip: the necessity or otherwise of taking money, and whether or not Godwin should pack the collapsible rubber bath he had brought from England. They agreed to visit the Legation the following day in order to outline their intended route, a necessary formality.

When they arrived at the Legation they were ushered straight into a large room on the ground floor that acted as the Minister's office and Godwin was surprised to see Sir Thomas himself present to go through this routine and relatively petty procedure with them. Straker was there as well, standing next to the desk, and he nodded seriously as the two men entered. The walls of the room were hung with a series of popular engravings depicting the Labours of Hercules; the muscular hero, bearded and twisting, meeting his appalling tasks with mature even-mindedness. The body of a primitive animal, Godwin thought, and the mind of an Englishman. It was a familiar way of viewing the ancient heroes of Greece.

Behind Wishart, as he rose from his desk and approached them, Godwin noticed three portraits: the Queen (a crude copy of a famous original) and on either side two giants of British foreign policy, Stratford Canning – hero of the modern Greek nation and stalwart opponent of Russia, and Lord Palmerston, still the embodiment of Britain's forceful-ness and extensive power overseas. In front of this triptych of imperial might Sir Thomas looked like the caricature of a minor official as he shook Godwin's and Pierrepont's hands, and muttered his few words of greeting. He was quite definitely in his role as crown clerk today and wasted no time in getting to the business in hand. He arranged his spectacles on the end of his nose, went through the details of their route, and finally issued his standard warning about the dis-comforts of travel. He then turned his attention to Godwin.

'Mr Pierrepont has of course had considerable experience of conditions upon the very primitive roads of Greece,' he said. 'But it is my duty to inform you, Mr Tudor, that, although the dangers of travelling to the interior of Greece should not be exaggerated, we should take upon ourselves grave responsibility were we to advise travellers to underrate the risks. There are some very disreputable characters still out there.'

'You mean bandits?'

Sir Thomas looked awkwardly towards the door on the other side of the room. He did not particularly want to discuss the matter but the question still hung in the air between them.

'I cannot deny that mischief has happened before,' he said.

'The Greek government had a purge against brigands two years ago, and since then they've been at pains to let the world know that Greece is completely safe for travellers.'

'But you think there's a risk?' said Godwin.

'At any event you should take with you a revolver, if for no other reason than to show that Englishmen are not ignorant of the dangers.'

'Mr Brooke gave us directly contradictory advice,' said Godwin, whereupon Wishart closed his eyes and pursed his lips.

Straker now came forward. 'Mr Brooke's opinions are not always of the type that we should be seen to endorse,' he said.

'I had gathered that much,' replied Godwin, smiling, but Straker was in a sober frame of mind and did not tune in to the humour. He clearly had something to say and had found his opportunity of saying it.

'Before embarking on this visit, and because of your family connections—'

'Am I to be haunted by my father even in the wilds of Greece?' Godwin interrupted, in a flash of reckless irritation, to which Straker replied by clearing his throat before continuing as if the comment had not been made.

'Because of your family connections, you should visit Mr Brooke with the foreknowledge of certain matters. Most importantly, you should be made aware that Mr Brooke has a number of opponents. Enemies, even. Some of them in positions of power in Athens. And he does little to improve his standing in the estimation of certain eminent statesmen. Gentlemen he would do better to woo.' Godwin made to answer again, but Straker interrupted him. 'And it has nothing to do with his lack of courtesy or refinement.' Sir Thomas remained gazing at the wood of his desk as Straker continued, 'You have heard one or two details about the Brooke family, but there is more you should know.'

'You sound as if you would put me off the visit,' said Godwin. Straker did not reply directly, but went on regardless.

'Edgar Brooke has sought to reverse his father's misfortunes in this country by doing something his father would never have done. He has bought into Greek politics and openly throws his weight behind one of the main political parties in order to benefit from a system of loyalties and liaisons that stretches from the highest levels of government down to the meanest village labourer. He is caught up in the network of corruption, political bullying, bribery and dubious dealings on which the Greek state operates.'

'Should any of this be my concern?' asked Godwin.

'Only inasmuch as it is our duty to inform you about these matters,' Straker added sombrely, 'so that you are aware of your host's standing. From the point of view of Athens. And that of London, of course.'

'You don't approve of Mr Brooke?' asked Godwin almost teasingly, amused at Straker's clerical formality.

At this point Sir Thomas looked up and snapped the awkward dialogue to a close. 'Nothing of the sort,' he said. 'Mr Brooke may have his eccentric ways, but we are all old friends. And he is our countryman.' Straker looked to the floor and remained silent.

Sir Thomas then went on to advise Godwin and Pierrepont that they need not go in person to inform the police of their travel plans. He would arrange permits personally and have their passports *visés*. There was also the matter of introduction letters, one for each of the regional demarchs and nomarchs in the districts they intended to visit, requesting and requiring safe conduct, assistance and hospitality.

'And do remember to avail yourselves of a box of Mr Keating's insect powder before you go,' he said as he shook their hands. 'The bedbugs in those village inns are most impertinent.'

Within the hour, Godwin was back at his hotel, where he found the lobby full of activity. A group of German gentlemen travellers, recently arrived, were gathered around a table, while a Greek tradesman placed before them various antique pistols and swords, which he lifted from cases on the floor. They were genuine artefacts, all dating from the war of independence, Godwin heard the man explain as he ceremoniously unwrapped a purple cloth from each one. The Germans examined the pieces with feigned expertise and superior expressions. Godwin already felt he had graduated from the ranks of such travellers, and was thankful for it. A door had been opened for him, a way into the heartland of the country and its people.

And hovering behind his new aspirations and hunger for adventure was the enigmatic figure of Edgar Brooke, a man whom Godwin could now clearly see was anathema to both Straker and Wishart; a liability as well, perhaps, to their masters in London, and, therefore, distantly, something of a thorn in the side of those polished, influential gentlemen who populated his father's circle. Godwin liked the idea that Brooke was the type of creature his father would have regarded as a natural enemy. Indeed, he welcomed the advent of Edgar Brooke into his acquaintanceship to the same degree as he acknowledged – not without a hint of mourning, surprisingly – the departure of Sir Harold from his immediate circle of influence. Of the two men Brooke was the younger, but, for all his excesses, he shared a quality with Godwin's father. It was something tyrannical, a dogged charisma that drew attention to his wishes and demanded compliance. It was a trait entirely alien to Godwin's nature, and he did not aspire to possess it but curiously pined for the assurance that it guaranteed. Since leaving England he had felt as if a great and noble monument had been removed from the landscape of his thinking. The view was clearer as a result, the air fresher, but the empty plinth had left him searching for something on which to pin his upward gaze; and, at times, to shelter beneath.

Chapter 5

Elias Lambros was finishing his bread and oil particularly slowly that morning and in silence. His wife glanced over her shoulder from where she worked, and aspirated prayers of frustration to the Mother of God to grant her patience. She made no attempt to hide her annoyance, though she would not dare voice any criticism of her husband openly to his face. They had been married for twenty-nine years now and, by the standards of the village, theirs had been a good marriage, one that had brought four fine children (all now grown and gone), and dignity to both their families. Elias had managed his affairs cleverly, so that when he was elected mayor of the village of Thasofolia, two years previously, his status as a man of consequence had become incontestable; and Katina, his mean-eyed, rotund wife, known for her sharp tongue and careful ways with money, basked in the rank it afforded her. Their new house was nearly built and it would be the finest in the village – apart from the house of the master, Kyrios Edgar, of course, up on the hill, but that hardly counted.

It had not always been easy. There had been dark times when enemies had emerged as if from nowhere: neighbours, kinsmen, people they had known all their lives, whose loyalty to the master had seemed to evaporate overnight. Elias, as Kyrios Edgar's foreman, had remained true even when it looked as if they might lose everything. Their sheep had been stolen, stones thrown at their windows and their crops burned; Katina had been spat at by other women in the street and someone had even tried to sell her poisoned bread, but Elias did not waver even for a moment. There was never any question about it. The old master, Kyrios Thomas, had stood godfather to him, and Kyrios Edgar himself had been sponsor at their wedding. They were spiritual kin.

And then came the election, three years ago, when their man, Solouzos, had been returned as Deputy for the island with a mighty electoral victory over the opposition. The skies had cleared and life on Pyroxenia had returned to normal. Solouzos was known to have the ear of the Minister for the Interior in the capital, and Kyrios Edgar was like a brother to Solouzos. Within a year of the election a chain of steel had been reforged, and those who had previously threatened them vanished as quickly as a wave that breaks on a hot beach. But dirty water leaves scum on the sand, thought Katina, and she had no pity for those who subsequently found themselves out of favour. Autumn swells the olive but rots the peach. There were some who withered in the new climate, who found themselves taxed into poverty, or who woke up to find their donkey's legs broken. They had cast their vote, made their enemies and had to live with the consequences.

Elias Lambros of course did not talk to his wife about his problems. They were no concern of hers, just as her own meddlesome ways and petty intrigues were of no interest to him. He pretended to take no notice of her tuts and impatient mumblings on the other side of the room as he finished his breakfast, though he secretly and silently scorned her for it. Little did she know. Had he chosen to tell her what was on his mind she would have been silenced on the spot, the blood would have drained from her pudgy, drooping cheeks and she would have made to steady her bulk by grabbing the table.

He finally rose to his feet and walked over to the fire, gouged and then expelled the snot from each nostril, before wordlessly departing. The house faced south-east, and his face creased from force of habit as he opened the front door, in anticipation of the familiar blaze that would meet him full on as he stepped outside.

Unusually, for a man of his age, Elias had not ballooned at his midriff, and he still retained the strong rectangular features and fierce brows that had made him a striking young man. A slight weariness about the eyes and a tightly sealed mouth, down-turned at the corners from a long-standing habit of keeping his counsel, were the only signs of the care-worn times he had weathered. Over the years he had stifled a naturally sensitive nature, and there were few now, if any, who remembered him as the dreamy boy who would sit under the plane tree near his father's livestock, passing the time by flicking black beads of animal droppings across the parched soil. As a youngster, the sour, cheesy scent of the goat pen – the *mandri* – had permeated his clothes, his hair, his skin, the dimples and folds of his flesh. To this day he associated that smell with everything that was truly intimate and homely, unlike the far more familiar odour of his wife's body, which even after so many years still struck him as alien, an almost unwelcome intrusion in his bed.

Elias had set himself apart from the other men of Thasofolia by abandoning the traditional *fustanella*, and donning instead a smart grey suit, like an Athenian gentleman, the first mayor in the history of Thasofolia to do so. That it was sometimes an impractical garment to wear (if he happened to be milking the sheep or rounding up the goats at the hillside *mandri*) was an inconvenience worth bearing for the status it signified. He had been photographed along-side Kyrios Edgar just last year, and what a fine figure he had cut – more than a servant, more than a foreman: the master's friend, no less. Katina had a copy of the picture framed on the wall of their house so that she could share her sentiments with everyone who visited. Unfortunately, Kyrios Edgar must have blinked as the picture was taken, and Katina, whose print of it was very large, had needed the services of the village sign-writer to cover the defect and paint in the master's eyes. It worked rather well, she thought, though his stare was a little too penetrating.

Elias had saddled the mule earlier, so there was nothing else to do, no little chore to delay the unavoidable. It was a two-hour ride from Thasofolia to his nephew Demetrios' house, along a track that followed the small stream heading out of the village, down towards the eastern seaboard port of Akrogiali. He dreaded what was in store, but could not put the responsibility of this on to anybody else; it was his own idea, and whatever the outcome, he would have to live with the consequences until the end of his life. He climbed, side-saddle, on to the mule's back. A couple of clicks of the tongue and a heel in the ribs set it off at a trot.

As he rode, Elias recalled the events that had brought him to this. First, the visit of the two German gentlemen at the end of the summer. They could not have been clearer. They were representatives of a mining company in Saxony and had come to Greece with the approval of the Athens government to prospect for what was rumoured to be the richest source of lignite in the country, spanning several miles of Pyroxenian forest on land belonging to the Englishman named Brooke. They had first been to see Edgar, who granted them no more than a few moments of his time before dismissing them with a minimum of courtesy but not before they had secured his permission, thanks to a pleading note from Deputy Solouzos, to perform an initial survey on the site. And so, at dusk a week later, equipped with all the necessary information and accompanied by an interpreter, they arrived at the door of Lambros' house.

One of them was large, balding and sweaty, with a permanent half-smile, and he leant forward into the light of the single candle to do most of the talking, while the other, pale and silent, sat back in the shadows, his dark eyes fixed, unblinking, on Lambros. The results of the survey had been sensational, said the fleshy German, there was enough lignite for at least fifty years, probably more, of open cast mining over an area of thousands of acres. It would be nothing less than an industrial coup for the island, not to mention the Greek nation as a whole. There would be new roads, shipping routes, hundreds, perhaps thousands of jobs, they would have to import more manpower, build a new village, and above all there would be wealth for the area. The eyes of every ambitious Greek, he added in a way that he thought would be irresistible to the jumped-up village mayor, will look towards the people of Thasofolia with envy. Katina, listening from the hearth, stoked the fire so that it crackled joyously.

The German went on at a pace: the Minister for the Interior, under pressure from Solouzos, had stipulated that Brooke must be in agreement before any deal could be struck, but, he added, raising his eyebrows and turning to his colleague, 'governments in young, turbulent countries are made or broken by the way they handle an opportunity such as this one, and if Mr Brooke makes trouble he may find himself bereft of a friendly representation in Athens, and we all know where that could leave him. And you, for that matter. That is why we are here today.'

Lambros pondered for a moment and then turned to tell his wife to leave the room so that they could talk in private. When she had gone he asked what they wanted him to do. The man replied that they suspected from their earlier interview with Brooke that he might prove difficult; they would return in a few weeks to try again, but in the meantime he had to be made to see the devastating consequences for him of a refusal. On the other hand, the benefits of compliance would be great: they could see to it that the contract for mining rights would leave Brooke imperishably wealthy, so that no future government or local faction would dare to threaten his position. They gave Lambros a moment to digest this information, and then it was the turn of the other visitor, the thin sinister one, who leant forward slightly into the flickering candlelight, binding Lambros with his cold stare. 'We have spoken to those who do not count themselves Mr Brooke's friends,' he said, 'and they have assured us of their unerring support should Mr Brooke choose not to co-operate.'

Lambros had thought about little else since the meeting. He feared the effect this news would have on the locals – allies and opponents alike – should word of it get out. There were several ways to a man's heart, Elias had learnt, but money was the surest. Forget women, God, home; forget nationhood, political allegiance or hatred for Turkey; money was the one passion harboured by every man he knew that overrode them all, and its insuperable allure could now turn everything upside-down. A new industry, an influx of well-paid newcomers, the possibility of quick advancement – these would upset the balance of power in the village and undermine the network of patronage as it currently existed. Within months of the mine's inauguration Elias Lambros could be a nobody, or the protector of just a few old half-wits left cleaning their rusty ploughs because they hadn't the imagination to recognize new opportunities when they arrived. There would be new overseers, foremen, chiefs and barons of industry, men who understood railways, engines, steam and gas, men with silver-headed canes, umbrellas, new shoes and a change of suit. The sounds in the air would change, the landscape would change, as would the smells on the hillside, the sheep's pastures, the mountain paths and the flight of the bees. The hills would be gouged for plunder, the steep valleys criss-crossed for roads, the rocky coastline harnessed and smoothed for jetties. His own sons might leave their flocks and fields to go and work in the mine, and he would be alone, outcast and impotent because of his attachment to a vanishing way of life.

And what of Kyrios Edgar? The future of the area, as ever, rested in his hands. In the weeks that followed the Germans' visit Lambros met with him many times to talk about the matter, but never once succeeded in getting through to the grit. His patron and employer had a way of brushing aside subjects that did not appeal to him, of talking on at a tangent in a manner that made it impossible to return to the matter at hand. Lambros knew him well enough to realize that the idea was an abomination to him, but there was something preventing him taking a decisive stand one way or another, and Lambros could not for the life of him work out what it might be.

The Germans returned to Thasofolia and Lambros was present as they were shown into Kyrios Edgar's study. The larger man acknowledged the estate foreman with a con-spiratorial smile, while the other ignored him, his steely gaze reserved for the landowner alone. Lambros had been asked to withdraw and so did not hear what was said at the meeting, but was there at the close when the Germans came out. The talkative one was buoyant and shaking Kyrios Edgar's hand like an old friend. Had the deal been approved and sealed? No information was volunteered, and for the moment Lambros did not think it his place to ask, though he threshed his thoughts day and night to work out what might have made his master ease his position on the matter. It was so much out of character. And then, a fortnight ago, he had quite by chance made a discovery.

Katina had been out in the yard blunting the horns on some young goats, when Maroula, the chambermaid up at the big house, stopped for a chat and let slip a fragment of a domestic crisis that had reached her ears. Lambros happened to hear her as he walked past. It was a small piece of gossip, the sort of blabbering bilge that he had heard and scowled at a thousand times through the years; but on this occasion it sparked a fuse and suddenly the entire situation about the mine deal was put into perspective. 'He's in all of a pickle at the moment,' said Maroula. 'The descendants of old Kyrios Hill have hatched like a plague of ants and want their share of the whole place.'

So that was it. Lambros could no longer stop himself. He turned on his heel, went straight up to Thasofolia, his wife watching bemused as he disappeared up the track, and presented himself to his master, repeating what he had heard. Kyrios Edgar, from behind his desk, then explained everything, unperturbed, a slight frown crossing his brow, as though it were a tiresome annoyance he was having to report to his foreman, like a hornets' nest under the eaves of the south wing, or a torn belt on the sawmill's flywheel.

Lambros listened as a ghostly personage from the past returned to their midst. It was not as if everyone had entirely forgotten about Samuel Hill and his share in the property at Thasofolia, even though he was long dead and had only visited Pyroxenia once, in the early 1830s. Lambros himself had a vague childhood recollection of the man, but it was probably informed more by the portrait of him that still hung in the hall of the big house than by actual memory. Not a prepossessing face, Lambros had always thought, very little manliness about it, a thin beard and rather too much suspicion around the eyebrows. The old master, Thomas Brooke, had been a dreamer with light in his eyes and love in his heart, whereas his business partner, Samuel Hill, was a practical man: he had methods, schemes, and a natural talent for managing finances. He had been a small grey man, who shied away from the sunlight and could spend days on end locked in his study, and yet the plans he had devised for the management of the crops and forest were still in place today, standing the test of time.

Edgar now told Lambros that the Hill brothers, grandchildren of Samuel, having fallen on hard times, had discovered by chance in some family papers that their grandfather had possessed a stake in a speculative property deal in Greece, which entitled him and his descendants to sixty per cent of all income derived from the estate, though no right to the land itself. At the time the agreement had been drawn up, and for several years after, Samuel Hill had lost interest and disappeared from the scene, such income as it referred to was non-existent or negligible. Nearly half a century later, however, the amount accrued was a large sum indeed. Hill's grandchildren now sought to reclaim their share and had stated their willingness to be bought out of the arrangement altogether, so long as they were satisfied by an up-to-date and independent valuation. They had already been in communication with an agent in Athens about the matter. There is no question that they had a legitimate right to the money, Kyrios Edgar explained, but the only way he could raise the funds required would be either to sell the property outright or to accept an advance loan from the mining executives. And he needed to act quickly. It appeared as yet that the Hills were unaware of the German project, but it would take nothing more than a rumour about the mine and the value of the share they demanded would escalate beyond imagining. One way or another they must be paid off speedily.

Elias was flattered that his master could speak to him openly about a matter of such calamitous importance and privacy without even once mentioning the need for discretion. It was not the first time in their long association that he felt a rush of love for the landowner so powerful that it threatened to overwhelm him. Even the memory of it, as he rode his mule along the river valley towards Demetrios' house, brought moisture to his eyes. He had to look up to the rocky crests of the mountains and the tops of the pine trees all around to stop the tears spilling on to his cheeks.

Demetrios lived in a small house next to a watermill, on its own at the foot of an overhanging cliff, surrounded by woodland. It was an unusual dwelling, hidden from view under a canopy of plane trees but easy to find because the golden rockface that towered proud and handsome above was a notable landmark for miles around. It was similarly disguised by sound: every noise that came from the house was muffled by the river cascading through the adjacent millpond, but that very roar betrayed the house's presence and informed anyone who happened to be passing or searching for the mill that it must be very close by.

It was the same with Demetrios. He was a shadowy, elusive figure, always one step ahead of the authorities and difficult to incriminate, while at the same time the most notable and ubiquitous outlaw on Pyroxenia. He was still a relatively young man but his many exploits had left him with an almost mythological reputation for brutality and panache. The last time Lambros had used his services had been during the elections, when Demetrios visited all the outlying home-steads and hamlets in rotation, to ensure, with bullish good humour and a threatening glint in his eye, that votes were cast in the right way. Just to make certain, he had positioned himself by the ballot box on election day, greeting everyone as they trooped through to vote. He inspired a peculiar blend of terror and hero-worship in the province. 'Here's one your grandchildren will sing songs about,' mothers told their little ones as he rode through a village, before bustling them indoors and bolting the door.

He was the son of Lambros' eldest brother, Constantinos, who himself had been something of a wild card, cutting his teeth at the age of twelve with the murder of a local tax collector in the pay of the Turks. When he was just twenty-five Constantinos died as he had lived, ambushed and shot down by the gendarmes as he took his first piss of the morn-ing outside a whorehouse in Páparis. Demetrios, his only child, was shrewder. Since the government had begun to crack down on brigandry, he had kept a low profile, biding his time, grinding corn and living a quiet life with his new bride in the shadow of the mountain. His many enemies were poised and ready for the first scrap of evidence that would drag him to the courts. They rejoiced that he and his type had been chased back into their holes at last, and eagerly awaited the time when their heads would hang by the hair from racks in Athens for the photographers to commemorate.

It had been almost a year since Lambros had seen his nephew and they embraced long and hard, swaying slightly, anticipating the manner of lovers in a type of dance neither of them would ever know but which would become a mainstay for courting couples in the same village of Thasofolia more than a century later. Demetrios seemed genuinely pleased to see his uncle, and Lambros could not help but return the warmth. Demetrios had an open, engaging smile and a healthy complexion, but it was more than that: he pinned you with his eyes as he conversed, and had the power to bestow a sense of privilege on those he smiled at; it was easy to see how he won the hearts of his followers, who would, and sometimes did, willingly go to their graves in his service.

Uncle and nephew sat and talked pleasantries for a while, of how the heavy rains had not helped this autumn's olive crop, of Yianni Petraki's daughter who was said to have a demon but improved after the priest performed an exorcism, of Lambros' own eldest son, also called Demetrios (after the shared grandfather) who had stunned everyone by leaving the village with his wife last year and moving to Athens. It was an ordinary family chat, with its share of manly camaraderie, raised eyebrows and sympathetic nods. There was no reason for Demetrios to suppose that a darker purpose lay behind the visit, though it hung heavy like a sack of carrion around Lambros' neck. He thought maybe he should drop the whole business and leave after coffee with a smile and a wave; what a relief that would be. His face lightened at the idea. Demetrios appeared to be content and relaxed with his new wife; it seemed a pity to threaten their wholesome idyll. And she seemed a good girl – a pretty eighteen year old, who averted her eyes and called Lambros 'master', as was appropriate for a young bride addressing her husband's senior male relative, at least until the birth of her first child.

As soon as she had left the room to fetch water from the

stream for the coffee, Demetrios put his question and Lambros felt his heart jump.

'So. What is it you want me to do this time? I can tell it must be serious. You look like someone bringing plague to the village. Relax, old man!' He patted his uncle on the knee with a smile and went over to fetch his pipe, humming a tune. He seemed no more perturbed by the prospect of what he was about to hear than if someone were to tell him there was rain on its way. Lambros glanced to the floor before looking up at his nephew. Their eyes met and all doubt left him. He knew that this was his man, his hope. He began to tell him the plan.

Chapter 6

The cold and draughty lobby of the Hotel d'Angleterre was sparsely lit by oil lamps at five o'clock that Friday morning. The heavy wind outside was pressing its assault on the fabric of the building and rejoiced in the discovery of invisible slits and needle holes, exploiting them as highways to invade the interior, so that the lamps' flames danced nervously on their wicks and a mournful wail swept from the entrance up the stairwell to every corner of the building.

When Godwin met Fortinbras Pierrepont in the flickering half-light of the lobby, a quarter of an hour before leaving for the journey, he was a little apprehensive. The reality of their departure now was dull, bleak and cold and he felt rather contemptuous of the boyish excitement that had played on his imagination in the past few days. He observed himself for a moment as if from a distance, an audience seat, some way removed from the stage of real events. He could see a rather awkward but well-intentioned man, bleary-eyed and dressed for travel, like some character in a music hall melodrama, the sort who walks innocently into a situation contrived by others, deaf to the audience's howls of warning, blind to the obvious pitfall that awaits.

It was time for them to leave, and they headed through a waiters' parlour, past the kitchens – as yet pitch black and inactive – and down a brick-lined passage to a pair of swinging double doors, on the far side of which was the rear tradesmen's entrance. Pierrepont had suggested they would be better off leaving quietly from the back door so as not to attract the crowds that usually gathered to gawp at the departure of a tourist party. There, waiting for them, in the darkness, illuminated only by a pair of lanterns up on either side of the driver's box, was a four-horse carriage.

'I thought we were going on horseback,' said Godwin.

'Only after Thebes,' replied Pierrepont. 'Athens to Thebes is about the only carriageable road in the country. Panayiotis will have arranged for all the horse changes along the way.'

'You know him?'

'Of course. You could never forget him. Splendid fellow,' said Pierrepont going over to a figure who emerged from the shadows on the far side of the lane.

Panayiotis acknowledged Pierrepont with nothing more than a wave of his hand to beckon him towards the carriage; on being introduced to Godwin he nodded expressionlessly, holding the door open and ushering them quickly inside. He was barely five feet tall, dark-skinned, with thick black hair that fell across his forehead, half obscuring a pair of pale hazel eyes. The shock of their colour lent his face a halting poetry. Despite his diminutive stature, he was stocky and nimble, and lifted one case after another up to the rack as easily as if they had been empty. There was an absence of ceremony about him and, while not exactly intolerant of his guests, it was obvious he preferred to waste as little time as possible.

The other two members of the party were already seated and waiting in the carriage. The most striking and un-expected aspect of Dr Schillinger was his blindness; this together with his great age and frailty. Godwin had imagined this classicist, whose eagerness to visit certain less celebrated sites was the reason for their journey's extension, would be a dynamic travelling academic, the type that is single-mindedly dedicated to his quest for sources and unperturbed by any discomfort or obstacle that might block his path. The vulnerable and sightless figure opposite him could not have been more different from what Godwin expected. He had a thin and ancient face with long white hair parted in the centre, and where his eyes should have been the lids lay sealed; the skin of them was delicate gossamer, and served merely to line two circular cavities. It was as though the miniature bowl-shaped swellings that nature had intended should be there had been reversed, like inverted orbs, looking back into the depths of his head. They lent his face a skeletal, deathly presence.

Next to him sat the student, an unusually pale-skinned boy of about twenty, with long, bland cheeks, each splashed crimson across the middle. He was reading a book, and scratching the end of his nose, but could not stop himself stealing a few glances at Godwin and Pierrepont as they settled down opposite him.

Pierrepont leant forward, held out his hand and introduced himself with his customary warmth. The boy managed a vague smile and then turned to say something quietly to his teacher. The old man replied in heavily accented Swiss German, employing few if any consonants. His voice was rough and high-pitched.

'Dr Schillinger speaks only German, ancient Greek or Latin,' said the student. 'And my English is unpractised.'

'Ah,' said Pierrepont, nodding and smiling, at a loss what to say next. Godwin took the message to mean that further intercourse with the learned doctor was perhaps not invited, but Pierrepont did not pick up on this, and continued in a louder and clearer voice.

'Then please tell Dr Schillinger that I wish him a very good morning, that I hope he has a pleasant journey, and that I greatly look forward to partaking of his scholarship as we progress.'

The student sat and stared at Pierrepont blankly for a few moments. His mouth hung open slightly so that the bottom row of teeth was just visible. Then he turned to say another quiet word to the doctor, who answered him without a pause.

The boy returned his thick-lipped gaze to Pierrepont. 'Dr Schillinger says he does not wish to talk.'

Pierrepont, lost for a reply, shuffled back in his seat.

The dull dawn mist had now receded and the wind rocked their carriage, sometimes violently, as the road ran along the sea shore around the Bay of Eleusis. Through the closed windows they could see the celebrated straits of Salamis, site of the famous battle, where the courageous little Greek fleet had routed one thousand Persian ships. Dr Schillinger was being fed a quiet commentary by his pupil, who broke off every so often to consult one of several volumes open on his lap. Godwin wondered what the blind doctor might be picturing as they rolled along, and almost envied the imaginary classical vistas spreading before him, his awareness limited to the scent of the sea breeze, his pupil's commentary and the grind of wheels through the rubble.

Panayiotis now turned the carriage inland, and his pace was slowed by the uphill gradient and stone-strewn surface of the road. It was a landscape of interlocking hills and valleys, ridge upon ridge of rugged, rocky wilderness, covered with myrtle, lentisk and the occasional gnarled pine tree. All signs of human occupation disappeared, except for the odd collection of goats by the road, that would look up inquisitively as they passed and reluctantly step out of the way, the bells around their necks idly tinkling a shared note.

They came at last to the small village of Mandra, a designated station on the Athens-to-Thebes road for changing horses. There was a small *khan*, or inn, by the side of the road, nothing more than a two-room farmer's house, where the travelling party had an early lunch of boiled eggs, onions and cheese. Panayiotis snatched a bite for himself as he unbridled the horses and bartered a price to have them fed, watered and walked back to Athens before the end of the day.

The road now ascended and descended the slopes of wooded hills in sharp zigzags, the highest points of which gave them distant views to the south-east of the mountain heights around

Athens, Hymettus and Pentelicus, before these last reminders of the city vanished altogether. Aside from the crunch of their wheels and the occasional encouraging noise from Panayiotis to the horses, they were now in a silent landscape of arbutus bushes and wild stunted oaks.

Godwin turned his attention to the young pupil, whose name, he had ascertained from Dr Schillinger's insistent repetitions of it, was Hermann. The boy was certainly far from handsome, and yet there was a poignancy about his looks. He seemed shy and withdrawn because he feared the world, as if he had quietly suffered much injury in the past and the circumstances of his life had turned him in on himself. Godwin could picture him alone at his desk, shunned by other students as too earnest and dull-tempered, working instead, buried in books and deprived of fresh air, perhaps pausing occasionally to play solemn Protestant chorales on the wheezy harmonium in the corner of his study. The picture fitted. But of his neighbour, the aged doctor, whose face allowed for no window through which to catch the least glimpse of a story, Godwin could form no picture whatsoever.

In the middle of the afternoon they negotiated a precipitous pathway towards the pass of Eleftherae, an ancient way through the seemingly impenetrable wall of Mount Cithaeron ahead. High above them, perched on a precipice, crumbling fortifications indicated the position of the old garrison, now hardly discernible except for a series of buttress towers that cut the horizon. Dr Schillinger's sightless face was turned towards the window; he was becoming increasingly animated and firing questions at his pupil, who did not seem to be answering them quickly enough. Godwin wondered what the great significance of this place was to the old man, and consulted his Murray guide to find out, but the sum of what was written was not as fascinating as the phenomenon of the strange old man with the thin curtain of white hair falling over his ears, whose enthusiasm for his field of study was entirely joyless.

Soon after passing the fortress they arrived at the highest point of the road and looked down over the vast panorama of Boeotia, an enormous plain encircled by distant mountain ranges topped with snow. Over to their right, due north, they caught their first glimpse of the Pyroxenian peaks, their destination, and the channel that separated the island from the mainland.

They now descended at full gallop down the winding road, and Godwin caught a look of anxiousness in Pierrepont's face as he gripped his seat. A mishap on a corner, an unexpected rock or a horse wrong-footed, could have catastrophic results. But as the sun sank on the horizon, they rumbled safely into the village of Plataea, stiff, hungry and rather dizzy from a whole day's jolting. News of their arrival had preceded them, and a large crowd of villagers was there, not exactly to welcome, but to look at them. The children were particularly amused by the spectacle, dancing around and shrieking with a freedom that their gawping, expressionless parents seemed to lack. Panayiotis pushed his way through the gathering to lead his guests towards their lodgings.

As Godwin later wrote in his diary, the *khan* in which they were to spend the night could hardly be described as an 'inn', with that term's connotations of cosy hospitality, warm beds and hearty pies. It was a two-storey building, the lower part of which was given over to livestock. To reach the upper level, the precinct for humans and only marginally better equipped than the lower, they followed Panayiotis up an exterior stone stairway. The animals' snorts, bleats, shuffles, and the free splatter of urine against a hard clay floor below could be heard through the single layer of wooden floorboards that separated the storeys, as if they were one and the same. As with the sound, so with the scent, which was everpresent, permeating the very fabric of the building.

It was a single room, divided in the middle by a low partition, on the far side of which the elderly innkeeper, known as the *khanji*, who also happened to be the village priest, lived with his wife. The remainder of the room was entirely bare of furniture and given to the use of travellers. Here the foreigners' mattresses were now rolled out, in lines, and these would serve to accommodate them as they ate as well as slept, there being no chairs or tables in the house. A fire was lit at one end of the room, and an iron cauldron was suspended from a tripod over its embers. Steam from the pot merged with the fire's smoke and rose up to blacken the hearth and coat the rough-hewn rafters of the ceiling with grime. To the right of the doorway was a little niche cut into the whitewashed plaster of the wall, in which a small icon of the Virgin was propped up behind a lighted candle in a red glass jar.

They had been offered a chicken for dinner, but Schillinger, adamant that he was not prepared to pay the extra premium, had vetoed the suggestion, so they had to make do with the standard fare of cabbage soup, rice and olives, together with a glass each of resinated wine. It was the coarsest that Godwin had yet tasted but he was coming round to the flavour.

'Look at the state of the fellow,' said Pierrepont nodding towards their host who approached, carrying their food in a pair of tin bowls. 'Quite takes away one's appetite.' The bearded *khanji* was dressed in a long black cassock and his greasy hair was tied in a knot at the back. He gruffly deposited their bowls, muttering to himself and sniffing repeatedly. As soon as his hands were free he wiped his nose on his streaked cassock sleeve, but this did not improve his temper. With a 'Ya, ya, ya, ya', he lowered himself stiffly to the ground and settled next to the guests to watch them eat, every now and then stretching a hand over to grab some part of their clothes, a handkerchief, watch or cuff-link, and ask how much they had paid for it. Pierrepont managed to answer each query in adequate Greek, but every reply seemed to irritate the *khanji* further, and he would shake his head, tutting with disbelief, or spit into the fire.

Dr Schillinger, who sat cross-legged, comfortable and upright as a Buddha, was fed morsel by morsel by his pupil, a slow process, as the old man would chew every mouthful to a pulp before swallowing, after which he would nod wordlessly and open his mouth to receive the next portion. Later, Hermann helped him undress for the night, after which he was instructed to lie down beside his teacher, spooned in for warmth. There were no sheets, but coarsely woven covers were provided, together with a sheepskin for each guest. The blush of the boy's cheeks spread and intensified beyond its usual splash as he climbed in beside the Doctor, aware that the others were watching him.

The two Englishmen talked on until they fell asleep where they lay, as the fire fizzed and spat. It was cold outside. Athens and the Hotel d'Angleterre seemed to belong to another world.

Chapter 7

The next morning was dazzlingly bright, with a slight frost on the ground, and when Godwin emerged from the *khan* he discovered a small group of villagers had already assembled to view the strangers. Panayiotis was also waiting, next to a line of horses, together with two baggage mules. The four travellers had a horse each, a small, hang-neck plodder of a beast, with bony shoulders where the fur had rubbed down to leather and ears that sagged horizontal from the temples.

It was a glorious day, and Godwin was looking forward to the quiet, slower pace of horseback travel. They progressed from a landscape of mountains and ravines, hanging behind them like silent giants, towards a marshy plain that ended at the Pyroxenian channel. There, by late afternoon, they were to cross over to the town of Páparis, on the shores of Pyroxenia, to spend the night. Godwin fancied he could already smell the sea on the morning breeze that came in from the east, enlivening the last remnants of the night that clung in dewy combes and gullies behind them.

Panayiotis travelled by foot and sang ballads as he led a baggage mule, swinging the husk of a cow parsley stalk with his free hand. Aside from his pleasant tenor, and the whisk of the breeze through the evergreen foliage of wild holly and arbutus, there was utter silence.

Mid-morning they arrived at a dome-shaped hillock where a crowded collection of houses, little stone and thatch huts, together with some scattered hovels and crumbling pieces of antique masonry constituted the modern town of Thebes.

After they had inspected what remained of the legendary site, and had some lunch, they continued with a ride which was as uncomfortable as the early morning's had been pleasant. They were mounted on traditional Greek saddles, carved from wood, broad and high above the back of the animal, with a handle at the front. Locals would sit side-saddle on them, but to ride with legs splayed, which was the only way the foreigners felt safe, was an uncomfortable stretch, and the result was bruised bones and an aching pelvis. There was no bridle and no need for one, because the old horses had long forgotten the joys of deviation, and followed one another slavishly nose to tail. So blind was their choiceless progression, they would indiscriminately pass between juxtaposed boulders or leaning tree trunks, so that the rider was regularly buffeted or scratched by obstacles along the way.

By the early afternoon Godwin felt thoroughly battered, a condition not helped by the gradual deterioration of their track, now nothing more than a path, if that. Their problems were compounded by a sudden worsening of the weather; the sky darkened, rain began to fall heavily and there was a distant rumble of thunder. Panayiotis told them they would have to abandon any hope of getting to Páparis by the evening because a storm was on the way. There was a village some two miles along the river where they might be able to find shelter for the night, but they must move on at a pace.

They progressed along a dried-up river course, a deep, gloomy gorge, as the light faded beneath black clouds. The boulders planted along the twisted way were rounded smooth from centuries of pummelling water, and scattered all about was a collection of debris belched up from the surrounding countryside. The rain now turned into hail, the force and weight of which seemed almost to defy nature. Godwin had never experienced weather like it, and felt a tinge of alarm.

They arrived at the small hamlet after a short ride, during

which the weather showed no sign of relaxing. Peals of thunder resonated through the river valleys, tumbling on into damp, spring-fed dells and gullies, finally absorbed and silenced by a hillside cushion of drenched myrtle and oleander. The air was sharp with the scent of soaking bark and foliage.

There were no more than five dwellings in the settlement, and Panayiotis led them, with his quick assured step, straight to one of them, a single-roomed stone and thatch house with one small window on either side of the tiny wooden door. He explained their predicament hurriedly to a woman with a colourful apron and headscarf, who was squatting inside. Her face was locked into a habitual frown of complaint, and she looked at the group of foreigners, huddled and dripping on her threshold, as a cloud of ice balls the size of marbles bounced and danced a fresh assault in the muddy yard beyond. With a tut of reluctance, she beckoned them inside, and led the way to a slightly raised wooden platform that took up half of the room, the other half being given over to livestock. There was no flue for the fire, or even an aperture in the roof, and the atmosphere was thick with wood smoke that found its only escape through two glassless windows. The woman threw some dried pine cones on the embers which immediately burst into flame, illuminating the room.

The party of travellers was by now decidedly subdued. They hung their heads like sad dogs as they disrobed in front of the woman and handed their clothes over to be dried as best they could. Soon the fire was blocked from sight by a curtain of steaming garments and a semicircle of boots, sodden at the creases. They sat on their bed rolls, which Panayiotis had had the foresight earlier in the day to have wrapped in felt to protect them from the rain, and their hostess provided them with blankets to wrap around their shoulders. A glance through the shutter showed that the hail had turned to a steady heavy downpour, the relentlessness of which seemed to defeat the day itself, as the light yielded to an early dusk.

Pierrepont was shivering, but turned cheerily to Godwin. 'Believe me, you'll be pleased one day to have done this. There are no hardships in this simple and uncomfortable travelling life but that in later years will make you look back on them with pleasure.'

'I don't doubt it for a moment,' replied Godwin, smiling.

They slept, guests and hosts alike, one squeezed alongside the next, so close to the animals they could feel the warmth of the donkey's breath. Godwin was aware of Pierrepont's broken sleep next to him, and could feel waves of uncontrollable shivers take hold of him throughout the night. Cats wandered carefully between the prostrate humans and leapt silently across roof timbers in the darkness, while the fire flickered on into the early hours and the rain pelted the thatch above. The smoke clogged their throats as they tried to sleep, while in all the bedding, the rugs and the sheepskins, there was a sense of things crawling.

Godwin woke early. The flapping of wings above in the darkness had informed him repeatedly in the night that some fowl were probably roosting in the eaves, and his suspicions were confirmed from a very early hour by a piercing crow that cut through the air every few minutes. The sound seemed to alert all the dogs of the hamlet at the same time, and a chorus of discordant howls and barks from near and far began. Godwin gave up hope of sleeping and crept from his covers, picking his way between the animals to the door, through which he could see that the rain had stopped. It was dull outside, but fresh. Everything was dripping. The sun, barely risen, was obscured by fog, but it might yet turn out to be a fine day. He could hear nearby the flow of a stream, and decided to follow the sound in the hope of finding fresh water to splash his face and drink. His eyes felt swollen and inflamed by the dust and smoke of the night, and patches of his skin were raised in itchy bumps from insect bites.

He made his way carefully between the bushes, down a bank from the village until he could see the river nearby beneath him. But something else caught his sight, making him stop in his tracks and instinctively move for cover behind a tree trunk. There in the river below him stood the bent and naked figure of Dr Schillinger, knee deep in the water, his hand supported by Hermann, who was also undressed. With his other hand, Hermann was washing down his teacher with a lathered flannel. The old man, thin, white and stooped, did not appear to be suffering from the cold, and as Hermann emptied cup after cup of water over his head he neither complained nor flinched. Godwin watched the little procedure, gripped by its bizarre quality. It was both sensual and ritualistic, almost baptismal, though the roles were reversed: pupil was anointing teacher.

When Godwin returned to the *khan* Pierrepont was up, and although he attempted a smile it was quite clear he had hardly slept. There were dark circles underneath his eyes, and he had developed a cough. Panayiotis said to Godwin that they should leave as soon as possible and get Pierrepont to the relative comfort of Páparis.

The village was still shrouded when they mounted, but by the time they stopped for lunch the sun was high in the sky and they had an uninterrupted view of the channel that separated Pyroxenia from the mainland, now stretching out in front of them. The sight of a coasting steamer making its way along the wooded headlands and sandy beaches of the shore reassured them all.

By three o'clock they had crossed the bridge which spanned the narrow isthmus and had entered Páparis. Once the pride of the Venetian empire, it was now a quaint town of ruined battlements, cottages and mosques converted into churches, their minarets decapitated and now serving as bell-towers. Panayiotis explained that they should go direct to the house of Mr Solouzos, a politician and friend of Brooke's, where they had been expected the previous evening. They made their way along the southern edge of the crumbling town wall before turning inland on a narrow lane, and eventually arriving at an imposing old stone gateway. They passed through the gates into a courtyard planted with pomegranates, figs and orange trees. Here they were received by Mrs Solouzos, a small, homely woman in her forties, with the manner of a solicitous but kindly school matron.

The travellers followed her up an external wooden stairway that led on to a wide, shaded gallery strung with vines along its length. The bedrooms led off from it. Mr Solouzos was at a political gathering, they were told, but was looking forward to meeting them at dinner. Pierrepont said he would retire immediately, and declined Mrs Solouzos' offer to call a doctor, saying that a good rest would set him to rights by the morning. Schillinger also announced that he and Hermann would not be dining, which Godwin thought inexplicably rude, given the hospitality that was being extended to them.

Panayiotis went off to the town to dispatch a rider on to Thasofolia so that Brooke would be warned of their delay, while Godwin changed into his spare set of clothes and relaxed in a comfortable wicker chair on the gallery. It was a mild and sunny evening, and he wondered at the fickle personality of the Greek weather. All of a sudden a church bell began to ring out, followed by several others from various quarters of the town. He remembered that it was Sunday and that people were probably on their way to celebrate the evening liturgy. He leant his head back against the top of the chair, grateful that his membership of an alien race exempted him from tiresome Sunday duties. A bath was being prepared for him. In the meantime, while the bells rang across the town, a dusky servant boy brought him a saucer of olives, and a glass of some devilishly pungent spirit.

*

Later that evening, Godwin, sole representative of the travelling party, sat dining with his hosts. After the meal, Mrs

84

Solouzos retired early, leaving the men to their cigarettes and a bottle of Madeira that her husband had been keeping in a dusty corner of their kitchen pantry for a special occasion. Mr Solouzos was the grandson of a Scot on his mother's side, and spoke English almost perfectly. As if to compensate for his missing slice of racial purity he was doubly Greek in every aspect of his personality, passionate in all that he said and free in his use of expansive gestures, especially when he spoke about the nation or his home town. His limbs had a fluid range of movements and his manner was at once informal and fraternal, the body language of one whose politics were naturally rather liberal, and came from the heart.

Solouzos had carved for himself considerable local influence, but despite his role as one of the most notable burghers of Páparis, his appearance was dishevelled to the point of absent-mindedness. His clothes were worn and tattered, his round, cherubic cheeks unshaven, his hair rather too long for its shape and unkempt. Beneath a pair of almost comically bushy eyebrows, his eyes stared hard and bright at Godwin, barely blinking, fixing him with an intense enthusiasm while they conversed. Vanity was clearly not amongst his priorities, his energies being taken up with public works and political science, about which he talked incessantly, perhaps hoping to find in Godwin someone who understood such things and shared his enthusiasm.

It became clear during the course of their conversation that Edgar Brooke was a good family friend and political ally. Solouzos referred to him with a mixture of affection and veneration, and always in the warmest terms, to the extent that Godwin wondered whether he was talking about the same man he had met at the Legation dinner. Solouzos explained that the Brooke family had struggled against the odds from the start. Edgar's father had been a remarkable, very industrious man, revered and loved by all, but had suffered continuously while he lived here, as had his wife. He eventually left the country, a tired and broken man.

'The old people of Thasofolia,' said Solouzos, 'still talk affectionately about Thomas, the old master, as they call him. Though they have a new father in Edgar Brooke.'

'That's how they regard him? Like a father? Such devotion?'

'Absolutely. I cannot think of another man so widely loved.'

'Edgar Brooke?' asked Godwin, his surprise getting the better of tact.

'Of course. Why not?'

Godwin sought a way to disguise his reaction. 'I just thought it peculiar that a foreign landlord could command such affection from the indigenous people.'

'But he is so much more than a landlord. And not exactly foreign. He has all the qualities of his father and more. He is employer, friend, inspiration. But above all, he is a man of principle. He has built for the village a church and a school. He has medicines and hospital books sent from England, and the sick line up outside his house for cures. He has become quite skilled as a doctor.'

'And his land is productive?'

'Of course! And improving all the time. Only last month he opened a new sawmill at the river, so his timber production is now hugely increased. He has drained the marshes, dammed the river, dug wells, cleared the river valley and introduced new crops. He leads his people like a captain. And a brother. And they are happy to be taught by him.'

'And so he prospers?'

'Aha! This is more difficult to answer,' Solouzos laughed and tapped the ash from his cigarette. 'A man in his position is continually beset with problems. He has to be aware that every bee making honey in the hive also carries a sting in his tail. The secret is to persuade him not to use it!'

Godwin liked Mr Solouzos even though his clothes smelt

stale as if they were hardly ever changed, merely sprayed with scent to cover up something worse.

'Have you known the family a long time?' Godwin asked.

'All my life.'

'Can you tell me what happened to Mr Brooke's wife? I heard she died some while ago.'

At this, a slight frown seemed to puncture Solouzos' buoyancy. 'She and her horse were found at the bottom of a ravine on the estate,' he said. 'Perhaps the horse bolted and went over the edge. Nobody knows for certain.'

'A riding accident?'

'She loved Thasofolia and did many wonderful things for the people. A beautiful woman. She was always full of plans, never resting.' His voice trailed off and his eyes lost their focus.

Later, as Godwin lay in his bed, their conversation about Edgar returned to him and hung there in the etheric territory between wakefulness and sleep: the Brookes' long struggle against the tide of fate, their misfortunes, the beautiful wife's death. He drifted away, and his imagination unshackled itself, calling here and there at shadowy silhouettes in his recent memory, as a bee flies indiscriminately from flower to flower. He tried to focus on Edgar and his peculiarities, to form a comprehensible profile of the man, but exhaustion overwhelmed him. His thoughts, unmarshalled, danced and spun like seeds in a wind, most of them falling on barren land, the occasional one sprouting wildly in rich turf, growing chaotic and shapeless before vanishing, all in the space of a split second. And then a rigid thought emerged through the haze: Brooke the man of principle, Brooke the benign philanthropist. This was what Solouzos had talked about. The incongruousness of the description registered with Godwin momentarily. He felt himself pulled back out of the mystery world of sleep like a piece of rusting iron salvaged from the silence of the sea-bed, brought to the surface, dripping and heavy, up into the noisy world of open air. It was a lamentable return to thought, a dreary world compared to the restful weightlessness of the depths, and so he let go once again, this time dropping irretrievably into the abyss.

Chapter 8

There was a knock on the door. It was Panayiotis. The mules were packed, breakfast was waiting, and Godwin was required immediately to pass judgement on whether Mr Pierrepont was fit to travel. There were just the three short sentences barked in Panayiotis' usual abrupt tone, to which no reply was expected, before the door clicked shut and Godwin heard the diminutive man's footsteps retreating along the timber gallery outside.

Thin slits of light pierced the joins and edges of the shutters, faintly illuminating his room. It was comfortable and he wished he could stay for another day to soothe his various aches and strains. He pressed his fingers into the symmetrical bones on either side of his groin, and felt the painful but irresistible bruising. Far from having subsided with grace to allow for another day's riding, the bruises were defiantly inflamed, rebelling against the prospect of what lay ahead.

Pierrepont's room was further along the gallery, and as Godwin hurried there he met Mrs Solouzos returning with an empty tray, looking concerned. She had just given Fortinbras some breakfast, and said that he had been sweating with a fever for most of the night. Godwin found him lying on his side, breathing heavily. He smiled and raised his head as Godwin approached, but he looked pale and tired. He was keen to persevere with the trip, thinking that he would be able to recuperate more comfortably at the Brookes' house, and so Godwin left him and proceeded to the dining room for breakfast. As he entered, the spooned cavities of Schillinger's eye sockets turned to meet him, and he felt a pulse of alarm at the sight, despite his familiarity with the old man after their journey together. He greeted him and Hermann but received no word in reply.

Solouzos was there to see them depart. A slight breeze in the air that morning freed the curls of Godwin's hair, giving him an unruly look, less formal than before, the constraints of city behaviour evaporating as they bored deeper into the countryside's heartland, across the coastal marshes, zigzagging uphill along sheer-sided paths.

The mountains were now wilder and more craggy, the presence of nature more enveloping; dark gullies led away from the travellers on both sides, their dripping rockfaces fed by moss-covered springs and kept in permanent shadow by evergreen shrubs and overhanging trees. This was a landscape less frequented than that which they had so far crossed, and at times the path disappeared completely into thickets of scrub. At one point they had to dismount to protect themselves as they passed through a tunnel of brambles; all except Pierrepont, whom Panayiotis covered with an animal skin and leant forward against the mule's neck, steadying him with his own arm as he walked along beside, taking the scratches and thorns without complaint to protect the sick traveller.

After several hours of rough travel they reached the summit, which offered them views out to the north and eastern horizons towards the grey silhouettes of several other islands peppered across the distant Aegean. Panayiotis allowed little rest but urged them on down a route of interlocking valleys. The forest became thicker and the smell of resin more pungent, as they curved their way down, tracing the course of streams and rivulets, to a dramatic gorge at the foot of the mountain.

On the ravine's far side, cliffs fell sheer to a torrent deep below, while on this side they could see their track curving away in front of them, cut into a barely less precipitous flank. Nature had carved its own bottleneck here, forcing all who wanted to pass north to cling like fragile insects to this one narrow ledge for a mile or more. Previous generations of inhabitants had clearly noted its strategic potential, and Godwin saw, towering like a nest on a distant rocky outcrop far above, the ruined remains of a fortress. Hermann was flicking through a volume at the sight of it, egged on by short waspish comments from his teacher.

Their quiet progress was interrupted by a call from ahead, and their animals came to a halt. Three men advanced on Panayiotis and surrounded him, one of them taking hold of his bridle. A simple wooden shelter had been constructed to the side of the track, against the trunk of a massive pine tree. There were rugs and stools in the shelter, and a small fire was burning on the ground in front of it. The men who had accosted them wore dirty *fustanellas* with billowing sleeves. Their leather leggings were lashed to their calves with criss-crossed ropes, and sheepskins were tied to their backs in the manner of cloaks. Each wore a woollen pillbox hat from under which their hair, matted into thick dense locks, bushed out, shoulder length, a wild frame to their strong, unshaven chins. They did not seem to understand, or want to listen to what Panayiotis was telling them, but stared at him, frowning and shaking their heads from time to time as he spoke. The one in front had a pistol in his belt. It was of an old type, an heirloom, perhaps, the brass inlay polished bright.

Godwin heard Panayiotis mention the words 'Solouzos' and 'Brooke' several times; the pitch of his voice was raised, and there was a hint of anxiety in his eyes, like a schoolboy accounting for himself. Whatever he said seemed to satisfy the men and they stood back to let him through, appraising each of the foreigners closely as they walked past. There was no hostility in their look, but it was more than curiosity. These local guardsmen of the mountain pass, or whatever they were, had experience in their gaze, the sort that could strip a man naked without touching him, could size him up for worth or strength. Here at this far-flung outpost, Godwin sensed that his rank and citizenship of a powerful nation far away counted for little. At this moment, on this pass, his life was in the hands of these rough-looking men, and for now, it seemed, thankfully, they were allies; but their eyes promised no guarantee for the future.

The valley began to open and the sound of the river subsided, turning from a roar to a gurgle as it spread towards a broad, gravel-banked bed. From here on it was flanked by a plantation of mature plane trees, their blotchy trunks smooth and circular in girth, the branches spread outwards like limbs on a voluptuous sculpture. Passing a tiny white-washed chapel, where a shepherd rested on a stone bench, Panayiotis called out that they had arrived at the boundary of Kyrios Brooke's land.

Although the sun had by now sunk low in the sky, the fertile plain into which they now passed was bathed in a golden late afternoon light. The backcloth of mountains, laid out in the shape of a horseshoe behind them, was densely forested and cleft by deep ravines. Looking back, it was as if the doors of the mountain were closing, dark and impenetrable, while before them lay an enclosed sanctuary. No-one said a word, but the mules, which had for some time been ambling exhaustedly, now began to trot, sensing the approach of their stable. The travellers, all except Schillinger, whose head was bent low as if in humble acceptance of his inability to share the sight, looked around in wonder at the change of scenery. The distant snow-capped summits hung protectively above the farmland basin. Their stony slopes, thick with brushwood and thorn bush, were turning a soft blue in the evening haze, and their wave upon wave of pine trees appeared from this distance like a vast fur lining, spread nonchalantly across the breadth of the range.

At the foot of the mountains the cultivation began, a tidy

arrangement of fields, paths, vineyards, ditches and meadows, unlike anything Godwin had yet seen in Greece, leading back, on either side, to the river, the main thorough-fare, artery and lifeblood of the landscape. Straight ahead of them, along the course of the river and clinging to the under-side of a pine-crested ridge, was the village of Thasofolia. The evening fires had been lit, and a horizontal film of smoke hung like a low ceiling across the valley. A little to the right of the village, perched on a knoll which set it above and distinct from the surrounding farmland, shrouded with cypress and cedar trees, they could make out the terracotta tiles of a large house. Their destination.

'Well, what do you think?' asked Pierrepont, whose spirits had rallied with the end in sight. It was the first thing he had said in hours, and the effort of it made him cough.

'So this is it,' replied Godwin softly.

'Thasofolia. The house is over there on that hillock. Appropriately named, don't you think?'

'What do you mean?'

'Thasofolia means woodland den. Forest hideaway, that sort of thing.'

'That's almost too cosy,' said Godwin looking around at the backdrop of mountains. 'This quite takes the breath away.'

About half a mile from the village the track parted from the river-bed and curved up to the higher ground on which the majority of the houses were clustered. They were almost all of the same design: single-storey, tiled cottages, one wooden-shuttered window on either side of the door, the walls coarsely mortared and painted with lime. As ever, word of their arrival had preceded them, and a handful of spectators came out to their doorsteps to watch them pass by. The little children, both boys and girls, had close-cropped hair and wore thick smock dresses; the older girls, like their mothers, had long headscarves covering their hair and wrapped around their necks, so that their faces peeped out

93

from the shadows behind a circular swathe of white cloth. All the men individually called out a greeting to Panayiotis, who responded with a nod and a wave. The road then passed out of the village and descended slightly before curving round and up a tree-lined avenue to the main entrance of the house, on the hill, half a mile beyond. It was almost dark now, and Panayiotis called out to the pair of guards from a distance so that they would open the tall timber gates in advance to save them stopping. This they did, and the little procession of mules, with their weary load of foreign travellers and dusty bags, trooped past a large pine that spread above the gates and into the courtyard.

The main building of the house, immediately facing them as they came through the gates, was the largest Godwin had seen since leaving Athens, though by English standards no bigger than an average country rectory or small manor. It was built in the local style, with rubble mortar walls, tall, shuttered windows, and a balcony around its entire perimeter at first-floor height. The lower windows were obscured by a vine-covered structure, protruding from the base of the balcony, which formed a shaded veranda all the way round the house. Two colossal flares, set in steel sheaths and collared either side of the main door, blazed wildly in the breeze, their huge flames lighting them down to a set of stone steps that marked the way to the entrance. On either side of this principal building, and stretching the full length of the courtyard down to the entrance, were two lower structures which served as workshops, stables, barns and store rooms. Around the edge of the settlement, delineating its boundary, tall cypress trees loomed black against the evening sky. The view of the mountains and the plain around was now obscured by mist and darkness. It was going to be a cold night.

A male servant in a white *fustanella* came down the steps to help Panayiotis unpack the animals, and Godwin assisted Pierrepont to the ground. Panayiotis had already called to a young woman, another household servant, who wore a thick, waistless cream dress down to her ankles, covered at the front by a colourful embroidered apron. She ran up to Pierrepont but seemed shy to take his arm and help him up the steps until Panayiotis snapped at her, and she hurriedly complied.

Godwin and the others followed on into the spacious wood-panelled hall. Its walls were hung with smoke-darkened portraits and hunting trophies, the most impressive of which was a bear, truncated at the ribs, its arms opening out into space, as if it had come down from the surrounding forest and burst through the wall to settle an old score. The hall was comfortably warm because of a fire that blazed beneath a massive stone lintel half-way along one wall. It was a fireplace of baronial proportions, with small benches inside the inglenook where one could sit and watch whole logs crackle and spit on the crested iron grate.

The smell of burning pine permeated every inch of the house, and this scent, more than anything, became for Godwin, in retrospect, inseparable from his experience of Thasofolia. It was a variant of the smell that hung over the entire area: the living firs of the forest, the fresh-split firewood outside every cottage, the resinated barrels, the wine, the mountains of amber dust at the sawmills, the beams and rafters hidden under the tiles.

'And you must be Mr Tudor? Is that right?' The question caught him off guard. His host was there in front of him. It had been eight days since their last meeting, Godwin thought, surely not long enough for Edgar Brooke to doubt who he was. There he stood, that virile, well-bred face, the same unruly greying hair, the bushy eyebrows and pale blue eyes. But there was a hunched, put-upon air about him that had not been noticeable at the Legation dinner, an uncertainty in the eyes. He was dressed in a worn brown waistcoat and there were patches on the knees of his trousers. He looked at Godwin, eyebrows slightly raised but otherwise without any expression whatever, hands clasped together, waiting for an answer.

'Yes,' said Godwin, extending his hand. 'How do you do, Mr Brooke?'

'I'm very well, I'm very well.' No hand was offered in return, as he shuffled around on the spot to look at the other new arrivals. He was wearing a pair of ankle-high coarse wool slippers, an unusual sort of footwear that Godwin thought must be local. 'Has someone taken your bags, would you like me to take your bags? I'm very strong, you know, and good at building fires, don't you like this fire, Mr Tudor?' He pointed at the inglenook, grinning widely and revealing a set of brown teeth. Godwin did not remember this smile or the teeth. 'I built it myself, and there's a nice one in your room, you're in the blue room, do you know where it is? I can take you there if you like. How do you do, and who are you?' He addressed the last question of his rapid patter to Dr Schillinger, looking straight at the hollow pink-skinned eye sockets. Hands together, he waited for an answer, but Schillinger was none the wiser. Hermann spoke up, 'This is Dr Schillinger, and I am Hermann Kopfling.'

'Very good, very good, follow me, you've all got nice fires, someone will bring your bags.' He started muttering something to himself in Greek as he turned and shuffled off in the direction of the staircase that led from the hall to a balustraded gallery above.

'Wait a moment, Percival,' a female voice called, and the man stopped where he stood. An elderly woman had entered from another room across the hall. She had grey hair, cut short like a schoolboy and topped with a small lace bonnet. Her dress was made of plaid wool, buttoned tight at the front and spreading in widening layers to a pleated hem that trailed some three feet behind her. 'Percival!' she called, and then turned to the visitors. 'How do you do?' she said generally to them before continuing, 'Percival! Come back.' The man Godwin had taken to be Edgar Brooke turned and walked back to her, mouth hanging open slightly, hands still clasped together.

'Yes, dear?'

'Ask Maroula to take a warming pan to the pink room at once, then to prepare me a basin of boiling water – the smaller of the two Welsh ones, please, and she must take care, those basins are irreplaceable. And I'll need six tumblers, eucalyptus oil, some dry yarrow flower, dry elder-flower and peppermint leaf. And a teacup. Will you remember all that?'

'Yes, my dear. Why, is there something wrong?'

'Mr Pierrepont has a nasty cold.'

'Aha. Poor Mr Pierrepont. Shall I check his fire?'

'After you've seen Maroula.'

'Right,' he said, and turned to hurry away.

'And have you greeted our guests, Percival?'

'Yes, I have,' he said opening a door on the far side. 'Mr Tudor's here, and Dr Schillinger and Mr Kopfling. I've made them all fires.'

'Dinner in an hour.'

'All right, my dear. Yarrow flower, elderflower and pepper-mint leaf,' called the man from the next room, and continued muttering to himself, out of earshot.

Godwin held out his hand to the woman. She took it – a delicate touch, more feminine than her appearance would have indicated. She had small hands, well preserved for her age, and ringless.

'Good evening. I am Miss Brooke. Magdalen Brooke. I wish you to call me Mag. So, it's Mr Tudor,' she said, looking him over like a piece of second-rate furniture left by a dead relative and now needing to be fitted in somewhere around the house. 'You don't have the build of a Tudor.'

'I'm sorry?'

'I was expecting someone looking like Henry the Eighth.'

Godwin smiled. 'I suppose the blood has been watered down a bit since then.'

'Horrible man. Horrible family, all in all.' There was not the smallest trace of humour either in her voice or expression. She turned to the others and introduced herself in faultless German. The servant who had unpacked the mules then came in, laden with bags.

'George, here, will show you your rooms. Just follow him and be down in time for dinner at half-past seven.' The others followed George up the stairs, but Godwin paused. 'Miss Brooke?'

'Mag.'

'I'm sorry. Mag.' The impropriety joined with the ugliness of the monosyllable made it stick in his throat. 'Was that not Mr Brooke with us a moment ago, who greeted us as we came in?'

'Of course it was.'

Godwin felt awkward. 'Mr Edgar Brooke?'

'Good gracious, no. That was Percival, my other brother, Edgar's twin. Senior twin, as it happens.'

'I didn't know. I mean, nobody told me.'

'Well, I don't suppose anyone necessarily would have thought to tell you. You mean about his peculiarities?'

'Of course not. I didn't mean that at all.'

'Don't mind him. He's perfectly harmless. You'll get used to his ways.' At this, she turned and was gone before Godwin could offer any further explanation.

Godwin settled into his room gratefully. Its high white-washed walls rose to a timber-boarded ceiling, and two sets of large double doors opened on to the balcony. They were shuttered on the outside, with slats to allow the cool air through in summer. Otherwise the room was heavily reminiscent of England, furnished with some old pieces in the style of Chippendale and decorated with a series of West Country hunting prints. The luggage, including his photographic equipment – mercifully undamaged – was brought up by the servant they had called George, and the chamber-maid, Maroula, eventually knocked at the door with a jug of hot water for his basin. After washing and changing his clothes he put another log on the fire and went downstairs. He was a little early, but thought he might have a look around.

He made his way from the hall through a morning room and into the dining room, laid out for dinner exactly as it might have been at an English country house. The candles were lit and a fire blazed, the light from both dancing through the table's dense population of glass and silver, across to the gilt-framed pictures and dark red walls behind. Godwin felt the warmth of the place like an infusion, the sense of a homely outpost cocooned from the gathering winter, in the cradle of forest and mountains. The shutters were closed and Greece was at bay. That wild and threatening scenery, its tempestuous elements and dangerous people. And yet if they weren't just there, beyond the shutters, the spirit of the place would be lost. Indoors, by the light of fire and candle, all was safe and well; the Levant was outside, a war-torn landscape, thick with history and legend. The romance of it was almost suffocating.

Beside the flutter of the fire the only other sound was of subdued voices from the room beyond the dining room, on the other side of the door that faced him. Thinking that perhaps some of his party might already be assembled, Godwin made his way to the door and went through. The voices fell silent and the three men sitting there turned to look at him.

There could be no doubting him this time. There stood Edgar Brooke, his heavy frame leaning over a desk, arms like temple pillars supporting his weight on clenched fists. He raised his face towards the door and his blue eyes now fixed on Godwin. Next to him stood a shorter man of about the same age, with a defiant expression. Beside them, a little way off and seated, was the third, younger, dressed in a *fustanella*, with long tousled hair and black eyes that almost smiled a welcome as Godwin entered. He tossed some beads backwards and forwards over his knuckles and looked back at his two companions with a slight smirk.

'Yes?' came the slightly throaty, deadpan voice of Edgar Brooke.

'Mr Brooke!' beamed Godwin. 'How do you do? How very good to see you!'

'This is neither the time nor the place, sir. Please be so good as to close the door behind you as you leave.' He indicated the exit behind Godwin's shoulder with a nod. 'Good evening.'

Godwin quickly withdrew and hurried back through the dining room and out into the hall. It was empty. Still reeling from the shock of his host's manner, he looked around in a sort of daze. A pair of knots in a wooden panel facing him were shaped like eyes, gazing out, and as he stared back he began to construct a face in the grain around them, a smirking face with a twisted mouth that seemed to take pleasure in his misfortune. The wood itself mocked him.

He crossed the hall to the drawing room, which he assumed would be empty, intending to sit and digest what had just occurred; but he was caught by surprise because there was somebody else already in there.

He would never forget the moment, this event that was to be so central to his life. Everything about it remained forever etched with perfect accuracy in his mind's eye. Perhaps it was because he had developed the perception of a photographer that he recalled such pivotal events as if viewed through the lens: the precise composition, light and texture of the scene. He was standing in the doorframe and she was sitting on a stool to the side of the fire, stoking it with a hooked iron. He could not yet see her face, just the spreading mass of golden hair, with a darker texture woven in its depths, and lightly curled, so that she had to hold it in check to stop it getting in her way.

She looked around as he came into the room and he realized instantly who it must be. She had her father's blue eyes and wide forehead.

'Hello,' she said, and with a smile returned to her fire. 'Are you one of my father's friends? You don't look like one.'

'I doubt you mean that as a compliment, but I may yet improve in your estimation. You must be Lydia.' Although she looked older, Godwin remembered from his conversation with Pierrepont that she was just sixteen and there was no need for formality. 'I am Mr Tudor, but you can call me Godwin, if you like.'

'I'll be able to see you rather better when you come further into the room. I'm afraid my eyes are not very efficient at discerning objects at a distance.'

'Am I a mere object?' said Godwin with mock injury, while his heart melted at the news of her infirmity.

'That is my meaning. At present, yes.' He walked towards her and she smiled approvingly as he came into focus.

'Have you met my Aunt Mag yet, Mr Tudor?'

'Yes. Earlier. When we arrived.'

'What do you think of her?'

'How am I supposed to answer that? We hardly exchanged two words.'

'Come, come, Mr Tudor,' she said looking at him with teasing mockery, 'can't you permit yourself a visceral response? You have the air of a romantic. Don't disappoint me at this early stage. Let me know your thoughts on Aunt Mag.'

'Very well,' said Godwin, approaching her and pulling up an adjacent stool. 'I suspect she possesses wit, and certainly strength, both to a considerable measure. She has authority but also kindness, though softness she probably lacks. No, really, this is too absurd. I do not know her!'

'Beautiful?' she smiled up at him. Her front teeth protruded very slightly beneath her upper lip. It was a full mouth, a ravishing mouth.

'Handsome.'

'You lie, Mr Tudor.'

'No,' he insisted, now rather enjoying the game, 'handsome

101

is appropriate. Beautiful is not a word that would have sprung to mind, but handsome is fair.'

'Foul is fair and fair is foul,' she quipped with a grin, and Godwin smiled at her brightness. 'Have a look on the mantelpiece up there,' she said: 'the daguerreotype, do you see it?'

Godwin stood up and moved in front of the fire to look into the little oval picture. It was set in a morocco case, leather-bound, the inside of its hinged door lined with velvet. There was a shadowy figure etched into the silver plate behind the glass, but the light and angle were wrong and he had to bring it down to the oil lamp to get a better look. The image was sharp and clear. It was a girl, probably no older than Lydia now, standing in a doorway, leaning to one side, her hands and cheek pressed to the doorframe. Her features were even, fresh and sensuous, her long dark hair parted in the middle and falling on either side of her face. She wore a sleeveless blouse and no shoes. Her large dark eyes looked up from under her brows, the smallest fragment of doubt betrayed in their expression.

'You're going to tell me this is her. Yes, beautiful. You are right.'

'The man who broke her heart was standing just behind the camera when it was taken, apparently. She was looking right at him. It was that door over there–' Lydia pointed across the room. 'It leads straight to the garden.' Godwin looked at the girl in the picture again and wished he could travel back and scoop her into his arms. She was lovely. She did not deserve to have her heart broken.

'What did the man do to hurt her so?'

Lydia gave him an arch look over her shoulder. 'Now, Mr Tudor, is that an appropriate question for a gentleman to ask? Should we really speculate about the power of passion to soften the boundaries of propriety?'

'You are right. I do not need to hear more.'

'Suffice to say Aunt Mag left Greece for some years after the incident and went to live in England. To work at a charitable institution. To atone, perhaps.'

'I have heard enough. Please.'

'Have you been a soldier, Mr Tudor?'

Godwin blinked at the unexpected and not entirely welcome change of subject. Lydia's conversation had the minute aggression of a needle point, and a host of unpleasant memories formed rank in his mind. 'I tried to be, once. In order to please my father. It didn't last long. I wasn't – how shall one say? – temperamentally suited to the soldier's life. But I did stay long enough for them to teach me how to draw. Which has been useful.' Silently he bade the young Magdalen Brooke farewell for ever and put the daguerreotype back in its place.

'And then?'

'And then,' he sighed, 'I tried to comply with my father's second choice. The Church.'

'Ah, so you're a Christian?'

'That didn't work for me either.'

'You did not have enough faith?'

Godwin smiled, though once more he felt uncomfortable with the line of questioning. 'It was a matter of temperament, again.'

'But you are a Christian?' she persisted.

'Yes, Lydia, of course I am. Are we not all?'

'You concur that Adam and Eve mark the beginning of humankind, that the Book of Genesis is historical truth, that Mary conceived as a virgin, and the rest of it?'

Godwin felt the moment called for a magisterial approach. 'Do you think it's appropriate for a young lady to be talking about such matters, and in such a manner? Who has been putting these ideas into your head?'

'Now that is amusing, Mr Tudor. Someone put an idea into my head! My head!'

'I take it, then, you do not concur with the opinions of all the archbishops, bishops and the manifold clergy of Britain,

103

many of them great scholars, heads of our foremost schools and universities, not to mention the cardinals and popes of the past thousand years and more, and of course the convictions of our own monarch? How so, child?' But he was smiling. She was a plucky creature. The slight upturn of her nose a classicist might see as a flaw, but Godwin thought if she did not lose it as her face matured, it would become highly attractive, perhaps seductive.

'Next year it will be eighteen seventy,' she answered. 'We are modern people who can travel the world. We have science, industry, medicine. We can judge for ourselves the folly of our predecessors. We don't have to cling to religious superstition for fear of burning in hell. The revolution in France taught us something, did it not? All that pomp, lace and priestcraft is just a big show to furnish the palaces of corrupt states and rulers.'

'This is dangerous talk.'

'Do you believe that any man on this planet who does not profess the name of Jesus Christ is damned for all eternity? Every Hindoo, Mohammedan, Jew, every savage, even the people who bow their heads to a lump of stone, are they to burn because they were not read Bible stories as children on wet Sunday afternoons?'

'So they tell us.'

'Do you think it?'

Godwin hesitated and glanced at his feet. 'Of course not.'

'I am glad to hear it,' she concluded victoriously, returning her attention to the fire.

'Let me help you with that.'

'No, thank you. And so, Mr Tudor. What brings you out here?'

Godwin was no longer smiling. He heard the question but was looking at her soft cheek. Having arranged the embers in the shape of a pyramid, she took the bellows and started pumping air rhythmically into their core. Within seconds a healthy blaze was established.

'I have long fostered a passion for travel,' he replied after a pause, 'and I have always wanted to see Greece.'

Lydia tutted. 'The usual affliction. Sentimental yearning for the good, clean courageous world we learnt about in school-books.'

'Partly,' said Godwin. 'And a fascination with the new nation. The defiance of the people. The beauty of the landscape.' There were voices from the hall outside. Others had arrived and were walking through to the dining room for dinner.

'As I said,' sighed Lydia under her breath as she poked the fire, 'the usual English affliction.'

Once again, Godwin was tickled by her spirited outspokenness. 'You think I am deceived?' he asked.

'You will certainly not find Greece as you supposed it to be.'

'That much I have already discovered.'

'Are you a passionate man?'

Godwin was taken aback but sought to hide it. 'I used to be.'

'You mean your passion has gone? Why so?'

'Because age has taught me a degree of humility. I now see my passions for what they are.'

'Which is?'

'An irrelevance. To the world and its workings.'

'But even so, is that not why you have come to Greece? To ride the beast of passion?'

'It is. Or, at least, it was. Goodness, Lydia, how you question me. Do you think I should not have come?'

She sat up suddenly and dusted some ash from her hands. 'Of course not, Mr Tudor,' she said, looking up. 'I think we shall have much amusement here together, you and I.'

The door opened abruptly and Mag appeared. She spoke tersely.

'Mr Tudor. Lydia. We are waiting for you.'

Godwin made his apologies and they progressed through

the hall. As they went, he brushed close to Lydia and could smell the skin at the curve where her shoulder met her neck. A clean, herby smell. 'We must talk again, Lydia,' he said quietly. She did not answer, but sucked on her lower lip and danced ahead of them across the hall towards the dining room.

Edgar was not present at dinner. His place was laid at the end of the table but he did not arrive and no mention was made of the fact. Mag sat at the other end with Dr Schillinger and Godwin on either side. Hermann sat next to his teacher and helped to feed him, betraying the occasional spasm of impatience on his face as he waited for the nod after every tiny spoonful. Lydia was there, together with Percival and Daniel, Edgar's twenty-year-old son, a cheerful, dark-haired youth, full of talk and laughter. Mag spent most of the evening in conversation with Schillinger, a dialogue Godwin could not understand. He had the impression the ageing spinster had taken a dislike to him. Daniel may have sensed this when he said, as if to soften her unapologetic manner, 'Aunt Mag spent some years in Switzerland as a girl. It's quite an opportunity to practise her German again.'

Godwin felt uneasy. He understood that his host was a maverick for whom ordinary rules did not apply, and who continued his rumbustious course leaving wreckage in his wake. Yet they had travelled out here in response to his specific invitation. He wondered whether he had made a mistake in coming and searched through the possibilities of how best and quickest to get away.

Lydia was now rather withdrawn, seen and not heard, smiling occasionally at some shared understanding with Daniel, in the way of siblings, Godwin thought, but otherwise taking no part in the proceedings except as an assistant maid – something he found peculiar – standing up at the end of a course and helping Maroula to clear the plates.

'Your father was a very handsome young man,' Godwin

said to Lydia, indicating the exotic three-quarter-length portrait above the fire. The face was unmistakable, though about thirty years younger, and perhaps exaggeratedly Byronic in its dreamy beauty. He was dressed in a Levantine costume, turbaned and festooned with crimson silk, a jewelled ring of pontific proportions adorning the index finger pressed to his cheek. Behind, a horse with wild eyes was being bridled by a negro servant, and behind that, in the distance, was the Parthenon at sunset.

'No, that's Percival, not Edgar,' interjected Mag, showing that little slipped her hearing, even though she was in mid-flow with Schillinger. 'He did so enjoy dressing up in those days. You don't so much nowadays do you, dear?'

'No, that's right,' chimed Percival without looking up, the first words he had said all dinner. He was busy with the juices of his stew, tipping his plate up to collect them in a pool before spooning them in.

Lydia smiled affectionately, stretching a hand across the table. 'You see, Uncle Percival? Mr Tudor says how handsome you were. It's true. Princely!'

'That's right,' said Percival in the same voice, hardly appearing to register her words, and still lapping up the liquid. Then he paused and looked up at Godwin with a huge grin. 'Do you think I look princely in my picture, Mr Tudor?' A drip of gravy hung off his chin.

'Absolutely,' said Godwin. Percival beamed widely at Lydia and Daniel in turn before returning to his juices. 'It was painted in Athens, you know,' he added, without looking up, 'in eighteen hundred and forty-two, between September the fifteenth and November the twenty-second. A very nice painter. Monsieur Duchamps, from France. There we are,' he finished, wiped his mouth on the napkin and got up to carry his own plate out. Godwin studied him. The physical differences from his twin were now clear. Percival's shoulders were rounded, giving him a slight forward tilt that made him jut out his chin a little to keep level. He was also shorter, or so it seemed, but it might have been an illusion caused by his small shuffling footsteps.

'I'm so envious of it,' said Daniel. 'I wish I could have my portrait painted like that. Have we still got the costume, Aunt Mag?'

'You vain peacock,' said Lydia.

'Well, that's fine and comical from you,' replied Daniel, reproachfully, 'with your pretty gowns sent from London.'

'Father prefers that I dress beautifully. Then he doesn't miss Mama so badly.'

'That's an easy excuse.'

'It's a truth.'

'It's a waste of money.'

Aunt Mag clapped. 'Quiet! Enough. Daniel, why don't you take Hermann to the olive harvesting in the morning and then ride down to the beach and show him the new *apothikia* there. It's a splendid building – our new sea-front warehouse. He would find it very interesting, I'm sure.' Hermann's eyes widened behind his glasses and skittered around with alarm.

'No,' he stumbled hoarsely, the flash of red across his cheeks beginning to blaze, 'I must help Dr Schillinger.'

'Nonsense,' said Mag. 'You look half dead. You must spend some time with the children. Dr Schillinger will be well looked after, you can be sure of that. Daniel, have the horses ready at seven.'

Pudding was brought around, again with the help of Lydia, who placed a bowl in front of Godwin. It was dried figs with honey on a bed of a cold rice pudding.

'Mr Tudor,' said Mag, turning to him for the first time. 'What would you like to do tomorrow?'

'I was rather hoping to meet my host,' replied Godwin, making his point but trying not to sound petulant.

'Well, that's quite impossible,' said Mag without the slightest pause. 'Tomorrow is Tuesday and Edgar has his surgery in the morning. And I know he is very busy after that. He may be going away for a few days.'

'For a few days!' repeated Godwin, his tiredness from the day's travelling getting the better of him. 'But it was he who arranged that we should come at this time.'

'Well, I'm very sorry about that. I can arrange for you to return to Athens, if that is what you would like. I suggest you stay a little while longer. You may yet find you like it here.' She munched a fig as she looked at him, in the complete and merciless knowledge that she had him pinned.

'Of course I shall like it here, Miss Brooke.'

'Mag.' She swallowed her mouthful.

'I shall like it here very much. You're very kind.'

'Good,' she concluded, and got up, barely having finished. 'That's enough for me. Good-night to you all. *Gute nacht, Herr Doktor, auch du, Hermann.*'

She bustled out of the room, talking Greek to the servants on the other side of the door, followed by Percival, who wished everyone a good-night. Lydia had gone earlier, on the pretext of taking a dish to the kitchen and had not yet come back. The door opened several times before the end of the meal, and each time Godwin looked up in the hope that it might be Lydia, but returned his tired eyes to the table with disappointment as it became more and more clear that she would not be coming back.

Within two hours all the candles and lamps had been extinguished, and the main house at Thasofolia was nothing more than a deeper black shape against the paler black of the night sky. The straight angle of its roof pitch contrasted with the irregular, rambling silhouette of the mountain beyond, into which it merged at one point, sharing the same blackness without boundary.

At the far end of one of the branching courtyard annexes a single window frame shone yellow in the darkness, and above it smoke still billowed from the chimney, dissipating into the shadows of high pines behind. It was the estate management office, not often used at night, and inside Edgar

Brooke stood with hands on hips in front of a map of the island. It was a huge map, six feet tall by eight feet across, one of three copies of an original drawn by himself years before. The data contained on it had been informed by every conceivable chart of the area he could find, but principally Turkish and Venetian sources, together with his own comprehensive surveys of the coastline, his explorations of the mountains and vast accumulation of knowledge on the topography of Pyroxenia. It was surely unique at the time amongst maps of the Greek islands for its detail and accuracy. Every headland and rocky spur had been accounted for, every homestead and enclosure, every road, track, path and stream, and where, through years of changing weather, shepherds' migrations or goats' meanderings, some courses had altered (or reports of suspected alterations had come back to Thasofolia) all copies of the map had been carefully amended with contrasting coloured ink lines, some of them dotted, others bracketed. Daniel suggested to his father that it was time to draw a brand new edition because so much had changed and there was a danger of it looking muddled. Edgar had told him to go on and do it, a good idea and an excellent education, but to leave him with his own map, because this was Pyroxenia as he knew it, as he had walked it for nearly half a century. It would seem wrong to wipe away the old lines; it would be like erasing memories or old associations, pretending they were not relevant to the present way of things, and how very short-sighted that would be.

His jacket was thrown across a table, and the sleeves of his heavy cotton shirt billowed out from where they were gathered at the shoulder and cuff, rather in the style of a *fustanella* blouse (not surprisingly, as the shirt had been tailored in the village). His gaze was fixed, through a pair of scratched pince-nez, on an area in the upper central part of the island, a place well within the thick pink line that marked the boundary of his and Percival's estate. Ownership of the property, and the income derived from it, was shared equally between the brothers, according to the terms of their father's will, a document composed and ratified by lawyers in Athens when the twins had been infants and before anyone had found out about Percival's disorder. For formality's sake, and in order to simplify the lawyers' documentation, Thomas Brooke had nominally split the land geographically on a north–south axis, bequeathing one half to each brother, although the income from both was to be pooled and divided equally. The one condition placed on this egalitarian arrangement was that both sons should reside for at least half the year at Thasofolia. If one of them should decide to return to England or settle elsewhere, ownership of the complete estate would revert to the remaining brother, while the income would continue to be divided. If both brothers left, the property would go to their children, or, if there were no children, to Magdalen, or else to her children, should she have any, but all on the same proviso: that they remain living and rooted on the land itself. Thomas Brooke had clearly not intended to let his beloved estate disappear while he had descendants left living.

But, of course, it was not just the Brookes' estate, as Edgar had recently been compelled to recall. The Hill brothers had discovered their legal entitlement to a majority portion of the property's income, an entitlement that had been over-looked for many years, and they were now trying to reclaim the debt. Edgar well knew that if the Hills were to be paid, a sizeable portion of the estate would have to be liquidated. And the inevitable consequence would be ruin for scores of his dependants. If Edgar could not remedy the situation – in the same way that, as the people's doctor, he was weekly called on to cure illness – the whole community would face a future of uncertainty, through no fault of its own. The mining proposal offered a solution, of course; but Edgar would rather go to his grave than allow his land to be raped and his people torn from the fields. No. The alternative must be given serious consideration.

Eyebrows tense with concentration, he reached out a little finger to one point on the map, spread his palm and marked somewhere else with his thumb. Then he reached up with the other hand and traced a route along one of the forest paths, an old one, drawn in black ink from the very first draft, pausing every so often to take something into account. He chewed his lip and shook his head, still staring at the map. Lambros was confident it could be done, and Lambros was no rash fool. Even as a very young man, when the rest of them were mad hotheads Lambros had been the voice of well-reasoned caution. Just like his father, and thank God for the pair of them, Thomas Brooke had used to say: so long as the Lambros family survives, Thasofolia will survive as well.

But Edgar could tell that Lambros was cornered, that in his heart he was wary of the plan. It was different with the boy, Demetrios. Nothing would stop him now, he was ablaze with ideas and could not easily be pulled to heel, even if they were to change their minds. It was an enthusiasm that had to be watched but not dampened as it could still work to their advantage when the moment came. Of course, Edgar had known Demetrios since he was born, him and all his cousins. He knew of the political work that had been done on behalf of Solouzos at the last election and the means applied to achieve the desired result. But things were different now, and in many ways it would be better for all if Demetrios were to stay out of trouble and retire quietly to his mill. If something were to go wrong, and Demetrios were found to be involved, the whole situation could catch fire.

If they were to go ahead with this audacious plan, there would be less than four weeks remaining before the enactment.

He picked up the lamp and made his way back to the house. It was now two o'clock. The first patients would arrive

112

tomorrow morning at about eight. He would be through by midday and could leave before lunch. He would have to go up the mountain for a couple of days at least. Panayiotis would go on ahead to clean the hut up a bit, get everything ready, store some bread, cheese and bottles, and light a fire. There were a few men who would have to meet him there if this thing was to go ahead, men whose loyalty and assent were crucial to a successful outcome. They would be more comfortable meeting him on the mountain than here at the house. Up there it was men with men, a matter of honour and kinship. They could all forget for a while that he was a foreigner who lived in a *palati*, the possessor of wealth unimaginable to them. They would come to him on the mountain as they had in times past, and they would eat, drink, and warm themselves together by the fire; they would sing the *tragoudia*, recite verses about heroes, and talk of men they had known, long dead; then Edgar would put his case and they would listen; they would nod, smile, they would embrace. And then they would state their price.

PART TWO

Chapter 9

For the next few days at Thasofolia the sun shone, the air was clear and cold, and for Hermann Kopfling life had never been so exciting. Daniel Brooke had been his guide, companion and friend. He had never known such friendship from a boy of his own age. Ever since boyhood he had been a peculiarity to his contemporaries, an oddball, both physically and intellectually. The problem was sparked around the time of puberty when it became obvious that his genital development was not the same as other boys'. The large steaming washrooms, with their regimented lines of baths and painted brick walls dripping with condensation, became a hell for him, and he would never forget the cries of other boys' glee echoing around the heights of that big room as they tormented him. He had had an unusual deformity of the foreskin that compressed his penis, a condition that was agonizingly rectified without anaesthetic at the local clinic when he was sixteen, but until that point his penis had looked so small that when he sat down or leant forward it disappeared completely into a heavy bush of pubic hair, causing the other boys to tease him mercilessly, call him a girl, and routinely strip his trousers down to gratify their curiosity. Added to this, he was anti-social, small, physically weak, with a large lower lip and a mouth that hung open. While the other boys at boarding-school were tumbling over each other in the corridors during dull winter afternoons, he was hunched over his Herodotus or Thucidydes, deaf to the sound of their boisterous scuffles and laughter. He would stare out of his window at the featureless flatlands of Lower Saxony, oblivious of the dull light and incessant drizzle, and form vivid images of historical places and characters. His boyhood imaginings had been populated by a pantheon of heroes, lit by a blazing Hellenic sun, and tuned to the metre of ancient verse. In the light of this magnificent fantasy his own mean existence and daily sufferings were ameliorated.

Thus it was a pleasant surprise to find such friendliness extended to him from so splendid a person as Daniel, who was as different from himself as he could imagine, just the sort of boy, he thought on first meeting, that might have led the ranks of his persecutors at school, not because he appeared cruel, but because he was so obviously of the handsome, confident and muscular mould.

The first day after their arrival, Daniel had met him early and ridden with him through the fields and across a small area of woodland, down to the sea, where his father had just had a new warehouse, or *apothiki*, built. He had never allowed their conversation to lull as he showed Hermann the fine new two-storey building, with its jetty and moorings, explaining how the ships would come here to take their timber, cotton, honey and grain off to Smyrna, or up through the Bosporus to Constantinople and Odessa. He had his own ambitions, he said, for a real port on this side of the island, more than just the marine staging post his father had built. Two headlands down was a perfect natural harbour, protected from the vicious *meltemi* wind, and deep to within a few feet of the shore. The ancient Greeks and the Romans had used it, and, by God, when the day came that he took over the running of this place, the Brookes would use it as well, he declared, with fire in his eyes, always smiling and alert, and never quite serious enough for his enthusiasm to come across as arrogance.

Daniel lent Hermann his own horse and raced against him along the beach; he showed him crumbled remains on a hill where only a month before he had found some ancient coins and a statuette of a fawn just beneath the surface; he took him to the new sawmill and showed him the extraordinary watercourse his father had constructed, circling down from high mountain springs to supply not only his own house and fields with water all year round, but also the cottages and farm plots of the village. And all the time Daniel seemed genuinely pleased to have Hermann's company; the language barrier was not so much an impediment but added intrigue and a certain amount of humour to their conversations. Within a few days Hermann felt he had made a friend as he never had in his life before.

But Daniel was only one cause of the general sense of thrill that he felt at being there. Something else even more wonderful had happened, something that illuminated and sanctified every thought and circumstance of his daily life. Hermann was in love. She was the most beautiful person he had ever seen. He was even in love with the thought of loving her. When she came into the room the light of heaven touched him and everything was immeasurably enriched, when she went out the magic slipped away like water down a drain. The sound of her habitual humming as she skipped, light and quick, down the stairs, brought on a flutter of miniature bird wings in his stomach at the thought that she might at any moment appear. When she was absent the minutes dragged and he gnawed at his nails, listening to the tick of the clocks, taking comfort in touching a handle or table edge where he had recently seen her hand rest, and wondering if some tiny remnant of her moisture might still be contained there. He had found one of her hairs on a cushion. He kept it safe in his wallet and brought it out when he was alone at night, placing it on the table next to his bed, which by its grace now became a shrine, and he would stare at it, imagining her, his heart squeezed with pain and happiness. He was utterly, overwhelmingly and obsessively in love with Lydia.

At night he would spend hours in private debate, listing to himself, in order of their substance and conspicuousness, the signs he had detected that she might be in tune with him. They were the fuel of his joy and he loved to remember them and dwell on them individually: things she had said, the language of her body, her glances and gestures. It had to be more than coincidence that their eyes met so frequently, and just when he was brimming with feeling. Surely she could feel it too and shared the secret.

The occasion that had unplugged the lava of his passion was the stroll they had taken, as the light faded to evening, down to the village to visit Eleni. This old widow had been part of the household at Thasofolia until her recent retirement, having started service as Edgar and Percival's nanny. She was now almost blind, and lived by herself at the heart of the village in a comfortable house built for her by Edgar, her supplies and needs seen to on a daily basis by members of the staff at the big house. That Lydia should invite Hermann to walk with her unchaperoned was astonishing to him – especially as it was dark by the time they walked home; but she was a free spirit, refreshingly unencumbered by the sort of restraints that shadowed his own life.

He had sat and watched as Lydia talked Greek with Eleni. Occasionally, she would translate some question directed at him by the old woman, or share an interesting observation. She also helped with one or two household tasks as they talked, sweeping the floor, stacking logs and putting pots away. The seamless flow of their conversation, incomprehensible though it was, warmed Hermann, its lilting rhythm, glottals and legatos, its rises and falls in dynamics. Lydia, it seemed, was at ease with everyone, always had the right word to say, the very opposite of himself. How he hated the gauche, stumbling way he spoke, and what a pig he felt, brush-chinned and blushing, beside her refined beauty. Towards the end of their visit, Eleni had approached him, and put a hand out to find his cheek, her eyes quivering and clouded. She found him at last and rested her palm there for a moment, finally smiling and saying something over her shoulder which made Lydia laugh but which she did not translate. Hermann's heart rushed at the possibilities of what it might have been. Had the old woman suggested he was a good boy, the right sort of boy for her, had she even intimated they were lovers? And then, on the walk back up to the house, Lydia had rested her hand on his arm. It was the very first act of physical intimacy Hermann had ever experienced with a girl, and for their short ascent up the poplar avenue towards the lights and chimneys of Thasofolia, he walked as if cushioned on air, his heartbeat throbbing in his ears.

The worm of doubt had come later. And with it the torment of selfish love. It began with the unpredictability of her attention. There were times when her smile indicated a silent and secret acknowledgement of the intimacy they had shared. She would seem to dally after others had left a room, in the hope, he thought, of exchanging a word or a glance with him. And yet, on other occasions she barely seemed to notice him or inexplicably took the opportunity to absent herself, even at times when they had the chance to be near each other. The plunging disappointment that he would feel, the nagging, impatient loathing of everything that ensued from her apparent negligence, knew no bounds. Sometimes it was her nursing of the sick Englishman, Mr Pierrepont, that kept her away. This Hermann could bear, but only just, as it endorsed her status as an angel; but her intimacy with the other one, Mr Tudor, was a different matter.

He had seen them together on a number of occasions and was alarmed at the evident pleasure this sophisticated English gentleman (a description edged with poison in Hermann's thoughts) derived from her sharp mind, and the obvious delight she took in his mature company. Beside Godwin, Hermann felt like a novice, an ill-bred oaf, and, of course, a foreigner. His anger at their friendship had become sharp and brittle, so that when he found them together in the library it was more than he could bear.

It was a quiet, panelled room with little natural light, on the north side of the house, lined from floor to ceiling with leather-bound volumes, most of which had originated in England and had made the perilous journey out here, across rivers and ravines, wrapped and packed in saddle-bags. Some might have said that it was folly to assemble such a collection in such a place, though the room itself lacked the humour and effervescence that the word 'folly' would imply. On entering the library, one was struck not so much by its owner's boast as by his earnestness. This was a shrine to learning. Hermann had gone in on the pretext of seeing his tutor but secretly hoped that he would meet Lydia there by herself. She spent much of her time reading there, or writing notes in a little blue book he had frequently seen in her hand, and three times already he had met her in the library where they would have short, highly charged interchanges before she would toss her hair, snap shut her book and tell him that there was something she had to go and do. He had begun to wonder whether she went to the library specifically because she thought he might come to find her there, that she shared his thrill at those snatched meetings, and it was with this fabulous hope that he now made his way there.

She was there, but not alone. Godwin Tudor, whose monopoly of Lydia's attention over the past few days left Hermann extremely uncomfortable, was with her, and they were close to one another; worse, agonizingly worse, they were in contact with one another. A silent stab of anguish ripped across Hermann's abdomen at the sight, and blood rushed livid to his face. Tudor was seated at the large table with some papers in front of him. His face was bowed forwards into his palms and he seemed almost to be weeping; it was difficult to see, because he got up and turned away as soon as Hermann came in. Lydia had been standing beside him with her hand cradled around his head, as if to pull him towards her bosom. When the door opened she took her hand away and let the smile drop from her lips (had she been in rapture?), whereupon Hermann muttered something about Dr Schillinger, asking them if they knew where he was (as if he cared a jot for that vile, shrivelled, disgusting old man). Lydia looked up slowly, smiling again, as though it mattered not at all that Hermann had interrupted them, as though she had never given him or his feelings a second thought. She shook her head gently in response to his transparently manufactured question and returned her attention to Mr Tudor. Hermann said something by way of an apology for his intrusion – a hopeless, guttural remark that hardly made sense – and, with cheeks throbbing (how he loathed his own juvenile complexion and the ugly hanging lip that made his chin dimple if he forced it shut), he withdrew. He closed the door on whatever it was that was happening in there, and his hell was complete.

Just then he was called from the hall by Mag who told him that Dr Schillinger needed him urgently, and he had been compelled to spend the rest of the day in the old man's room, massaging oils into his emaciated naked body, in between performing spontaneous translations of Virgil's Georgics, not because Schillinger needed to be reminded of these texts but because he took a mean delight in turning the academic screw on his pupil when there was nothing better to do. So for some hours he had to hold at bay the tide of misery, knowing it was hanging there waiting to plunge his world into darkness. When he was finally released he went to his room and sank on his bed, sobbing face down into the pillow to suppress the sound.

Over the next few days Lydia went off several times with Godwin after breakfast, on horseback, and would arrive back, smiling and happy, after the rest of them had already begun lunch. And so Hermann decided to punish her for her insensitivity by self-consciously ignoring her. He could not switch off his obsessive passion, but needling her might just bring the result he sought. He would look away from her when their eyes met and pretend mild uninterest when she spoke to him. Once he could not stop himself going to the library when he knew for certain that she would be there alone, but instead of engaging her as he had done in the past, he formally greeted her, went straight to a bookshelf, feeling her eyes following him, took out a volume (a difficult one, that would impress her and make her envious of his erudition), and left the room without another word. When the opportunity arose he would gravitate towards Daniel instead, talking with him and giving him his full attention at mealtimes, to the exclusion of everyone else, though he stole the occasional glance at Lydia to see if she had noticed.

His plan seemed to be bearing fruit when he noticed one evening that she was visibly subdued. When she asked him something, he answered with the barest, coldest mono-syllable and thought he saw her eyes moisten, which made his heart leap. The next morning she came up to him purposefully and demanded that they have a talk.

'Why?' he said.

'Because you have been avoiding me all week and I don't know what I've done wrong.'

'You have not done anything. Why do you think that?' He stayed ice cold, though he had to put his hands in his pockets in case she saw how they trembled with excitement.

'I thought we were friends.'

'Why do you think I am not your friend?'

'You don't talk to me any more.' Her eyes now filled with tears and her voice rose in pitch. Hermann felt a flood of joy. He had come to know that she was not a person circumscribed by the manners of conventional society, but if there did exist fragile boundaries that constrained her behaviour, he sensed them crumbling.

'Don't say that,' he said, holding a quivering hand out to her, hardly believing his own courage. 'Of course I am your friend. I am your very good friend.' He was a shaven edge away from declaring it all then and there, swamping her with his love, but managed just to hold himself in check. Then it did not seem to matter anyway, because, as the tears spilled simultaneously on to her cheeks, she put her arms around his neck and rested her head on his chest.

'Are you really? I thought you didn't like me any more.'

'I like you very much,' he said, hardly aware of his words. Every fraction of this moment deserved months of joyous reflection. He had survived on less than the smallest particle of this for a week now.

The moment passed and they were parted once more, she to her aunt's desk to assist in the management of the household, and he to the side of Dr Schillinger. But Hermann had reached the crest of life – not without shadows and hidden snares, but an experience unparalleled in the repertoire of human joy.

Chapter 10

Mag sent Panayiotis down to the village with a note for Elias Lambros, the estate manager. She had waited long enough for answers and now wanted her old friend to come up and visit immediately. It was not long before he was there. He had dropped whatever he was doing and walked back up with Panayiotis. She greeted him at the door and led him through to her private parlour, a room down towards the kitchens at the rear of the house where even Edgar knocked before entering. She kept it like a chapel, with oil lamps burning in front of icons, a large crucifix pinned to one wall. Her desk at the far end, which resembled an altar, was spread with white linen, decked either side with candles, and in the centre an austere antique German statuette of the Virgin. An upholstered kneeling stool, neatly decorated with needle-point, in the English country church tradition, was placed in the corner of the room facing a striking icon of the prophet Elijah, who was pictured writing a manuscript in the desert and turning his head to commune with a raven. No-one questioned why Mag, who in no other respect expressed religious conviction or ever attended church, should choose to bedeck her room in such a hieratic fashion. Her manner and guardianship of privacy precluded discussion of the matter.

She gestured for Lambros to take a seat at the far side of the desk. They spoke in Greek.

'How is Katina?' she asked with a teasing smile. He returned the smile, nodding, and began to roll two cigarettes. Lambros was the only person who ever saw Mag smoke. Aside from their occasional private meetings she would not touch tobacco, but they never met without enjoying it together. It had been their secret ritual for thirty years.

'She doesn't change,' he finally said, his face turning more serious as he handed Mag her cigarette.

'It could be worse. You could be married to Irini.' At this they both burst out laughing, and Lambros nodded again, pulling his lower lip into a droop. Irini, once the village beauty, had developed into a bony toothless hag, whose daily high-pitched berating could be heard across the village and beyond into the fields, making her husband an object of derision and no little pity to the other menfolk.

'That's true,' he conceded.

'She was after you once, you know.'

'No!' Lambros gasped in disbelief, leaning back in his seat.

'Don't give me "no". The whole village knows. It's only thanks to my mother you got out of it. She was wise. She could see the viper taking shape in that little woman's head.'

'She was wise, your mother, that's true.'

Mag sucked on her cigarette. She sat on the edge of her seat, her knees spread wide beneath the woollen folds of her dress, like a village woman. She leant an arm on her desk and relaxed. Lambros always helped her to relax. They had flirted a little in their teens, nothing serious, but enough to seal a lifelong understanding. That was before Iain had even come into her life. Her friendship with Elias Lambros had weathered that storm, and every other vicissitude of the intervening decades, including her failed attempt to build a new life in England. When she sat here opposite him, hunched over her desk, breathing in the smoke and suspending her habitual sense of decorum, she was glad it had failed. She had felt compelled to return to Greece and look after the family after her mother's death, but it was the right decision. Her place was here.

'So. Are you going to tell me what's happening?' she asked.

As if having anticipated the question, Lambros put his hand on his heart, leant back and closed his eyes.

'You know you cannot ask me that.'

She scowled impatiently. 'All right, all right.' She waved her hand loosely above the desk, cigarette trapped between two fingers. 'Just tell me if I need to be worried. He's been away for ten days. I know something important is up. I'm no fool.'

'You're cleverer than all of us put together,' smiled Lambros.

'You think you have to tell me that? If you weren't such a pack of halfwits I might be flattered.' They laughed again, but not for long, as the cloud of more serious business descended between them. 'Go on, then,' she said.

'He'll be back soon. Maybe tomorrow. Everything's all right as far as I know. Just business that has to be seen to.'

There was a long pause.

'Is that it?' Mag asked, taking a final draw on her cigarette and stubbing it out irritably on a shared saucer in front of the statuette. 'Is that all I get? I know I'm a woman, but I deserve better from you, Elias.'

'It's not because you're a woman,' he replied and patted the air soothingly in front of him. He paused again and scratched the back of his head with a grimace. 'There are people in the house. Word can get about. This is too important.'

'People in the house!' she scorned. 'A blind old bat and his lovesick shoeshine, an invalid, and a lost soul looking for purpose in life. They'll be gone soon.'

'Which one is the politician's son?'

'The latter,' she replied stonily. 'What of it?'

'Nothing in particular. Politicians can be dangerous, that's all.'

'Now, in English they would say that is the pot calling the kettle black!'

He smiled. 'The pot should know.'

'You needn't worry about this one. He's not interested in politics. Just art.'

'A pansy?'

'By your standards, perhaps.' They exchanged grins. 'But I don't think so. You can be sure whatever you tell me will be safe.'

He looked her plain in the face. 'I wouldn't be the man you know me to be if I told you any more. You understand?'

She conceded with a sigh.

'This is the big one,' he continued. 'The big one. If it goes well we'll be all right for a century or more. If not, well . . .'

'Well what?'

'We may barely get away with the shirts on our backs. Any of us. Perhaps worse.' Mag let a moment pass to take this in. Through her mind there flashed memories from her childhood. The attack, the smell of hot oil and scalded flesh, the brigands' blades glinting and the shattering of glass against the flagstones.

'Is there going to be blood?' Her voice was quiet, almost tremulous. Lambros made no answer. His head was bowed and he looked at his hands clasped together on his lap.

'Just tell me this,' she went on. 'Is it in good hands?'

'The best we can manage.'

'Can Kyrios Edgar cope?'

'Like an emperor. Don't worry.'

This was as much as Mag could hope to hear, and so they turned to lighter matters and shared another cigarette. Mag could have gone on for longer and would have enjoyed a drink with her friend, but the sun was low in the sky and they both had families and duties to attend to. Lambros kissed her hand chivalrously before departing, and, as ever, bemoaned the rarity of their meetings nowadays.

After he had gone, Mag put out both candles but left the icon oil lamps alight. Percival made sure they were always topped up. Evening was settling in outside. It was a short distance down the passage to the kitchen, and thence to the main part of the house; she knew her geography of the building well enough not to bother with lighting a lamp for such a brief walk. But on opening the door of her parlour she took a sharp breath as she saw a figure emerge from the shadows on the other side. In the darkness she could not make out who it was, but a quick deduction of the possibilities brought just one name to mind.

'Mr Tudor? Is that you?'

'Yes.'

'What on earth are you doing down here at this time of the evening?'

'Going out.'

'Through the back door?'

'Yes.'

'Without a lamp? Or a coat, it seems.' She could see him better now.

'I'll be all right.'

'Well!' She had recovered from her shock, had plenty of things to do and was not of a mind to dwell on the vagaries of young men's moods. 'So long as you're back within the hour for dinner. If not, we shall start without you.' Shaking her head, she bustled past him.

Godwin made no reply but continued on down the passage to where a small door opened on to a short stairway and a grassy slope behind the house. It led down past a water cistern to a cotton field, and thence to the river.

Chapter 11

Her wit is tuned to a melody as agreeable as it is arch; breathtaking in its range and equally mercurial, Godwin had earlier recorded in the pages of his journal. Her wit, indeed, had been the first snare. That and the speed of her reasoning. And the unexpected course of her arguments, a quality that he found as unnerving as it was invigorating. Perhaps she reminded him of what he formerly possessed and had lost to the iron will of his father all those years ago. He pined to rediscover the kind of passion and originality that seemed to underpin her every utterance.

And he was intrigued by the infirmity that softened the perspicacity of her vision. He felt a grain of shame at this, in case he was attracted because of the sense of charity that it aroused, but reassured himself that Lydia was anything but vulnerable. No. It was another gift that she possessed, as if to compensate for the mist in her eyes: a sense of a world beyond what ordinary folk were able to perceive. It was in her gaze, her detachment, her dissociation from all things banal.

The night had a bracing edge. The stars were out, it would be bright and beautiful again tomorrow. He stood near to the river's edge and listened to the burbling water in order to clear his head a little. He felt a danger within himself, a deep and personal alarm, but determined to resist it. This was not a time to yield to the whisperings. All these years he had held them in check, even taught himself a method, a form of exercise, to silence the inner demon's voice, to hold fast his clarity of thinking. He wanted now to reflect rationally, like an ordinary man, on the extraordinary things that had happened today, but he struggled to bridle his thoughts. He would have preferred not to have been noticed slipping out the back way, but Mag had been there and something in the quick judgement of her expression seemed to endorse his own old and secret fear that he was not an ordinary man, and would never succeed in winning a place in the ranks of ordinary men.

The sequence of events that had led to today's cataclysm had begun earlier in the week, when he and Lydia had been talking about his first rather unsatisfactory photographic experiments. He had been a little peeved at her comments. Admittedly, the pictures had been flat, lacking in character and hardly worth the glass plates he had sacrificed to produce them; but he had expected – and wanted – her to be rather more impressed. After all, she had watched with wonder, by the light of the ochre-filtered lamp, as he had processed the prints in the house cellar, and had asked a stream of questions all the while, like the most impressionable *ingénue*. But then, when the moment arrived and he presented her with the finished result, she held them up close to her eyes, smiled rather patronizingly, and commented on how the real places were so much more beautiful than the photographs. Partly because he was disappointed with himself, he felt less appreciative of her abrupt frankness than usual.

'Well, thank you for your words of encouragement,' he said tersely.

'I do not mean to discourage you. It's not your fault. That sort of beauty can't be caught by a wooden box. And without colour. I'm not at all sure that a photograph can be artistic. Not in the same way as a painting.'

Godwin was decidedly needled by this. In one bumptious sentence the child had swept away the entire purpose of his enterprise. 'What on earth do you mean? Of course it can. There are plenty of examples of magnificent art photography.'

'I mean, how can anything that represents so plainly what is beheld by the naked eye contain the equivalent level of feeling that is possible in a painting?'

'Do you think the naked eye fails to appreciate feeling in a scene?'

She thought for a moment about this, her brows knitted. 'I think the eye sees without feeling or judgement; it is the mind that imbues a scene with both. A painting shows the mind's interpretation of a scene. Unlike a photograph. That is why a painting is art and a photograph is not.'

'You show your immaturity,' said Godwin dismissively, but immediately regretted it. Lydia's argument had logic and intelligence, even if it was flawed, and it was mean of him to squash her with so condescending a remark. But she did not seem deflated and, before he had a chance to say anything else, looked up at him brightly.

'Would you like to see Father's watercolours? I think they would illustrate my meaning.' For a moment Godwin thought she must be joking. Edgar Brooke had been absent from the house since the night of their arrival, and Godwin's opinion of him had been sinking by the day. The idea that this uncouth brute could paint or produce anything that might illuminate his own understanding of art was not just preposterous but laughable.

'Your father's what?'

'Watercolours. They're very good. Although he doesn't think so. As soon as he finishes one he says he's going to throw it away, and I have to go and rescue it. But I think he secretly likes me to. I've put them all in albums. There are masses of them, dating right back to when he was a boy.'

'You're not serious.'

'Of course. Why should I not be?'

'Your father is not interested in art.'

Lydia looked around the room and went to the table to

start gathering up the photographs. 'You underestimate him.'

'It's not that,' began Godwin but she interrupted him.

'I have noticed it from various other remarks you've made. I don't know what he's done to make you think ill of him in this way, but you clearly don't know him very well yet, and certainly you underestimate him.' Godwin did not reply in words, but let out an explosion of air from his lips that implied contempt for what Lydia had said.

'You say that *I* show immaturity. You will live to regret this attitude,' she said; a bold statement from a girl to a gentleman, Godwin thought, especially a girl half his age; but they had been communicating as equals for a week now, and had allowed themselves to speak more frankly than convention usually permitted, so she could be excused. She bent down to a shelf at the bottom of a bookcase and pulled out a large bound album. 'Come,' she commanded, and Godwin approached the table to have a look. He would humour her.

'So these are they,' he said, the corner of his lip curling into a smile: 'your father's works of art.'

'They are, indeed,' she replied in the same tone, and opened the heavy book.

One by one Lydia turned the pages of her father's album until Godwin, wordlessly, because words failed him, stilled her hand. Some of the scenes he recognized, having attempted without great success to capture the same views in his photographs. There was no exaggeration in Edgar's representations, no deviation from truth for effect. In proportion and topography they were precisely accurate, the draughtsmanship detailed, the perspective faultless. But it was in the entire effect that the power of these pictures rested. As Lydia had earlier argued, accurate representation of a scene cannot attain the heights of art until reviewed through the veil of a sensitive eye; and every one of these paintings was a poem. In his journal, Godwin was to conclude: *Mr Brooke is a rare and exceptional artist, no mere dilettante in pursuit of pastoral diversion. He has the skill of one who can behold the commonplace and yet depict it with mood and ambience thereby transforming it, while the pictures remain faithful representations of real places. What he sees with his eye he ennobles with his brush. I was profoundly moved, as much by the quality of the works as by the depth of my own former complacency.*

Godwin was staring at the paintings, head hanging. 'They are quite wonderful.' He consciously supressed a tremor in his voice to conceal the shame that he felt. 'I had no idea. They are amongst the finest watercolours I have seen.'

'It is his favourite pastime. In the spring he will go off alone into the hills with a mule and a few provisions. He has a hut up on the mountain. If he doesn't come back within three days, Panayiotis rides up with more supplies. Look, here is this house when he was a boy. He painted it from the chapel of St Catherine up on the hill.' Godwin shook his head with a sigh and sat down at the table. 'Mr Tudor! I do believe you are upset.'

'What must you think of me?' he said quietly, and turned to look at her. She responded with a smile that possessed a resonance well beyond her years; her eyes silently absorbed his concerns and reduced them to vapour.

'But Mr Tudor, I only think the best of you. Truly.' She was standing above him and now gently put a hand to his head, stroking it through his hair.

Suddenly the door of the library opened and Hermann was there. Lydia instantly retrieved her hand and Godwin stood up from his chair. Hermann said something about Dr Schillinger and left the room. Godwin turned to the window, momentarily at a loss, and they remained that way for a short while before she spoke.

'You must come with me to my pool.'

'Oh yes?' he said, though his eyes were straying back to the album.

'My favourite place. My secret place. It is the heart of the world. Will you come? Tomorrow?'

'Hmm.' He was flicking through the paintings again. 'If I

were not so completely dumbfounded I would say you had planned this to laugh at my expense.' But Lydia's thoughts had moved on.

'We'll leave at seven and be back in time for lunch. If you put all the equipment you need in the hall tonight, I'll make sure Panayiotis has it packed and ready by the time we leave.'

'My equipment? You want me to do a photograph. Where?'

'At my pool. You cannot deny me.'

The next morning was not as clear and sunny as it had been earlier in the week. The cloud hung low and there was fog in the valley, obscuring the village below as if it had been swallowed overnight by an Arthurian lake, peopled in its depths by sleeping knights and sword-bearing maidens. Godwin did not acknowledge the mystical quality; he was in a scientific mood and judged the morning from the perspective of classification and measurement. He observed the light, sniffed the air and wondered if it might not be possible to take a photograph at the pool after all. Water was difficult to catch because of its movement and ripples. It would have to be a long exposure in this light, and mist drifting across the image could be a problem.

Panayiotis was supposed to have accompanied them, but when they emerged into the yard after breakfast they found the horses packed, saddled and ready, with an old man waiting beside them. He was short with thick white hair and a broad, close-clipped moustache. It was Barba Stamos, the chief cook at Thasofolia who was also father to Panayiotis and the chambermaid, Maroula. He had heard that they were going to the pool and insisted on taking the morning off to accompany them. It was some time since he'd talked to the spirit who lived there, he explained in a high-pitched babble to Lydia. She translated for Godwin: 'and being so old now he'd better go while he can, or he might die without completing his business. He still has much to sort out with that spirit before he goes to his Maker. That's what he says.'

'Is he joking?' asked Godwin, who wondered if the old man's grin was indicative of humour or just habitual good-will.

'Of course not,' said Lydia.

'Spirit? You of all people believe in spirits?'

'I can at least admit there are things I don't know.'

Godwin felt chastened and dropped the sardonic tone in his voice. 'Have you met this spirit?' he asked.

'Not in the sense that you may be thinking. But it is a very special place, you'll see.'

Barba Stamos insisted on walking on foot beside Lydia's horse, despite her protestations, and they conversed in Greek for most of the hour-long journey. Godwin was glad that they were occupied with each other. He felt slightly guarded, not quite as confidently adult in relation to Lydia as he had before.

They started out on the wider eastbound track but after a mile cut up a steep rocky path that eventually came out on an open treeless ridge covered in grass as lush and thick as an English meadow's. At one point a herd of goats blocked the path; their colossal horns threatened a savagery long bred out of their nature, and they stared through peculiar elongated pupils, gormlessly indignant at the intrusion; all of a sudden their mood gave way to cowardice, which spread through the herd like an epidemic and sent them cascading downhill into scratchy thickets, bells tinkling.

The path now led sharply down towards a full and noisy torrent. The horses were nervous of the river's roar and unsure of their footing between the boulders, but Barba Stamos' expert clicking kept them going until they reached more level terrain. They were now in a narrow gorge, with sheer cliffs on either side, into which the light barely entered.

Barba Stamos said something to Lydia in an almost absurdly theatrical, high-pitched whimper. He tutted and looked at the ground, shaking his head.

137

'What does he say?' Godwin asked, smiling at the caricature peculiarity of the old man's voice.

'He is lamenting the fickleness of fate.'

'Why so?'

'We are near the spot where they found my mother,' Lydia replied. Godwin closed his eyes.

'I am so sorry. How terrible for you to come here.'

'Absolutely not,' said Lydia, looking straight at him. 'This was one of her favourite places as well. I honour her by returning.' Godwin now joined them in silence as they passed through the gorge, and his horse fell behind Lydia's of its own accord. The animals gave off a more pungent scent in the damp air; the steam that puffed from their nostrils as they clambered through the fallen needles had a distinctive tang that was not there on dry days.

The gorge was at its narrowest at the point where it terminated, and the party emerged through the overhanging trees into an open basin, protected around its entire diameter by a sheer rockface that stretched up some hundred feet all round. It was an almost perfect circle, cut cylindrically into the rock of the mountain, about two hundred feet wide. Across its span spread a sheet of dead still water. Around the edge of the pool the ground was carpeted with ferns and wood spurge, and an occasional deciduous tree sprouted from this dense greenery, its bark blanketed with moss and sprigs of polypody. Random drips fell from high overhanging rocks into the black water, momentarily disturbing its surface with circular ripples. The smooth cliff face was streaked with the marks left by moisture oozing down through the centuries, slow streams of drips that deposited minerals, stains and sculpted stalactites. High up, at the crest of the cliffs, where the forest reclaimed the turf around the edge of the gigantic hole, bushes clung precipitously to the earth. Here and there a pine tree had seeded itself just too close to the drop, its trunk distended and twisted in a tenacious attempt to right its balance and hold on to life.

The geology of the area seemed to have suspended itself for this cavity. The wildness was tamed, the disorderliness temporarily levelled and silenced. There was a monumental quality to it, like a place of worship.

'This is a most unusual location,' Godwin said, reaching for his pencil and notebook, but Lydia stilled him with a finger at her lips. They dismounted and stood motionless beside the horses for a while, looking round. There was a thin mist spread low across the surface of the water and an unearthly quiet, broken only by the hollow, abnormally amplified echo of droplets all around. It was a sound that had barely been touched or polluted for millennia, thought Godwin, except for the occasional distant cry of a hawk or the ubiquitous summer drone of the cicadas.

'I'll be back shortly,' Lydia whispered to Godwin. She had removed her boots and walked off to the right, raising the hem of her dress a little so that he could see her bare ankles wading through the ground bedding of maidenhair. He watched her for a while, slowly circumnavigating a portion of the pool, until she disappeared from sight behind an outcrop of juniper.

Godwin then turned to the packhorse and began to unload his equipment: the camera, tripod and plates, together with a collapsible tent, assorted instruments, and various boxes of bottled chemicals. The quilted black-out tent was erected, its interior filled with equipment, and the camera screwed on to its tripod. He was clad in a hide apron and rubber gauntlets, and all the while observed by a grinning Barba Stamos, who made the occasional cheery remark to him in Greek, not seeming to care that the foreign gentleman understood nothing of what he said. Godwin accepted the comments with the goodwill that they appeared to transmit, and smiled back.

Once everything had been set up, Barba Stamos approached and had a look at it all close to, bending low and prodding his nose forward, as if to check its scent. Satisfied, he turned to Godwin and rattled off some more sentences that could either have been question or statement, and then turned away with a long high whistle, walking off on his own, still chattering to himself every now and then, until he, too, disappeared from sight and hearing.

Godwin sat in the ferns, for he did not know how long. He put a hand down to feel for his watch but found that it was not there. More time slipped past with nothing more to mark it than the fall of watery drips and the circling of an eagle high above. He wondered if the old man had gone to seek out his spirit friend. It was a fecund place. The droplets' isolation complemented the silence, gave it greater depth and definition, as a single lit match will do to a blackened hall. Time passed as if suspended.

'Hello.' It was Lydia. She had returned without him hearing and was standing right next to him.

'Did you have a pleasant walk?' he asked, smiling up at her. She did not reply, but turned in the direction of the water. After a few moments she pointed to a smooth flat-topped rock positioned about thirty feet from the shore.

'I'm going over there. You stay and watch.'

'But how can you? Is there a boat?' She walked away from him, with a slow, measured pace. 'Lydia! That water will be very cold!' She approached the water's edge, hitching up her skirt to see where she would place her feet. 'Lydia, please!' But his words went unheeded. Time held back its pace as she tiptoed to the water and appeared to walk across its surface, step by step, away from the shore. Godwin watched in astonishment and rose to his feet. She was at one with the stillness, her movement slow and deliberate. She was lost to him in grace.

'Lydia!' Godwin called again, coming to his senses. His voice echoed around the stony bowl and he felt the sweat rising in his pores. She turned to smile at him.

'Don't worry,' she said softly, but her voice carried. 'There's a secret causeway of stepping-stones across to the rock. Father had them put in for me. For my birthday, when I was ten.' Step by step she crossed the water and finally sprang on to the rock, where she settled herself, her skirt ballooning. She hugged her knees and looked out across the pool. Her face was tilted slightly, the neck and profile sharp against the darkness of the water, her golden hair spread out behind one shoulder. Godwin could hear his own breath discolouring the silence as he watched her.

And then it occurred to him. There was no plan, no prior thought or manufactured design. It was serendipitous, perhaps, that he had set up the tripod at that particular spot, though what he had intended to photograph he did not know; it had filled the time while he was left alone with Barba Stamos. And now she was there, and he was permitted to behold her in this state. It felt like a privilege. He thought about calling across to her to say what he intended, to warn her to hold still for the exposure, but as he looked out at the rock he knew it was unnecessary. Words would be an intrusion. This was no stage. The magic was the moment as he felt it this instant, unpolluted and immaculate.

The silence seemed intensified as he went about his process, and every sound he made cut the air like a knife. The slip and click of the oiled brass runners on his tripod as he adjusted the legs to the precise height; the smooth slither of the Dallmeyer rectilinear lens as he twisted the retractor knob to bring the subject into sharp focus. The scene on the rock, reflected by internal mirrors, appeared upside-down on the smoky glass plate at the camera's rear, but Godwin could see sufficient to know the quality of the composition. She was close enough, the gentle upturn of her nose, the slight exposure of her upper teeth. The patterning of the distant rockface was magnificent, the water surface like glass, the light mist hovering still, like smoke from a thousand elvish homes.

He prepared the plate with iodized collodion in the darkness of the tent, immersed it in light-sensitive solution, and, while it was still wet, locked it into the shield case so that it could be carried outside to the waiting camera. All was set. Then, just as he had his hand on the cap to remove it, she turned her face and looked him full on. Her gaze was sightless, unengaged. He did not think to stop his hand or ask permission, but took away the cap. Motionless they remained, eye to eye and unblinking as the image fizzed itself into the plate's silver solution. The chemistry, the scene and the time span all linked in a curious dance of meta-morphosis to steal the moment and preserve an aspect of it for ever.

It was past. The cap was replaced and she turned back to stare out across the pond again. Godwin went into action, removed the shield, and disappeared into the dark-room tent to attend to his wet plate. While he was in there, Barba Stamos returned, and Godwin could hear him start up a con-versation with Lydia as he prepared the animals for the return ride.

When Godwin emerged from the tent, Lydia was back from the rock and tying up her laces. The plate had come through vividly, a complete success, but he did not say any-thing, nor did she ask. In a peculiar way he did not want to look at her, and would have preferred to stay in the darkness. Their eye contact during the exposure had led them to an intimacy Godwin had not anticipated. It was alien, he thought, a little embarrassing, and had no place in the relationship they had built up to this point. He glanced at her as he dismantled the tent in silence. Her movements had a grace he had not noticed before, a womanly contentment, like a young mother who has breast-fed her baby to sleep and lays him quietly in his cot. She was in a warm rapture of her own. Godwin felt peculiarly drawn to her serenity, and yet excluded from it. She needed no external stimulus to complete her enchantment: it was entirely self-contained.

When the moment came for them to leave, Godwin noticed that Lydia was having trouble mounting her saddle.

It was a tall horse, and something in the ribbing of her skirts was preventing her getting a clean lift off the ground. Without stopping to think, he stooped beside her, on one knee in the damp earth, offering her his shoulder as a step. With a wordless smile she accepted the offer, and he cast his eyes down in respect of her modesty as she placed her foot and lifted herself into the saddle.

They arrived back at Thasofolia a little late for lunch, but feeling hungry and enlivened after their outing. The silence of the others in the dining room Godwin interpreted as disapproval.

That same afternoon he made his way down the flag-stoned passageway, past Mag's private study, past the kitchen, the scullery and the meat pantry, with its carcasses hanging on great iron hooks from the ceiling, to the cellar. He had to step through a wooden hatch and climb down a ladder. It was cold and damp, but spacious and there was little chance of being disturbed. The only light down there was from an oil lamp which he shielded with a piece of yellow muslin, the same that he would use in his black-out tent. In this murky ambience, which drained colour from every-thing and replaced it with sepia monochrome, he removed from his box an appropriate-sized sheet of albumenized paper, soaked it in a tray of silver nitrate to make it light sensitive, and hung it by a peg to dry. He enjoyed the smooth coated surface of the albumen paper, it was precious and sensuous to the touch, almost inviting a lick because of its derivation from egg whites. He had read that the Dresden Albumenizing Company, one of the biggest manufacturers of the paper, required sixty thousand eggs a day to cover their needs, and employed factories full of girls who did nothing but separate the whites all day. The yolks were sold on to a patent leather company.

Once the paper was dry he laid it on the varnished side of the glass negative, clamped them both tight within a wooden frame, secured the hinged back of the frame with two brass springs, and took it out of the cellar into the courtyard. This was the point where the egg surface of the paper cooked, like a cake, in the daylight, the silver solution visibly clouding dark over the surface as the exposure time elapsed. Maroula, the chambermaid, came past him and quickly glanced at the contraption he was bending over. He looked up at her and smiled, thinking he might beckon her over to have a look, but she cast her eyes down and hurried on with quick little steps beneath her heavy skirts.

Once the cake had browned to Godwin's satisfaction, he took it back down to the cellar and plunged it face down into a salt bath. The purply quality of its darkened patches now turned a dull red. He then washed it and laid it face down again in a solution of gold chloride. Now the shadows turned to a darker brown, with greater definition and variety. The signs were promising, the texture and contrasts spectacular, but he would not be distracted by the content of the picture, tempting though it was. For the moment he was a chemist and the priorities were timing, co-ordination and dexterity. The image was finally fixed for a short spell in soda hyposulphite and then washed. He looked across the room as his cold fingertips lightly massaged fresh water over the smooth surface of the picture, and he deliberately turned the print away from him when he hung it up to dry, so as to deprive himself of full satisfaction until later.

'You can keep this copy. I made two.'

Lydia held the print up to her face, tightening her eyes into focus, and drew a sharp little breath. He glanced over her shoulder. It was neither entirely landscape nor portrait; formal, and yet immediate, spoke volumes and yet evaded title or classification. It might be history, romance or nursery tale, it was the start of a rambling text but it was impossible to say of which genre. There was a girl alone on the rock, a girl looking fixedly out at the viewer, her eyes wide with expression, but silent, her message withheld, almost secret.

The light and mystery of the setting was enhanced by the monochrome, which united the figure with the water, the young flesh of her arms with the ancient, mottled stone beneath her. Their textures were distinct but their tonal palette shared. The eternal nature of the setting contrasted with the spontaneity of the subject in an orderly balance of opposites. And there was the sheer entrancing beauty of her face at the centre of it all, thought Godwin – as Lydia, now inches from him, surveyed the picture, inch by square inch. Her approval was silent, though her face beamed with delight.

Suddenly, she pulled away from him, her mood changed by a new idea. 'Would you like to try another?' she said. 'I know some other wonderful places on the mountain and in the forest. You can build on your new discovery.'

'I think I should like that. Very much,' said Godwin, sensing a golden thread unravelling before him. 'But,' he hesitated, 'I think, for everyone's sake, it would be best if nobody else were to know of the photographs we are making. Do you not agree?'

'If you think so.'

Thereafter, they did not take a guide with them on their morning rides, and no one thought to question where they were going or for what purpose, except Hermann, who would come out into the courtyard and watch as they were packing up, his face a picture of reproachfulness. 'I think he's displeased with me,' Lydia said one morning, 'because he would like to spend more time with Daniel and prefers me to look after Dr Schillinger.'

'Does Daniel mind?'

'No, I think he enjoys it, although he has things he wants to do on his own sometimes. Hermann's an interesting boy. And very sensitive. Almost too sensitive. He's very upset with me.'

'Have you talked to him about it?' Godwin asked.

'Do you think I should?'

'It would not hurt you.' Lydia considered for a moment, smiling into space.

'All right,' she said, 'if you think so, I shall.'

They had made three expeditions, and completed two exposures on each. Lydia standing centrally, draped around the twisted trunk of a two-thousand-year-old olive tree; Lydia standing precipitously on a craggy spur, hair catching the wind, the plains and sea stretching beyond; Lydia lying in the moss; Lydia seated by a waterfall; Lydia curled in a dell; Lydia, still and incalculable; her face, the depth of her expression, her vivid eyes – and her skin, the only smooth tone in each photograph.

Godwin busied himself in the cellar most afternoons, processing the results with a sense of mission that was almost manic. None of the others at Thasofolia saw the results or had any idea of the growing portfolio that he kept locked in a box under his bed. He had less and less interest in their dining-table small talk, preferring to spend time in his room, looking at the prints, writing up the results in his journal, and wondering what new perspective or mood he might include in the next photograph. Yet the more he looked and thought, the more he came to realize that his subject was dictating its own ends, and he merely followed. It was all Lydia. Everything else was incidental. She was the one and only subject of every picture. He was there to co-ordinate the other elements into her matrix. And it was her apparent lack of self-consciousness that provided the key. She, the core of each composition, was simultaneously subtracted from it – a detachment which engendered, for the eventual viewer, a curiosity, a hunger, almost, to be allowed into her world. One must attribute this disengaged quality to her short-sightedness, Godwin argued in his journal, clinging to the tabulations of comfortable reason.

And then this morning came, this bright, mild, almost summery morning, when she had had a new idea, an inspiration, it seemed. It had turned his world upside-down, and it was to contemplate this sudden development that Godwin had needed to escape the house through the back door after dark, when he had hoped to slip out past the kitchens and pantries unnoticed, but had been apprehended by Mag.

This morning he and Lydia had ridden to a circular woodland clearing on level ground at the foot of a mountain, surrounded by ancient pines. High up, the fresh growth on the trees swayed brilliant green in the breeze against a backdrop of clear blue sky. Down below, it was a different world. Their huge trunks stood shoulder to shoulder like silent sentinels in the gloom, immobile and regimented. On every trunk a bag had been hung beneath a heavy gash in the bark, from which the trees bled a slow but incessant stream of resin.

Godwin observed the setting as he went through the familiar procedure with the tent, the camera, preparation of the solutions and the plate. The weather was glorious and he knew they would make a spectacular plate. It should be full of youthful energy – the soft vitality of her face in the generous light would blaze out against the dark encircling pines: hope and life springing from the depths of the earth. He mentioned as much to Lydia before entering his tent to sensitize the plate, but she did not reply, and he wondered if she ever took any notice of his preambles.

Emerging, a little after, he had to close his eyes for a few seconds and stand still to acclimatize to the extreme brightness. There was never time to waste at this point in the process because the plate must not be allowed to dry, but he could not risk stumbling half-blind across the rocky ground to his camera. However, when he opened his eyes something other than sunlight pinned him to the spot, so that for a moment the valuable seconds ticked past and he could neither move nor speak.

She was naked. Positioned perfectly still in front of the camera and ready for the photograph, but naked. Her weight rested on one leg, while the other relaxed with a slight bend at the knee. An arm rose up vertically from the shoulder above her left breast, and doubled back at the elbow, falling behind her head, which was turned to the side, eyes skyward. It was a pose he thought he recognized from a celebrated statue, though if she was imitating this deliberately he did not care to know. Her skin was flawlessly smooth and had a sheen that would translate into a soft marble grey in the photograph. Her form was limpid but athletic, like a resting cat roused from slumber; from raised elbow to ankle it formed a straight line, softened by the slight undulations of her hip, thigh and calf. As an object of art it was incomparable.

But she was more than an object of art to him, and he was a fool not to have acknowledged it until now. Ever since that first exposure by the pool he had become an open book to her. In a reciprocal drama of soundless intercourse she had become his muse and he her worshipper. The whole woman was now revealed to him, the complete form with nothing hidden; and there could be little doubt that she was inviting him to partake of her beauty in its fullness, knowing how he would feel, sensing his appreciation and his hunger. It would have required a titan's resistance not to have construed this situation as anything but a lover's gift. If ever there were a yielding of gentle womanhood to the toiling search of a man, it was in this moment of unconditional revelation.

He stood astride the tripod in shirt-sleeves, his jacket discarded on a nearby rock, sweat gathering on his forehead, and bit into his lower lip as he removed the brass lens cap. She had astonishing control of her limbs. There was no discernible sway, not the smallest quiver or tremble for the entire ten-second exposure. Once the cap was replaced, Godwin removed the shield from the camera and went back into the tent to complete the development. By the time he came back out she was fully dressed, seated on a rock and prodding the soil with a stick she had found. She said nothing as they rode back to Thasofolia, either about the photograph or the new territory into which they had graduated.

He did not see her that afternoon. She had told him she was going to read Byron to poor Mr Pierrepont, who did so seem to appreciate her visits, and he wondered when or if she would express a desire to see the new print. By six o'clock he had it in his bedroom and was examining it in detail by the light of seven oil-soaked wicks. It was everything he had hoped for, and more; but the effect of it, and the day as a whole, and the week leading up to the day, was to drive him out of the house by the quickest route. The cool evening air would clear his head.

Chapter 12

Petros Cameron Solouzos, so named after his Scottish grandfather, Peter Cameron, was not looking forward to Daniel Brooke's visit. He had known him since he was born, of course, and was fond of him, with his bright eyes and engaging smile, but this was the first time Daniel had requested a private meeting, and the last sentence of his letter, which said that it was essential his father should not be told about the visit, had made Solouzos uncomfortable. The eminent Páparis politician had no children of his own (a source of profound sadness for him that he exorcized over the years by throwing himself into his work) and therefore had romantic notions of how loving families should be; a young man arranging a meeting behind his father's back, particularly a meeting with one of his father's oldest and closest allies, was not behaviour that he condoned or wished to encourage. However, he decided to give the lad a hearing.

Daniel was not at all like his father as a young man, Solouzos thought. Edgar had been much more ponderous, almost abstracted, and perhaps lacking in humour, which his son possessed in abundance. They both had tremendous energy, but while Daniel's was of a spontaneous and flamboyant type, Edgar's was less demonstrative. He would make his decisions quietly and act on them, often with no reference to others, and expecting nothing in return for his actions, whereas Daniel liked everyone to know what he thought and what he was going to do about it. The boy's mother had been more like that, very dynamic and outspoken. She and Edgar had frequent quarrels, although it was only her screaming voice that could be heard echoing around the house or wafting on the breeze across the valley to the edges of the village. Having said that, Solouzos doubted there could ever be another woman for Edgar Brooke. She had provided the counterpoint to his life, a life which, since her death, had become a plodding dirge, ground out remorselessly.

But then it would have been impossible not to adore Eliza Brooke, as Solouzos knew only too well. Her volatile nature was as prone to affection as to fireworks, and it came straight from the heart. Solouzos would always cherish the memory of his own secret passion for her, a love that never broke the surface or caused even the faintest breath of suspicion from his own wife, thank God. Once, in a fit of desperate longing, he had written Eliza a letter, a great outpouring of his heart, laying his whole life and career like a mat for her feet, but he had wisely put the letter into his stove instead of sending it, and his secret remained intact. On one or two other occasions, when he had had too much wine, he had held her gaze for a fraction too long, but only so much as to provoke her into laughing at his drunken stupor, never a hint of anything else. No-one ever suspected that he was waiting for the merest blink of acceptance, and that if it came, he would throw away everything – wife, prospects, possessions and personal honour – to be with her. It comforted him now to reflect that he had never caused her to face that calamity; he bore the pain all himself, leaving her, for the remainder of her pitifully short life, with the gentlest and sweetest friendship a man had to offer.

Perhaps it was for her sake he had agreed to meet Daniel today, and also because the sight of him brought back to life a faint aspect of Eliza, something in the mannerisms, the eyes and the slope of the forehead. But the temperament did not translate so well from mother to son. Daniel's impetuosity, which in a beautiful woman can be interpreted

151

as spirit, was immature in a gentleman. The time had come to grow out of it and the boy would have to learn to keep his counsel. Perhaps he had begun to learn, and that was why he had arranged this clandestine meeting. Solouzos would not be too hard on him.

He was on time, and that was a good sign, Solouzos thought, as he looked out of his first-floor study window into the courtyard and saw Daniel handing the reins of his exhausted horse to the servant. Solouzos checked his watch. Eleven o'clock. The fastest he had ever known anyone complete the journey between Thasofolia and Páparis – including a change of horse half-way at the village of Agia Anna – was four and a half hours; and that was travelling at full gallop where it was possible. If anyone was going to beat that time, Daniel was as likely a candidate as any. He must have left home before dawn, and if he hoped to get back in daylight today he would have to be gone within a couple of hours. Solouzos thought he had better organize some lunch that the boy could eat as they talked.

Daniel came into the study and embraced his father's friend warmly, ignoring the tangy smell of ingrained dirt and the dusting of dandruff over the older man's shoulders. They exchanged pleasantries and news about the family. Although Solouzos spoke perfect English, they both felt more relaxed speaking Greek. Coffee was brought, and some cheese, bread and meatballs ordered for Daniel.

'And so what do you think of your guests?' Solouzos asked.
'I was impressed with Mr Tudor.'

'I haven't talked to him a great deal. He's very busy with his photography, and I'm not sure if he likes us very much.'
'Oh?'

'Lydia thinks he disapproves of Father. And that he probably regrets having come at all. He's very upset that Father went away as soon as he arrived and hasn't been home since. Anyway, she's taken him under her wing to cheer him up.'

'That's very kind of her.'

'Well, you know what she's like,' said Daniel, smiling: 'she can't resist a lame duck, someone to impress.'

'Now that's not kind. Or true,' said Solouzos returning the smile and offering Daniel a coffee, 'and besides, Mr Tudor is far from being a lame duck, I assure you. He's intelligent, wealthy and well-connected. He would make a good husband for your sister.'

'Is that all you Greeks ever think about?' Daniel laughed in mock scorn. The Greek jokes were always good ones, Daniel being every bit as Greek as he needed to be when it suited him, but able to stand apart and pretend the higher moral perspective of a European. Their goodwill established, they allowed the humour to settle and became more serious.

'You know all about the lignite mining prospectors, of course, and their approaches to my father, as you must also know about the Hill grandchildren's claims?' Daniel asked.

'Before you proceed, Daniel, I will tell you as an old family friend to be careful what you are about to say.' But Daniel was in no mood to be careful. His frustration boiled over.

'Say what you like to Father! You're the only person I can talk to. He's going to ruin us all. We've got a real chance here. We could make more money than we've dreamt of and still have enough land to do great things. If he doesn't act soon the Hills will be down on us and the government will throw us to the dogs. We either get on the winning side, which in this case happens to be the Germans with their mine, or we go down. But if we are shrewd in our dealings we could do so well out of it. Thasofolia could become a very important place, an industrial centre, and just think what that could do for all of us! It's the way forward, the future. For you too! If you stand against the tide, you'll be swept aside as well. Our enemies will see their opportunity and in no time snatch the prize from us. Their thugs are probably sharpening their blades as we speak.'

'Don't exaggerate.'

'Why is Father being so pig-headed?' Daniel slammed his

fist on the table, spilling the coffee. Solouzos saw the boy was too far gone to take a reprimand.

'Have you spoken like this to your father?' he asked.

'Of course not! He wouldn't give me the time of day!'

'So, how do you know what he's planning to do?'

'I know something's up. He's thinking of a way around it. It's obvious,' replied Daniel. 'He's always having private meetings with Lambros and Demetrios—'

'Demetrios Lambros? Elias Lambros' nephew?'

'Yes.'

'Demetrios comes to your house?'

'Yes.'

'Often? Recently?'

'Yes. And now Father's been up in his hut for over a week, meeting all his mountain cronies and preparing the way for something, and don't tell me he's sounding them out for their opinion on the mining rights.'

'He could be. They would have an opinion.'

'Only in terms of how many bags of silver they can get out of it.'

'Well, that might be relevant. And it is their mountain after all.'

'No it's not, it's ours. Ours! The sooner they learn that the better for everyone.'

'That's where you differ from your father. And your grandfather.'

'And I want to differ, because he's going to ruin us, and we've been offered a chance to make ourselves a fortune. I have been born to this place and I deserve a future here. What's he doing up the mountain, anyway? If he wants to be a shepherd or a bandit and hang around with the likes of Demetrios I'll happily pension him off and take over Thasofolia myself.'

'Now this is dangerous talk.'

'Well, maybe it's time to be dangerous. Look what he's doing to the family. And his drinking!'

154

'That's enough.'

Daniel paused for a moment and took a deep breath, allowing his emotion to subside.

'Well, that's why I'm here,' he said in a quieter, more measured voice.

'What do you mean?'

'I want you to support me on this. You and I together. Persuade Father to retire. He should go to England, like his father, and leave me to take care of everything. He had his chance, now I should have mine.' Solouzos let out a puff of laughter.

'You're lucky I don't throw you out by the scruff of your neck. If you weren't such a child still, I would.' He sounded more angry than he was. Daniel had a point. In his heart, Solouzos did not share Elias Lambros' apocalyptic fear of the future industrialized Pyroxenia. He did not assume it would bring disaster or upset the network of political allegiances they had spent so long constructing. He was by nature more of a radical politician than a conservative, and he rather relished the possibility of change on the island, transforming the lives of peasants imprisoned in the poverty trap, opening the doors of opportunity, a revitalized economy, closer links to Athens, a flashpoint of political influence – it all appealed to his natural ambition and lust for revolutionary adventure. On the other hand, he was getting older and things were good as they were. If he wanted to be sure of a rounded, comfortable conclusion to his career, followed by a prosperous retirement in a community that looked to him as elder statesman, he would do well to oppose too dramatic an upset to the local economy just now. It depended on developments in the capital, of course, and if his friends in government really started putting on the pressure he might have to change his mind, but for the moment he would stand by his old friend Edgar and the status quo. He certainly would not show any of his doubts to this young stripling.

'If that's your attitude, I'm sorry I bothered you,' said

155

Daniel. 'I had thought you and I could usher in a new era for Pyroxenia. Perhaps I have overestimated you.'

'You overestimate yourself. At the expense of your father.' At this moment there was a tiny knock on the door and the servant brought in food for Daniel, who excused himself politely and said that he should return home immediately. Solouzos entreated him at least to have a quick bite before his ride. Daniel accepted, allowing the atmosphere between them to ease a little.

'I do apologize if I have appeared disloyal and pre-sumptuous,' he said formally as he took his leave. 'It is not meant out of disrespect. I have nothing but admiration for you, and that is why I came. I take it I can trust you to keep the contents of our discussion private?' Solouzos nodded, taking the boy's hand, and putting his other arm around his shoulder.

'So long as I can trust you to contain your madness and work out whatever you need to work out quietly with your father.'

'At least put a word in for me,' Daniel retorted, 'so that he will listen to me seriously. Without disclosing that we've met.'

'I can try,' replied Solouzos. 'It's only natural you should want to be heard. You're a man now, a man with a great future. Your father will only begin to treat you like a man when he agrees to listen, you're right. But it will take time for him to change. He's always had to rely on himself alone, his own judgement. He's played a difficult game over the years and played it like a master. The family is still there and things are going well. You can't expect him to let it all drop at a moment of crisis, just when he's most needed. The family, the land, the villagers, the herds, the crops, the forest, every-thing he's built and lived for. Go and retire in England! I'm sorry, Daniel, it is not going to happen, or at least not until he's had years of calm, until you have proved your-self, until Lydia is married, and he is resting one day in the

156

sun on his terrace, with his hat over his eyes and feet up, and he suddenly wakes up to brush away a fly and says to himself, "Yes, the time has come." But now? No.'

Daniel pursed his lips and looked to the ground, accepting the lecture. Then he mounted his horse, leant down to shake Solouzos by the hand, and galloped away, in the direction of the beach road.

Chapter 13

Fortinbras Pierrepont's health was on the mend but in his mind he wrestled with the Furies. While the fever spread in waves through every joint and sinew of his body, wringing the juice from his flesh and depositing it in damp circles on the sheets, his thoughts returned again and again to the problem he'd been trying to avoid confronting these past few months. In his delirium it took shape as a venomous creature that would arrive to jeer at him as his carcass submitted to the shivers and the sweats broke out.

Edgar Brooke had not had time to visit him before setting off from the house on that first morning, but had left some powders with his sister, which, along with the various infusions, teas, oil vapours and the slow passage of time, seemed to contribute to the general easing of the symptoms, to the point where Fortinbras decided that this would be his last day in bed. And with this decision came the resolve to write the letter that had to be written. The time had come. He could post it when they returned to Athens in the new year, which would mean that it would reach its destination, his home village of Frobisham in Berkshire, some time around the end of January. He would prefer it to be sent earlier and have done with it, but that would mean entrusting it to the hands of others, at least as far as Páparis, which was a risk he dared not take. The merest glance at the envelope, a quick reading of the name at the top of the address, and his secret would be out. Too much was at stake. He hoped with all his heart that he might be able to bury the whole mess at home without anyone being the wiser, and make a new start in Greece. No-one must find out about the life he had left behind. No-one must know that he had a wife.

The thought of Marie, the image he carried of her in his mind, her voice and narrow eyes, the way she tilted her head to speak, the short, tapered fingers and the particular configuration of her earlobes, all of it, all of her, the whole woman, from head to toe, repelled him – disgusted him. And he loathed himself for feeling this way because Marie had done nothing wrong. It was not her fault, but then neither was it his own. He had never wanted to marry her, but as a twenty-year-old boy he had allowed himself to be persuaded by his bone-thin and overbearing mother that the neighbour's niece, a girl seven years older than himself, would be the one to look after him and give him a good family. Love would come in time, they said.

But it had not. Nor had the smallest seed of affection or mutual empathy. The first few nights of their forced intimacy had sealed the fate of the marriage project. Fortinbras would never forget the cold of their room, its dank air and drab brown furnishings; he would never forget how he had preferred to shiver under the counterpane on the floor, flicking off the woodlice, than lay himself next to her repulsive, quietly sobbing hulk on the bed above. The sight of her naked flesh was utterly repugnant to him, the wobbling fruit-peel texture of it on the thighs, the meat folds that lapped down from the waist, the delta of massed silvery vein marks that laced her upper legs. And the shape of her form. He had never imagined such disproportion possible in a woman – the slack fall of her pot belly, with its twisted umbilical wart protruding gracelessly from the middle, her mountainous, jellied hips, that rolled on an axle of their own with every step she took; but far and away the worst of it, the most shocking, the one flaw for which no work of art he had ever laid eyes on had prepared him, was the hair – the dense, impenetrable clump rooted in her groin and sprouting in all directions, a thicket of no particular shape that thinned only as it rose to her navel and spread symmetrically across both upper thighs. He forced himself to approach it on one of their first nights together, so as not to seem impolite or unmanly, but had to pull himself away, retching as he caught the smell of it. With this rotten kernel of a secret at the core of their marriage, Fortinbras and Marie Pierrepont had managed courteous friendship at the best of times, mutual contempt at the worst, but for the most part complete lack of interest in one another's activities and well-being.

Fortinbras had spent most of his time away from home. He had been an associate engineer for James Whimple Esquire, and helped to construct sections of railways leading to Cotswold quarries. Afterwards, more ambitiously, he worked on spanning the multiple estuaries, rivers and canals of Schleswig-Holstein, where he travelled for successive three-month tours. His brief visits home to Marie were bleak affairs, times when his habitual bonhomie – which Marie had hardly known – was crushed by the weight of his entrap-ment, an inescapable weariness that left him feeling old before his time.

It seemed far away as he lay in his bed at Thasofolia with the sound of the village in the distance below, a cock's crow, dogs barking and the wind in the cypress. He loved this country. Mag had just been to visit and check on him, as she had several times every day since his incarceration, her practical intolerance of self-pity or small talk aiding his will to recover and restore equilibrium to his thoughts. She would leave the more menial tasks, such as emptying the bedpan and changing the sodden sheets, to the Greek chambermaid, but stayed in the room to supervise proceed-ings without thinking to turn away as Fortinbras climbed out of bed or changed his nightshirt. She had treated the sick for as long as she could remember, first as a girl here in the village, helping her mother with herbal concoctions and traditional Greek country remedies, and then in Bath, at Miss

Hawthorne's Institute of Mercy and Redemption. She was no stranger to the sight of a patient stripped of dignity, and through her plain manner and unabashed assumption of control – which was not devoid of compassion, though few tender words were uttered – Mag made it clear that the ordinary rules of propriety were temporarily suspended. When they were resumed, her unspoken contract decreed that no memory of degrading procedures or unseemly sights would be retained. The consequence of her spartan but unfailingly attentive care was that Fortinbras developed a filial fondness for her, a sentiment which, if reciprocated on Mag's part, was apparent only in the faintest of occasional smiles.

Which was not at all the style adopted by her niece, Fortinbras' other regular visitor. Perhaps it would have been better for all if Lydia had been less warm, if she had learnt from the long experience of her aunt, who would doubtless have known that a man laid low by sickness and dependent on others for his needs is vulnerable to more than just the illness that afflicts him. Coming round from his delirious purgatories to see her fresh, smiling face beside him, or to hear her voice reading *Childe Harold's Pilgrimage*, childishly holding to the lilt of the metre at the expense of some of the word emphases – which was charming – affected him in ways he would prefer to have suppressed. Her feminine wholesomeness, fabulously abundant, seeped into the spongy recesses of his consciousness, and though he was not aware of anything particularly out of the ordinary to begin with, the moment he closed his eyes and fell prey to dreams, she returned in an altogether different guise. As he tossed and flailed against the asphyxiating heat of the bedclothes, she would be there, naked with him, her body smooth and golden tanned by the firelight, as finely shaped as a polished cello. The nape of her neck was all softness, the curve of her uplifted breasts swollen with womanly kindness.

Every time he fell asleep she would come to him, so that

he could even smell the health of her skin, the dense, trapped scent at the roots of her hair. If the dreams had ended like this, as they had begun, close and cosy, the memory of them in his waking hours would have brought nothing more than a pinprick of wicked amusement. But the dreams did not end here. They progressed inexorably along a defined track, accelerating in rhythm and vigour, like a train as the throttle opens, boilers stoked and ablaze. Her body, which began the unfolding drama as a silken source of warmth, nestled quietly into him, became a thing of livid voluptuousness. It writhed beneath him, knees spread wide, and her face was lost behind a mass of hair tossed from side to side. Twice already Fortinbras had woken to a powerful pulse in his scrotum, and found himself doubly shamed: the lingering dream (so disappointingly ethereal) and the sticky mess cooling on the sheet above him. He had had to creep from his bed, joints aching and head throbbing, to scrub clean the sheet and hang it in front of the fire before Mag or her maid arrived in the morning.

The more he thought about her, and encouraged by her frequent visits to cheer him up, the more debauched the imagery of his dreams became, to the point where his host's teenaged daughter, who in actual life was the very picture of innocent, cultivated girlhood, was transformed into a whore of the utmost lasciviousness, whose imagination and skills in the mechanics of sexual union knew no bounds, astonishing him with their originality and torturous brinkmanship. And so, as the patient slowly recovered from one ailment, he fell prey to a second, a more insidious enemy that crept up on him camouflaged with sweetness and promise. He had hoped that daytime would bring reason, that his obscene imaginings would disappear in the wintry morning light, and that when he saw Lydia in person – the child nurse who came to see him with a cup of tea and a heart full of good intentions – the madness of the night would evaporate and he would be able to laugh at himself for his own silliness. But it was not so. As she read to him and he looked across at her, he was disturbed at how close she seemed to her invented double, just a word or a particular glance away from the luscious spectre he had come to know so well by night.

> ' "'Tis to create, and in creating live
> A being more intense, that we endow
> With form our fancy, gaining as we give
> The life we image, even as I do now." '

He watched her, now aware only of the peculiarity of being so close and yet unable to enjoy her. The dart of her tongue as she pronounced the verses recalled so closely the same organ's teasing agility in the dark. The cup shape of her constricted breasts as they rose and fell with each breath gave him a flutter as he pictured their darling naked roundness and softness to his kiss. He imagined her legs parting to welcome him in and felt himself harden at the thought. It tortured him to restrain himself. He felt it was nothing more than an artificial veil that kept them apart, and despite himself he considered springing from the bed to rip it down.

> ' "Yet must I think less wildly:– I have thought
> Too long and darkly, till my brain became,
> In its own eddy boiling and o'erwrought,
> A whirling gulf of phantasy and flame." '

She paused and stared at her text for a moment before looking up and fixing him with serious eyes. His heart thumped and he felt a wave of sweat rise on the pulse of it.

'Fortinbras. There's something I think we ought to talk about. And this last verse makes me think of it.' His mind flashed back to the last verse as he tried to remember it, but he had been distracted. The words 'wildly', 'boiling' and 'phantasy' still hung in the air. God, had she read his thoughts?

163

'I had thought not to say anything about this,' she went on, 'because it is of a private nature.' She hesitated and had to look down to gain courage. 'I hope you won't think worse of me for mentioning it.'

'How could I?' he replied gently. She smiled at him, encouraged. His penis was engorged and prodded at the bedding. He raised a knee to conceal it.

'Thank you,' she said, 'I knew I could trust you. You see, it's about Mr Tudor. I've grown very fond of him, as you probably know, but I'm worried about him.' Fortinbras felt his manhood wilt, the sharp prick of his feelings instantly lose its menace, melted down to a flat pan of disappointment. 'He's sad. I don't know why. Well, I think I might know partly why,' she tilted her head and looked away – 'but there's more, I'm sure. He has become distracted. Lost in a melancholy dream.'

'I know what you mean,' Fortinbras said, trying to sound interested, 'I've noticed it as well.' Lydia looked up at him, her face a picture of animated concern.

'I knew you would understand,' she said. 'I have a theory about it, and I'd like to know what you think.'

'Yes?'

'I think Mr Tudor is feeling things here that he has not recognized in himself for many years. And it's making him sad.'

'Why?'

'Because it reminds him of what he's lost. Youthful happiness. Joy. Romance, perhaps.'

'Oh yes?' Fortinbras could not have been less interested. At this moment he might even have loathed Godwin.

'Just like the narrator in *Childe Harold*. He feels'– she checked the text, pointing to it with her perfect index finger– 'that the springs of his life are poisoned. Like this—' she traced her finger across the page again, back a couple of stanzas. 'Here: "Since my young days of passion – joy, or pain, perchance my heart and harp have lost a string," and—'

'I think you shouldn't concern yourself with it,' interrupted Fortinbras, attempting to stifle any show of impatience. 'Mr Tudor is a grown man, of much learning and experience. *He* can work out his own problems, if he has any, and *you* could not and should not attempt to do so on his behalf.'

'You disappoint me, Fortinbras.' She looked into her lap, closing the book.

'You did ask my opinion.' Lydia managed a smile, but with little heart in it, and rose from her chair.

'I'm glad to see you're feeling so much better. It will not be long before you can join us downstairs.' Fortinbras felt wrenched inside. He could not bear that they should have a misunderstanding, and at the same time wanted to violate her there and then to make it better, just as he had done every night for more than a week.

'Lydia,' he called to her as she neared the door. He felt confused and wished he could shut himself up, but the words came. 'Please forgive me. I mean nothing but well for you. You cannot understand how well I mean for you.'

She stopped in her tracks. 'What do you mean?'

'I can't bear that you should be upset with me in any way. I really could not bear it. You are—' Lydia stared at the door for a moment. Fortinbras checked what he was saying, it was too emotional and completely improper. Such powerful feelings, she would not understand where they had come from and why. Idiot! He spluttered the first thing he could think to cover his tracks and set her mind at ease. 'I'm not completely better, you see. Still a bit sorry for myself, and talking a lot of nonsense. Don't tell Mag. She'd rap my knuckles. And I'll think on about Mr Tudor. You may be right.' Lydia smiled and it seemed as though the situation were saved.

'Have a good rest,' she said, and walked quietly from the room.

Fortinbras covered his face with both palms. He had to do it, and do it now. It was the only way out of this madness, and it should have been done ten years ago.

He climbed out of bed, put on a cotton robe and went over to the little walnut desk. The fire was dying. Percival, who took such great pride in making sure all the fires of the house were kept alight and healthy, might well be up again soon to stoke it.

He took out a sheet of writing paper and dipped his pen in ink. Then, with a sigh, he began his letter to Marie.

Chapter 14

The light of the rising sun spread across the garden lawns at Thasofolia to reveal an expanse of grass bleached by the early morning frost. The garden was terraced on several levels down the southern slope of the hill, with tucked-away benches, secret nooks and shady retreats swamped by foliage. Each private little cul-de-sac provided a refuge from the blazing sun on hot summer afternoons, but at this time of year they were seldom visited. The garden had been lovingly sculpted by Edgar Brooke's mother, who saw it as the single compensation for her otherwise lonely and trouble-ridden life here. Mag kept her mother's achievements in order but lacked horticultural flair, so that the effect was now rather tired, as though it had all seen better days – the statues flaked paint, the benches and tables wobbled at their dowelled joints, sections of stone balustrade cracked and crumbled in the frost.

The tiles and roof timbers of the house on the eastern flank of the building creaked at the change of temperature as the sun rose above the horizon. Inside, the occupants still slept in their shuttered rooms, unaware that, from the village below, the tall windows on this side of the house were ablaze with the reflected crimson of the dawn sky. The Brookes' home, set on its hill, was flooded with light a good twenty minutes before the rest of the village, and at the end of the day enjoyed the last of the sunset for some time after the workers' cottages had submitted to dusk and their evening fires were burning well in the hearth.

Percival went into the dining room at six-thirty, as he did every morning, to light the fire beneath his portrait so that it would be warm by breakfast time. Normally, he would also draw the curtains and open the shutters, but this morning he saw as he went in that the sun was already casting a glow on the opposite wall. Somebody had beaten him to it, and the familiar steamy citrus smell told him immediately who it must be. There on the table was the usual huge cup filled to the brim with boiling lemon water, and the man himself was stooped in front of the fire, blowing at some embers and kindling wood.

'Hello, Edgar,' said Percival in his usual detached way. He gave the impression of never being surprised or particularly interested in anything that occurred, so long as his own activities ran smoothly, according to established routine and plan.

'Good morning Pea,' replied Edgar. Although most people thought Edgar's nickname for his twin referred to the first letter of his Christian name, it actually derived from an old brotherly jibe: the ten-year-old Edgar had habitually teased Percival that he had a brain the size of a pea. 'And how has everything been?'

'Very good, thank you. Can I do that for you?' Percival asked, kneeling down beside his brother. The timbre and pitch of their voices were indistinguishable.

'No, it's all right. I think I've got it going.'

'Did you get on all right?'

'Yes, thank you,' replied Edgar.

'Have you been in the hut?'

'Most of the time.'

'Are Stefanos Iannara's beehives still up there by the *rematiá*? He said he was going to take them away before the *panighíri* and that was last month, have they gone?'

'I don't think I saw them.'

'Well, that's good. He said he would take them away by the

panighíri and that was last month. That's good, if they're gone. You didn't see them?'

'No.'

'Do you think he's taken them away?'

'How are our guests?' asked Edgar.

'Very well, I think, yes. Mr Pierrepont has been ill but is much better now. I've kept his room warm all the time. And Dr Schillinger is very busy with his work. He must be a very clever man, Dr Schillinger, is he very clever?' Edgar gave the fire a last long blow, and, satisfied that it was burning well, leant back and turned to embrace Percival, giving him a kiss on the cheek. 'Mr Tudor is busy as well,' continued Percival, seemingly oblivious to the affectionate greeting, 'he has been going out every day to take photographs.'

'Photographs? Of what?'

'Mostly of Lydia, I think.'

'Really? What are they like?'

'I haven't seen any,' continued Percival in his matter-of-fact way. 'No-one has, but I'm sure they're nice. Mr Tudor's a very nice man, don't you think?'

'How do you know he's been photographing Lydia?'

'The goatherds saw them. Have you written to the Swiss Minister about my music box?' Edgar closed his eyes. He had forgotten all about Percival's music box.

'I'm sorry, I haven't,' he said. Percival pulled back from the fire looking suddenly very perplexed. His voice rose in pitch and his forearms shook from the elbow.

'You said you would write. You promised me you would write. How am I going to do Christmas if my music box isn't working?' Percival's old Swiss music box, his pride and joy, and for which he owned no fewer than twenty-seven different six-tune cylinders, was broken. The spring had gone. It was a Christmas Day tradition at Thasofolia that Percival would entertain the whole family after lunch with a formal recital on his music box, dressed in his best clothes and with prepared introductions for each piece. He relished the occasion, and always performed with great panache, beaming with pride, much to everyone's amusement and enjoyment. Six weeks had passed since he had begun to panic about Christmas, and Edgar had assured him he would write to the Swiss Legation to see if they could recommend a way of having the contraption repaired. With six weeks to go now it seemed impossible it could be taken to Switzerland and returned in time.

'I apologize, Pea, I've had a great deal to attend to. I'll write today.'

'It's probably too late,' continued Percival, the tension in his voice mounting, 'what am I going to do at Christmas if the music box isn't working?'

'I've told you,' said Edgar calmly. 'I'll try to sort it out.'

'But what if it's too late?' He was clenching and unclenching his fists at speed. Edgar got up.

'Maybe we should ask Dr Schillinger to have a look at it. He is Swiss, after all,' he said, smiling.

'Well, that wouldn't be very sensible,' Percival retorted angrily, 'he's blind. That's not a very sensible idea, Edgar, is it? A blind man can't mend a music box. You do say some stupid things sometimes.' Edgar turned away, picked up his hot lemon and made his way to his study, as Percival left the room talking to himself crossly in Greek, hands clasped together in front of his stomach.

Within a few minutes there was a knock on the study door. Elias Lambros had arrived. It was early, but Edgar had sent for him, aware that his foreman would want to know the news as soon as possible. Elias took a seat on the opposite side of the desk and they spoke in Greek with lowered voices.

'All of them were in agreement?' asked Lambros.

Edgar smiled. 'You know what those old men are like. Hard as rock and sharp as thistles. Like the mountain they were bred on.'

'But the salt of the earth.'

'And old fashioned,' added Edgar, 'and that's what swayed

them. They like to think the old days are not completely over. This sort of plan reminds them of the past. They didn't make it easy for me, though. They took some persuading. But in the end I got what I needed.'

'So they agree to let Demetrios have free passage?' asked Lambros. 'Not to interfere at all?'

'More than that. They guarantee him shelter, respectful treatment, food, drink. As it used to be in the old times.'

'Within what boundary?'

'The usual limits. Demetrios knows them.'

Elias drew down the corners of his mouth in surprised appreciation. 'What do they want in return?'

'There's the money, of course,' replied Edgar. 'And a couple of conditions.'

'What conditions?'

'That Demetrios sticks to his word and asks for nothing more than the amnesty.'

'That's all he's ever wanted.'

'And there's to be no looting or bullying along the way.'

'We all know he's not that sort.'

Edgar paused and scratched the side of his nose. 'There is something else.'

'What?'

'They want him to leave the island when it's all over. And never come back. They say that if he's given an unconditional pardon by the government or the King he'll be safe to go and live in Athens. They want him off the island for ever.'

Lambros looked shocked and opened both palms. 'But this is his home,' he said.

'It's a small price to pay,' said Edgar.

'What if he refuses? What if he returns home to a quiet life when it's done? To have children and tend animals.'

'He would lie in bed every night in fear of his life.'

'Fear is not in his nature.'

'That is their deal. Demetrios may be a strong young buck,

171

but these old men have more real power than he has in his little finger.'

Lambros frowned and paused before continuing. For a moment he could not bring himself to look Edgar in the eye. His voice went down to a whisper. 'There has been a problem, Kyrie,' he said. 'Something happened while you were away on the mountain.'

'What sort of problem?'

Now Lambros looked at him. 'Solouzos has got word that Demetrios has been coming to the house.'

'How did he hear?'

'I don't know. But it might have been Daniel.'

'Daniel?'

'Daniel went to see him. I don't know what was said. The servant told me there were heated words. All I know is that Solouzos' suspicions are raised. He sent me a message asking why Demetrios has been coming so often.'

'A blunt question.'

'He's worried. If things get rough, I'm not sure we can count on Solouzos any more.'

'He's stood by me all my life.'

'This time it's different,' replied Lambros. 'You know how important it is that he keeps his record clean in Athens. If it's discovered that he's got any connection to Demetrios, that he had any idea in advance that this whole thing was planned, he would be finished.'

Edgar tutted and bit on his lip. Lambros waited, eyebrows raised, for his master to digest the news. At last Edgar sat back, with a sigh.

'Well, we might just have to manage without him,' he said.

'Without him?'

'He may not join us, but he will never betray us. I would stake my life on it. The worst he would do is sit out on the side and claim complete ignorance.'

Lambros moved in even closer, looking hard at Edgar from beneath his heavy brows. He spoke quietly, with deep

172

sincerity. 'Kyrie. All our futures depend on this. Can you be so sure?' Edgar did not answer, but picked up the lemon drink, now cooler but still with bite in its flavour, and drained it in one mouthful.

'Have you spoken to Demetrios since I've been away?' he said at last.

'Once.'

'His plan?'

'It's all worked out.'

'And if he doesn't immediately get what he demands?'

'He keeps his blade sharp. Unless you order otherwise, it will be done the traditional way.'

'We must hope it doesn't come to that.'

'Hope and pray.'

Edgar smiled and sat upright, checking the watch in his waistcoat. 'Prayer is a waste of time, Elias! Another snare invented by the churches to make people feel better. There's never been a bigger piece of delusion!'

'Kyrie, as long as it makes people feel better, I'm for it.'

An hour later all nine members of the household were assembled around the table for breakfast. Edgar, having been absent for so long, added zest to the occasion by his presence, even though he sat in silence at the head, with a book open beside him; it was some sort of gazetteer in Greek, and he read it through a dainty pair of spectacles. It was as though the others had been summoned before their senior officer with the expectation of a thorough briefing but in the event found he had nothing to say to them. He behaved as if he had been there every morning, barely raising his eyes to greet the guests as one by one they entered the room. Nevertheless, a quiet atmosphere of anticipation hung over the table, which Godwin felt he should not trivialize by introducing conversation, unless of a high or necessary nature.

Edgar was in reality far from unaware of his family and

guests' presence, and his quiet detachment concealed momentous stirrings as he geared himself to make the announcement that was to commence the unfolding of his plan. Finally, he closed the book, removed his spectacles and inspected the warm milky bread pudding that a manservant had brought to him. He dusted cinnamon over it from a silver quail and began to eat with a spoon. In between mouthfuls, and without looking up, he now quietly addressed the assembled company.

'We are expecting visitors next week, on Wednesday.' He ate another two mouthfuls, savouring each with his tongue at the front of his mouth, as if separating edible from inedible particles, but swallowing the lot. 'Eminent visitors,' he continued. Mag, at the other end of the table, did not look up but rested her lips against clenched hands, elbows on the table. 'Some of you will have to move rooms to make way for the great and the good. The penalty of lowly birth, I fear.' If this was said as a joke, there was no hint of a smile on his face. 'There will be five in the party and a servant: Sir Thomas and Lady Wishart, a Mr George Farkas – an industrialist from Liverpool and a guest of the Greek state – together with his wife; and Prince Leopold of Würtem-something-something, who is said to be a distant cousin of our Queen's late husband; also somehow related to that wastrel on the throne in Athens, don't ask me how.' He chewed on another mouthful as the others digested the news. 'It is this last person,' he said, now wiping his mouth on a napkin, 'that all the fuss is about. They'll arrive and depart with a platoon, I don't doubt. They will not be staying with us for more than five days before heading back to Athens.'

'The Queen's cousin! And braving a journey at this time of year – how unusual,' said Daniel. 'That will be exciting. Uncle Percival, what do you think of looking after a relative of the Queen?'

'Yes, very nice,' said Percival in an automatic, bland way.

Edgar looked down the table to his son with mild

174

curiosity. 'Are you impressed by those who hold rank merely through an accident of birth?' he asked.

'Very impressed,' said Daniel, undaunted. 'I think it will be splendid and very grand to have Prince Leopold here. He may become a friend and invite us stag shooting at his *Schloss*. I wonder how old he is. Do you know, Father?'

Godwin guessed that Daniel was being deliberately provocative, as it was well known that Edgar did not approve of hunting. However, he appeared not to hear his son, and turned to his left, where Godwin and Pierrepont sat next to each other. 'I have some business to attend to round and about the estate this morning. If you would care to ride with me, Mr Tudor and Mr Pierrepont, I should be glad to show you something of my property.' Godwin glanced across at Lydia. It was another perfect day and he had thought that she might suggest going on a photographic expedition. There was no reaction from her and so he replied, politely, 'Thank you, yes, I should enjoy that very much.'

'It's a very kind offer,' said Pierrepont, 'but I think it would be wise for me to stay indoors for another day or two.' He too now looked at Lydia, who again did not respond. 'I was wondering, perhaps, if I might be granted another canto of *Childe Harold*. To seal my recovery.'

Mag spoke up. 'Daniel has suggested taking Dr Schillinger and a party to the beach, which I think is a splendid plan. The wind is down, the sun is out and it will feel quite like spring. It would do everyone good. Hermann! You will of course go along?'

Hermann's cheeks rose in colour and he pulled up his lower lip. He had the sudden sensation of a hot and poisonous thing swelling within, and with a spasm of pain his feelings burst into words: 'I think . . . I mean . . . you . . . Miss Brooke,' he stammered nodding in Lydia's direction but not daring to engage eye contact, 'Miss Brooke has kindly offered to accompany me in the forest. For a ride.'

'Have I? Did I?' said Lydia in singsong surprise, looking

around with amused embarrassment as she chewed a dried fig. 'Sorry. Did I say that?' she said to Hermann. 'Where did I say we would go?'

Hermann hung his head and spoke low across the table, just to her. 'To a special place for you. A lake, you said.'

Godwin shot a look at Lydia.

'Nonsense,' said Mag. 'The beach it will be. Will you go with them, Lydia?'

'No,' she replied airily, 'I think I shall stay and write in my room today. I would like a quiet time.' Hermann blinked into his untouched breakfast and his lip fell open.

'I'll have the carriage ready in an hour,' said Daniel. 'Will you be joining us, Aunt Mag?'

'No. I have George Skordhas coming this morning,' she answered, switching her attention from Daniel to Edgar, mid-sentence.

'Oh yes?' Edgar said between mouthfuls, without looking up.

'He's very insistent that he should be allowed to put in an offer for the Howards' house. And I think he's quite right. It will fall down unless someone moves in and starts taking care of it. The whole of the downstairs is used as common stabling for any animals in the village at the moment.'

'Then why doesn't he come to me?' Edgar's voice was deep and grainy, with the same airy distractedness of tone that Percival had.

'He has often tried.'

'Oh yes?' Edgar frowned, not looking up as he sliced fruit on his plate.

'Well,' said Mag after a pause, 'shall I encourage him?'

'Certainly not,' he replied, removing a pip from his tongue.

Mag sighed. 'Why not? Do you want the house to fall down?'

'We don't want any Greeks in there. Let's find an Englishman. What about you, Mr Pierrepont?' He looked at

176

Fortinbras. 'Would you like to buy a very pretty little house close to here? You could settle down.'

Fortinbras looked animated. 'A house? Which house?'

'A house that at one time belonged to some friends of my parents, the Howards. Poor wretches. It has been empty for ten years, ever since old Mrs Howard, the last owner's mother, passed away.'

'Why poor wretches?' asked Pierrepont.

'They died,' said Edgar.

'They were butchered,' interrupted Lydia, 'and it's a horrible house. You can feel the murders hanging over it like a cloud. I hate to go anywhere near it.'

'You're imagining it, of course,' said Edgar. 'You quite happily went there as a little girl to visit old Mrs Howard before you knew anything about what had happened. You played in the very room, on the very floorboards where their blood was spilt, and you didn't bat an eyelid.'

'Edgar!' said Mag.

'Father, how could you?' said Lydia.

'Butchered?' asked Pierrepont. 'By whom?'

'By a young man they trusted,' said Lydia. 'A villager they entertained regularly out of the goodness of their heart.'

'How terrible,' said Pierrepont. 'Why?'

'The usual,' replied Edgar, sighing. 'Money.'

'Shot as they lay in their beds,' said Lydia.

'And their infant son barely survived four weeks after the ghastly event,' added Mag. 'No-one has wanted to go near the house for years.' She looked down the table to Edgar. 'If Skordhas is so keen to have it, why not let him?'

'I think the property would suit you very well, Mr Pierrepont,' said Edgar, and Mag raised her eyes to heaven. 'Particularly if you intend to remain in Greece for some years. Let us go on a visit when you are feeling better.'

'I should like that very much,' said Fortinbras enthusiastically.

'What shall I tell George Skordhas?' said Mag, wearily.

'Tell him to come and see me. Or if he can't be bothered or can't find the patience to wait, tell him straight that it's not for sale. Mrs Howard's will was quite clear. I have complete say in the matter. There's an end to it. Now, Mr Tudor, shall we leave in half an hour?'

As it turned out, the two parties were in the courtyard and ready to depart at the same time. Dr Schillinger had hold of Daniel's arm as he climbed into the carriage, and Hermann stood behind him, book in hand. Panayiotis was arranging the buckles on the horses for Edgar and Godwin. Edgar's own horse was a magnificent creature, a good five hands taller than any horse Godwin had yet seen in Greece, black, muscular and well groomed. With its tight-plaited mane and tail, its fine saddle and gleaming tack, it could have stepped out of one of the finest stables in England. Just as they were all about to leave, Lydia came running from the house into the yard and approached Edgar.

'May I go up to the hut for the day?' she asked him. 'It would be so lovely up on the mountain. Please, Father.'

'I don't think so.'

'Why not?'

'There's no reason to go straying so far from the house on your own.'

'I'm perfectly able to look after myself. I love it up there. It's inspiring.'

'You require no more inspiration than you already possess. You should perhaps spend less time with the fairies and more time helping your aunt.' Daniel, who had been about to climb into the carriage, now wandered across to listen in on the conversation. There was a frown on his face.

'I find time for both,' said Lydia. 'I find time for everything. And if I have a love of spending time with the fairies, it's something I've inherited from you. That was unjust, Father.'

Daniel interposed. 'Why don't you just do as Father tells you, Lydia? Why do you always have to dispute the matter?'

Lydia whipped round at him. 'This has absolutely nothing to do with you,' she said, her voice venomously transformed.

'How dare you talk to me like that? I am your elder brother, and senior to you in this family.'

She let out a laugh, but there was no humour in her tone when she spoke. 'You? Senior to me? From the moment I learnt how to speak I left you grovelling beneath me. I've known dogs with more sense.'

'Children,' said Edgar.

Daniel went pale. 'I would prefer the company of a dog to yours,' he said through his teeth. 'At least a dog knows something of loyalty. At least a dog will not toy with people. It has no wiles or sly craft.'

'That's right,' she continued without pause, her eyes ablaze, 'a dog just sits there gawping and barking at the moon until it's hoarse, and wagging its tail in the hope that someone will notice it and throw it some scraps. Does that sound familiar?' Daniel walked up to Lydia and it looked as if he was about to strike her. Edgar leapt from his horse.

'You had best find yourself a husband before you fall into my care, madam,' Daniel spat, 'because all this will weigh heavily against you when you come begging at my table.'

'Isn't it the dog that does the begging?' she replied into his face.

'Only if the bitch is in heat.'

Edgar came between them and pushed them roughly apart so that Daniel staggered and almost lost his balance. He advanced on his son, who now took a step or two backwards. Godwin noticed the formidable breadth of Edgar's shoulders compared to the wiry boy. 'Don't let me hear you talk like that to your sister,' he said with total control in his soft, deep voice. 'And don't be too hasty to plan the state of things after I am gone. I am far from finished here.'

Daniel cowered with his hands before his face but cried back at him, 'Perhaps it would be better for all of us if you went now, before you destroy everything.' At this everyone fell silent, including Lydia, who watched open-mouthed. Edgar walked slowly up to Daniel who had now retreated as far as he could against the far wall of the courtyard. He stood inches from his son, stone-faced and silent, staring without blinking into the boy's tear-streaked face.

After a moment he turned and walked away, leaving Daniel doubled up, sobbing. Edgar came over to Lydia and put his arm around her shoulder. His face was soft, though he wagged a thick forefinger in front of her. Godwin overheard some of his words, something about her having to be kinder to her brother, about his not being as strong as her. She nodded resignedly and he kissed her on the cheek before returning to mount his horse.

He and Godwin walked their horses out of the courtyard, with Panayiotis riding beside them on a mule. He had a large box strapped to the rear of his saddle, resting against the animal's rump, which Edgar explained was Percival's broken music box. Panayiotis was taking it to Páparis, where Solouzos would arrange for it to be sent on to Athens immediately.

Godwin observed his host with cautious awe. How far behind that powerful, bullish front was the man of sensitivity and vision who had produced those watercolours? The quiet brooding of his blue eyes gave a clue to what might lie beneath, but it was still something of a mystery.

When they reached the crossroads at the bottom of the hill, Panayiotis turned off towards the mountain pass, while Edgar and Godwin went straight into the heart of the village towards the square that was flanked by the church and the school. Godwin remembered Solouzos telling him that both buildings had been donated to the village by Edgar.

'That is a fine church,' Godwin said, 'and unusual for Greece not to be built in the cross plan.' But Edgar was not to be drawn, and he nodded without even looking at the building. On the other side of the road, some schoolchildren, who had been playing outside their classroom, were called into a line by their teacher as Edgar approached; they waved at him as he rode past, and he raised his riding crop in acknowledgement. Godwin waved too.

'A handsome group of children,' said Godwin, 'and they seem pleased to see you. It is marvellous to see a prospering village school in so remote a place.' An identical nod was his answer but nothing more. If this was Edgar's idea of companionship, Godwin thought, it promised to be a lonely and difficult morning.

As they walked on through the village every householder called or waved a greeting, men raised their caps to Edgar, and those who passed close, even if they were burdened with heavy loads on their backs, stooped to lower themselves beneath the level of his boot. A medieval pontiff would have received no greater show of respect. Those who were some way off, too far to make a personal greeting, stopped what they were doing, stood still and stared as the two Englishmen progressed through. Edgar's visits to the village, no matter how frequent, Godwin thought, were clearly quite an event.

Without warning, a woman came running up to them shrieking in a high-pitched voice. She prostrated herself on the ground in front of Edgar's horse to make him stop, and then came to his side, weeping with emotion and stretching up to grasp his hand. Edgar placed his palm on the woman's head and said some words to her before passing on.

'What on earth did she want?' asked Godwin.

'She didn't want anything. She was thanking me.'

'For what?'

'It was just a little local nonsense. Nothing of great consequence.'

'Of great consequence to her, surely. I hope you do not mind my asking?'

'Very well,' Edgar said as they walked on. 'That woman is married to her cousin, not a unique occurrence in this area, but nonetheless in breach of Greek ecclesiastical law. They are well liked as a couple and no one sought to notice the flaw until last month, when her husband's vote was required by the demarch for some local political matter. He refused. A week later he and his wife received a visit from a representative of the diocese who announced their marriage was non-existent and that they should henceforth live apart. These people have three daughters.'

'How terrible. What happened?'

'It was simple enough. I went to visit the demarch and the matter was sorted out. Their marriage is safe again.'

'The man agreed to change his vote?'

'No. We could not allow that. He kept his honour and it was settled in the usual way.'

'The usual way?'

'Money. We call it a loan rather than a gift. The agreement in all these cases is that they will pay me back one day. Of course they can't.'

Godwin was moved by the story, but could not help wondering if Edgar's philanthropy was entirely altruistic. Was it not also in his interests to keep the village in his debt? But it was nothing more than a fleeting thought, because Edgar had relaxed, and as they progressed out of the village he began to talk more freely of the various enterprises he had undertaken here over the years. Crop rotation, new housing, irrigation, ploughing techniques – his passion for the project was boundless, and Godwin, thankful that his host's previous reticence had finally lifted, willingly sat and listened to the compelling narrative.

Daniel drove Hermann and Dr Schillinger the fifty-minute journey to the beach in silence. When they reached the nearest point where it was safe to take the carriage to the sand, he stepped down, tied the reins to a tree, and opened the door for his passengers. He was surprised to see them engaged in an earnest conversation. They did not usually speak much to each other, except when the older man was giving instructions and barking demands at his pupil; but this time Hermann was doing the talking. He was questioning his teacher with a raised voice, almost whining, his eyes full of resentment. Dr Schillinger was obviously angry. His anger did not find expression in shouting or gesticulating but in the percussive twist of his consonants; he hissed and spat as he spoke, while his cheeks twitched and his tongue flicked like a scorched viper.

Hermann was sitting forward on his seat with both his hands out, palms up, staring at Schillinger. He pushed his head forward and his eyes widened at whatever it was the doctor said next.

'What's the matter?' asked Daniel, forgetting his own problem for the moment. Hermann did not answer or move, but, still staring at Schillinger, repeated a question because he could not believe the answer he had received.

'*Sofort. Morgen,*' came the snapped reply.

'Huh?' Hermann gasped incredulously, to which his teacher made no response. Hermann now turned violently on his seat and pushed Daniel out of the way to get out.

'Hold on,' said Daniel, but Hermann stalked on past him, out towards the sea-front, arms swinging as he struggled to keep his footing in the soft, yielding sand. Daniel looked back at Schillinger, who sat implacably and without expression, showing no intention of moving from the carriage.

And so they waited, for an hour or more. Daniel sat barefoot on the beach, sleeves rolled up and forearms on his knees, looking out towards the massive blue horizon, until Hermann eventually came back, shuffling ankle deep through the sand, his shoes pale and cracked. Daniel jumped up and hurried over to him.

'Hermann,' he said, 'please tell me, what's happened?'

'He says we must go.'

'What?'

'We must go. Tomorrow.'

'Go?'

'Leave this place.'

'Why?'

Hermann did not answer, but walked on, head hanging and cheeks ablaze, staring at the ground in front of him. He climbed into the carriage and closed the door.

Chapter 15

Fortinbras Pierrepont looked out of the windows of the drawing room and saw Lydia leave the house on foot. She was carrying her blue notebook and he noticed her glance up at the sky with an anxious look. He watched, wondering where she was going, in her matching cape and hat, until she disappeared beyond the gates. He decided he would go to the library, but as he walked through the hall he saw the chambermaid, Maroula, hurrying towards the stairs, her arms full of folded linen. She rarely looked up from the floor when people were around, he had noted, but this time she did quickly raise her eyes from under her headscarf, and when he said good morning returned his friendliness with the faintest of smiles. She had large, dark and very beautiful eyes, Fortinbras thought, and her shyness was charming.

He had seen a certain book on the shelves the day before and wanted to go back to have a closer look when no one was about. The house was pretty much empty now; Mag might be around, but she usually stayed in the staff quarters during the morning; and so, emboldened, he went straight to the shelf to find it. He felt a pulse of dangerous excitement as he took it down and opened the title page: *The Passage of Maidenhood. An Academy for Woman*, from 1772. There were engravings. He had never seen anything like it before. Bodies coupled, half dressed, in the countryside, in the boudoir, spread, wrapped and twisted; men in wigs with gargantuan members; stockinged, double-chinned ladies with large wigs, dainty feet and gaping apertures. He shut the book, his heart beating and his breath shorter, and then reopened it at a page of text.

> *From the position of a man at the high point of excitement, the sexual act is concerned only with the place wherein to accomplish his deposit. This is a command of nature. Having reached the point where this becomes his sole concern, the person of the woman within whom he has intention of accomplishing his deposit, her soul and her intelligence, have no relevance. In the same way nature commands that a woman's satisfaction is to be found in achieving the man's deposit, thereby heightening her opportunity of conception. Sexual pleasure for a woman depends upon her success or otherwise in coaxing the man into an emission of his seed. Thus it follows that there is no greater joy known to woman than to accomplish by her own skill, and eventually witness, the eruption of her male's fluid.*

Fortinbras shut the book again and put it back on the shelf with a shaking hand, his feelings uncomfortably caught between savage excitement and shame. He walked out of the library and headed back to his room, trying to erase the images that had formed in his mind.

When he opened the door of his room, he found that Maroula was there, changing the sheets. She looked up and there was the smallest hint of a smile again before she returned her attention to her work. Fortinbras walked towards her. Although the fabric of her dress was thick and heavy, he could just make out the form of her behind and upper legs, as she leant over to tuck in the sheet. Her waist was narrow and her chest pronounced.

'Let me help you,' he said, taking the other side of the sheet. She did not look up now, but her actions took on a slight urgency. Her busy fingers were short, the skin and nails a little neglected, almost like a child's, he thought tenderly. She worked fast and smoothed out the blanket at the base of the bed. Fortinbras turned down the sheet and walked around behind her to tuck in the other side. He was looking at her shape as he went around, and a slight turn of her head as he passed behind showed that she was aware of his gaze. He had stopped. She whipped around to face him, and her eyes darted nervously from one of his to the other.

'Don't be afraid,' he said, taking a step forward and holding her by the shoulders. This was a lovely girl, he thought. Perhaps he should marry a girl like this and turn native. She did not deserve to be a servant, he could save her, elevate and ennoble her, and she would worship him all his days in thanks for it. A future vision of himself surrounded by a huge Greek family flashed through his mind, angelic dark grandchildren crawling around his ankles, a lamb on the spit outside, handsome tanned sons-in-law coming back smiling from the fields, and this gorgeous woman growing old at his side. He could smell her now, a wholesome spicy scent, like cinnamon and nutmeg. But she was moving away from him, her face a blaze of terror.

'Why are you frightened of me?' he said, pushing himself against her and feeling his own hardness bump into the cloth at her navel.

'Please,' she said in a little high-pitched voice.

'So, you can speak?' said Fortinbras, smiling, and cupping her cheek in his hand.

'Please!' She had nowhere further to retreat and was forced to lean back over the bed.

'I'm not going to hurt you, little one. I can be very nice to you.' He grabbed at her long skirts with both hands and began to hitch them as he pushed her further back on to the bed. She let out a tiny shriek. 'No, don't do that,' Fortinbras said, still with a gentle voice, though it now betrayed a slight quaver, and he pulled up the swathes of fabric. His own hands were shaking and his fingers touched flesh. The angle was too much for her and she fell back against the bed as he pushed between her knees. The grey skirt was up around her waist and he could see that she had no underwear. Her flat belly, above the hair, was heaving up and down with every sharp breath.

'Please!'

'Please what?' he almost whispered as he forced her arms down and out by the wrists. There were tears in her eyes.

'Please. No.' Her voice was feeble.

'Don't say that, my dear. I want to be kind, believe me.' His own breathing was heavy now, and his jaw shuddered. He took his hands from her wrists for a moment to fumble with the tops of his trousers. Freed for an instant, Maroula went into a frenzy, arms and legs struggling, lashing, slapping, kicking, like a trapped animal. It was all Fortinbras could do to protect himself from the ferocity of her movements. He shielded himself as he recoiled, trousers falling. A blue and white vase was sent spinning to the floorboards, where it smashed. With more room to manoeuvre, Maroula flung her limbs at him aimlessly, letting out gasps of anger and misery until she was clear of him enough to return to her feet and push down her skirts, after which she ran to the door and fled, sobbing.

From the depths of the house, Mag had heard the crashing vase, and, after she had finished the paragraph she was writing, she came out of her room to see what had happened. Passing the kitchen and glancing inside from force of habit, she noticed Maroula on a stool, her face in her hands, leaning into the embracing arms of old Barba Stamos, her father, the chief cook. He saw Mag and gave her a reassuring nod, as if to say nothing serious was up and it was best leave well alone, and so Mag returned to her room, convinced that the crash had been the silly girl dropping something; she did not give it another thought.

Chapter 16

Edgar Brooke and Godwin progressed along paths and across ditches that separated fields now stripped bare; fields which in different seasons yielded crops of tomatoes, tobacco and wheat. Plantations of walnut and fig trees spread up the slopes to the east where the gradient made ploughing less comfortable, punctuated by silvery olive groves. They were on their way to see a woodman who lived in an isolated hut on the lower slopes of the forest and their approach was by a steep path which wound its way between prickly arbutus and lentisk bushes. They emerged at last at a level clearing that commanded expansive views of the forest.

At the far side of the clearing was the small timber shack that constituted a home for the man and his family, surrounded by piles of wood, with a larger enclosed pen for livestock adjacent to it, and a tidy kitchen garden to the front. A huge black dog, leashed to a wooden post, barked wildly when it sensed the intruders, jumping hopelessly into the air and almost throttling itself in defence of its patch. As the two Englishmen approached at a slow walk across the grassy clearing, it became clear that all was not well at the homestead. They heard the sound of a female voice shrieking with panic and then saw a woman come running out towards them, arms in the air. Edgar quickly swung from his saddle and went to her, pulling her to her feet as she lowered herself before him, her words a babbling high-pitched stream.

'There's been an accident,' was all he said to Godwin as he

strode quickly towards the hut, the woman at his heels. Godwin tied both horses to a tree and followed. Inside the hut a man lay twisted on the mud floor, his shirt removed. The angle of his arm was wrong, mechanically reconfigured, so that it seemed as if it could flex in reverse. A bulbous white protrusion in the shoulder showed that his bone was pushing up against the skin. His stocking was torn and blood dripped from a gash in his thigh. Next to him, staring at the sight in silent, frozen fascination was a boy of about seven.

Edgar threw off his own jacket and ran over to the man, snapping orders at his wife, who hurried off to find some cloth.

'He fell from the tree,' said Edgar by way of explanation, and then began to talk in Greek to the man on the floor, feeling along his arm and shoulder in various places and asking questions all the while. The forester could barely talk from the pain, and held his breath to contain it.

'Take the boy aside,' Edgar said quietly to Godwin, who then attempted to pull him back by the shoulders, but the lad shook him off and remained rooted to the spot. Now Edgar positioned himself over the man, wedged a knee against his chest, and took a firm grip on his arm. He remained like this for a moment, pinning him down beneath the weight of his own barrel girth, and feeling for the perfect grip. He said a few words to the forester which must have been humorous because the man responded with a brave smile, but before he had even finished what it was he was saying, Edgar suddenly wrenched up and out with a violent jerk, so that the man let out a roar of agony and slumped on to his side, breathless. Edgar patted him on the back and got to his feet. The shoulder had been relocated and the arm returned to a natural shape. Edgar reached for his jacket, took a silver flask from the side pocket, and drained it. The wife now came in, piping her concern, and handed over a bowl of water and a length of muslin before hurrying to her man's side, where she held his face between her palms.

Edgar then proceeded to wash the leg wound, expertly tear the cloth into strips and tie a bandage. Noticing the young boy still standing there with a glazed expression, he called him over, breaking his sombre reverie, and had him put a finger on the bandage knot while he tied it into a double bow. When the job was complete he put an arm encouragingly around his shoulders, and Godwin noticed how the lad slumped and melted into Edgar with a sort of dazed relief as the strong arm enveloped him. It was clear that the landowner was as much employer as member of the family to these people.

Godwin helped to carry the forester, whose name was Dhimos, over to a sheepskin rug by the fire. He was already feeling better and enjoying some joke with Edgar, who had settled himself on a low stool in front of the hearth and was resuscitating the fire as if it were his own home. That task accomplished, he disappeared outside the rear of the building and returned a few minutes later carrying a large pile of logs, which he stacked next to the fire. Dhimos called his wife to bring over a bottle and offer a drink to the visitors. It was the first time Godwin tasted *raki* and he thought it was like liquid fire, but it was a good, heartening drink, and it pleased him in a masculine way to raise his glass in a triumvirate mutual salute with Dhimos and Edgar.

He continued to feel elated during the ride back to Thasofolia, in contrast to Edgar, whose euphoria began to ebb, so that by the time they rode through the gates of the house he had become brooding and silent once again. Godwin knew that the retreating effect of the *raki*, which Edgar had consumed liberally at the hut, would leave him dull and lethargic, but there was something else in his demeanour as he returned home to resume his duties, something troubled and lonely – a man shouldering his burdens

191

alone, like Atlas, because no one else had the strength and stature to share the load.

They had missed lunch and there was no one around as Edgar led the way into the hall. He made for the staircase, instructing Godwin to wait for him downstairs and he would have something prepared for them to eat shortly; but he disappeared to his room, and in the event never re-emerged.

Godwin waited in the dining room for a while, looking at the pictures on the wall, some of which were by Edgar's father; small, dark and moody oils, rather pleasing, but not of the quality of his son's. Tucked in the far corner there was one simple frame he had not noticed before, its mount divided into four equal-sized squares, each containing a curled lock of hair mounted in a silver clip. They were labelled underneath in black ink, a fine, spider's-web script: Magdalen, Alithea, Percival, Edgar, three of them an identical fair colour, while the fourth, Alithea's, was mahogany brown. It was the first and only relic Godwin had seen at Thasofolia that pertained to Edgar's other sibling, the girl who had died of a nervous condition brought on by the brigand attack. He looked at it for some while, and at the other three locks, until it became obvious that neither his host nor any food was coming.

That evening at dinner, Edgar sat at the table's head dressed in a long cream caftan, belted with an ornamental rope and fastened with jewelled hooks. On top of this he wore a full-length tan gown made from coarse silk, together with a matching pillbox hat. The effect of the voluminous costume was to exaggerate further the impression of his breadth, the mountainous curve of his shoulders and thick, bare neck, as he leant forward over his soup. There was nothing remotely ostentatious in his manner. He had dressed for comfort, not effect, and was as oblique to the proceedings and remote from the social dimension of the meal as ever. He drank only water and volunteered no speech.

Hermann did not come down for dinner, but Mag made a little announcement to the assembled company. She explained that Dr Schillinger had completed his work and would be returning to Athens with his pupil earlier than expected – the following morning. The old academic seemed cheerier than ever before, and although the upper half of his skull remained fixed in his usual expression of slight surprise, his mouth and cheeks more than once during dinner tightened into a smile. It was not clear whether his habitual humourlessness had been eased by having achieved his goals or by a sense of relief that his departure was imminent. Either way, Godwin detected a not entirely wholesome quality in the Doctor's lightened spirits. It was pleasure of a sort that feeds on the misfortunes of others.

'We will all be sorry to see you go,' said Mag, to which Schillinger nodded an acknowledgement.

'Must Hermann also leave?' said Lydia to her aunt. 'He seems so much to be thriving here. I went for a walk with him this afternoon and he was terribly upset at the thought of having to go.'

'That's right,' concurred Daniel, 'he's a changed man since he came. I say let Hermann stay on for Christmas and I'll see him back to Athens personally in the new year. What do you say, Father?'

'I have no opinion,' replied Edgar, spooning his soup without pause.

'Aunt Mag?' said Daniel.

'Of course he must leave. How else can Dr Schillinger manage? Shame on you for suggesting such a thing, Daniel. And Lydia.' There was so little conviction in her tone that the two siblings exchanged a quizzical look across the table, after which Mag added, amelioratively, 'Anyway, it is entirely a matter for Dr Schillinger to decide.'

At this point, Schillinger, who had always protested his complete ignorance of English, spoke up in an irritated, almost shrill, bark.

'The boy will leave,' he said, 'and that is the end.' His manner cast a dark atmosphere over the table and they ate in silence for a while. In the end it was Percival's voice that cut through the air, relieving the tension.

'Are you fond of music boxes, Dr Schillinger?' The old man turned his head towards Mag, and she translated, after which he replied with a single negative syllable.

'Well, never mind,' Percival said, and added, a few moments later, 'I'm very fond of music boxes.'

'I think we should all benefit from a little music,' said Pierrepont. 'Lydia, will you play for us after dinner?'

She smiled her assent. Godwin had several times during dinner unsuccessfully tried to attract Lydia's attention to himself, but every attempt went unnoticed. He had hardly exchanged a word with her all day. She was either embarrassed and trying to pretend yesterday had never happened, or had given up on him for whatever reason, or was capriciously oblivious to any particular duty she might have to offer him attention. All three possibilities made him uneasy.

When the company rose to go through and hear Lydia play, Edgar remained in his seat and silently engaged eye contact with Godwin, by which Godwin assumed that he was being asked to remain. Edgar took a cigarette from a silver box on the table and poured himself another glass of water. Once everyone had gone, the door had closed and the two men were left alone, Edgar lit his cigarette from a candle on the table. A pustule of resin popped and fizzed from the fire. 'Help yourself to some Madeira,' he said, breathing out a cloud of smoke, 'and then be so kind as to fetch me the photographs you have been making of my daughter.'

Godwin felt a throb of guilty shock at the request. He almost asked how his host knew about the photographs, but thought better: any intimation of intended secrecy would only serve to incriminate him.

'I fear what I have accomplished is of an experimental nature,' he said. 'It would little interest you.'

'My watercolours are also experiments, and trivial ones at that,' Edgar came back quickly, 'but I gather you have shown an interest in them.'

Godwin had to conceal his surprise for the second time. 'You are an accomplished craftsman, sir,' he answered. 'My efforts pale in comparison.'

'Pray spare me the flattery. It means nothing to me. There has never until now been a photograph of Lydia. I have an interest.' Godwin was left with no choice but to accede to the request, which he did with a silent nod, and left the room to fetch the box of prints. His feelings were mixed as he returned down the hall stairs. He trod softly but the creak of the wooden boards sliced discordantly against the pretty keyboard tones resonating from the drawing room. It was one of Mendelssohn's *Songs without Words*. As well as everything else, he noted, Lydia could play the piano very nicely. The immediate prospect for himself contrasted darkly with the gentle moods conjured by Mendelssohn's melodies. While she, the heart of it all, lost herself in gorgeous legatos next door, he must now steel himself to reveal all to her father.

Edgar was still there at the head of the table, waiting, with heavy eyelids and an expression of dismal detachment that made his face hang. Godwin sat down, brought another candle over for better light and, without introduction or explanation, handed over the first exposure of Lydia, the one taken at the pool. He could not deny feeling a certain dangerous thrill that so rare an eye as Edgar Brooke's should be the first to appreciate the sequence of images.

Edgar's face seemed concentrated on what he saw, the pale blue eyes darting across the surface of the print under slightly knotted brows, finally resting for a brief moment on the central subject. He put the picture to one side, after no more than a few seconds' assessment, and his voice had that dry, questioning timbre of distraction again: 'Aha.' Godwin handed him the next, which was given a similarly brief perusal, then another, and another. In a matter of minutes, with little more than a handful of syllables expressed, neither in judgement, surprise or approval, there was one final print remaining to be passed, the one taken only the day before. Godwin's heart thumped and he hesitated to place it in the open, waiting hand. He now silently questioned why he had not left this picture hidden in his room upstairs. That would have been the easier course. Did he possess some perverse or innate desire to ignite the older man's outrage in the same way that he always managed to infuriate his own father?

'What is the matter?'

'This picture is the most recent. And it is different.'

'Aha.'

'I must tell you that the form it has taken was not prescribed by me. It is the result of a voluntary action on Lydia's part.'

'Aha.'

'And that I was taken by surprise.'

'I wish only to see the print.'

Godwin hesitated still longer, blinking repeatedly in the direction of the table, his hand momentarily paralysed.

'I can assure you that I am insensitive to shock,' said Edgar.

'That may be so, sir, but I am not.'

'Then you should do your utmost to rid yourself of such a childish sensibility. It will only serve to restrict your outlook.' With that, he leant forward and snatched the print from Godwin's trembling grip. His eyes scanned the faultless nude body of his daughter pictured in the woods with no more or less discernment than the other pictures, and then he put it with the others on the pile. 'Is that all?'

'It is.'

Edgar sniffed and leant forward, cigarette in hand, to sip his drink. He cut an impressively exotic figure behind the thin haze of rising smoke that hung in the air; the expatriate patrician swathed in silk, an Englishman like the pioneers of old who embedded themselves for years in distant colonial outposts, almost forgotten by the administration that had sent them, and spawned broods of mongrel children; they became lords of all they surveyed, governors turned princelings turned minor deities. Edgar at this moment seemed cut from that cloth.

Godwin spoke quietly. 'You may well consider, sir, that I have acted in an improper manner.' Edgar seemed not to hear Godwin's comment, and when he eventually spoke his voice was dry.

'I had thought the camera might bring us within a whisper of the Godhead. But of course it will not.'

Godwin was taken aback. Edgar's face was sculpted desolation.

'I did not grasp the substance of your remark, sir.'

Edgar roused himself from his meditation. 'We will never translate the immediacy of nature into form until we learn to shed sentiment. I had thought a photograph might be free from pretensions but I am disappointed. I am more persuaded than ever of the inefficacy of art.'

'Do you not like the prints?'

Edgar tutted disparagingly and shook his head. 'It has nothing to do with like and dislike. I am talking about the object of art.' Godwin stared at Edgar, who was facing down the length of the table. In the curve of the cheek and the turn of his nose Godwin could now recognize a heavier and coarser replication of his daughter's features, something he had not noticed before.

'What do you see as the object of art?' Godwin asked.

'To frame a glimpse of the Godhead.'

Godwin felt innumerable miniature tremors spreading from the roots of his hair. As if in possession of some metaphysical map, Edgar had found his way to the attic of his house guest's mind and stumbled in. The door was flung open and light cast into the dim recesses for the first time in years. This was territory heavy with significance for Godwin. 'The object is to represent God?'

'Which cannot be achieved. But art is the attempt. And man's undying urge through centuries to achieve that end is the most glorious and moving of his attributes. The closer he reaches, the more tragic his failure.'

'You believe we have an urge to portray God?'

Edgar raised his head and looked towards the far end of the room. In the distance, from across the hall, was the sound of clapping and a man's voice cheering. Meanwhile, a candle at the other end of the table coagulated in the mutant build-up of its own wax deposits and let out a rhythmic popping sound which was echoed by a flicker in its flame. 'A truly gifted artist is a creature who is fortunate enough to glimpse divine benediction and uses his skills in an attempt to enshrine it,' said Edgar. 'It is a form of worship. It makes the tragedy of his failure all the more poignant.'

'Why do you say he fails?'

'Because he seeks to render permanent and static a truth which is by its nature in perpetual motion.'

'But cannot a photograph depict one moment stolen from that perpetual motion, and thereby hint at the divinity you mention?'

'Not without degrading the truth. You may write out a recipe, you may describe a dish in a thousand volumes, but you can never substitute a description for the experience of taste.'

In a few sentences Edgar had defined the purpose of art and simultaneously dismissed it as a stillborn pursuit. The authority of his reasoning was crushing.

'Is there not something else attainable through art?' Godwin asked. 'What about the expression of feeling?'

'The baggage of human sentiment must not be confused with true art, which is a divine calling. For the rabble these pleasing story-pictures'– he indicated the pile of photographs – 'might pass as art, I grant you.' Godwin cast a look at his precious work, so much wasted paper.

Again, applause could be heard from across the hall, and now several voices cheered.

'I think you should join the others,' said Edgar, and rose to leave. They parted company in the hall, Edgar saying nothing more than a dry good-night before climbing the stairs to his private world above.

Godwin waited by the massive inglenook hearth until he heard the door of his host's room upstairs close. He knelt in front of the fire and poked at the embers. The shadows of the hunting trophies shimmered high above on the wall, antlers, a pair of boars' heads with yellowing tusks, and the open-armed bear, mounted in the centre. He wondered when this great beast had crashed its way, oblivious to all, through the pines and snowy peaks of Pyroxenia.

The fire had expired and would need bellows and fresh kindling to reignite, and so Godwin gave up on it. He did not want to join the others. He did not feel part of their company. And so he picked up the box of prints and made his way upstairs.

Chapter 17

Edgar's comments had stirred the deep waters of Godwin's memory – a dark well that had been sealed and stagnant for longer than he could recall. He sat in his room and reluctantly allowed himself to journey back to boyhood, to that pivotal summer morning during the school holiday; and his heart sank. He had thought never to dwell on it again, but acknowledged with resignation that a ghost like this could never simply be banished, merely screened for a time. The incident was as clear and immediate here in the wilds of Greece as it had been at the time, seventeen years previously. He had been summoned back; back to his father's desk.

He was standing at a respectful distance in front of the massive figure of Sir Harold before his presence was acknowledged, while the great man finished whatever it was he was writing.

'Good morning, my boy,' his father at last said, not unkindly, putting down his pen.

'Good morning, sir.'

'Godwin, I do not intend to dally. I have here a letter from your housemaster that perplexes me in more ways than one. Is this something you would have expected?' Godwin thought hard and quickly. He had an equal choice: of affirmative and negative, one or the other, and on the instant he had to assess which would give rise to the least damage.

'Yes, sir.'

'Ah, so you know of your deficiencies?'

'I do, sir.' He hung his head.

'Look at me, please.' The words came softly but were no less terrifying because of it. 'So, what, in your opinion are the deficiencies?'

'I am too easily distracted, I do not work hard enough, I am lazy, I do not try well enough in sport, my handwriting is untidy, I am late for fixtures, I do not concentrate when the master talks, I—' he paused, blinking, trying to think of more sins to add to the litany.

'All this and yet you spend your holiday time painting pictures in the nursery? Do you not think you should be improving yourself?'

'Yes, sir.'

'We shall see to that in due course. But first, there is another matter. The particular item in your housemaster's letter that causes me the most distress.' Godwin looked up wide-eyed, wondering what shortcoming was so far and above the others to deserve special treatment. 'Let me ask you this, and take your time, because upon this question hangs everything. It is not to be trivialized, underestimated, or regarded with anything less than the supreme relevance which it has in every single department of your life, present and future. And it is this: how do you describe God?'

'God, sir?'

'God.' Sir Harold lowered his brow and observed the boy with deadly seriousness from underneath his eyebrows.

Godwin looked around the room for inspiration. 'Our Lord Most High, Eternal Mighty King, All Merciful, All Terrible, our Shepherd, er,' he struggled to remember more lines from the hymns, 'Blest Creator, Holy, Holy, Holy—'

'That is how others have described Him,' interrupted his father, 'now take your time and tell me how *you* would describe Him. Your own words.' Godwin bit his lip and closed his eyes for a moment. He so wanted to say the right thing. When he spoke it was hesitant.

'The property of all creation, part of everything.'

'And his appearance?'

'Dazzling light? And goodness.'

'Is goodness an appearance? Think, sir! If our Lord God were to reveal Himself to you, how would He appear?' His father's eyes showed a flash of irritation. There was no room for error now.

'I don't know, sir.'

'What colour is His skin?'

'I don't understand, sir.'

'It's quite simple, boy, you speak English, well, listen.' He leant forward and spoke slowly as if to an imbecile: 'What colour is God's skin?'

'Well, like us.'

'Like *us*?'

'Not like us, sir. But, rather, we are like Him. He made us to be like Him. In His image.'

'Does He have a beard?'

'I don't know, sir. Sometimes He does.' Godwin hurriedly thought of a way to justify his comment, 'Jesus does, and Jesus is God as well, and so sometimes yes, sir.'

Sir Harold folded the letter and put it back in his drawer with a sigh. 'Your housemaster says you questioned the representation of God in the east window of the school chapel. That you questioned whether He would appear like that, would be dressed like that, or bear any of the characteristics depicted in that ancient and hallowed representation. Is this true?'

Godwin remembered the incident now, and felt his stomach fall away. 'I wondered how anyone could fashion a picture of God when no one has seen Him.'

'And how do you, a thirteen-year-old child, who has barely been out of Surrey in your short life, dare to claim knowledge of who has and has not, in the entire history of mankind, seen God?'

'I don't know, sir.'

'I sat in that same chapel more than a thousand times as a boy, looking at that same window, and I say, sir, that the image of God represented there is as fine as any in Christendom. Do you agree?'

'Yes, sir.'

'Well, either you lie or your housemaster lies, and as the latter is inconceivable, we must assume that the former is our problem.' He pursed his lips and scanned the desk. 'For which we must devise appropriate punishment.' He looked up at his son. 'Come closer, sir.' Godwin approached. 'Am I an unreasonable man, Godwin?'

'Certainly not, sir.'

'Then you will consider that the punishment I am about to prescribe is not unreasonable, either. As you are confident in your own understanding of divine physiognomy, and as you prefer painting to study or sport, you will have three days, during which time you will emerge for meals and sleeping only, to produce for me your own representation, in ink and watercolour, of Our Lord God Almighty. We shall then compare and see whether your interpretation is more successful than that achieved by the anonymous master responsible for the school chapel's east window. Three days,' he looked at his watch, 'seventy-one hours fifty-nine minutes. And I want an image no less than three feet by two feet. You may go now, Godwin. Thank you.'

'Thank you, sir,' he said, and turned to leave.

For the following three days Godwin endured a purgatory of indecision and muddle. He racked his brain for ideas and tried out a number of them, but by the middle of the third day found that he was once again facing a blank sheet. The torn and scrumpled detritus of his failures lay all about him on the floor. It was at this point that he was visited by his mother. Lady Tudor was a brilliant and unusual woman in her way, who read widely and had a vast repository of knowledge at her disposal, but was not naturally maternal, preferring to cultivate her intellect rather than her children. A century later she might have made a formidable academic – a quality that Sir Harold found attractive, though he never admitted it – but as a woman of her time she was obliged to subjugate herself to the career and opinions of her eminent husband, and seemed content to do so. However, she would not entertain the idea of further pregnancies, despite Sir Harold's longing for a daughter. He never made a secret of the disappointment he had felt on hearing the news that his second child was not a girl.

Lady Tudor's visits to the nursery were rare, but because of her interest in the subject of theological iconography and her genuine concern that Godwin might be in a quandary, she took the opportunity to see how he was getting on. She secretly admired her younger son's originality, and his comments at school about the inappropriateness of the stained-glass God had brought her no little amusement; but these were sentiments she did not dare to express, nor was it appropriate, given the response of the housemaster and her husband.

'Good afternoon, Godwin,' she said. It was the first time she had seen him all day. 'Well, how far have you got?' Godwin attempted a stoical response, but then his courage failed and he dissolved into tears, confessing that he had achieved nothing. He had no idea what God looked like, and was plain terrified of what his father had in store for him.

It was not in his mother's nature to soothe his upset with loving words or embraces. Far from it – she could not bring herself to give him more than a quick pat on the shoulder with the tips of her long, manly fingers. Her way was to isolate the heart of the problem, think of a solution, and implement it with the minimum of delay or emotional distraction. To this end she gave her advice.

'The only honest way to address your task is to be true to yourself, and thereby you will fulfil your father's prescription. He wishes you to show honesty and he wishes to see your ideas on the matter. Anything less would be mendacious.'

'But I fear he does not wish to see my ideas. I fear he wishes me to put myself to rights.'

'Well, given that in this situation you only fear and do not know what his intentions are, your safest course is to show complete integrity. And, in any case, I should like to know your ideas. Now. How do you perceive God?'

Godwin looked down and spoke in a low voice. 'You would be shocked to hear.'

'I am not shocked by anything.'

'I do not mean any irreverence.'

'Of course you do not.'

'I do believe in God.'

'Enough preamble.'

Godwin paused to summon courage.

'I perceive God as, as nothing, or rather no thing, complete and empty simultaneously. I think the best picture would be an undrawn page.'

'Well, that would be convenient for you,' his mother said without hesitation, 'though I dare say we would be poorer as a civilization if every artist had taken your view.'

'Anything else would be blasphemy,' Godwin continued, voicing the conclusions of his hours of thought on the matter. 'I would not presume to put pen to paper with such a subject. An empty sheet is perfection. And limitless.'

'A nice thought, Godwin. You are a clever boy, let no one persuade you otherwise.' In its veiled defiance of her husband this was the most affectionate and moving remark he had received from her. 'But it may not be enough to persuade your father. You will have to decide, and the process of making the decision will build your character. You have a choice: an honest representation of your thoughts, or an ameliorative remedy to your father's displeasure. Now, I have said enough, quite enough.'

The following morning Godwin was too nauseous with anxiety to eat breakfast. His appointment with his father was at nine o'clock. He arrived five minutes early at the study door, with the sheet scrolled under his arm, tied with ribbon, and gazed at his watch until the precise moment came, before knocking. He was called to enter and felt his knees weaken as he walked across the threshold, closing the door behind him. He had not seen his father since their previous meeting.

'Good morning, my boy.' His tone was friendly. 'So let us see what you have for me.' Godwin walked forward and handed over the scroll, unable to stop himself mumbling, 'I'm sorry, sir.'

'Sorry?' his father replied with a smile, pulling open the ribbon bow. 'I'm sure there's no need for apology. I am not a monster to reward hard effort with unkindness.' He gripped the paper by the top, between his massive thumb and forefinger, and unrolled it downwards, blocking Godwin's view of his face as he first caught sight of its emptiness. His arms fell to the desk, the paper crumpling beneath the weight of them into a creased heap. For a moment he said nothing, and Godwin stood there, his frame juddering with each thump of the heart.

'I am waiting to be enlightened.'

'I did try. Very hard. But I found that every attempt was presumptuous in the extreme. It seemed a mockery of the subject.'

'You will recall the origin of this exercise,' his father said through his teeth. 'Try to imagine yourself as the school provost who first commissioned the construction of the chapel's east window. Indeed, in recollection, I believe it may have been the monarch himself. Your kinsman. Imagine his reaction if he had arrived on the day of the unveiling to find, instead of God depicted, several hundred square feet of plain glass. What would you, as king – a laughable notion – have said to the pale-faced, self-obsessed and not particularly intelligent little artist who thought to disappoint thousands of worshippers for centuries to come because of a vainglorious contention, in the face of all tradition, that the divine cannot be depicted?' The insults made Godwin flinch. 'You talk of mockery. You have mocked me. With your conceit.'

'No, sir.'

'Yes, sir. And you shall pay for it. Do you expect me never to resist your boundless mendacity? What sort of father would that make me?'

'I have never lied to you, sir.'

'What's that you say? What of the illness? Your months of boudoir indolence!' His eyes bulged with a fierce energy but remained fixed coldly on Godwin. 'Did you expect me to believe your fanciful inventions? Voices in your head! Whose voices, may I ask?'

'I don't know. It felt like the devil.'

'Well, that part at least does not surprise me. Away with you now, out of my sight. You will remain in the nursery until I have considered what to do with you.'

Judgement was passed and the course of Godwin's summer thence defined. His father was not a whipper. The fear he could impart was reliant on more subtle means for its effect. For the remaining weeks of holiday, when Godwin would have been playing cricket and tennis, accompanying the family first to their grouse estate in Scotland and then to their coastal house at Great Yarmouth, he was compelled to remain with a member of staff who hardly spoke and whose cooking was abominable, in the nursery at Epsom, where his days were spent producing exact watercolour reproductions, one after the next, of the complete set of illustrations in his Children's New Testament. There were forty-two, most featuring a blue-eyed, golden-haired and bearded Jesus, walking gracefully, in a white robe, through little crowds of dusky Middle Eastern people, performing miracles and blessing as He went.

By the time he returned to school at the close of the holidays, Godwin's ways had been mended. Not once did he express another unconventional attitude towards the opinions he received and was required to adopt, nor did he lapse in his studies or flag at sport. He was an adequate, perhaps even promising student, who kept his head down and his profile low; but the incident that had sparked his change left a scar both on him, and, he suspected, his father. Sir Harold never entirely trusted his younger son from that time, despite the letters of satisfaction from school, the reasonable academic achievements, and the apparent disappearance of the illness. He seemed convinced that it was all a sham, an elaborate deception on the part of Godwin to hide his true nature, which was lazy, petulant and troublesome. There was nothing Godwin could do to change his mind, and the old man never tired of taking opportunities to criticize him.

As he lay on the edge of sleep in his bed at Thasofolia, Godwin wondered how different his life might have been had Edgar Brooke been his father. Such far-reaching thought, such neglect – disdain, even – of boundaries. Just a day in Brooke's company and he felt unshackled. And, in a sense, redeemed.

Chapter 18

Early the next morning the upstairs corridors at Thasofolia rang with the howls of Dr Schillinger. Daniel (who slept naked even in winter and had to throw on a nightshirt as he ran from his room) was first to arrive at the old man's bedroom, and despite the piercing screams coming from the other side of the door he hesitated and knocked before going in. The Doctor was in his nightclothes and stumbling around on all fours, bumping into furniture and catching his toes on rucks in the carpet, one arm outstretched in front like a trunk-sized antenna. Daniel leapt across in front of him to push back the shutters and let in the light, by which time Lydia and Mag had arrived at the door.

'Whatever is the matter?' said Mag.

'I know as little as you,' replied Daniel. 'I found him like this.' Dr Schillinger had sunk to the floor, his wails subsiding into whimpers. His thin white hair was messed, and tears seemed to be seeping through the sealed joins of his eyelids. Mag knelt down, put a hand on his shoulder and spoke to him in German. His head was slumped back to one side but a reply of sorts came through his crying, to which Mag responded by barking an order at Daniel.

'Go at once to Hermann's room and see if it's true.'

'See if what's true?' asked Daniel.

'Go and see if he's there. Not you, Lydia!' she added as her niece made to follow Daniel out.

'What's happened?' asked Lydia, approaching, hand over her mouth as if to protect herself from an infection.

Schillinger was still muttering pathetically and Mag had to lean close to hear what he was saying.

'He says Hermann has gone.'

'Gone? Where to?'

'Just gone. He should have been here an hour ago to wash and dress him, and he's never late.' Daniel was back at the door, out of breath.

'He's not there,' he said, 'and Barba Stamos is downstairs saying the pantry has been robbed.'

Within an hour the extent of the crisis was known to everyone in the house. Hermann had disappeared in the night, had taken a few spare clothes and a bag of food, but otherwise left no clue as to where or why he had gone. Edgar and Panayiotis left promptly after breakfast at the head of two search parties, while Daniel, who felt wounded that his father had chosen Panayiotis rather than himself to lead the second mission, agreed to accompany Dr Schillinger to Páparis. The old man, who surprised everyone with his uninhibited and drawn-out display of emotion at the loss of Hermann, had decided to leave as planned, partly because Percival had warned that if he did not leave today, while the weather was dull but mild and dry, he might be stuck at Thasofolia for days. So it was that after breakfast, rather later than planned, and still whimpering to himself, with a handkerchief held to his nose, Dr Schillinger departed on horseback through the gates of Thasofolia, southbound for the mountain pass.

'I think he may be in love with Hermann,' said Godwin to Lydia as they watched him disappear around the corner.

'What a funny idea,' she said glibly and hurried indoors. Godwin followed her, and had to take long strides to keep up, a fact of which she must have been aware, because he was there, coat flapping, at her heels, though she made no move to slow down until they reached the hall door. As she paused to open it, he came close to her ear and said, almost conspiratorially, 'Your father was none too impressed with our photographic efforts. He insisted I show him the collection last night, but dismissed them as little short of blasphemy. He knew the comment was an exaggeration and his jocular tone as he said the last word implied as much, but Lydia would not be drawn by the humour.

'And does that bother you?' she said.

'Well, I confess I was hoping for a little more approval. Do you not think the photographs deserve it?'

Lydia frowned a little impatiently. 'Deserve?' she said, 'I think Father deserves to have an opinion.' They were not angry words, or even emotionally fuelled; if they had been it might not have been so bad. But they were said with discursive flippancy and she was off on more important business, leaving Godwin standing there, at a loss what to think.

That evening, after the search parties had returned unsuccessfully from their mission, and heavy clouds gathered in the night sky above the cypresses of Thasofolia, dinner was a low-key affair, with simple food, sparse talk and an early dispersal of the company to bed. But Fortinbras Pierrepont and Godwin moved to the drawing room, where they shared a carafe of *retsina* in front of a blazing fire. Fortinbras was buoyant, and wanted to share his impressions of the Howards' house that he had visited earlier in the day.

'You would not believe the place. It is perfect in every way. Like a much smaller version of this house, more deteriorated – because it has been unoccupied for so many years – but proportionally equivalent, with magnificent mountain views and a courtyard. The villagers would welcome me with open arms.'

Godwin smiled at his boyish enthusiasm. 'But why on earth would you want to have your home out here? Your work is in Athens. And don't you intend to return to England when you've finished?'

Pierrepont now beamed at Godwin, savouring the moment.

211

'Ah, there, my friend, you bring me to a matter of momentous importance. I have been waiting for the opportunity of telling you, and now would seem to be the moment. You will be the first to share in our happiness.'

'Whose happiness?' asked Godwin, genuinely baffled.

'Mine and Miss Brooke's. I am going to ask Lydia to marry me.' Godwin was speechless and could do no more than stare open-mouthed at Pierrepont. 'And the Howards' house will be perfect for us,' he continued. 'I tell you, I can think of nothing else but acquiring it and making it our home. I know I will have to be in Athens a good deal, or else in other parts of Greece, but I could arrange to be here for several months of the year, and Lydia would have her family so close by, so that it would not—'

'I do hope you're joking?' asked Godwin.

'Joking? Of course not. What is the matter?'

'Well, to begin with, she's no more than a child. And you barely know her. Has she given you any sign that she might accept you?'

'No question about it,' replied Fortinbras, waving aside the objections with a flick of his hand, 'I can tell. She'll accept. And her age is an irrelevance. She's not typical, I think you'll agree. In fact she sometimes makes me feel like a young fool. I was wondering . . .' and here he looked down with a smile, almost too shy to bestow the compliment, 'I was wondering if you might stand by me when the time comes. As witness.'

'How can you entertain such a notion?' interrupted Godwin in disbelief.

'You will not?' said Pierrepont, looking rather injured.

'Have you declared your intentions?'

'Not yet. You are the first to know. The future is glorious. Really, Godwin, you should come and see the house with me. You will love it.'

'I have not the slightest interest in the house or your preposterous ramblings,' snapped Godwin but, seeing Fortinbras' look of genuine hurt and surprise, softened his tone. 'Listen. I will take a long ride with you tomorrow and we can talk.'

'I won't change my mind,' replied Fortinbras quickly, as if such a thing should be obvious. 'I'm resting my life on this.'

'Will you at least spend the day with me? To talk.'

'I can't. Lydia is taking me for a ride tomorrow, if the weather holds.'

'What?'

But Pierrepont did not have the chance to reply, because at that moment Percival came into the drawing room and shuffled quickly over to where they were sitting.

'Hello Pea,' said Fortinbras, availing himself of the nickname that had until now only ever been used by Edgar.

Percival did not seem to notice, but went straight to the fire, knelt down and expertly rearranged the logs, talking all the while, almost to himself, about Hermann. 'I wonder where he can have gone, Dr Schillinger was very upset about it, poor Hermann, and it will rain tonight, though it may clear by the morning, do you think he will be all right, Mr Tudor?'

'I hope so,' replied Godwin, on the edge of his seat, facing Fortinbras and trying to retain his attention. Percival then stood up, clasped his hands together at his navel, and said, 'Would you like me to recite some poetry for you? I'm very good at Gray. "The Curfeu tolls the knell of parting day, the lowing herd wind slowly o'er the lea." Do you like Gray, Mr Tudor? That's the beginning of his *Elegy Written in a Country Church-Yard.*'

'Very beautiful,' said Godwin with less enthusiasm than he would ordinarily have shown. Fortinbras had the expression of someone who was settling in with lazy delight for some humorous entertainment.

'Splendid!' he said. 'Some more!'

'Moore?' said Percival. 'Yes I can do some Moore. "At the mid hour of night, when stars are weeping, I fly to the lone vale we loved, when life shone warm in thine eye—" is

213

that right?' He was grinning widely at them, and nodding.

'This is marvellous,' said Fortinbras, clapping his hands, 'Percival, you are magnificent!'

'Would you like a song, I'm rather good at singing, my mother taught me, do you like singing, Mr Tudor? Could you accompany me on the pianoforte?'

Godwin sighed. 'Very poorly. But perhaps.'

'I have a book of Italian songs. I very much like *Per la gloria d'adoravi*, shall we try it?' He looked expectantly at Godwin.

'Very well.' They made their way to the keyboard, while Fortinbras whooped and clapped from his seat. Godwin began the accompaniment and Percival took up the vocal line in a slightly hoarse baritone. 'A–*man–do pe–ne –ro, ma sem–pre v'a–me–ro-*' Godwin glanced across at Pierrepont. He was looking skyward with a relaxed smile, beating time with his finger, '*si, si nel mio pe-na-re . . .*'

At one point Fortinbras looked straight at Godwin but either ignored or failed to interpret the seriousness of his return expression.

Chapter 19

As he sat alone in the empty room above the innkeeper's kitchen, waiting for his men to arrive, Demetrios Lambros reflected on the short, unhappy lives of brigands he had known. Some he had loved, some he had betrayed, others he had known only through tales of their exploits, their fearlessness, honour and glorious deaths. The truth, as he knew only too well, was less romantic than the legends. Theirs was a weary, pain-ridden, filthy life, of bruised feet clambering miles over rocks at night, of unstitched boot soles in winter. Wherever they went they were greeted with despair, and misery followed in their wake. Their tools were terror and pain; their rewards the silent compliance of widows, orphaned children hunted into corners, husbands humiliated and brought to their knees by blade and barrel. These were the hallmarks of a brigand's life. And an early death – slumped on the ground, a mouth full of blood, eyes still and sightless.

It was time to stop. Times had changed and the brigands of old, kings of the mountain, were no more. The modern Greek state was being born, with regiments of real policemen, with roads, railways, telegraph connections, and machines to do the work of fifty farmers. The wilderness of Greece would soon be charted on map and grid, and the brigands' fiefdoms brought to order. This was to be Demetrios' last job. The biggest, perhaps, and therefore the one that offered the greatest chance for what he needed above all else: a royal amnesty. It would be a sweet finale.

He was meeting his men at a safe *khan* in the fishing

village of Petrohori, some miles from Thasofolia. Of course, nowhere was entirely safe for a man of his reputation, with all the enemies he had accumulated, but for every enemy there was a stalwart who would put his life on the line to protect him, and for every tale that cast him as a villain, there was another that put the fear of God into any that might dare to turn him in. All five of the hand-picked men who joined him in that upstairs room at the *khan* were as sure as granite, courageous, and ruthless if the need arose. He knew that each one of them could be relied on to stand alongside him to the end if needs be (their end, that is, because he would always find a means of escape, alone, if necessary; Demetrios was a God-fearing man and firmly believed that he would smell the nearness of death only when he knew the Lord's goodwill had turned from him; but until now he was convinced that, for reasons unknown to the small minds of men, the Almighty had looked with favour upon his activities). He had known comrades who vowed eternal brotherhood, who bonded bleeding wrists to his and wept tears of friendship, and yet whose loyalty could turn like the fickle midsummer weather. They had paid for their treachery. Demetrios was not one to trust lightly, perhaps because he knew how few could place their absolute trust in him, but with these men, these good, sure warriors – who in another age would have been the heroes of ballads or the founders of nations, like the *pallikars* of old who fought the Turks – with these men his plans rested on rock.

'We're not going to see each other again until the morning of the action,' he said to the men seated around the table. All of them sat forward, elbows resting on the surface, apart from Christos, the veteran warrior from Epirus in the north – handsome, tanned and rugged – who leant back in his chair, arms crossed, his face half in the shadows. The air was thick with the rich scent of Livadia tobacco smoke and the aroma of fresh coffee. 'We've been through the plan a hundred times, and haven't met here today to piss about any more. We all know there'll be surprises, things we haven't prepared for, changes to the plan. There always are.'

'Let it happen,' interjected Theodoros, grinning, his heavy hands clasped under his chin, 'we'll be ready for anything.' Theodoros was a fine bullock of a man, with massive shoulders and a neck built to pull a cart; and he was hungry for the chance to prove himself. Demetrios loved this boy but feared for him. He had seen his like many times before; eager and heroic, running on ahead; they were always the first to fall, their beautiful young blood soaking through the pine needles before their brethren had even caught up.

'I have never failed,' said Demetrios. 'Follow what I say and everything will run smoothly. I will not tolerate any questioning of my authority. I want this clear now. If anyone has a problem speak up, because there will be no room for this discussion after we begin.' He turned to Christos and held out a hand. 'I'm sorry, friend. You are my senior. You're a legend, and every man in this room would gladly fall in behind you, but with this job—' he opened his palm and shrugged his shoulders. Christos acknowledged the gesture with a slight nod, silently closing his eyelids in assent. He had taken more lead balls in his flesh than any man alive; his indestructibility was the subject of wondrous rumour and there were some who said he had sold his soul to the devil; he could accept a few days under a younger man's command without feeling the wound too deeply.

'Good,' continued Demetrios. 'So, the basics: there will be no mutilation or killing without my specific authorization. And no abusing the power of the gun. A man who gets his pleasure taunting the innocent by pointing his gun is a man with nothing between his legs. Are we agreed?' Everyone sniggered and shuffled on their stools. 'We're professionals, with a serious objective. Second, we understand the difference between stealing and robbery. The one is demeaning to us as men, as fathers and neighbours: the other is a way of life and a gateway to glory. We are not thieves. Thieves are scum. We do not steal from those who supply us, we treat all, apart from our declared enemies, with respect and gratitude. Never forget that we are being watched at all times by the Lord and His saints. No drinking until the job is done, and absolutely no womanizing.' The brief silence that followed was punctuated by the sound of tapping on the table. It was Adonis, the shepherd from the north of the island; he was making a circular pattern in the wood with the point of his knife, and stared wide-eyed and unblinking at his work as he chipped away.

'Go home now to your families,' concluded Demetrios, 'fuck your wives and make sure you do it well because I don't want to hear anyone tossing themselves off in the night when we're camped up on the mountain.' They laughed. 'What about Theodoros?' said one of them, putting an arm around the young man's shoulders. 'He doesn't have a wife.'

'Then let him take a goat,' said Pandelis, smiling.

Demetrios smiled across at Pandelis. Of all the assembled company this was the man he would depend on the most. Pandelis was clever, daring and sly. He was a cousin of Panayiotis and Maroula, who both worked for Kyrios Brooke. He would find out, through Panayiotis, exactly what was going on at Thasofolia, and could provide precise updates on everyone and everything there. He also spoke excellent English, which meant that he would perform the vital role of translator.

'Thank you, my brothers,' said Demetrios. 'Let us drain our coffee – because we have nothing else – and drink to a better tomorrow, to a nation that will one day salute us, and to the children and future peace of our beautiful island. It will be a privilege to work alongside you all.' They raised their cups to a man, but found little left to sip other than the bitter, tepid granules beached up from the coffee they had finished a while back, the taste of which brought a slight grimace to their faces.

Chapter 20

Percival was absolutely correct about the weather. From about eleven o'clock that night it rained savagely. The wind roared through the trees near and far, filling the valley with a blustery rumble; it was a noise that made them curl up small in their beds through the dark hours at Thasofolia, grateful for the warmth and comfort. Suddenly, at about six, the rain stopped, but its presence remained as the grey dawn light paled. The morning had a leaden, ominous feel, as if the weather had no more than agreed a temporary truce, on sufferance, and the threat of an onslaught remained ever present.

The search parties – farm workers, household staff, unwilling volunteers – left that morning in silence with sombre faces and heavy limbs, scanning the featureless sheet of cloud above them for signs of a fissure, some assurance that they might be spared a drenching. There was little comfort in the skies and less in their hearts as they set off, and more than one of them muttered inaudible obscenities about the foreign wretch who had caused them all this bother.

Godwin had come down early and loitered in the hall in the hope of seeing Lydia, steeling himself to ask directly what she intended to do about Pierrepont. He was surprised at his own nervousness as he waited to hear her light footstep on the stairs. But there was no sign of her.

The dining room was filled with the scent of hot lemon, and there, at the head of the table, leaning over his steaming, pint-sized cup, was Edgar. He greeted Godwin cheerfully and announced, in his habitual style, which allowed for no contradiction, that the two of them would form their own team in the search today; he had an idea of where Hermann might have taken himself, and it was a place that he would like to show Godwin anyway, and so would he kindly prepare himself to leave at first light, in half an hour's time, at about seven o'clock?

Neither Lydia nor Pierrepont had appeared by the time Godwin reached the courtyard at the prescribed hour. Edgar was dressed in a coarse goat-wool coat, short-sleeved and tailored without buttons, like a knight's tabard, and with a hide cape buckled across his shoulders. He wore high boots and a thick woollen skull-cap, and looked to Godwin every inch a falconer in the pay of some Renaissance prince. His saddle was packed full, as if for a longer expedition, leather pouches bulging, a holstered rifle and a pair of decoratively embroidered *tagari* bags slung across the stallion's neck. Godwin, in his tweed jacket, light cap and checked trousers, felt that he had perhaps underestimated the strains of the day ahead, but justified his attire with the recollection of just how limited was his traveller's wardrobe.

The matter of Lydia still preyed on him and he could not concentrate properly on anything else. Even as he mounted his horse next to Edgar, helped by Panayiotis, his glance was drawn continuously to the front door of the house, or the balcony above, in the hope of catching sight of her. In the event Lydia did not appear, and he silently despaired as he rode through the gates. His day was to be long and uncomfortable, and the spectre of Lydia's proposed outing with Pierrepont would never be far from his thoughts. He secretly prayed for the coal-ash cloud that pressed down on them to discharge its heavy load on the valley and prevent any further expeditions from Thasofolia. Then, at least, they would be contained together indoors at the house, with the ever-watchful eye of Mag upon them.

'I will not conceal from you, Mr Tudor, my lack of interest

in the mission upon which we are embarked,' Edgar commented buoyantly from the fore. They were riding north-west away from the village on a gradient and seemed to be heading to the heart of the forest.

'You mean the mission to find Hermann?'

'I think that we should leave the boy to meet his own destiny.'

'Surely you would not have him die of cold on the mountain? Anything could happen to him out there.'

'The boy made his own decision to walk out, and he can decide to return if he wishes. The best service we can render him is to respect his decision. It is quite possibly the first action of true character he has ever taken. There would be something heroic in his dying in such a manner, heroic in an appropriately German sense. It would show conviction.'

'There is nothing heroic about death,' said Godwin.

Edgar's brows knotted slightly. 'How would you interpret the event of Hermann's death?'

'As a tragedy.'

Edgar scoffed. 'Tragedy is nothing more than an attitude of thought.'

'There is no escape from such attitudes of thought,' Godwin said. 'It is the stuff of our working minds.'

'Then let our minds be stilled.'

'Then tragedy would cease to occur?'

'Cease to exist. Along with other preoccupations and anxieties.'

They had ridden high enough now to have their view ahead curtailed by the mist that clung to the mountain flank from this point upwards. Edgar led the way along a narrow pathway until they reached a level plateau in the middle of which was a grassy clearing. As they rode to the centre of this, Godwin saw a small wooden structure which he took to be their destination. It was a single-roomed cabin, constructed from logs, with a door and two windows that faced them, and roofed with a type of thatch. The surroundings of the hut were difficult to define through the vaporous shroud.

'Welcome, Mr Tudor,' said Edgar, dismounting and making his way straight to the door, 'welcome to my personal Thasofolia, my woodland retreat. Come inside. Let us warm this place up a little and chase away the mournful spectre of damp. Hermann!' he raised his chin and shouted as he opened the door, 'are you in there?' But even as he spoke the words he turned to chuckle at Godwin, as if the joke had been for his benefit. He was rubbing his palms as he led the way in, like a hungry man arrived to a warm welcome at his kinsman's feast.

'Logs, we must have some more logs,' he said. 'Mr Tudor would you please split some logs while I light the fire with what we have here and unpack the horse?'

Godwin, who had never split a log in his life, wordlessly received the steel wedge and mallet in his slender fingers, and turned to assess the large stack of dripping pine trunks beside the hut. Edgar, humming a tune, brought armfuls of bottles and muslin-wrapped parcels indoors from the saddle-bags. Half an hour later, with a sweat on his brow and blistered palms, Godwin felt he had mastered the task; having stacked up a good supply of logs to dry beside the hearth, he settled himself indoors on a wooden stool next to his host and splayed his whitened fingers to thaw in front of the fire.

'That's a good blaze, a good blaze,' said Edgar, smiling broadly and pouring two tumblers of *retsina*. Godwin looked around at the cabin. It was tiny and basic but endearingly cosy. There was a high bed built into the timberwork along one wall, like an elongated wardrobe, with curtains that served to enclose it from the room. A woven patchwork bed-spread of pretty fabrics stretched from the foot up to a set of lace-edged pillows at the head. Next to the bed stood a small bookcase, which served as a bedside table, with a brass oil lamp on top, and which was packed full of leather-bound books in English and Greek. A small table, a cupboard and a few chairs made up the rest of the furniture, and for decoration there was nothing but a huge map of the island, expertly drawn and inscribed by hand, that took up almost the entire span of one wall. The windows were small and allowed through barest glimpses of daylight. It was an inward-looking, hearth-centred place, which appealed to the primal need to be insulated and protected from intrusion. A view of the world beyond would almost have been unwelcome.

'What do you do for water?' asked Godwin.

'There's a spring just a few yards up the hill, back there,' Edgar indicated approximately with a wave of his fingers. 'Water is the first requisite. No water, no dwelling. The old boy would never have chosen this spot unless he'd been sure of decent water, all year round. A lot of places dry up in the summer.'

'Which old boy?'

'Mitzo. The old goatherd who used to live here when I was a boy. Used to live on this spot, but not this hut. I had this built after he died. No, his house was rather more simple. I used to escape from my governess and come up here to see him whenever I could. Poor woman despaired of me. Then the brigands came and she was one of the ones they amused themselves with. I was sorry afterwards that I hadn't been kinder to her.' Even the horror implied in his brief tale could not dampen his merry state of mind, and he barely stopped himself chuckling at the recollection of his own past misdemeanours as he poured himself another glass.

'He was a truly splendid fellow, old Mitzo. A dear, wise, settled man. I could sit here with him for hours in the spring-time, bees buzzing through the wild flowers, and hardly exchange a word, but yet come away with a better understanding of the world. How can a man do that to the mind of a child without even talking?'

'He must have set you an example you admired, I suppose.'

'I still admire him,' said Edgar, draining his glass in one. 'If I were half the man old Mitzo was I'd be a hundred times better than I am.'

He talked long and agreeably about the benefits to humanity of humble living, of country folk he had known, and husbandry. As ever, Edgar's mercurial temperament had set both the tone and the mood, and in the face of so persuasive and irresistible a force, Godwin's former pre-occupations once again evaporated. What power this man wielded, he thought as he watched Edgar empty another glass, to crush or to energize those in his orbit. The fire crackled and the rain began to pelt the thatch above as Edgar applied his iron grip to a knife to cut a slab of cheese. He tore the bread in two and passed a hunk to Godwin, along with some more wine, which was gratefully received.

Godwin had not yet seen Edgar so relaxed. There was nothing forced or stilted in their dialogue, and Edgar partici-pated with gentle humour, listening as much as he talked, all in a spirit of intimacy that was almost fraternal. The slipway of his euphoria, its fuel and ballast, doubtless derived from the glass in his hand, but Godwin was nevertheless buoyed and flattered by the friendship that seemed suddenly to have spawned between them. He tactfully pretended not to notice Edgar's hand dipping occasionally to reach for the pocket flask – his private supplement, which it did not even occur to him to share.

As the morning waned and Godwin's pocket watch told him noon had passed unnoticed, he began to wonder whether Edgar would be in a fit state to remount and make his way across the difficult terrain back to the house. A return by lunch was now out of the question. The rain had stopped some while earlier, and Godwin walked over to look through the dripping window panes to consider what should be done. He was getting keen to return now, and find out what Pierrepont had been up to. He turned from the window and looked towards where his host sat, half slumped in front of the fire, head hanging to one side, glass in hand at a danger-ous tilt. Edgar had begun to talk less, and was sliding gradually towards troubled depths. As if having heard

Godwin's thoughts, he roused himself with a jerk and drained the glass.

'Come back, dear boy,' he called, without looking round. His consonants were thick and rounded, and he filled another glass.

'We must return to the house,' said Godwin. 'I thought I just heard some thunder in the distance. If we do not leave we could be stuck here for the night.'

'What of it?' The three words drawled into one, a tripartite, slurred syllable.

'They will worry about us. And with Hermann missing we do not wish to add to Mag's concerns.'

''The devil take them all,' said Edgar, flapping a wrist above the shoulder. His chin sank forward. Godwin sighed and looked around the small room for inspiration.

'Would you like a little rest? Come, Mr Brooke, come and lie down a while.' Edgar muttered inaudibly and pushed Godwin away. A long roll of thunder boomed far off around the mountain, confirming Godwin's fears. He looked out again, but still the rain seemed to hold off. He tried once more: 'Mr Brooke, we really must be on our way. Here, let me help you.' But this time Edgar did not even notice the arm that attempted in vain to haul him to his feet. Godwin possessed neither the strength nor the aggressive determination to move the older man. He raised his voice. 'Come, sir, I beg you. There may be a storm.' The noise jolted Edgar from his reverie, unbalancing him so that he slid in a heap from the wooden chair to the sheepskin rug on the floor. Godwin raised his hands to heaven in despair and observed the slumped form at his feet. There was no way he could transport the man home without assistance. Even if he managed to get him mounted, the movement of the horse and the steepness of the route would unseat him after a few paces. There was little option. He would have to leave him here. He guessed it was not the first time such a situation had arisen.

After making the fire safe, covering Edgar with the

bedspread and sliding a pillow under his head, he went outside to untie his own horse. The mist had risen and he had a greater sense of his bearings. He saw that he was in a clearing, closely backed on the far side by a precipitous tree-covered slope that encircled him. Looking up, he saw that the sheer slope led to a vast triangular landslip of boulders, a feature he clearly recognized from earlier outings. It stood out from afar like a colossal gash in the mountain's flank, and from close to, with its displaced rocks and vomit spread of grey rubble, it appeared even more hostile and threatening than it did from a distance. But it was a marker that allowed him to calculate approximately the direction he would have to head in for Thasofolia. The clouds were turning from grey to black and billowed dangerously in a fresh wind that had arisen from the north. Again thunder rolled far off, though he suspected it sounded closer than it had earlier. There was no time to lose.

He picked his way across the pathless terrain, his horse stumbling every so often on a loose rock or shying to avoid a prickly bush. After fifteen minutes of steady riding Godwin felt he should be on a downward gradient, but the ground ahead continued level, with no familiar landmark or feature to jog his memory. Every arbutus thicket and tree stump resembled the thousands of others all around, the same carpet of bronzed bracken clinging to the stony ground. Turning around to equalize his bearings, he saw to his dismay that the mountain backdrop he had earlier recognized had once again vanished behind a veil of cloud. He was anchorless. A peculiar silence that was almost deafening in its void descended with the mist. And then, from nowhere, came a colossal roll of thunder, far closer than before, that echoed round and round the vast invisible basin of mountains behind him. The horse tossed its head free of the reins and stared wildly at the sound, and Godwin leant forward to pat its neck before progressing on at a trot. The sound of bells to his right alerted him to the presence of livestock nearby, and he stopped to scan the greyness in the hope of seeing a goatherd. He heard his own breathing and the thump of his heart as he searched, but saw nothing. The only presence on all sides was the ghostly regiment of pine trees in the damp mist – ephemeral, unworldly entities. A bell sounded again, but now fainter, and so he started on again.

He knew that at some stage he would have to head left, south, and downhill, and so decided now to take fate in his hands and follow a goat track that led that way, knowing full well that in this forest such pathways could evaporate as suddenly as they began. The passage between the wild shrubs and bushes was narrow, and thorns pulled threads from his jacket. His horse stopped abruptly at the sight of a large black goat standing in the path ahead, staring at them curiously. It had twin white stripes the length of its muzzle and a pair of horns that twisted back in elongated spirals towards their points. Seeing the animal encouraged Godwin, but a moment later it was gone, collar-bell jangling dissonantly with others of the same kind on a lower, hidden slope, and his sense of abandonment intensified. He dug his heels into the horse's flank to urge it on, but it refused to budge. He tried again, lashing the reins encouragingly, but whether it was the goat, the apparent absurdity of forcing a passage through ever thicker foliage, or a sense of its rider's mounting panic, the horse would not move. Though damp, it was a mild day, and for some while Godwin had been uncomfortably warm beneath his tweeds. His forehead now broke out in a sweat as he cursed and angrily kicked his heels sharply in the horse's ribs. Just then, quite suddenly, and with a violence that was almost biblical in its grandeur, there was a savage clap of thunder, right above them, that continued in a long, burbling crescendo, swamping the mountain, valley, trees and rocks with unbounded resonance. The whole earth was instantly dwarfed and seemed to cringe in horror at the power of the outburst, and Godwin's horse, panic-stricken, raised its nose to the sky in a terrified neigh.

As it did so, a flash of forked lightning cracked down from the heights, which sent the animal into a frenzy. It danced and kicked on the spot, every muscle flexing, tossing its head free of the reins, wild-eyed, its powerful neck taut and swaying.

'Down, sir, calm down!' Godwin cried ineffectually, gripping with his knees as the mighty torso beneath him jostled and twisted. 'Stay, stay,' he called again, but the horse was regardless of any attempt at mastery. It had returned to a primal state, all memory of man's dominion and taming obliterated by the urgent resurrection of its own raw nature. Its hind legs tightened and it raised both front hoofs in a defiant punch at the air, before bursting into a gallop and smashing through the bushes ahead, oblivious to obstacle, rider or ground beneath its feet. Godwin leant forward and gripped with both arms around its neck, fighting to keep a footing in the stirrups. He was aware of cloth tearing as they crashed forwards, of branches snapping; his cap was ripped off and something sharp flashed a graze across his scalp. The ground raced beneath him as the hoofs sent clods of earth and stones up, splattering indiscriminately around, pelting him. It was all he could do to cling to the animal. The speed was terrifying, the frenzy of the livid hulk beneath him relentless. At any moment, he imagined, he would be thrown, smashed against a boulder or run through by a branch. In a blind panic he suddenly recalled the fate of Eliza Brooke. It would not have been far from here, in perhaps the same circumstances.

He yelled into the hellish tunnel ahead as the horse careered onwards, crashing, thundering, at full stretch.

All at once the bushes on either side stopped tearing at his clothes, the undergrowth was left behind him, and the horse ran free, unrestrained, ears flat, across clear open ground. It all happened in a flash. Godwin could see the lie of the land ahead. The open ground beneath him was nearly done, but it was not forest or bushes beyond, it was the end, the land

228

falling abruptly away, the earth truncated. Images flashed past him, thundering hoofs, black sky, the bowels of the earth ahead, and then, from above, another clap of thunder, partnered simultaneously by a streak of lightning, as if the sky had cracked open for an instant to reveal the dazzling light of heaven beyond. As the horse heard the noise and saw the light, it reared high on its hind legs, throwing Godwin clean off its back so that he fell heavily on the ground, just a few feet from the edge. It was a precipice.

He lay there, panting, waiting for the agony to dawn, the snapped bones that would take his breath away, the stream of blood that would soak his clothes, or worse still, no sensation at all, no hot or cold, no movement. But as he lay he became aware that he was not seriously hurt; he had fallen into a bed of bracken, sandwiched between two rocky outcrops. A yard further in either direction and his body would have been dashed. Or a few yards ahead, he remembered, raising his chin and looking towards the precipice; had it not been for the clap of thunder, this would have been his grave by now.

He crawled towards the edge, shaking, breathless and grazed. It was some kind of chasm, and although he could not yet see the extent of its depth he could make out the continuation of terrain on the far side, a few hundred feet away, on the same level as where he now lay. For that matter, he noticed, looking from side to side, the ground continued to the left and right as well. It was no gorge but a circular hole, cut and plunged into the earth. All of a sudden the realization struck him and he scrambled forwards urgently, like a hunted beetle, to the very edge of the drop; he stretched out his neck to see what was below, to confirm his guess.

There was a dreadful inevitability about what he saw next; before his reasoning interpreted it, even before his eyes beheld it, he knew it would be so, and the full horror of that knowledge ripped across his chest as he looked down between the overhanging bushes at the pool, her pool, and saw the two of them together, far below, so small from this distance. Lydia and Pierrepont.

They were standing, face to face on Lydia's rock. Motionless. Pierrepont had shed his jacket, and she was dressed in white. Godwin could not see if they were talking. It did not look like it. There was no sound other than his own panting and the rustling he made with his every move. He dipped his head into the heather so as not to be noticed. It was prickly and uncomfortable. Had his life been spared so that he could witness this? Had the entire day been orchestrated to culminate in this torture, this unspeakably cruel coincidence? It was like a drama in which he had been cast as the low-life worm, the hunchback who loves from afar, plotting misfortune from the shadows on the golden young couple. It was a demeaning realization, and he felt humiliated even by the thought of it. And yet his anger was there, welling and boiling so much that he wanted to yell out and dash their reverie, he wanted to hurl a rock from the heights so that the water below would burst and the noise would scare the wits out of them. The magic at this pool was his and Lydia's. He had the photograph to prove it. Did it count for nothing? Was there nothing in the air that morning when she stood for his exposure? Would she have been the same for anyone? The next thought made him close his eyes and bury his face in the ground. Would she offer her nakedness so lightly, as well?

When he finally looked up they were gone. They must have slipped quietly away, their tryst concluded. He turned on to his back and waited a while longer, lying in the moss and bracken, the ants crawling over his wrist, and the pain of the deep graze on his head throbbing. They would have set off for Thasofolia and he had no intention of meeting them on the way. The cloud had mostly lifted now, the storm had passed rainlessly overhead, and the contours of the surrounding landscape had come back into clear view.

He would have no difficulty finding his way home from here.

The horse stood calmly nearby, chomping at the heather, its fit forgotten, like the thunder that had engendered it. After a while, Godwin got to his feet and led it slowly away by the reins, his muddy boots wading through miniature fields of bright pink cyclamens, whose prettiness, in any other circumstances, he would have considered a gift from God. But now they seemed to mock him.

Chapter 21

Later the same evening, after the sun had gone down and the wind dropped, an even layer of cloud settled in for the night above Thasofolia, blocking the stars and insulating the valley. It was almost too mild for fires in the house, but Percival lit them anyway, because he always did after the fifteenth of September. Godwin had retired early in order to nurse his wounds, but he could hear the remainder of the household having dinner downstairs, especially Pierrepont, who was entertaining them all noisily and hooting with laughter. They did not include Edgar even though, to Godwin's surprise and relief, he had managed to get himself back from the hut before seven o'clock, just as the last light faded in the west.

What neither Godwin nor anyone else in the house knew was that outside the walls of Thasofolia, at that very moment, hidden and crouching in the heavy growth of laurel on a lower garden terrace, a man waited and watched patiently as people moved from room to room, until eventually, at a late hour, all downstairs lights were extinguished and his eyes were raised with longing to one window on the upper storey, and one window alone. That man was Hermann Kopfling, and he had come to this spot for a second night to serve silent vigil on the damp, dewy ground at a safe distance beneath the bedroom of his beloved.

A passing glimpse every hour was enough for him: a shoulder paused for a few seconds here, a shadow on the wall there, four or five quick sightings, perhaps, at best, was all he could expect, before it was time to close the window shutters – that glorious, climactic moment when she was there in full, her heavenly face and presence framed by the window, leaning out first to the right and then left, to release the pair of catches. After that it was his pleasure to watch the cracks at the shutters' edge and see that the light was still on, to know that her darling mind within was still in motion, that she was doing, knowing and feeling. And then, after darkness finally descended and all the lamps were doused, there was still joy to be had just gazing up at the space where she dwelt, where she slept, where she dreamt, guarding her tenderly from afar. It was reward enough just to live out his life on this spot, adoring her every move. It was a thousand times better than living in comfort and prosperity at another place. He had some food left, was not too cold, and had found a patch between the rhododendron trees where he could lie at night after retreating from the laurel, even shelter from the rain, and still, whenever he woke, glance up at the dark square of her window.

There were less happy times, when she left the house for hours on end, as she had done today, when she was beyond his reach, and he was forced to take refuge in a crumbling gardener's siesta hut beneath an abandoned lower terrace vegetable plot. He had seen the search parties heading off in the mornings, and because of this had expected quite early on to be discovered and packed off to Athens to join Dr Schillinger, but, to his bemusement and growing sense of triumph, no one had thought to search the house compound, all of them assuming that he would have fled further afield. Did none of them guess what he was about? Had nobody, not even Lydia herself, considered that he might have dedicated his life, and perhaps even his death, at the altar of love, and that there was no place on earth that he could be but here, within calling distance of his angel beloved?

He had observed, with satisfaction, that Mr Tudor had been apart from her for two days, and he even dared hope it was a sign that his former fears and devil-pronged fever had been misplaced. However, there was reason to be disturbed about the other, the handsome blond-haired one, Mr Pierrepont, who always seemed so annoyingly happy, so irresistibly charming. He, now, had been spending more than his fair allowance of time with the beloved. They had ridden together this afternoon, and returned at tea-time full of laughter and chat. It irked Hermann to the bone. He would sink to his knees after her departure, staring aimlessly at the damp soil, lost and without purpose, until the need for discretion forced him to return to the shadows.

The blackest moments were when he would wake in the night, convinced that dawn was just a couple of hours away and his vigil could recommence, only to discover, by turning his watch this way and that to catch a glimpse of the hands in the dull light, that it was just gone midnight. In those hollow, cold and solitary moments, when he reflected with despair on the course he had taken and where his future lay, Hermann would meet his demon face on. He would lie on the ground, curled and embryonic, arms wrapped around himself, inadequately self-mothered. And it was all too clear that Lydia was not there to help him, to nurse or cherish him. She did not even know he was waiting for her. She might not even care.

*

Daniel arrived back from Páparis, having delivered the ageing Doctor safely aboard a steamer to Athens, and he brought with him news just telegraphed from the capital. Sir Thomas Wishart would not be joining the expected party of visitors because of urgent business that required his attention in Athens, but his wife would still be coming, accompanied and represented in Sir Thomas' place by the Legation secretary, Mr Straker. They and the remainder of the party would be arriving for dinner the day after tomorrow.

Godwin spent the afternoon in the cellar, packing away his bottles, trays and tongs. He thought how good it would be to see Straker again. The business with Lydia had been leading him towards a dangerous calamity. His fall from the horse had woken him up to the madness of it and he thanked God that he had come to his senses before it was too late. With Straker he would talk of past times, of home and old friends, and the walls of his shaken fortress would be restored to strength by the warmth and familiarity of it all.

And so he completed his task in a resigned and settled mood, and was even whistling when he came up the cellar steps as the dusk began to settle. It was all the more surprising and disorienting, therefore, to find Lydia standing there, blocking his path along the passage. She had hold of his camera, which she must have silently retrieved from where he had just a moment before left it, in its oak case near the cellar hatch. She was barefoot on the flagstones, with the camera held delicately between her fingers, pointing the lens directly at him as he emerged from the darkness below. It was an arresting sight and Godwin's former equanimity was instantly fractured.

'Will you allow me to make an exposure of you, Mr Tudor?' she said, with a hint of mischief in her eyes. The tone of her voice seemed to inform him that she had observed every nuance of his feelings of the past few days, and that he had been worrying about nothing – it was all hot air. Godwin stood on the brink of the chasm once more, and any resolve that he might have made during his afternoon of reflection in the cellar now slipped away like warm oil, leaving not a trace of itself behind.

'I have never been photographed before.'

'No? How peculiar. Would it not amuse you?'

'I have little interest in my own appearance,' he replied. 'Please be careful with that.' He leant across and took the camera from her hands, his fingers brushing against hers as

235

he did so. 'How have you been, Lydia? I seem hardly to have seen you this week.'

'I have been mostly with dear Fortinbras,' she replied with a sigh. 'He is so amusing.'

'He is.' Why *dear* Fortinbras, thought Godwin urgently as he replaced the camera in its box, whilst I am forever a Mister?

'But one can have only so much amusement,' she added. 'The weather has improved again.'

'Not in the cellar,' he said.

'Which makes me think,' she continued, turning back and looking at him, 'that we should resume our project. From where we formerly let it rest. Do you not think it would be a pity not to continue? Just as we were making such progress?'

Godwin's heart jumped at her words, but he deliberately paused before answering, all the while holding her gaze.

'From where we formerly let it rest?'

'Yes,' she replied without hesitation. 'It is almost like summer. Like an English summer, at least. We must make the most of it before it turns. Winter can arrive almost overnight in this country.'

'I can well believe it.'

'Oh, poor Mr Tudor. Was it terrible for you in the storm? Are you badly hurt?'

'Thankfully, not at all. But I could have been.'

'Thank God, then.'

'If we are to believe He cares for our thanks.'

'Ha, ha, Mr Tudor. You have learnt the ways of my thinking!'

'Were you out in the storm, Lydia?'

'Yes, I think so,' she said, turning on the spot to walk away, as ever defining both the start and the termination of her encounters, 'but it passed before we had particularly noticed it.'

'We?' called Godwin to her back.

'Fortinbras and I. We were on an outing. Shall we leave at first light, as usual?'

'Of course. I shall have my equipment prepared. I have only five plates left.'

'Then we must make them each special.' She was gone, and he was left standing there, at a loss, eyes fixed on the flagstones.

Godwin slept fitfully that night, the projections of his mind amplified by the dark and exhaustion. Images of Lydia returned to haunt him, though misshapen and menacing. When morning came, and the ghosts of the night evaporated, he prepared his equipment with tired eyes but was out in the yard by seven, ready to ride. He had borrowed clothes from Daniel while Mag had arranged for his own to be stitched and repaired by the village tailor.

Lydia was already there, waiting beside a third horse.

'This is not the estate's finest steed, by any man's description,' said Godwin, stroking the neck of the spare animal, a thin, rather dwarfish creature with its head hung low. 'Is there to be another in our party?' he asked, and could not stop himself from adding 'Can dear Fortinbras not bear to be apart from you for a single morning?'

'The other horse is for Daniel,' she replied. 'He very much wants to come, and I told him I felt sure you would not mind.'

'Well, did you?' said Godwin tersely. 'As it happens, I do mind. Very much.'

'Why so?'

'Is it not obvious?'

'No.'

'You wished us to continue from where we formerly left off.'

'Yes.'

'With Daniel present?'

Lydia looked genuinely puzzled. 'Why on earth not?'

237

Godwin felt his head spin as yet another perspective on all the events leading to this moment flashed before him. Had he been completely wrong about her astonishing gift? Had there in fact been no gift at all? His thoughts were cut short at that moment by the appearance of Daniel, handsome, bright and smiling, his obvious enthusiasm instantly dousing Godwin's show of displeasure.

They rode in silence, Daniel leading the way, for some distance. It was warm and they were following the course of the river, under the cover of planes, southwards. Leaves were falling from the trees all around in the breeze, like gigantic golden snowflakes.

' "*And we round about a spring were offering on the holy altars unblemished hecatombs to the immortals, beneath a fair plane tree, whence flowed bright water*" ', recited Lydia, smiling at Godwin. 'That's Homer. Relating the preparations of Iphigenia's sacrifice at Aulis. Not far from here, as it happens.'

'Fair virgin daughter of the King,' commented Godwin airily, 'beloved of the gods.'

'I have in mind a location by the river,' said Lydia. 'The light coming through the trees will be interesting.'

'Unless the breeze drops I fear these falling leaves could foil your plan.'

In the event, the place she chose was a shallow gully, protected from the wind and unusual because of a uniquely large and flat-topped rock, something like a giant toad in shape, that all but formed a complete bridge across the river.

'Toad rock!' chimed Daniel with delight. 'I haven't been here in years. We used to come here as children and leap from its nose. There's a deep pool below it, Mr Tudor. Would you come for a swim after your business is complete?'

'I have not come prepared,' was Godwin's reply. He was nervously setting up his equipment. The thought of what Lydia might be planning made his hand jitter. How had it come to this? he asked himself. That he should be intimidated by the machinations of a young girl.

'This is all fascinating,' said Daniel, watching the technical procedure closely. 'Great heavens, what a lot of bother for a photograph.' His cheery humour was in stark contrast to the morose quietness of Godwin.

'It gets better,' said Lydia from the toad's head, sitting with her knees pulled up to her chin. 'He puts up a tent.'

'A tent!' exclaimed Daniel. 'Will we be required to stay for the night?' Both siblings giggled like children at this, while Godwin, hot and serious, continued his tasks feeling like the only adult on a class outing.

When the equipment was eventually set up and ready, the tripod and camera in place, the chemicals unstopped and the plate-box poised within, prepared for action, Godwin went across to discuss the composition with Lydia.

'Allow me to surprise you,' she said in response, smiling. 'Go into your tent, now, and come out to see me when you're ready.'

'I would rather talk about it first.'

'Don't you trust my sense of art? After all we have achieved together?'

'Of course I do.'

'Then do as I ask. Please.' Godwin paused, hands on his hips, and looked around, perplexed. The graze on his scalp ached. He winced up at the sun that was beating down on his lightly freckled skin, and then returned his worried eyes to Lydia. He was tired from his restless night. Silently, he begged her to feel at one with him, but right at this moment it felt as if every objection he raised became a target for her derision, an amusing absurdity.

'All right, then,' he said. 'We will do as you please.' She smiled triumphantly and he turned to go into his tent.

Inside, where the heat was doubled, he clutched his face and wiped away the sweat before going to work. It was a delicate procedure in the pitch dark and he took deep breaths to calm himself, but after a few minutes he had locked the wet plate safely in its shield. He unbuttoned the

239

tent entrance and stepped outside, ready to face whatever caprice the girl had in mind for him. As ever, he stood still for an instant, a hand shielding his eyes, while he acclimatized to the light, and then looked towards the great rock that stood before his camera.

They were both there, brother and sister, still and composed on top of the rock. And naked. This had been their plan from the start, he suspected. She stood, sideways on, balanced on one foot, her other leg raised at a right angle and tightly flexed at the knee. Once again, her stillness and control of carriage were masterly. Her hair flowed loose and her arms were raised in front, above her head, wrists limp. He, magnificently formed and muscular, stood opposite her, like a god, fingertips touching hers, and posed as if straining forward to push a colossal weight. His sinews were tense, skin tight, flesh engorged with the effort of the strain – in opposition to her form, limpid, slender, her head slightly angled to one side, as if yielding to his power. It was, again, an irresistible image – male and female in essence, Aphrodite and Mars, matter and spirit, together with the strangely mutant rock, the plane trees, the river beneath. Despite his fear that he had become a pawn in their game, Godwin could do nothing but play along, so entrancing was the opportunity, so perfect the bodies in relation to one another. He made the exposure while they stood motionless, spellbound. Once the brass cap was returned to the lens, Godwin uttered a hoarse 'Thank you,' and they let fall the pose, turning to face each other, and giggling again. Godwin felt embarrassed, like an intruder, and quickly removed the plate, returning to the cover of his black-out tent as soon as he could.

They went on to make two further exposures in the same manner, from different angles, and with slight variations of pose. Daniel then suggested they all have a swim. Godwin, appalled at the suggestion, declined and busied himself with spurious, invented jobs, arranging and rearranging his bottles, repacking equipment, examining wooden and brass components in full daylight, to check for non-existent flaws. Meanwhile, brother and sister, still unclothed, jumped repeatedly from toad rock into the river pool below, splashed, laughed and swam, before finally drying themselves, dressing and remounting their horses for home.

Chapter 22

On the morning of the big day, the house was in an uproar of preparation not eased by Barba Stamos' discovery that the food waste bins outside the kitchen, where he kept all the leftovers to feed the pigs and chickens, had been ransacked in the night. He attributed the violation to a roaming pack of dogs that had been spotted a couple of times lurking beneath the rear garden wall, down by the sheep pens. The old cook's roars of fury could be heard resonating down the corridors from the kitchen, much to the amusement of the other staff, who huddled around corners, out of his sight, stifling giggles into their palms. He swore by the mother of God to lay traps for the dogs before nightfall, sharp and rusty traps, he said, a set he knew he had somewhere, that would give them a particularly slow and nasty death. That would teach them.

From his study, Edgar Brooke heard the yelling distantly but a knock on the door and the entrance of Fortinbras Pierrepont brought a recollection of the unpleasant business he had set himself to address this morning.

'Mr Brooke,' said Pierrepont, 'a very good morning to you. You asked last night that I should call to see you, and so'– he shrugged his shoulders and opened both palms to the heavens – 'ecce homo!'

Edgar sighed, and turned for a moment to glance out of the window. It was a glorious day; the forests and mountains behind basked in a summery haze that lent the distant peaks and ranges a variety of shades of a shared pale blue. His eyes took in the beauty but his expression betrayed not the smallest appreciation of it and the grim set of his mouth spoke of a man resolute in the face of deep and hidden burdens.

He explained briefly to Pierrepont that it was a busy day for the household, but that there was a certain matter he wanted to settle before the eminent visitors arrived, and so was about to ask his guest a straight and simple question to which he expected an answer of the same genre. Did he, or did he not, have intentions of a romantic nature towards Lydia?

Pierrepont smiled from where he sat, and glanced briefly at his shoes while he sought the right words. His cheery, carefree face could not have contrasted more with that on the other side of the desk, the one that belonged to the man he hoped to make his father-in-law.

'I was waiting, sir, to find an appropriate moment to approach you, and you appear now to have provided me with it,' he said. 'Yes, my intentions are as you describe. I love Miss Brooke, and will always love her. And I can think of no greater happiness than to spend my life with her at my side, as wife, as mother of my children. With your permission I should like to announce these feelings and aspirations to Miss Brooke. When the time is right.'

Edgar looked at him expressionlessly. Pierrepont returned his gaze but, as the pause grew longer, began to blink uncomfortably.

'You want to marry Lydia?'

'Yes, sir. And if she agrees to make me the happiest of men, I propose to buy the Howard house and make it our own. So that she would be able to spend her life close to the family and the property she loves.' Pierrepont looked pleased with the way his statement had come out.

'Thank you,' replied Edgar, returning to his work. 'Good morning, Mr Pierrepont.' The smile dropped from Fortinbras' mouth and he uncrossed his legs.

'But have you nothing to say to me, sir?' he asked.

'Not at present,' replied Edgar, searching for a particular sheet in the jumbled mass and eventually finding it on the floor beside him. 'You will, of course, not mention anything about this matter to Lydia until I have had the opportunity to talk with her.' His voice was characteristically flat and deep-grained. 'I take it I have made myself clear?'

'Yes, sir, of course. If that is what you want.'

'Do you not consider her a little young for wedlock?'

This was a question for which Fortinbras seemed prepared, and he answered confidently. 'I think, with respect, sir, that she is mature beyond her years. And I have a cousin, Harriet, who married at the same age and who has become a most happy wife. And mother.'

Edgar did not say another word, but looked from Pierrepont's face to the door behind him with the slightest nod. It was indication enough for the younger man that their conversation was at an end.

Godwin joined the other guests in the hall that evening when word was announced that the expected party of visitors had been spotted emerging from the pass at the far end of the valley. The mounted gendarmes accompanying the visitors were galloping ahead, flares in hand, to ensure a clear passage for the final leg of the journey; from the house the flames of their torches looked like distant comets. Thasofolia's manservants, dressed in freshly laundered and iron-pleated *fustanellas*, lined up by the front entrance, while the women continued to work behind the scenes, making last-minute preparations for dinner. Lydia was in white, her dress made from several layers of fine muslin, belted at the waist with a crimson silk band. Her hair was knotted tight on top of her head and decorated with white silk roses. She was standing under the open-armed bear, beside Pierrepont.

Godwin, who was wearing his own tweeds once more (miraculously restored, with very few noticeable traces of the accident), watched them from across the hall. He had not spoken to Pierrepont again about the issue that divided them, and had tried not to express too openly the keen sense of resentment he felt, but he could no longer make the pretence of being a good friend. If Pierrepont had noticed the change, he gave no indication, and continued to act with Godwin as though they had never exchanged a discordant view. His sunny obliviousness was no longer charming; at best, Godwin considered it insensitive, at worst, sinister.

Of Lydia's feelings nothing could be discerned, and Godwin had learnt that it was pointless even to speculate. She was, as ever, beyond category or prediction, answerable to none. It was as if everything she did or thought was justified according to a code of reasoning known only to herself. Could such a creature ever love another? he asked himself as he watched her talking to Fortinbras. Could she participate in that mutual exchange of trust, compassion and empathy that was for lovers a gift willingly and joyously offered and received? Her self-assurance was impregnable.

'Mr Tudor!' She was smiling up at him openly, radiant and gorgeous. He walked across the hall to where she stood with Pierrepont at her side. 'Fortinbras and I were just speculating. Do you think Hermann was in fact a German assassin and is at this moment lurking somewhere in the garden, waiting to leap out and murder the Prince when he walks though the gate?'

'I hardly think poor Hermann matches the part.'

'Ah,' said Pierrepont, raising a finger, 'but that's the skill of these people. They are schooled in the art of deception.'

'Even so.'

There was a clatter of hoofs as the party rode through the gates and into the courtyard. One by one they were helped from their horses, clearly tired and stiff after the long ride. Edgar, Mag and Percival were there to meet them, and a team of servants rallied round to take their luggage. A three-person musical ensemble, brought in for the occasion, played a rather oriental serenade of welcome as the travellers dismounted, but their tune finished prematurely at a signal from Edgar. The militia were already off their horses and slumped against the mounting blocks outside the stable, lighting their pipes.

Straker was the first up the steps and into the house, perhaps breaking protocol in his enthusiasm to greet Godwin. He was in high spirits and Godwin wondered at the transformation of the man he had visited just a few weeks earlier. He looked fresher, revitalized. Perhaps it was the mountain air; or perhaps he was benefiting from escaping the turgid lethargy of his home

Straker withdrew to the courtyard again to accompany Lady Wishart and Prince Leopold to the door. The Prince was rather diminutive, but dapper, upright and smart despite the hardships of his day. He was followed by his personal servant, a tired-faced, thin man in late middle age, who wore the embroidered costume of a central European huntsman, with antler buttons. Godwin recognized straight away that the Prince belonged to that elite caste, educated from the cradle to master the art of good bearing, for whom deportment was considered an indication of breeding; and well-bred he certainly was, as was demonstrated not only by his immaculate Prussian manners, but by his innate charm and ease of style.

'Before we familiarize ourselves with one another any further,' he announced to the hall of strangers within minutes of arrival, in excellent English, 'I wish to say to you all that I am here strictly as a common traveller.' There was general nervous laughter at this, over which he continued: 'It will be a great joy for me to have a short respite from my responsibilities in society. Please,' he opened his arms wide, 'in this beautiful corner of Europe, this refuge, let us treat one another as friends. Thereby you do me the greatest service.' Hearty applause followed these well-prepared words.

Next to cross Godwin's path were Mr and Mrs Farkas,

who had been talking to Edgar in the courtyard since dismounting, he, heavily moustached and aglow with excitement, she, nervous, pale and wide-eyed. Godwin had been wondering if Farkas would remember their short and tersely concluded conversation on the steamer from Messina, and the offence he had inadvertently caused. It was not a recollection he was going to bring to the new arrival's attention unless compelled, but apparently the incident had erased itself from Farkas' memory and they shook hands as if for the first time, the Anglo-Greek industrialist seemingly delighted to meet a member of so influential a political family. But Farkas could not disguise his especial interest in Edgar, and made his way to talk to him again at the earliest opportunity. He had heard something in Athens of the maverick landlord's efficient farming methods, and Godwin wondered how long it would be before the subject of Edgar's buying and importing Farquharson machinery was raised by the younger man.

Out of the corner of his eye (a corner that was becoming increasingly well exercised since his preoccupation with Pierrepont had begun), Godwin noticed Prince Leopold's personal introduction to Lydia, how he kissed her hand and looked into her eyes as she curtsied. He was a handsome boy, for all his stumpy stature, probably in his early twenties, with thick dark hair, and an air of gallantry that gave the impression, rightly or wrongly, of one capable of heroics in battle. He most certainly allowed Lydia's fingers to linger in his own in a way that Mag's had not. There falls another, thought Godwin, almost amused at his own extended despair. Is there no end to the capability for devastation allotted to a single individual? But he had expected no less, of course. What better prize could a healthy young man of rank and red blood hope to discover after a weary day's travelling to one of the loneliest and loveliest outposts of Europe?

Godwin noted early on, with something more than relief,

that Edgar had elected to drink only water for the evening. The result was that he spoke little and seemed tired by the evening's proceedings, but this, thought Godwin, was preferable to the alternative.

The first subject to pull general attention was raised by Prince Leopold, who called rather boldly down the table to his host.

'I trust I will find your park congenial to the sportsman while I am here, Mr Brooke. What game do you propose we look for at this season?'

'We do not hunt at Thasofolia,' replied Edgar quietly, without looking up from his plate.

'But the trophies, as we entered the lodge?' ventured the Prince.

'From a previous generation.'

'You do not hunt at all?' insisted the younger man, disbelief getting the better of his composure, while Godwin felt himself tense.

'That's right.' Edgar continued to eat.

'With all these forest and mountains?'

'I'm very sorry, Your Highness,' said Edgar, now looking up amelioratively to an almost audible sigh of relief around the table, 'there are no weapons in the house appropriate for sporting pursuits. If you would like, I could send to the village to find a man who would take you into the woods, perhaps.'

'It is of no concern,' said the Prince, smiling, and returning his attention to Mag beside him. 'It will be good to have a rest from the gun.'

Edgar's reluctance to communicate much with either of his neighbours meant that Daniel was compelled to entertain Mrs Farkas on his left. He appeared to be struggling, for all his uncontainable humour, because Mrs Farkas was exceedingly shy. Whenever she felt compelled to answer Daniel in more than a minimum of detail, she would dart her huge dark eyes nervously down the table to her husband, either for approval or reassurance, but Mr Farkas appeared ignorant of her dependency and chatted merrily to Mag.

Lydia, from the moment they sat down, made herself entirely available to Prince Leopold's attentions, ignoring Pierrepont on her other side. The attention was clearly appreciated by the young aristocrat, who leant in towards her, shortening the distance between them and fashioning a little niche for them both from the remainder of the gathering. Godwin noticed Pierrepont observing the pair with thinly disguised vexation, until, unable to bring himself to make conversation with anyone else, he excused himself and withdrew from the room.

Godwin himself was beside Lady Wishart, she of perfect features but a fidgety, almost nervous demeanour. She was drinking without restraint and more than once said what a relief it was to get away from her incessant social obligations in Athens. Her delight in Godwin's company was complete when she discovered that their paths had crossed as children, when he and she had accompanied their respective families on a shooting weekend in Dorset. She distinctly recalled him, the younger brother, too young to be allowed a gun, who had stayed in the house when the rest of the men went out for the day's sport. He had read books all day by the fire. And had he not been rather unwell? she asked. Until that moment Godwin had forgotten about this particular event – there had been so many weekend house parties, each as dreary and lonely for him as the others – but now that she mentioned it, filling in the details with colourful recollections, the scene returned to him, and he even remembered the gauche and lanky girl who had watched him from afar as he recuperated from his illness. She had seemed too shy to talk to him, while he, withdrawn and self-contained, quietly struggled to suppress the demons in his mind.

'If I am absolutely honest,' she said, sipping her wine, rosy-cheeked, her glance darting around the room, 'I was perhaps a little more interested in your older brother. Wasn't he very handsome and dashing?'

'He was, indeed. And is still.' Hers was a familiar sentiment.

'Look at those two down at the end,' Lady Wishart now said to him, nodding towards where the Prince and Lydia sat. 'Don't they just make the perfect couple? The handsome Prince and dear, pretty young Miss Brooke. She is such a darling. I have known her since she was really quite small, and feel quite maternal towards her. I shouldn't be at all surprised if they don't fall completely in love with one another during the stay. Perhaps her first love. How simply rapturous! This is such a romantic place. One can feel the breeze of passion playing on one's heart like wind through a lute. It's in the landscape, the woods, the air itself.'

Godwin was less than appreciative of her poetic sentiments, but feigned a degree of empathy with a hum of agreement. She drew breath to resume in the same vein, but he interrupted her before the words came out.

'Does your husband share your appreciation of Thasofolia?' he asked. Her smiling face seemed to fall fractionally, and the tone of her voice flattened.

'Oh Thomas is immune to romance,' she said. 'He was born in Calcutta, you know. His father was some official who filled out East India Company ledgers for decades. Thomas is never happier than behind his desk. I sometimes think he might prefer to live in his office.'

'I'm sure he is a busy man, and very efficient at his job,' said Godwin, smoothing down the apparent edge in her remark and continuing with a gentle lie, 'I have heard several speak highly of him in Westminster.' She received the news with a grunt and looked around the table, taking another sip from her glass.

Pierrepont had been absent now for some while, and a silent exchange with Mag persuaded Godwin that he should do something about it. He muttered his apologies to Lady

Wishart and slipped from the room. It was a relief to have a pause from the evening, and he climbed the creaking stairs, leaving behind the burble of noise from the dining room. The door to Pierrepont's room was open, and with a gentle knock Godwin put his head around to see if he was there. He was not, and Godwin withdrew to the landing, but only for a moment, because the impulse overwhelmed him to go back into the room. He recognized that it was improper, but he now had serious misgivings about Pierrepont's character, and this momentarily gave him the courage to ignore his own sense of propriety.

Fortinbras' day clothes were draped over a chair in the corner, his bed was turned down and a nightshirt lay folded on the pillow. Next to the wardrobe were his small trunk and saddle-bags, empty. Godwin walked over to the desk and looked down at the papers tidily arranged on it. Some notes and figures relating to the purchase of the Howards' house, a diagram chart of calendar commitments and work projects. Everything was regular, neat and organized, and told of a man who appeared to have his life and plans in perfect order. Too orderly, perhaps, Godwin mused, glancing at a tabulated analysis of Greek rocks and minerals; this desktop did not quite correspond with the light-hearted clown he had come to know. But there was no evidence here of a darker, unstable nature.

There was a shallow drawer to the desk, not quite closed, which Godwin now pulled open. Afterwards, he would question himself about the morality of what he had done. Was he motivated by petty jealousy, or was he merely trying to protect an innocent young girl? The action would not lie quiet with him and the jury within his thinking could not resolve the debate one way or another. Either way, he would reassure himself, the discovery he was about to make, though perhaps not the appalling chain of events that it precipitated, justified the questionable motivation that spurred him at that instant, as he inspected the contents of Pierrepont's desk drawer.

There was a tin of Carathanassis Samos cigarettes, bought in Athens, a small magnifying glass, a silver pillbox and a leather-bound book. He opened the book. Plain, unprinted paper, with a few jottings on its early pages. Nothing of any consequence: topographical statistics, distances, notes on terrain and gradients. It was a work notebook, no diary, to be sure. He flicked through the empty pages with a slight sigh. Then, at the rear of the book, the pages fell open rather heavily; a sealed envelope had been wedged there, apparently ready to post. He turned it over to look at the address. England, Berkshire, and a village called Frobisham. It took a moment for the full impact of what was contained in the top line of the address to burn itself into his eyes. Of all the possibilities he had considered, never once had his thoughts rested on the like of this. *Mrs Fortinbras Pierrepont.*

There was a noise on the landing. Someone was just outside. Godwin's hands were now shaking, and he quickly replaced the envelope, closed the book and the drawer, and walked towards the door. Before he reached it, Pierrepont was there, looking at him quizzically.

'What are you doing in here?' he asked.

'I came to find you. We were worried. You'd been gone so long.'

After the briefest of pauses the querying frown vanished from Pierrepont's forehead and he smiled broadly. 'Nothing to worry about,' he said. 'I just needed some fresh air. All these fires. Not really cold enough for them, if you ask me. I felt a bit muggy.'

'Better now?' asked Godwin.

'Absolutely. Shall we go down together?'

Godwin observed Pierrepont for the remainder of the evening, wondering at the secret that lay hidden. He searched the fine contours of his face, the flawless features, the sunny humour reflected in the smile that never left his lips. He remembered their meeting in Athens, Pierrepont's firm, reliable handshake, his apartment, his enthusiasm about their travel plans. Godwin mourned the passing of their understanding, the laughter they had shared, the adventure of their journey out to Thasofolia. But the moment passed and he began to make plans for the action he would have to take against this man.

Chapter 23

The house was silent, the lights downstairs all extinguished, and the last remaining flames in his grate had expired as Godwin sat writing his journal in the armchair of his bedroom, still dressed from dinner. The utter flatness of the quiet made the knock at his door seem all the more violent. It was Straker, in his evening clothes as well, despite the hour.

'I hope I'm not intruding,' he said. 'Saw the light was on and thought you might not be able to sleep either.'

'Aren't you flattened by the journey? I'm surprised you're not dancing with the fairies by now.' Straker smiled and did a little twirl, one hand in the air.

'I don't sleep much nowadays,' he said, pulling up a chair opposite Godwin, 'but it doesn't bother me. I read. Write the journal. Pore over old Persian texts. And other light pursuits.' Godwin smiled and offered him a glass of Madeira, which he refused. 'Life has changed for me since you were in Athens. I think your coming gave me the jolt I needed. Abdul's gone back to Egypt.'

'Good heavens, what happened? He's been with you for years.'

'He hasn't wanted to stay for some while, really. And to be honest, I didn't want him any more. It is time to move on. And I feel like a new man. I've left my old house and am renting an apartment in the middle of town, very near the Legation. I saw just how far I'd let matters slide. Do you see I've already lost an inch or two off my stomach?'

'So you plan to remain in Athens?'

'If they'll keep me. I realize I have to prove myself again, rebuild broken bridges. That's the reason I'm here. I can tell you, but don't say a word to the others.' He paused and relaxed back in his chair, puffing his cheeks and blowing into space.

'Are you going to explain that remark, or are you going to wait for me to ask?'

Straker laughed quietly. 'First of all, you tell me how you've been getting on with our Mr Brooke. You've been here a while. What do you make of him?'

'You may be surprised by what I say.'

'I doubt it.'

'Would you be surprised to hear that I think he is the most remarkable human being I have ever met?'

'That does not surprise me.'

'That his intelligence, masculinity, visionary sense of art, philosophy, agriculture, knowledge of the nature of man and his place within nature is second to none that I have encountered?'

Straker raised his eyebrows. 'I am beginning to sense a whiff of the unexpected.'

'That he commands those who surround him, peasants, farmers or guests, with an authority that is both complete and magnanimous, that this authority is repaid with devotion and an acceptance of his superiority as a man and as a master?'

Straker nodded. 'You have planted a seed of curiosity.'

'That he is at heart a retiring man who longs for a simplicity of life that is almost ascetic, and that in this sense he is one of the most religious men I have met, one who has sacrificed his own happiness to bear the burden for those who are dependent upon him?'

'Now I am approaching the realm of surprise.'

'And that he is an abomination, a creature bereft of manners or consideration for the feelings of others, who wounds and devastates without discrimination, and who I suspect – though I should need a qualified medical opinion on this – may not possess a heart in his breast.'

They both laughed. 'Now I am on familiar territory,' said Straker.

Godwin settled back once more and added quietly, 'I cannot begin to describe everything that has happened to me in this place. One day I will find it within myself to relate the tale. But it is still confused and unfinished.'

'I am intrigued,' said Straker, sitting forward and staring wide-eyed at Godwin. 'That you of all people, so calm, reasonable and – how shall I say it? – so *settled* in your thinking, should be swept into confusion by the wind of emotion. I should like to hear more.'

Godwin leant forward to rekindle the fire. 'And you?' he said, shifting attention away from himself. 'You say there is a purpose to your visit. Something other than as gallant escort to the frail and vulnerable Minister's wife?'

Straker was smiling again. 'Lady W would choose others before me to be her champion jousters. You, perhaps. She seemed delighted with you at dinner.'

'We met as children. So. Tell me your purpose.'

Straker joined his hands and moved to the edge of his seat. He paused before continuing, in a quieter voice. 'I don't know how much you have learnt yet about Greek politics and the economics of the country.'

'Barely anything. Except that the maintenance of power is the prime concern of any politician, rather than the pursuit of policy or ideals. And that the attainment of power is not always achieved by honest means.'

'Correct. That is the threshold on which the system operates. The situation is as follows.' He looked over his shoulder, leant forward and spoke in a half-whisper. 'The government at present is fighting for survival. A war is raging in the Athenian newspapers, which are more or less equally split in their political allegiance, and at the moment it seems as if those who support the opposition have the edge. That in itself is not an unusual situation, but those in power are getting anxious. Particularly the Minister of the Interior. And the Prime Minister, for that matter. And one of the issues currently aiding the rise of the opposition party has to do with a bid from a German mining company. You know to what I am referring?'

'No.'

'The proposition is to tap a magnificent vein of lignite recently discovered in north Pyroxenia – on this very property, to be precise. It is apparently of a quality almost equivalent to that found in Newcastle, and could produce a revenue for the Greek nation of five hundred thousand drachmas a year. That's more than fifteen thousand pounds. And if you consider that the entire revenue for the nation is close on five hundred thousand pounds, you will see the significance of the discovery.'

'And so, why is there a problem?'

'Because Brooke refuses to allow the mines on his land.' Godwin did not know the reasons, had no idea of the consequences for Greece and was wholly ignorant as to the economics of the situation, but at these last words from Straker he felt an eruption of warmth and admiration for his host. What defiance! he thought. What manly resistance to the plotting penny-pinchers.

'He must have his reasons. Good reasons.'

'Nobody knows what his reasons are. I was hoping you might provide a clue.'

'I'm afraid it's the first I've heard of the matter.'

Straker touched the fingertips of his hands together and raised his eyebrows at Godwin. 'It has not been discussed here?' he asked.

'Not to my knowledge.'

'A matter of such consequence?'

Godwin smiled with disbelief. 'John, I have answered. And even if I had knowledge of what you want, you would not

257

expect me to talk about the matter without the authorization of Mr Brooke.'

'Of course not.' Straker looked down.

'But you may be assured I have not heard it mentioned.'

'A pity. As you can imagine, the opposition are accusing the government of pandering to a foreigner instead of forcing an issue that would benefit the nation. And there is nothing that fires Greeks more than putting foreigners' needs before patriotism. It's no secret they hate all foreigners. And so, the government has been on to Westminster, demanding that the situation is dealt with by London. Which is why it has landed back on our desk in Athens. Which is also why, in case you hadn't guessed, Sir Thomas has not come on this visit. He cannot be seen to be too closely allied to a figure increasingly viewed by powerful people in Athens as an enemy of the state.'

'Can Mr Brooke be compelled to comply?'

'Through persuasion, perhaps. If we cannot persuade him we should have to support his resolve. As a British citizen holding legal rights to his own property, albeit on foreign soil.'

'Can the Greek government demand his compliance?'

'Only through legal action, which'– and here Straker let out a sardonic laugh – 'would open up a nest of vipers. The courts would be at it for years, and the lawyers pulling in the fees. The – let us call it *malleability* – of the Greek justice system knows few bounds.' He then added, 'And those bounds are invariably drachmaically defined.'

'And if he stands his ground, and defies both you and the government?'

'Then the government will most likely switch the island's political allegiance against him, and use every tool in its power to squeeze him out. Or the incoming new government will do it in its place. As one of the articles of its election.'

'What sort of tools?'

'Local politicians. Most importantly the Nomarch in

Páparis, who, in practice, is answerable to his minister in Athens, not those who elected him locally. At a word from the Ministry he would see to it that certain rural demarchs, officials and mayors are quickly removed – threats, property damage, that sort of thing, or worse – and would have them replaced with a league united against Brooke. Taxes would be imposed, lawsuits fabricated, petty, out-of-date policies invoked. Brooke would fall, and a local way of life would evaporate. Welcome the mines.'

'It would seem in Mr Brooke's interest to comply. He would presumably benefit financially.'

'Enormously.'

Godwin sighed and thought. Straker tightened his lips and nodded.

'His reluctance would seem to be a mystery,' said Godwin.

'One which you would perhaps help me unravel,' replied Straker, looking him in the eye.

'How on earth could I help?'

'You appear to have earned his friendship.'

Godwin smiled at him. 'Are you asking me to be your spy?'

'The alternative for Brooke is destruction. If we, the Legation, can work alongside him, in full knowledge of his claim and reasoning, we are in the best position to assist.'

Godwin shook his head in disbelief. 'That is your concern. Your job. Not the task of a friend.'

'Brooke does not even give me a minute of his time. He loathes me. And I need to return to Athens with an answer. To fail on such a mission as this would not be advantageous to my prospects in the service. Particularly at this point, when I hope to improve matters.'

'Shame on you, John,' said Godwin, smiling, almost affectionate. 'That it should come to this.'

'View it as an act of patriotism. Your duty as an Englishman abroad.'

'Now you sound like my father.'

'Just give the matter your consideration. That is all I ask.'

Godwin looked away without replying and Straker rose to his feet. 'I have stayed too long. It is late and I am probably more tired than I feel. Please do not judge me too harshly.'

'Of course not,' replied Godwin.

Straker was about to walk from the room when he remembered something. 'Did I tell you I received a letter from my mother? The first in some years.'

'You didn't. How is Lady Straker?'

'She is in excellent health and spirits, thank you.' He looked down, almost coy. 'It seems that she would like to see me. Our differences have worn away.'

'That is good.'

'I feel the weight of years lifted.' He drew breath heavily. 'Dear Mother.' He turned to go. 'Time for bed,' he said. 'Good-night.'

Chapter 24

Godwin finally went to bed some time after Straker's departure, almost delirious with exhaustion, so that when he distantly heard the disturbances in the night, he could not bring himself to get up and investigate. There were raised voices from somewhere below, and footsteps running along the corridor outside his room. Warm between his sheets, he decided whatever it was could wait until the morning. It was a decision that pricked him with guilt when at last he did rise and go downstairs, to be met by a haggard-looking Mag, and the coarse smell of a disinfecting agent. Two maids, one of them in tears, were mopping the floor, and Barba Stamos, his face white as a sheet, hurried past him from the dining room, heading back along the passage to the kitchen. Prince Leopold's servant, who was hovering in the passage with a worried face, stepped aside to let the old cook pass and then followed him down towards the staff quarters, confused at what was going on. Mag greeted Godwin briefly, informing him that breakfast might be slightly delayed. She had been up half the night along with Edgar and Lydia.

'What has happened?' asked Godwin.

'Hermann has been found, and he is terribly injured. His leg was caught in a fox trap by the waste-bins. The wounds are very deep. Edgar fears he may have to perform an amputation.'

Before Godwin could ask any more questions, Edgar himself came down the stairs, dressed for riding. His face was grim, but no more than usual. He nodded a silent greeting at

Godwin and explained to Mag that the boy was in a stable state, had lost much blood but the bleeding had now stopped. The bandages would have to be changed, but he himself would not need to attend the patient for a few hours. He would therefore take the guests on a tour of the farms, as planned. Hermann would be safe in the care of Mag and Lydia.

'And what is the condition of his limb?' asked Godwin.

'I had to amputate while his pain was still intense. To delay and then reoperate, perhaps after an infection had set in, would double the trauma and possibly finish him. He has lost his foot about five inches above the ankle.' Edgar's attention was distracted by Barba Stamos, who had appeared again, running back from the kitchen carrying dishes. His fingers were shaking as Edgar exchanged a few quiet words with him in Greek, resting a hand on his shoulder.

'How did it happen?' asked Godwin. Mag sighed as she watched the old cook weave a path between the mops back towards his domain. Edgar went through to the dining room, from where the familiar morning scent of hot citrus was already emanating.

'The cook put out some traps yesterday,' replied Mag, 'when he discovered the bins had been rifled. He had assumed it was dogs. He can't be blamed.'

'But it was Hermann. Looking for food,' replied Godwin.

'So it would seem. He must have been hiding near the house all the time.'

'Why?' asked Godwin in disbelief. 'Why should he endure the weather, the hunger, the discomfort? Surely not merely to escape Dr Schillinger.'

Mag's mouth tightened and she looked at Godwin with something less than sympathy in her eyes. 'I am surprised that you can ask that question, after all that you must have observed. The boy was hopelessly in love, of course.'

Godwin looked at her, opened-mouthed. 'You mean this has something to do with Lydia?'

Mag walked around him and made for the stairs. 'I must go and change for breakfast. Most of the guests are joining Edgar for a ride this morning and you are welcome to accompany them. I do not think they will depart until at least nine o'clock.'

Lydia did not appear at breakfast, but the rest of the party were present and were given the briefest of explanations by Edgar about the disturbances they might have heard in the early morning. Godwin was surprised at how Edgar could describe so calamitous an incident in such dispassionate terms. He could only imagine his host wanted to play down the affair so as not to disturb the smooth enjoyment of the Prince's stay. Lady Wishart, alone amongst the guests, looked genuinely concerned, and whispered urgently to Godwin after breakfast, 'Shall I stay and assist with the nursing?'

'I believe the boy is well accommodated. You would do better to leave with the others.'

'Will you not come with us?' she asked, with a certain emphatic appeal in her eyes.

'I think not,' replied Godwin. 'I have been on several tours of the estate and have some affairs of my own to attend to today.'

'I am not sure that I wish to go either.'

'Then stay.'

Lady Wishart looked him in the eye and smiled as if they had exchanged a wordless understanding. She then said that it was probably her duty to go with her host, and quietly turned away.

As they all assembled in the courtyard, Prince Leopold and Daniel were competing with one another in an attempt to mount their horses by running at them from the rear and vaulting into the saddle. Both young men eventually managed the feat, to the applause of all onlookers apart from Lady Wishart, who hardly noticed the display but glanced once or twice across to where Godwin stood in the doorway.

When the party, including Pierrepont, had gone, Godwin

made his way to the room where he had been told Hermann was lodged. He opened the door quietly and went in. Hermann was lying in a white quilted bed, its linen sheet perfectly pressed and folded at his chest; he was asleep, with his head to one side in the deep down of the pillow. Pale and drawn though he was, he appeared to be utterly at peace. Lydia was there beside the bed, lying back in a chair and holding the young student's hand. She looked tired, her hair was unbrushed, and she still wore her nightgown and robe. Her expression showed that her usual defences had been wiped away; those arts she could normally engage with such ease, to leap and dance around the clumsy manners of others, had abandoned her. When Godwin opened the door she looked up, straining her eyes to identify the intruder.

'It is I,' he said.

'Mr Tudor,' she whispered.

'My dear girl.'

'Come closer.' Her voice was choked with feeling.

'Is he in great pain?'

But she did not answer his question. As he approached, she slipped her hand out of Hermann's, rose from the chair and flung herself into Godwin's arms, wrapping herself tightly around him as the tears spilled on to her cheeks.

'Dear child,' he said, holding her, 'you poor, dear child.'

'Is it my fault?' she sobbed, trying to keep her voice to a whisper. 'Tell me if it is my fault.'

'Of course it is not.' Godwin turned his face sideways, and saw that the sun was shining outside. It was a fine day; the view seemed immeasurably beautiful.

'He has spoken of love a great deal,' she continued. 'He has developed a passion in secret, and I had no idea. Everything that has happened to him has been for love of me and I was blind to it. Am I heartless? Do you think me a freak?'

'Of course not,' said Godwin, stroking the tangled golden hair as her tears began to stain his shirt.

'I do not intend to hurt people,' she went on through her

crying, 'I try to do my best in friendship, but it never seems to be enough for people, and then they get angry with me, and I feel I have not got a heart, and I don't know what to do about it.' The last words were sobbed uncontrollably. Godwin tried to quieten her with a gentle 'Sshh', and glanced to Hermann, who was still fast asleep. He could feel the heat and moisture of her mouth as she pressed against him, trying to smother the sound she was making.

'You have done no wrong,' said Godwin quietly. 'You cannot blame yourself for the love you inspire in others. It is your gift.'

'It is a gift I do not want. I hate it! I don't know what to do with it. I cannot return this sort of love.' Godwin pulled her towards him and closed his eyes. Then, as if this new closeness caused her discomfort, she gently pulled away and freed herself from his embrace, quietly blowing her nose on a handkerchief and wiping her eyes. 'Thank you,' she said, 'I feel a little better now.' She returned to her chair and linked hands with Hermann once more. Suddenly, she smiled though her retreating tears, recollecting something. 'Prince Leopold came in here earlier. I think he was rather disgusted to see me like this.' Godwin smiled back. 'Perhaps he will now be less pressing in his attentions,' she continued, and then turned to look at the patient. 'Poor Hermann. He must have had so little sleep these past few days. He has lost weight. And he will never walk properly again. The poor, dear boy.'

'He is alive and safe,' said Godwin. 'And he is being tended by you. That will be a blessing beyond his dreams when he awakes. It will help ease the pain of the other.'

'I will never leave his side,' said Lydia, and with her other hand stroked the boy's forehead.

'Mr Pierrepont will miss you.' Godwin had tried to stop the words but they had emerged of their own accord.

'Fortinbras is a buffoon,' she said, and then turned to face Godwin. 'I am sorry for saying that. I know you are very good friends to each other, and he always speaks so highly of you. But his humour is irksome to me.' At these words an impenetrable heaviness that hung above Godwin crumbled, allowing sunshine and fresh air to circulate through and around him.

'You are being very frank,' he said, hiding his joy.

'Not intentionally. This is not a time to be frivolous, that is all.'

Godwin was moved, and walked towards her. 'Lydia, I want you to know that I think you are a remarkable and wonderful person,' he said, but when he saw a flash of alarm, the smallest pulse of a reaction, glance across her brow, he stopped himself going any further. 'I will leave you now. I will be in the house all day if you need assistance.' She thanked him, apologized for her earlier histrionics, and they parted.

The tour party returned late in the morning, with Mr Farkas in a state of great excitement. Dressed in his fur-collared coat, he followed closely on Edgar's heels as they walked through to the hall, and his voice was clearly audible even from where Godwin stood, on the landing upstairs.

'At last I am proud to belong to the modern Greek nation,' Farkas was eulogizing. 'With such magnificent men as yours, Mr Brooke, my faith in our motherland is restored. We must modernize the country's farms. Greece could become the breadbasket of Europe. We need to educate – educate and mechanize. Steam, coal and steel are the requirements, and we will increase productivity threefold, perhaps more in the nation at large. By thunder, if I were to make it my mission in life, I could transform Greece and the name Farkas would be etched into the annals of our great country's history as surely as that of Demosthenes.'

But instead, Godwin thought to himself, you will remain a small, self-important money-maker, develop a large girth, and spend your days boring all you meet with pompous claims and poorly informed opinions.

'My dear,' said Farkas, leaning his head back slightly in the direction of his wife, who he presumed was following close behind, 'were not those cotton carts the most quaint sight? Laden high as a tree with their soft, snowy harvest, and leaving pretty little trails of white flocculence on the bushes either side of the track? Mrs Farkas has an eye for the picturesque,' he added to Edgar.

'I rather preferred the olive harvesting,' she answered in a shy, piping voice, looking to Pierrepont, beside her, for support.

'I agree,' said Pierrepont. 'Whole families of peasants picking away at a tree like locusts, and the fruit falling on to those huge groundsheets. And the magnificent collection baskets!'

Farkas scoffed dismissively at the suggestion and flicked a wrist in the air. 'Olives are an inefficient crop,' he said, 'too little fruit, a biannual harvest, and a requirement for absurd levels of human labour. There will never be a machine to strip an olive tree. And where is the export demand? No. Olives do not have a significant place in the future food markets of Europe, take my word for it. Mr Brooke, we must introduce the potato to your estate. And perhaps the turnip and the carrot.'

'One would have to consider whether such crops would be suitable for Greece,' said Edgar softly, handing his gloves to Maroula in the hall and looking towards the landing, where his eyes met Godwin's.

'The soil is perfect for them,' insisted Farkas. 'And soon the railway will carry Greek produce like an artery into the Balkans, through to Austria-Hungary and beyond.'

'What news of the boy?' called Edgar, already climbing the stairs and disregarding Farkas, who looked up at his disappearing host in surprise.

'When I saw him he was sleeping,' said Godwin. 'But that was some hours ago.' Edgar passed him and proceeded to Hermann's room. Next came the Prince, who had been chatting animatedly with Daniel while his manservant removed his cloak and hat, and now leapt up the stairs two at a time.

'Where is Miss Brooke?' he demanded of Godwin. 'I should like very much to share with her my impressions of the estate.'

'I fear she is indisposed, Your Highness,' replied Godwin. 'She is attending the poor boy who suffered the accident.'

'The student?' asked Prince Leopold, his expression contorted with distaste. 'Cannot a servant perform these tasks?'

'I think Miss Brooke would prefer to lend her own assistance,' replied Godwin, adding, with hidden mischievousness, 'she has an attachment to the youth. It is endearing to behold.'

'Is that so?' said the Prince, the animation falling from his face as he stopped on the stairs. 'How vexing.' He decided to return to the hall, annoyed that his intentions should be foiled. 'In that case, perhaps I might be lucky enough to see her at lunch.'

'Perhaps,' said Godwin, inwardly triumphant. 'But I doubt it.' Prince Leopold pulled down his cuffs and descended the steps at a brisk trot, spotting Daniel along a passage and calling to him.

Lydia took all her meals in Hermann's room that day. Godwin, however, received a message from her, via Mag, late in the afternoon, to say that he would be welcome to visit the patient briefly, if he should please, and so knocked on the door about half an hour before dinner. Hermann was awake, lying with his head to one side, watching Lydia as she read out loud from a volume of Herodotus. She smiled as Godwin approached and put down the book.

'Hermann is the bravest man I know,' she said, now looking down at him as he lay, motionless. 'He never complains of the pain, or asks for anything at all.'

Hermann said nothing to Godwin except to answer his questions with the merest grunt and nod. The reversal of his fortunes in so short a space of time had quite disoriented him, and it was all he could do to fix his eyes on his beloved and watch the gentle movement of her lips as she read. The poor boy may as well enjoy it while it lasts, thought Godwin. The day would come, quite soon, when he would have to hobble downstairs to a waiting carriage, and thence be transported from Thasofolia, probably for ever. A similar departure inevitably awaited Godwin himself, though he tried to disregard its imminence.

One matter was clear to Godwin: Fortinbras Pierrepont must be persuaded to leave as soon as possible, perhaps joining the departing group of guests in a couple of days' time. There must be an end to his absurd plan of marriage and an end to his intention of buying the Howards' house. Godwin tried several times to take Pierrepont aside, but never managed to get his full attention. It would have to wait until tomorrow.

Once again, Godwin could not sleep, and he sat by his fire to think about what he would say to Fortinbras. Shortly after he heard the grandfather clock strike one o'clock, there was the sound of a muffled bump from one of the bedrooms on the opposite side of the corridor. He turned his head and listened carefully. There was a woman's voice, weeping quietly. And then, above it, came gruff masculine noises, followed by another knock and the woman's crying raised to a sharp yelp. The man's voice now became more emphatic – a thunderous monotone, occasionally pausing, as if expecting a reply. Then came a tremendous crash and a high-pitched shriek from the woman, a noise which propelled Godwin to his feet and out of the door to investigate. At the same moment, Lady Wishart also emerged from her room, dressed in her nightgown, and looked at him with an anxious expression.

Godwin held up his palm to silence her, and approached the Farkases' door. The man's voice could still be heard, bumbling aggressively, though now quieter.

When the situation appeared to have calmed down,

Godwin tiptoed back to his room, where Lady Wishart now stood in the doorframe.

'A domestic dispute, I fear,' Godwin said quietly. 'I think we should let them be.' She nodded with a slight smile, standing back to allow him through and then closing the door behind her. She turned to look Godwin full on, a nervous light in her eyes.

'Is there something—' he began, but she stopped him with a finger to her lips, and took a pace forward. For an instant, part of Godwin refused to believe that she could have improper intentions, but his resistance to the idea was swept aside when she raised a hand and touched him lightly on the face. She pressed closer in to him, moulding the length of her body against his, so that he could feel her firm contours through the nightgown. A hidden throb of eroticism flicked across his loins even as he took her hand in both of his and brought it away from his cheek. He smiled at her and shook his head, whereupon she lowered her eyes and pulled back.

'I must apologize,' she whispered, reclaiming her hand.

'Please,' replied Godwin, 'let it be as if it never happened. I will forget: you have my promise.'

She smiled up at him. 'You are kind. And I hope you will not think harshly of me. I have not done this before, I assure you.'

'Who am I to judge others?'

Lady Wishart faltered for a moment and looked down. 'Thomas is a good man at heart. But he is not a passionate man,' she began, and seemed to search for words to justify herself. 'And I, and I, as a result . . . am without a child, as you know. Do I make myself clear?'

'I think so.'

'I do not wish to hurt him. Or anyone. But my youth is passing, and I know that—' Godwin nodded. 'I hunger,' she whispered, and after a short pause, drew a deep breath and made for the door. As she placed her fingers on the handle she turned and smiled at him. 'You appear to have been drawn into the heart of the Brooke family.'

'What makes you think that?'

'Miss Brooke – Mag, that is – has spoken of your understanding with Mr Brooke. And his daughter. My husband has never succeeded in winning their confidence.'

'It is more difficult for Sir Thomas,' replied Godwin. 'I am merely passing by. There is no conflict of interests.'

'You have created a deep impression for a mere passer-by,' she smiled, before saying good-night and creeping silently from the room.

Chapter 25

After breakfast the following day, Godwin finally coerced Pierrepont into the library for a private interview. Pierrepont had elected not to join the others on an outing, in the hope, he now told Godwin, without the smallest show of restraint or embarrassment in his use of terms, of spending some time today with his betrothed. Godwin looked at him open-mouthed, astonished as much by Pierrepont's blindness as by his audacity. For a moment he was speechless, collecting his thoughts, as Pierrepont leant back relaxedly against one of the tables and began to scan a bookshelf for some interesting reading.

'Fortinbras, have you quite lost your senses?' he asked.

'Come now, Godwin. We know each other well enough now for you to call me Forty. All of my closest friends do.' He suddenly spotted a book. 'Now this looks interesting. Do you know anything about the geology of the Hebrides?'

'What do you mean by your "betrothed"?'

'My dear fellow, who do you think I mean? Lydia, of course.'

'Betrothed?' asked Godwin in horror.

'As good as. I have spoken to Mr Brooke.'

Godwin could barely find words to reply. 'Mr Brooke has given his approval?'

'Not exactly. But he has not refused my proposal. He merely wishes to discuss the matter with Lydia first.'

'And has their conversation yet happened?'

'I'm not sure,' said Pierrepont airily, leafing through his

272

book. 'I was rather hoping to find out today. Why so many questions?'

Godwin drew a breath and looked out of the window at the sunlit courtyard. Panayiotis was unloading some harvested cotton from the back of a cart; others then carried it by the basketload down to the animals' pens. A pair of dogs snarled at each other in a corner of the yard, one of them eventually submitting, and scuttling off through the gate, tail between its legs.

'Fortinbras, it is time for all this nonsense to stop.' Pierrepont laughed, either in response to Godwin or because he had been tickled by something in the text he was reading. 'Put the book away and sit down. I ask you. As a friend.'

'All right,' said Pierrepont, and did as he was asked with faint reproach in his eyes as he took a place at the table.

'It is over,' said Godwin.

'What is over?'

'Your delusion.' Godwin said. 'Lydia is not interested in marrying you. And you know you cannot delude her as well as yourself into thinking that marriage is possible for you. Another marriage.'

'What do you mean?'

Godwin looked him square on. 'Do I have to say it? Would you not prefer to concede, and leave the words unsaid?'

'I cannot think what you might mean.'

Godwin sighed. 'I refer to a certain person who awaits you in the village of Frobisham. Berkshire.'

Pierrepont made as if to answer but no words came out. He was looking straight at Godwin, mouth open, eyebrows raised, and he began to blink. After a moment, he closed his mouth and let out a long breath. It was as if a spiritual entity left his body with that breath, a phantom of geniality and light-heartedness that took with it some of the very substance of his form, so that he seemed almost to shrink in his chair.

'How did you discover this?' he asked.

'I am not at liberty to discuss the matter.'

Pierrepont buried his forehead in his palms. 'Of course,' he said. 'It must have been Straker. She has written to the Legation. Why did I not think of that? Marie has become suspicious and has written to Sir Thomas to enquire after me. Thereby putting an end to any freedom I might have thought I had in this country. And Straker has told you the news. When does he plan to broach the subject with me?' Godwin looked at him but said nothing. He had not anticipated this response, though it conveniently obscured his own wrongdoing. Pierrepont turned to the window, the colour rising in his face, and with a violent flash of anger stood up and clenched his hands. 'How dare she do this to me!' he spat. 'She has never been a wife to me. My first chance to find happiness and she does this to me. Spoiling everything!' He grabbed at empty air with both fists, squeezing tight, forearms shaking, until the fit passed and he turned back to Godwin, drained, his eyes moistening. 'What am I to do?'

The answer was direct and firm. 'There is only one thing to do. You must leave and return to Athens. At the earliest opportunity. The day after tomorrow, with Straker's party. You can still salvage your reputation. Go to see Mr Brooke, apologize, and beg him to say nothing to Lydia. All will be well. Then arrange for divorce proceedings and start a new life as a free man in due course. But first, and most importantly, leave this house. Do you understand?'

Pierrepont nodded, tightening his lips and looking to the ground. 'Could you persuade Straker not to mention anything to Mr Brooke?' he asked. A flash of guilt went through Godwin as he upheld the falsehood.

'I'm sure I can. He and I are old friends. But you must do as I say, or my assurances cannot be guaranteed.'

'Of course.' Pierrepont then looked Godwin in the face. 'You have been a good friend to me, Tudor.'

'Please.'

'No, I must say it. You have intervened in this matter before I had the opportunity to make a complete fool of myself. Imagine if Lydia had heard! You have stood by me, and now you offer your help to hide the facts of my situation, despite the risks involved to your own reputation.'

'Please, Fortinbras. I have done nothing.'

'Oh, but you have,' he replied, and advanced to Godwin, arms spread. 'You are a true friend.' He enfolded Godwin in a tight embrace and held him there while the tears trickled across his cheek and down to Godwin's tweed-clad shoulder. 'And I am a broken man,' he said, recovering his composure. 'But because of you I may yet not be perceived as a liar and a blackguard.'

He departed, leaving Godwin alone in the room to reflect on what had occurred. The incident had been nothing less than a detonation, and the shattered fragments of the former situation now began to fix themselves into a new pattern. A joy, the like of which he barely recognized, overwhelmed him. It was triumph, of a savage, masculine, competitive variety. He was grateful, victorious and jubilant all at the same time. And he was suddenly very hungry. The thought of lunch, which was imminent, made him rejoice. And he was also very keen to see Lydia.

He approached the door to leave the library, but to his surprise it opened towards him, and there was Daniel, with Straker following close behind. Something in the solemnity of their faces alerted Godwin's suspicions. What possible business could Straker have with young Daniel Brooke? After a fleeting pause Daniel digested the fact of Godwin's presence, smiled a greeting, and mentioned that he was going to show Mr Straker some maps of the area so that he could take himself on a walk without fear of getting lost. Godwin nodded, raised his eyebrows cheerily at Straker, and left them alone in the library.

Chapter 26

Daniel had thoroughly enjoyed having Prince Leopold to stay. He craved the company of young men, and here was one with whom he instantly felt an affinity. They rode, competed, chatted and cavorted with each other incessantly, and within twenty-four hours of meeting were sworn comrades, exchanging intimate thoughts and pledging an acquaintanceship for life. Daniel admired the Prince's fiery daring, his defiance of his father, and his esteem for the belligerent Bismarck; but, above all, Daniel envied and stood in awe of the young aristocrat's impressive record of romantic conquests. Daniel had never enjoyed a woman, in the sense that the Prince had on numerous occasions. He barely ever met eligible girls. Village Greeks were of course forbidden and his exposure to young females was therefore restricted to the occasional daughter of his father's acquaintances – a limited selection, narrowed even further by the disqualification of several through age or ugliness. His only regular experience of femininity since reaching manhood had been with Mag, who did not count, and his sister, who was both everything and nothing compressed into one.

He shared this very personal complaint with the Prince, and could barely hide his sense of shame in the face of the other man's disbelief and worldliness. Life would not be worth living, said Leopold, without regular visits to the well-spring of woman. It had priority, came before anything else, overrode all concerns and responsibilities. It was the single, throbbing, central target to which all his energies, cravings, hopes and joys were directed, at all times. All else was mere entertainment. He spoke of a world and a way of life Daniel had never dared contemplate, though with every claim and anecdote it sounded more attractive.

'How does your father expect you ever to choose a bride if you have not tried at least a score of women for every one you give consideration?' he asked Daniel as they paused between gallops and sat observing one of the estate's finest views in the sunshine. His servant was standing a little way off, in the shade of a large wild olive tree, holding the reins of the horses. 'And for every score of those considered, you select one for a little more serious consideration, until you have a score of them, and so on. But you should start soon. The list is shortening fast. You must find them young.' He lit a cigarette and looked across the valley, crossing his legs and perfectly tailored trousers in front of him in the grass. 'I myself must begin soon to narrow the field. One can defy the family for so long, but it would be madness to leave one's choice of wife until after the best fruit has been picked.'

Encouraged by the sympathy of his friend, Daniel began to vent other resentments concerning his life, especially the limits of opportunity afforded him by his father. He spoke with passion, describing himself as a man crushed, possessing talents untested, a man whose loyalty and natural ambition were given less consideration than the dog at his father's feet.

The Prince drew long on his cigarette and nodded expertly. Daniel's was a common problem, he said. But the time had come for action. No-one else was going to stand up to his father on his behalf. The one and only way to earn his father's respect was to demonstrate his capability. As soon as his father realized the young lion had reached manhood, he would step aside somewhat; not step down, perhaps, but step aside, allow another to share his place, which was the first stage towards the practical business of inheritance. From there on it would be easy and natural. Daniel must choose a project to prove his ability, must execute it with precision and without assistance.

Daniel listened, star-struck, to this manly advice. It filled him with noble ambition, and his thoughts began to race across the spectrum of possibilities. It was therefore with added interest and enthusiasm that he listened to John Straker's words one evening after dinner in the drawing room, when everyone else had gone to bed and the two of them were left alone with a decanter of port.

Straker treated him like a man and an equal, which Daniel appreciated. He asked questions about the estate on the assumption that Daniel would know answers, he delved into details of family history, land ownership, the terms and conditions of Thomas Brooke's legacy to his sons, all the while giving the younger man his rapt attention, filling his glass and offering him an endless supply of good tobacco. Daniel was flattered.

It was late in the evening and he had had plenty to drink when they strayed on to the subject of the estate's future prospects, his own role therein, and, inevitably, the matter of the German mining proposition. Straker claimed to have heard something of the debate in Athens, and asked what Daniel's opinion might be. The answer was immediately forthcoming and unequivocal. He had no hesitation in telling Straker that his own position was opposed to that of his father, and how he believed the fortunes of the whole island could be transformed for a century if only Edgar would see sense.

Straker deflected Daniel's attention from serious matters for a moment by asking him directly, with a mischievous smile, what he might do, in a single decisive action, if he were to have control of the estate and two hundred thousand drachmas at his personal disposal. Daniel raised his eyes to heaven as several possibilities flew before him, but he paused for effect before answering, to give his words greater weight and an air of maturity. He would resurrect the old

278

Roman harbour, two headlands down from his father's coastal *apothiki*, he said; it would provide a perfect staging port: protected, well positioned for prevailing winds and for overland access along the river course. He would build a quay, jetties, storehouses and a decent road to serve it. Perhaps even some dwellings for full-time marine staff, and then purchase a vessel.

Straker leant forward in his chair and looked Daniel straight in the eye, all trace of humour now absent from his face. How would Daniel feel, he asked, if the accomplishment of this dream were not so far away from his grasp as he might imagine, if there might be a method to secure not only the funds for such a project, but also the freedom to enact it? Daniel could see by the older man's sudden change of mood that this had been no joke. But when he asked for an explanation, Straker replied that it would be best for them to have a formal interview, free from the clouding influences of drink, smoke and tiredness; perhaps the following day, at eleven o'clock in the library?

Thus it was that as Godwin was leaving that same room with a spring in his step and a happy perspective on the world, he was met by John Straker and Daniel Brooke coming the other way, their minds fixed on weightier matters.

Straker ensured that his old friend had walked some distance off down the corridor before he firmly closed the door. Daniel then retrieved a few maps from a drawer and seated himself beside Straker at the table.

The older man drew breath. 'What I am about to suggest,' he began, 'I do only because your father leaves us little option. It has never been our intention to sow the seeds of family discord, but if the present situation remains unresolved, all who have considered the matter agree that the Brooke family's survival in Greece will shortly come to an end. And, of course, any catastrophe for British citizens within Greece, particularly citizens of high standing, is a

279

catastrophe for relations between the Foreign Office in London and the government of Athens. I apologize now for the shock that this news may occasion, but it is as well to make plain my reasoning before we begin.' Daniel was silenced by the absolute sobriety of his tone. 'However,' he continued, 'there may be a way to avoid catastrophe, for all concerned, excepting perhaps a single person, should he remain intransigent to the last.'

'My father.'

'Allow me to inspect a map of the estate.' Daniel then proceeded to spread across the table a chart, hand-drawn, about two feet square, showing the boundaries of the property. Straker leant over it, unfolding a pair of hinged gold spectacles from a little crocodile-skin case and wedging them on to the end of his nose. His breathing was quite heavy as he focused on the detail of the map, searching around for certain markers. 'I see,' he said, 'this is much as I had anticipated. We are agreed, then, that your grandfather left the entire estate to be divided between your father and your uncle Percival, and that he was specific as to the division: the north-eastern half to Edgar,' he delineated a rough circle towards the top right of the map with his index finger, then moved it diagonally across the page, 'and the south-western to Percival. This, I am pleased to say, suits our scheme to perfection.'

'I confess I am at a loss as to your meaning.'

'Dear boy, it is simple. Your fortune is within your grasp.' Daniel smiled but shook his head in confusion. 'Percival of course is not fit to govern his share of the property. A legal charge must be established, through the Nomarch of Pyroxenia and the courts in Athens, whereby you gain trusteeship for Percival's share.'

'But that trusteeship was assigned to my father many years ago.'

'Precisely. Many years ago, before the Greek Constitution was established in eighteen forty four, and before the change of monarch and the new Constitution in eighteen sixty four. The nation has been through two administrative revolutions since that document was drawn up. We are living in a new Greece.'

'Can that change the law? Are property rights dating from the former era now defunct?'

Straker smiled. 'Not the property rights. But the niceties of a disputed trusteeship are tenuous at the best of times, and, with the application of certain pressures, the tenuous can quite speedily become the fractured.'

'You mean the courts can be bought? To benefit me at the expense of my father?'

'They could, but that is irrelevant to us. In this instance, a little pressure from the government should seal the matter. You will have control of half the estate, which, by good fortune happens to be the half which is richest in deposits of lignite. You will grant your permission for work to begin on the mines immediately. From there it is but a short step to persuading the mining companies to forward you an immediate advance of some thousands of drachmas, as a gesture of thanks and goodwill. It will be but a fraction of your income from the project in the long term.'

'The government is so keen for this project to be advanced?'

'Indeed. And you can surely imagine how advantageous it would be, as you take up the reins at Thasofolia, to have the blessing and full support of Athens. This is a matter supported by both parties, the incumbent government and the opposition. You would begin your reign as a political hero. We might even be able to arrange for the King and Queen to visit the new enterprise.'

Daniel was dazzled by the terms and descriptions flowing with ease from Straker, a man whose opinions were no mere trifles but carried the endorsement of many years' experience in Anglo–Greek relations. Daniel's eyes shone. In the space of a few minutes he had begun to picture himself no longer as the glorified estate messenger-boy, performing errands on horseback, but as a landlord, a towering figure in the modern industry of Greece, the toast of the capital, a prize catch indeed for the most beautiful young women in society. He saw himself at the head of a strong new dynasty, a big family to fill the house, the Brookes finally secure and established for centuries to come, not scratching by on a dream and a hope as his father and grandfather had done.

'It is indeed a tempting vision,' he said quietly, looking at the map.

'Let us not lose sight of the obstacles in our euphoria,' added Straker, 'which I believe will be transitory, though painful. The estate will be divided for a period. You will perhaps lose your family and home. Your father will doubtless oppose your action to the point of open hostility, and he may or may not be joined by other members of the family.'

'Lydia will stand by Father, surely. I sometimes think she would prefer me out of the way.'

'We shall see. I think it would be both unwise and unkind to attempt to unseat your father from his home. You may be compelled to build your own new house within the territories administered by you. In due course your father will retire, perhaps return to live in England, or will die, whereupon you or your children will most likely inherit, and the divided property will be reunited. At worst, your trustee-ship of Percival's share will secure for you eventual ownership of at least half the estate.'

Daniel now leant back and stared blankly ahead, fiddling with a pencil between his fingers. 'You appear to have worked it all out. To the last detail,' he said.

'I cannot pretend to have been idle,' replied Straker, relaxing. 'If you are in agreement with the Minister's proposal—'

'The Minister? Has Sir Thomas Wishart something to do with the plan?'

'Of course,' said Straker, smiling at the boy's naïvety. He admired the energy and handsomeness of the youth. With a little responsibility and the calming effect of years, this boy could, given a sprinkling of fortune, develop into an impressive landowner. 'I do not suggest any of this out of a personal inclination, though I do firmly believe it to be the right course of action. No, this is Legation business, and you must interpret what I say as the advice of the Minister, the Legation, and, for that matter, the Foreign Office.'

Daniel thought for a moment longer. He tried to disguise the trembling of excitement that he could feel in his finger-tips. 'How do we proceed?' he asked.

Straker smiled and began to fold the map. 'We must get you to Athens, soon. Unfortunately, it may entail the pro-duction of an invented pretext. The formalities will take no more than a day or two at most, as I will have had everything prepared in advance of your arrival. But news will of course reach Thasofolia shortly after the new trusteeship has been published, and you may therefore wish to remain in Athens for a while longer, until the summer perhaps, to make plans for your future and to secure your alliances in society.' Here Straker let slip his formal tone and gave him an avuncular smile. 'You could reside with me, if you like. I have a capacious apartment in the city.'

Their conversation was brought to an end shortly after this by the intrusion of Lydia, who said she had a matter to dis-cuss with Daniel. Straker was content to let the subject rest for the moment, his point made, the seed sown on what appeared to be fertile ground.

He went to the drawing room to await the call for lunch. He was satisfied that his conspiracy was under way, but there was no room for complacency: not until the deeds and rights had been appropriately signed and sealed. The poor lad, in his vanity and ambition, had not even stopped to think what would become of his father, beached and left to rot. Godwin, of course, must be prevented from knowing about the plot. If enough time passed before the major events of the plan were enacted, and Godwin were to return to England, he might never discover that Straker had been instrumental in the downfall of Edgar Brooke. That would be happier for all.

* * *

Later the same day, Lydia sought out Godwin, finding him in the hall, where he was wiping his boots having returned from a stroll by the river. His delight in seeing her was unbounded. It had been a stunning sunset, he said, and went on to describe it in euphoric detail, his cheeks glowing from the clear wintry nip outside. He had not felt so happy for as long as he could remember. 'Who has need of man's paltry artifice,' he said, 'when divine nature can produce a canvas such as that, effortlessly, without cost to anyone? And how is your patient this evening?'

'Very much improved. He has been laughing. I believe we may hope for him quite to recover. And he is changed.'

Godwin stopped for a moment and looked at her. 'Well, that is good news indeed. Changed, you say?'

For an instant she seemed uncharacteristically lost for words. 'For the better, I mean. If you can credit such a thing. He has become a man. And strong, in a way. Despite the – the injury.'

'That is interesting to hear,' said Godwin, placing his boots tidily against the wall. 'And how do you account for this change?'

She averted her eyes. 'How should I know? He has perhaps awoken from his despair a better and a wiser person.'

Godwin smiled generously at her. 'As well as everything else, you appear to possess the healing powers of an angel. But that does not surprise me. I would have expected no less.'

Lydia put a stop to the discussion by introducing a plan she had devised.

'Am I not right in thinking that you have two photographic plates remaining in your box?' she asked.

'You are, as always, my dear, completely right.'

'Would it be very opportunistic and selfish of me to ask if you would be prepared to expend those last plates on an exposure of my designation? As a favour, from one old comrade in art to another?'

'Dear Lydia,' replied Godwin, with reckless elation, 'I could not deny you anything. The plates are yours to do with as you please.'

Her face broke into a huge, childlike grin. 'Really?' she said, and jumped in the air for joy. 'Mr Tudor, I do adore you!'

'And I you, you heavenly creature,' he replied with mock chivalry, bowing elaborately.

'You will not seek to alter my plan tomorrow?'

'You have my word.'

'And you will promise not to be shocked?'

At this last remark the smallest splinter of doubt pricked him, though his exhilaration was too great for him to give it more than a flash of consideration, nor allow it to reveal itself as he replied to her, in the same exaggeratedly humorous manner: 'Do you not think that I know you well enough now to be more surprised by the absence of a shock than shocked by whatever you are planning to devise?'

'Splendid!' she said, clapped her hands together and leant forward to plant the smallest kiss on his cheek. 'After breakfast, then, as usual.'

'As usual,' chimed Godwin, and went up to his room in a rapture of happiness to change for dinner.

For the first time in days, he slept long and well that night. Little now, he told himself as he turned his cheek into the huge downy pillow and closed his eyes, could impinge upon his state of peace and equanimity.

Chapter 27

The silence of the place was bewitchingly tangible. It was not emptiness or nothingness, but seemed to throb. The pool had a character of its own that demanded deference of sorts, but not of the type that required hushed voices or doffed caps, as in a cathedral. Those who came here answered to a religiousness invisible to the culture of man and his elaborate constructs of worship. They touched upon it willingly in the silence of the place. A sanctity uncontained by language; a sanctity that would not submit to the bridle of denomination, no matter how exquisitely crafted the bridle might be. It could no more be perceived in its immeasurable vastness than it could be overlooked in its entirety in a single speck of leaf dew. Such was the immaculate atmosphere that dwelt in this extraordinary place, where the earth had given way and formed its own sunken, watery, still and living sanctuary. And as Godwin quietly laid out the tools of his craft, he felt appropriately ennobled by the atmosphere.

Lydia had spoken hardly at all on their way there, and seemed serenely enveloped in a meditation of her own. Daniel, who was accompanying them, had ridden on some twenty paces ahead, apparently consumed in thought. Godwin, at the rear, was still riding high on his elation of the previous day, though now somewhat mellowed and settled, and he appreciated the clear air, the shafts of sunlight beaming through to the ground between pines, the birdsong, the crunch of hoofs in the bed of needles beneath. As they neared the pool, Lydia turned, smiling back at him, and spoke.

'These are very different conditions from when we performed our earlier exposure.'

'They are indeed,' said Godwin. 'It will make an interesting contrast.' Something within him recognized the opportunity to put a question to her, as if to seal a wound, a final, closing epilogue to a sorry tale that had turned out well. 'Have you been back to the pool since we visited it last together?' He asked it innocently, as if in connection to her comment on the weather, and she could surely not suspect his possessing any other motive.

'Once,' she said.

'Yes?'

'It was Fortinbras' doing. He had seen the first exposure. The extra print you gave for my keeping. I think perhaps he was a little envious. He insisted that I bring him on an expedition here, and would not let the matter rest until I agreed. It was the day of the storm, when you had your fall.' Godwin's joy would have been complete at this innocent confession, but her next words smoothed away any last trace of troubled memories. 'He did not understand the place at all. Not in the way that you do.'

After this remark Godwin concluded that it was in a spirit of more than comradeship that they now returned to the place where he had experienced his first moment of intense closeness with Lydia. He now had little doubt that her regard for him extended to more than mere friendship, more than a shared respect for art and beauty. For the first time he allowed himself to reflect on their intimacy in a way that before would have made him shrink with shame; but now he admitted that it was not so ridiculous to acknowledge the simple facts. Why not admit that he was in love with Lydia? Why not recognize that she perhaps shared the feeling? And why not allow that one day, perhaps still far off, he might be able to raise the question of marriage with this adorable creature?

These were his happy thoughts as he unpacked and

arranged his equipment on the fern-bedded banks of the pool that morning. It was two weeks since his previous visit, the two longest weeks of his life, during which time he had travelled over a landscape of crests and valleys, but had now arrived at a summit of equilibrium and contentment.

Daniel was ponderous, his expression grave, and in the present context seemed to Godwin to possess greater maturity than he had until now. There was a resonance of his father about him that had previously been unnoticeable; it was there in the knit of the brow, the purposefulness of his limbs as he moved, the turn of his wrist as he tethered the horses, the bend of his elbow as he lent a hand to his sister to help her cross to the rock. Lydia, meanwhile, seemed to grow in grace and radiance, just as she had on the previous visit here, her posture becoming almost regal, her actions slower, more deliberate, her usual peach-like loveliness trans-figured into untouchable beauty. She stood by her brother on the rock now, talking gently to him, consolingly it seemed, for his head was hung low, and she stroked his cheek with the back of her fingers.

Godwin looked up at the birds of prey that circled high above the great cavity, and the blue sky beyond all. He felt free and he felt absolved. There was neither right nor wrong at this place, no absolute truths demanded or imparted, an absence of authority. And for one piercing moment of liberation, when he felt the strains and guilt of years slip from him into the black, still waters all around, he realized that there were no eternal truths in creation at all; so-called moral certainties were nothing more than ideas, dreamt up and ennobled by people and cultures to justify an agreed set of standards and a particular way of life; and the same applied to the super-idea of them all: God, the ultimate authority, a grandiose invention of hot air.

The constraints of his former life cleared before him, like a malignant vapour in the breeze.

Lydia's quiet conference with Daniel seemed to be at an

end, and both siblings now looked across to Godwin as he stood waiting for them, beside his apparatus. He smiled at them. They surely understood what he was thinking. They and he were part of it together.

'We are ready now,' called Lydia softly. 'You may prepare the plate.' Godwin signalled his assent and disappeared inside the tent.

There was absolutely no noise from outside. Within that small pyramid capsule all was black. The sounds in there were the sounds of intimate, close confinement, a sniff in his nose, fingers flexed in a rubber glove, a dust brush stroked across the surface of clean glass, the hissing rush of chemical powder poured on to a tray. And it was at a certain point, in that cropped, blind world, as he prepared the components and mixed the fluids, that he became aware of the demon watching him. It was a small presence at first, hiding in the shadows, somewhere behind his shoulder, smiling cynically as he worked. He tried to dismiss it, tried to remind himself that he had just before reached a state of unparalleled peace and that there was no room in his thinking now for doubt and despair; but its hideous little snigger was persistent and refused to be ignored. And before long, cloaked from the air and light of day, confined in blackness, Godwin felt himself trapped in a breeding ground of suspicion and misgiving. The demon's voice murmured poison, an incessant flow of it, and there was nowhere to hide. Godwin listened in agony as it smirked at him, whispering its little song, like a warped nursery rhyme, that she was not the darling he hoped her to be, that there were impurities, that the situation was hopeless; and it cackled with laughter at Godwin's naïvety in having ever believed otherwise.

The plate was coated, wet and sensitive, the hinged shield neatly closed, its locking thread tightened as Godwin turned around to unpeg the entrance of the tent. His hand rested on the upper button as he paused, and an inevitability dawned upon him. This exposure would never be made. He knew, even as he stepped out, before he saw them, that the dream was shattered, could never have been, and therefore the shock that awaited him was somehow forestalled. There were two Godwin Tudors who now beheld the scene on the rock: one, a spectral personage, who, in the palm of his demon, forewarned, now nodded, almost smiling, who had known all along that no good would come of this business; and the other, the man of bone, sinew, learning and principle, who could barely hold himself upright at the sight of it, whose grasp of reality reeled for an instant as he stumbled forward into the tripod. His camera fell over and its oak casing splintered on a rock, but he barely noticed. He let drop the shield into the soft maidenhair carpet at his feet, where the wet plate cracked, and dripped chemical poison into the soil.

*

About an hour later, Edgar was sitting at his desk when he heard a heavy footstep approach rapidly across the floorboards on the other side of the door. Without a knock or any other formality, the door burst open and there stood Godwin, his clothes stained with dirt, his face streaked and sweating, a wildness in his eyes. Edgar looked up at him without saying a word, waiting for him to speak. Godwin walked forward and leant against the desk to regain his breath before beginning.

'Mr Brooke. I wish to tell you that I am leaving this house. I am leaving this island. And I do not intend ever to return. I leave with Mr Straker and the others for Athens at first light tomorrow morning.'

Edgar removed the glasses from his nose and observed Godwin. His reply was quiet and empty of feeling. 'I am afraid that is impossible.'

The anger returned to Godwin's eyes as they darted back and forth across the surface of the desk. 'I tell you now, sir, that I shall be leaving.'

'What has happened, Mr Tudor? What has occurred to

affect you in this manner?' Godwin found himself unable to give an immediate reply and hung his head. 'You are clearly inconsolable,' continued Edgar. 'Perhaps we should talk after you have allowed your passion to subside.'

'No!' said Godwin. 'There will be no more talking.'

'Then why are you here?'

Godwin paused to collect himself. 'I am here to tell you something about your children. If there is an ounce of moral stature left in you, you might yet prevent your family sinking irretrievably into a mire of sin and depravity.'

Edgar's response was almost impatient. 'Mr Tudor, sin is not a notion to which I give much consideration, except as a means of understanding the preoccupations of people whose perspective of living is circumscribed. By priestcraft and the like.'

'There must be limits to what you consider permissible.'

'Perhaps. But limits born of sound reason, not custom or superstition.'

'And would you consider it reasonable and sound to prevent your children committing a foul and unspeakable act, one that scorns nature itself?'

Edgar looked hard at him before replying. 'Do not blur your accusation with rash judgements and impassioned descriptions.'

For a moment despair seemed to get the better of Godwin and he retreated towards the door. But he changed his mind and turned back, resolved to impart his news to Edgar, even if it was to be their last conversation. 'I shall tell you what happened in as plain a form as I can. You must prepare yourself for the worst.' Edgar did not say anything in reply but cradled his hands, until Godwin was ready to speak.

'We had ridden to the pool at the end of the gorge, Lydia, Daniel and I, to undertake a final exposure for my collection. Lydia had personally requested the expedition, declaring a secret purpose, and she forewarned me not to be shocked at its nature. I will tell you now that I have always been surprised by the apparent ease with which she volunteers her own nakedness for my exposures, and that surprise was extended still further after Lydia insisted recently that Daniel should be included in our tableaux. I had wondered at the propriety of this. But I had also grown to know her ways a little. She exceeds the boundaries of convention.'

'My son has also posed for you?'

'He has.'

'With Lydia?'.

Godwin nodded. 'I had allowed myself to trust her intentions, and so this morning did not question her.' His voice was now soft, and he looked down as he spoke. 'I thought she might love me, you see. I was fool enough to think that it was all a gift of sorts. The photographs, her posing for me. I had believed it was a means whereby our intimacy could be extended and eventually sealed. I understood that this, our last exposure, would be that final seal, that she entertained a plan to leave me in no doubt about her feelings. How could I have been so wrong?'

'Your disappointment, then, is that of a wronged lover?' Edgar's words were said without feeling, merely as a statement of record.

'My disappointment? My disappointment! I do not speak of disappointment! I speak of a crime against nature.'

'I do not wish to belittle your hurt, Mr Tudor, but clearly such injury as you have experienced has had some bearing on your interpretation of what happened next.'

Godwin's head slumped a little to one side. He was tired of Edgar's warped reasoning. Let the brute hear the news in as plain a way as he liked to give advice himself. 'They are lovers,' Godwin said. 'They were locked in a close embrace. Entwined and . . . their mouths locked. And in movement. It was not a pose for my photograph. They did not still their . . . caresses when I appeared.'

A silence now descended between them. A distant cock could be heard crowing in the village, and the high metallic

292

voice of a housewife far off seemed to answer it. The clock in the hall chimed the three-quarter-hour bell, a quarter to twelve, and the clink of glass being laid out in the dining room next door indicated that it was not long until lunch.

Edgar shook his head, puffed his cheeks and sighed heavily. Godwin looked up at him, suddenly stung by a needle of remorse. He had perhaps been hasty in his choice of words and manner. For all Edgar's peculiar ways, he was still a father, a man with feelings, not impervious to wounding.

'I am sorry,' Godwin said quietly, 'that it is I who am compelled to tell you this.'

Edgar let out a grunt of a laugh, and looked at him, smiling. 'Is this the heart of your complaint?' he said. 'Only this?'

Godwin looked up at him, frowning. 'I do not understand,' he said. 'You don't think their behaviour to have been unnatural?'

'Unnatural? Hear yourself, Mr Tudor! Unnatural?' It was now Edgar's voice and tone that rose in feeling. 'The only unnatural part of this debate is your imposition of prejudicial standards. It is you who are unnatural.'

'I cannot believe I am listening to these words.'

'You disappoint me, Mr Tudor. We had travelled some distance in our conversations and I was of a mind that you were a believer in free thought and action.'

'Within certain bounds, yes.'

'But who sets those bounds? If it were you, I should not be so disappointed. But you have received them from others, and thereby you subscribe to the system that enslaves you all. Man is born free, Mr Tudor, and yet everywhere he is in chains. Is not this a sentiment you recognize and admire? At least so you have led me to believe.' His speech gathered pace as the heat of his feelings rose.

'Of course that is a theory I admire, but—'

'If you think it a mere theory it is of no use to anyone. We

293

aspire to lift the constraints of social slavery, Mr Tudor, not to theorize comfortably in armchairs between glasses of port.'

'But,' Godwin floundered for a reply, 'but is it considered social slavery for a brother and sister to refrain from indulging in, in . . .' The words failed him.

'If their action is wrong – if they find it to be wrong, rather than have it told to them by a spurious authority – if their action is wrong, they will cease to continue with the action, and will learn and grow as a result of it.'

'There is no "if" in this matter. It *is* wrong.'

'You are quite convinced of that?'

'Beyond any doubt.'

'You would stake your life on it?'

'Absolutely.'

'Then you have nothing to fear in what you witnessed this morning.'

'How so?'

Edgar paused a moment before replying. 'What you witnessed this morning was an experiment. These exposure compositions encourage a desire to experiment, do they not? And, in that sense, you yourself are to some extent responsible for having fostered the desire. But if, as you say, their experiment is unquestionably wrong, a travesty against nature, the action will not be repeated. The deed informs itself of its own moral feasibility.'

'But what if they do not recognize it to be wrong? What if they are in the grip of a disease?'

Edgar smiled. 'Mr Tudor, do not be hysterical. And have a little more faith in the mechanics of nature. The sexual act between a brother and sister is not widely practised because nature informs us that it is wrong, that it is against the interests of our species, not because we are told so in the bible and warned from the pulpit that God disapproves of it.'

Godwin pursed his lips and lowered his gaze. 'You are a

clever tactician with words, Mr Brooke. I cannot deny you that. But I cannot also deny my instinctive horror at what I beheld.'

Edgar pointed a finger directly at him. 'You are confusing your horror with the jealousy of a neglected lover.'

'It is still my intention to depart.'

'In good time.'

'Tomorrow.'

'Impossible. Please do not press me on this issue. Tomorrow is out of the question. We shall arrange for appropriate transport, guides and supplies at a date in the near future, but tomorrow, I repeat, is impossible.'

'And I repeat,' said Godwin calmly as he rose to leave, 'that I shall be departing in the morning. Along with Mr Pierrepont, who, in case he has not already told you, has also found himself in a position whereby an extension of his stay here is untenable.'

'Well, well,' said Edgar leaning back in his chair and holding his pen at either end, horizontal between his fingertips. 'I do not seek to minimize the significance of your respective dramas, but I cannot allow you to accompany tomorrow's party.'

Godwin looked at him. 'Are you going to tell me why not?'

Edgar held his gaze, eyes like frozen glass, before he replied. 'I am not at liberty to disclose the reason. You will have to believe me that it is not in your best interests.'

'I shall be the judge of that,' replied Godwin, now turning away and approaching the door. 'And I would recommend that you do not seek to impede my intention, lest I am placed in the position of having to declare to all the reason for my insistence.'

He walked out of Edgar's study, closing the door firmly behind him, and made for the hall, where he hesitated for a moment to collect his thoughts. But the moment passed when he heard the front door open and Daniel came in, returned from his expedition in time to take lunch. He looked up at Godwin, surprised to see him there but unable to find words to speak. He removed his gloves and riding coat, placed them on a heavy oak throne that stood beside the door, and walked hurriedly towards the dining room, nodding a greeting as he went. Godwin let him pass without attempting to say anything. Whatever there was to say could not be said here, or now, if ever. There was no sign of Lydia, but fearing that she might follow soon after her brother and be in the hall at any moment, he decided to slip quickly up the staircase to the refuge of his room.

Chapter 28

Godwin spent the afternoon in his room, for the most part standing at the window and gazing emptily at the landscape. The beauty of it seemed to have diminished. Perhaps it was the dullness of the sky, which had clouded over since the morning; or perhaps the deficiency had nothing to do with the view, but indicated a change in the viewer. The hills and forests were now bereft of promise. The contours and features of the landscape remained unchanged, but the magic had drained away.

There was not much to pack, and he had it all done in a few minutes, but there was a good deal to contemplate. As the hours passed, and the initial sting of the morning's events subsided into a deep ache, he went to lie on his bed. He was still there at around five o'clock when there was a knock on the door. Swinging his feet to the ground and straightening his clothes, he asked who was there.

'It is Edgar,' came the reply, and the door opened. 'I believe everyone is out of the house,' he said quietly. 'There is more to say.'

'I think I have heard enough,' replied Godwin. 'Unless you have withdrawn your objection to my leaving in the morning.'

'I have not.'

Godwin felt his indignation rise again. 'In which case,' he said, 'there certainly is nothing further to discuss,' and he made for the door.

Suddenly and without warning Edgar's palm hit the

surface of a table next to him with such violence that Godwin's whole frame jerked and he was momentarily frozen to the spot.

Edgar roared in an explosion of rage, 'Stay where you are and listen to what I have to say!' Godwin had never heard anything like it. Either because of Edgar's habitual equanimity and control, or because of the latent power of his mountainous physique, the effect of this volcanic expression of anger was primal and terrifying. Even his father could not communicate danger on a scale like this.

'Sit,' commanded Edgar, pointing to a chair in front of the table. Godwin did as he was told. Edgar then rubbed a palm harshly back and forth across his scalp, ruffling his hair as he walked towards the window and looked out, away from the confinement of the room. A silence followed, as his eyes rested on a certain point, and he remained like that for a while, without movement, apparently lost in thought, so that Godwin began to wonder what had snared his attention. At last Edgar turned back to the room, looked down at the floor for a moment, and then levelled his pale blue eyes at Godwin to resume the burden of their dialogue, fixing him with an unblinking stare, a look so penetratingly earnest it allowed for not the smallest flicker of levity or distraction. When he spoke, his voice had shed its unbridled edge and was soft again, his mood tamed, like a lion beneath the trainer's whip.

'I am not practised in the arts of false invention,' he said, 'and so will not attempt to deceive you, but will explain the situation in as abbreviated a form as I am able. However, by revealing all, I lay bare to you a matter of such grave consequence that should you choose to use the information to my detriment, it would result not only in my own downfall but in the destruction of everything that has been achieved at this estate, and the inevitable decline in fortune of hundreds of villagers. It would also endanger innocent lives. Do not compel me to reiterate the sincerity of what I have said. I cannot bind you to secrecy, though I believe you will not undertake to expose me without a thorough consideration of the consequences.'

'Expose you?' said Godwin. 'Are you involved in a criminal activity?'

'According to the laws of this country and our own, yes.'

'To what end?'

Edgar began slowly to pace the room and spoke in a subdued voice, though his words struck Godwin like a hammer blow.

'Tomorrow, about half an hour before noon, and at a point on the Páparis road some eight miles north of my boundary, the party of travellers recently departed from this house will be set upon by a band of brigands.'

'How – how do you know?' murmured Godwin, staring blankly ahead of him.

'They will not be harmed. The women will be escorted to a place of safety and thence sent on their return journey to Athens. Prince Leopold's servant and Panayiotis will similarly be separated from the danger. Panayiotis knows nothing of the plan.'

'What plan?'

'The abduction. The three remaining gentlemen, Mr Straker, Mr Farkas and Prince Leopold, will be held in as much comfort and with as much respect as can be afforded a fugitive band on the mountain, until such time as the brigands' demands are met. At that point they will be released unscathed and can return to their lives and callings.'

'And you are part of this conspiracy?'

Edgar continued his circular route around the room. 'The demands will be twofold. A ransom, and a royal amnesty for the brigands. It will be a straightforward matter to negotiate and could be settled within forty-eight hours if the recipients of the demands are compliant.'

'And if not?'

'Then it will take a little longer.'

'How long will be allowed?'

'A few days. It depends on the circumstances.'

'And at the end of that time?'

'The demands will be met.'

'If not?'

'Then the brigands will have to take steps to demonstrate to the authorities that their intent is serious.'

'Murder. Or mutilate the captives.'

'It will not come to that.'

'I cannot believe what I hear.'

'I shall explain to you my purpose.'

'God in heaven.'

'I am in an impossible position.'

'You would do this to your own guests?'

'Will you listen to my reasoning?'

'I suppose it has to do with the mines,' said Godwin, at which point Edgar stopped in his tracks and looked across the room at him.

'You know about the proposed mines?'

'You would risk the lives of three innocent men because of your stubborn resistance to the inauguration of a new industry on your territory. Because you cannot bear to relinquish power over your kingdom. Because you cannot countenance the prospect of a rival influence on the island, an institution, or worse, a person, with equivalent or greater strength and money than your own.'

'You are misled.'

'Three trusting gentlemen are to be put through terror and hardship, and perhaps even murdered, all for the sake of your fanciful notion of being a saviour to those who work for you, those who subsidize your life; when in fact your ways are polluted, as are those of your perverse family.'

'You do not know of what you speak.'

'I do not?' said Godwin, turning to look at Edgar. 'Then pray, sir, explain yourself.'

'Hold your judgement. You are grossly mistaken. The

mines are a matter of great concern to me at present, but this concern is not related to the matter under discussion – or not in the way that you think.'

'There is a connection between the two, then?'

'Of sorts. But allow me to explain and then you may draw your own conclusion.' Godwin did not reply, but held Edgar's earnest gaze.

'Contrary, perhaps, to your understanding of the situation,' Edgar began, 'I am neither wealthy, nor ambitious to become so. My support of this household hangs on a nail's edge, and always has done. It was the same in my father's lifetime. My personal finances make grim study and I am in a perpetual state of debt to a variety of banks and Athenian money-lenders – not people you would like to include in your acquaintanceship. I claim as my own the smallest share of the profits from the estate in order to uphold a living appropriate for a landowner of my status in the Nomarchy. I choose as simple a life for myself as I am able, in the circumstances. Everything else is returned to the benefit of the land, the farms and the people who work them. I tell you this not because I seek your pity or approbation but in order to explain the background against which the immediate crisis in my affairs has arisen. I have less than no money at present.'

Edgar began to explain the history of the estate's stock holding, and the old partnership between Thomas Brooke and Samuel Hill. The agreement, formalized nearly half a century before, entitled Brooke to the land itself and forty per cent of its income, while Hill would receive the other sixty per cent but have no stake in the actual property. Godwin listened to the story of how, nearly forty years ago, Mr Hill had visited Thasofolia for the last time, had declared a dislike of the climate and the people of Greece, had grown disillusioned by the project they had jointly undertaken, and had finally quarrelled with Thomas Brooke and returned to England, where he subsequently died without having further

301

corresponded with his former partner. There the matter had appeared to rest, and Thomas Brooke had composed his will either forgetting or deliberately neglecting to take Hill's share into account. The name Samuel Hill had not been spoken at Thasofolia again until recently, when his grandchildren had discovered, almost by accident, that they were entitled to the majority portion of whatever proceeds the estate had accrued in forty years, moneys which, as Edgar explained, were not materialized in a capital sum that could now be repaid, because everything had been reinvested for the benefit of the entire experiment. If he were now compelled to raise the sum required to repay the debt, he would have no option but to sell the estate outright, and return to a life of penury in England. The latter was the least of his concerns, but the abandonment of his labourers and tenants, their children and old folk, was a prospect he refused to contemplate. As it happened, an alternative had presented itself that would achieve the desired purpose and cost little more than a few hours' slight discomfort for three healthy and wealthy young men.

'And you are confident of raising such a mighty ransom?'

'Indeed. We had planned for Sir Thomas Wishart's capture, but I gather Mr Straker comes from a wealthy family, and will make an appropriate substitute. Mr Farkas and the Prince, of course, will command substantial value. It is unfortunate that it must be so. I do not refer to these gentlemen as commodities out of heartlessness. In my position I am continually required to disregard the personal pains of an individual, and frequently my own feelings, in order to accommodate the needs of the majority. My mind is fixed upon the benefit of my people, hundreds of them, and for a century or more.'

'How can you trust the brigands? With the money and with the lives of their captives?'

'Their captain is a godson of mine. He wants little more than to legitimize his life.'

'And he goes about it by committing an act of unlawfulness?'

'The majority of the money received will come to Thasofolia. A small portion will go to the band. After a reasonable period has passed, and all suspicions relating to the planning of the incident have subsided, I shall travel to England to negotiate a settlement with the Hill brothers. The brigands will be content with their amnesty, which is for them worth more than a mountain of gold.'

'How can you be so sure?'

'Their leader, the young man I mentioned, I have known from the cradle. I was brought up alongside his late father, his uncles and aunts. His grandmother nursed me, his family are my men. I can be sure.'

'And why will they embark on such a risk purely for the sake of an amnesty?'

'These are hunted men. They belong to a bygone time, when outlawry was not only excused by the authorities but actively encouraged. The country has changed. These outlaws are no longer seen as heroes of the mountain like the old warriors who fought the Turks. And they have lost their friends in politics.'

'Friends? What sort of friends?'

'Friends in government. Brigands were once vital for the achievement of political ends in the provinces. It was the accepted way in the old days. Brigand chiefs were widely celebrated, were entertained at the palace balls, would meet freely with ministers and be seen parading themselves with their gangs and weapons in the main streets of Athens. But all that has passed and those left live in fear of being brought to justice. An amnesty would remove that fear and allow them to live out their lives in peace.'

'Answer me this,' said Godwin. 'Assume, if you will, that I accept your argument, that I trust your action is proposed not for your own benefit but for that of your dependants.'

'That assumption would be correct.'

'Assume also that I believe your plan will have a successful outcome, that your ends will be achieved and the theft will be bloodlessly accomplished.'

'I do not think the sums involved would cause any degree of serious hardship to those who will be asked to pay; compared to the devastation that would overtake the lives of many if they do not.'

'But why should you choose to pursue this course,' continued Godwin, 'and realize the money you require by unlawful means, when there is a legal and honourable alternative open to you?'

Edgar drew a deep breath. 'I take it you are referring to the financial offer proposed by the German mining company?'

'Indeed.'

'There are two reasons,' he replied, 'one of which makes good economic sense, while the other requires a degree of visionary intelligence.' Godwin looked at him quizzically, as Edgar continued. 'If I were to accept the terms proposed by the engineers the result would be an immediate and quite cataclysmic increase in the value and yield of my land. As soon as the Hill brothers become aware of this increase they will lay claim not only to the forty years of back profits, but also to sixty per cent of the sum offered by the prospectors. Furthermore, they would most likely refuse to be bought out of the original partnership. The mines would bring them wealth beyond their dreams. I would therefore still be unable to repay the sum required, and henceforth would have to share all administrative decisions to do with the Thasofolia estate with partners unqualified for the task.'

'And the second reason?'

'The second reason you may not immediately consider valid, but that is because you do not occupy the position, for better or for worse, occupied by myself, and because you will not have formed the attachments and subtle understandings that derive from a lifetime spent in that position.' Here Edgar turned away and regarded the view from the window once more, his hands clasped behind his back, brows knit.

'As owner of the property?'

'More than owner,' murmured Edgar, his gaze fixed on the distance. 'As guardian. And it is more than merely property. We are speaking of a culture.'

Godwin paused for a moment and then broke the silence. 'I have observed your superintendence of this property. I have witnessed clearly the role you fulfil in these people's lives and welfare. I am not ignorant of your achievements and your ideals. And I am not unaware of the responsibilities that you carry.'

'But what you are perhaps as yet unqualified to notice,' continued Edgar, now turning back to the interior of the room, 'is the subtle path that I must tread in this place. I am compelled to maintain my life in a perpetual state of balance: the balance of my role as something between master, friend and saviour; the balance of preserving myself as an Englishman while proving to them that I am as Greek as the best of them; the balance of weaving the thread between honesty and corruption; the balance of political influence, which could overturn my achievements in the twinkling of an eye.' He spread a palm wide and placed it on the table. 'And much besides. You observe Thasofolia in a state of perfect balance, on a precipice at all times, but a precipice with a steel rail along its length, and therefore secure as long as the machine stays on the rail and we do not allow ourselves to dwell too much on the drop we perceive on either side. That is how things are at present, that is how they progress daily, and that is at the core of my responsibility as guardian of this place, this house, this family, and all those people.' His arm travelled in a wide arc in the general direction of the village, beyond the garden walls. As his eyes scanned the horizon he continued, 'When my father left this island all those years ago, I could see his heart was tearing itself apart. I was young and he probably feared what the future might hold, for me and for Thasofolia. Before departing he said to me that he was passing on the custody of a kind of kingdom. But no ordinary realm. It is a dominion of wilderness, he said, where bounds and order will never submit to daily management. It was a yoke rather than a crown that he bestowed on me, a life of service rather than ownership.

'Take a look out of this window, Mr Tudor,' he continued. 'Do you have any idea what the arrival of these mines will do to this place, to these people?'

Godwin rose and came up beside Edgar. 'It might not be as ghastly as you imagine,' he said. 'There will be prosperity for many.'

'Wrong. That is not the way of industry. There will be prosperity for a few. A few who as yet are unknown to this village, this island. The many will be degraded. Their lives will be choked with harsh noise and coal dust. They will tire, age young, die in horrible accidents. A generation will spend its life in airless subterranean tunnels, the farms will go to ruin, the belched fumes of fire and commerce will settle for ever in the valley, the forests will be razed, the hillsides raped, scarred and piled with slag. Hundreds will come from the mainland to join the degradation, new local leaders will emerge bristling with ambition, corruption will breed on a scale that will make what happens today seem quaint. Thasofolia will be swamped beyond recognition, a way of life, a wonderful way of life, will come to an end and darkness will descend.'

'That is an apocalyptic view,' said Godwin quietly.

'I believe my position has earned me the privilege of being able to predict with some accuracy such an outcome and pronounce such a view. And I assure you it is not one I wish to possess.' He sighed. 'And so, you see, I have my reasons for wishing to impede the inauguration of the mines.'

'Do you think you will be able to impede them? Is not the government determined?'

For the first time, Edgar almost smiled. 'The government I will deal with in due course. I must tackle my obstacles one at a time. In the first instance I have the matter of tomorrow's events. And your potential disruption of them.'

His statement at an end, Edgar now stood in complete silence watching Godwin, whose head was lowered in thought. They remained like this for some minutes, while the noise of activity – other members of the household chatting as they came in from their afternoon's expedition – could be heard from the hall downstairs

'Tell me this, if you please,' began Godwin. 'How do you propose to have the negotiations between the brigands and the authorities in Athens performed?'

'I will undertake the role of negotiator myself,' replied Edgar. 'I am above suspicion. It is on record that I have publicly denounced my godson's lawlessness. I have been careful these past weeks to arrange my affairs so as to give the impression of an ordinary continuance of life at Thasofolia. I have even gone to the trouble of arranging for other visitors to be present here at the time of the fateful incident, as witnesses to my innocence and ignorance.'

'Myself and Pierrepont?'

Edgar nodded. 'And the learned Doctor, though he has now departed.'

'Do you not think it will be a risk for you to be so closely involved with the enactment of the plot? At some point in the negotiations you might be exposed. A word slipped, a reference made. You elect a dangerous path indeed.'

'Perhaps. But I have little option. There is no one else.'

'There is,' replied Godwin quietly. He drew a deep breath, exhaled, and looked up at Edgar. 'I could accomplish the task.'

'What can you mean?'

'Mr Brooke, do not misinterpret what I am about to say. I am appalled by your conspiracy, but I have heard your plan now, and if I do not act to disrupt it I must be seen to be in

307

accord with it, at least within my own conscience.' He paused for a moment. 'I am resolved not to subvert the plan, because I believe your intention is for the benefit of others rather than yourself. But I am not content to allow my role in this matter to end there. I would never be able to live with myself for guilt. It is therefore my intention to accompany the party, as I had intended. With my foreknowledge and private information, I will be able to impart a degree of comfort to the victims, see to it that everything proceeds smoothly and that the prisoners are treated according to the standards you yourself would insist upon; and I shall act as negotiator between the brigand captain and Sir Thomas Wishart in Athens.'

Edgar's concentration was too intent to allow the intrusion of disbelief or any expression of surprise. His eyes were half closed as he stared at Godwin, assessing the content of his demand, and weighing up the consequences.

'Why should you volunteer such a course?'

'I have given my reasons.'

'You would not, I take it, reveal to the prisoners or the brigands the fact of your foreknowledge?'

'I would not. I wish only to assist in achieving a bloodless and speedy conclusion to the whole horrible enterprise.'

'You would protect my name from exposure in this matter? And take the secret to your grave?'

'You have no option but to trust me.'

'You would be prepared to insist that the demands are met in order to bring about a happy conclusion?'

'That would be my resolve.'

'And if I refuse?'

'You cannot refuse. I now know everything. If you refuse, the plot disintegrates before your eyes, at my instigation. And that would be the end of everything. Give me your answer this evening. Nor must Mr Pierrepont be dissuaded from departing, or suspicions will be aroused. He must be released with the ladies. He will hardly increase the value of your catch and will only add to the burden of the abductors.'

'I have no objection to his release.'

'If anything were to happen to him, I should feel a particular responsibility.'

They stood together in silence for an interval, until Edgar turned towards the door. His face was dark, his mouth set grim and tight. 'I will have an answer for you before dinner,' he said, and left without waiting for a reply.

It was not merely the guilt of foreknowledge that spurred Godwin in that impulsive moment to offer his assistance to the conspiracy. Nor was it purely his feeling of responsibility for the welfare of Pierrepont, whose planned departure he had himself so satisfactorily orchestrated. There was something else, and it was calling out to be recognized. As Godwin stared into the mirror and washed his face before dinner, he secretly confessed to another motive: he was in accord with Edgar. It was a silent and shameful acknowledgement between himself and the haggard man he beheld reflected. Not that he sympathized with the plot or could ever wish mortal danger on another person, but he had heard Edgar's words, his plea, and had recognized nobility in them. And, having heard and recognized, he could not abandon this place, this family, this man, to the precarious destiny that appeared to await them. Not without first leaping across the chasm to join them. It was a bond he could neither trace nor justify, and wordlessly he searched his features in the glass for an explanation. He hadn't looked at his own face so intently for months, perhaps years. Much had changed in it, a darkness had settled on the brows. The mark of experience; wisdom, even. Though he barely allowed himself to think it, the face now told him that allegiance is not necessarily born out of clear reasoning or moral clarity, and that a portion of his allegiance, despite his better judgement, now resided at the feet of Edgar Brooke.

Godwin knew that he would have to give a plausible performance that last evening, and an excuse must be put forward for his sudden decision to leave; he made up his mind to tell everyone that he feared a change in the weather. Wintry conditions might make travel across the pass impossible until well after Christmas. Percival was the only one who seemed genuinely disturbed by this reasoning. He prided himself on matters of hospitality and on knowing what the weather was about to do. He was confused to the point of annoyance that a house guest should pronounce on the matter without having first consulted him. Mercifully for Godwin, Lydia did not come down for dinner.

He hung back after the other guests went through to the dining room, and found Edgar waiting for him in the hall, half concealed in shadow, under the rise of the great timber staircase. They looked at each other in silence. And then Edgar nodded.

'My terms are accepted?' asked Godwin quietly. Edgar saw no reason to repeat his assent, but turned and went through to join his guests. That single nod was sufficient, and indeed carried greater weight and sincerity in Godwin's eyes than a hundred words of affirmation from a lesser man.

PART THREE

Chapter 29

The travellers assembled in the courtyard the following morning as servants buckled saddle-bags, girth belts and bridles on the horses that were waiting to begin their wearisome journey. The beasts stood still and patient, their flanks rocking with the tightening of straps, rump muscles twitching, their breath clouding the cold morning air. It was a fine clear day.

As Godwin waited in the yard, he nodded a greeting towards Prince Leopold's elderly servant, but the man knew his place too well to return the pleasantry with any degree of familiarity. His strained, weather-beaten and long-suffering face seemed a little brighter this morning, perhaps because he was glad to be away from this place where he was compelled to sleep like an animal with the other staff; no one here spoke his language or made allowance for his more refined tastes. He doubtless longed to return to the comfort of his palace apartment at home. Poor fellow, thought Godwin. He little knew what lay in store for him or his master.

While the others were thanking their hosts, Godwin cast a look up every now and then to the window he knew to be Lydia's. At one point he thought he saw her form disappearing into the shadows within, as if she had noticed his gaze and quickly withdrawn to the depths of the room to hide herself. But then Mag took him quietly aside to tell him that Lydia had been at Hermann's bedside since before dawn, reading out loud, and was refusing to come down to say goodbye; and so he assumed the spectre in the window had been an illusion. The story given to everyone else was that she was still feeling unwell and sent her apologies and very kindest regards to all those departing. Prince Leopold, who seemed to have rather given up on her, shrugged off the news but had the courtliness to write her a short note expressing his regret at not having had the chance to pay his respects. Pierrepont was not so unaffected. On hearing that Lydia would not be there as they rode away, his face, which had been haggard for the past twenty-four hours, now looked blighted, as though pain and sickness had been added to his disappointment.

'She has not even the grace to see me depart,' he murmured to Godwin as he mounted. 'And here am I with my very heart ripped from my chest. Perhaps I have been blind all this time.' Godwin did not answer.

Daniel was there, and after exchanging warm embraces with the Prince he approached Godwin. He extended his hand and grasped Godwin's firmly, though no words were spoken between them. Edgar and Percival were also there, as was the entire complement of household staff. They bowed and curtsied as the Prince walked past each of them in turn. Employing one or two words of Greek that Daniel had taught him, he thanked them all for what they had done to make his stay so pleasant. He went on to exchange a word of appreciation with the two-man gendarme escort that had been arranged to accompany them. They were an unshaven, dirty pair, with ill-fitting uniforms and unctuous smiles, who almost prostrated themselves at the Prince's approach. Godwin heard Edgar explain that the pair would ride with them only to the far side of the mountain pass, at which point they would be met by a mounted detachment of militia waiting to escort them to Páparis.

Edgar gave the impression of being in reasonably high spirits. He said little to Godwin other than to observe the appropriate formalities of a host on bidding farewell to his guest. Their last private exchange had been the previous night, at the end of the rather subdued final dinner. He had spoken to Godwin quietly in a corner of the drawing room, while the others stood near the fire talking amongst themselves with their cups of tea. He had mentioned the name of the brigand captain, Demetrios Lambros, who would be informed of Godwin's special status. There was also the matter of the military escort. Godwin was not to concern himself about it, he said. Their presence had been accommodated in the plan. Not another intimate word was spoken between Godwin and Edgar; no reference to the times and talks they had shared, no mention of Lydia, no expression of goodwill, no hopes for a fortunate outcome, and no hint that they might meet again in happier times. Godwin assumed that his relationship with Edgar, the series of revelations that had propelled his journey to the heart of this fascinating man, and whatever friendship they had accrued during his stay at Thasofolia, had been effectively annulled.

The moment arrived for Panayiotis to flick his stick and start the party upon its trail. It seemed as though the whole village had assembled along the track beyond the gates, to watch and wave as the travellers rode past. The guard escort rode out at the fore, with self-important expressions, snapping harshly at children who leant forward from the crowd to get a better view. The plan was to arrive in Páparis before dark, where they were expected by Mr and Mrs Solouzos for dinner and the night. The following morning they would embark on the steamer *Bosporus* which would take them in comfort back to Piraeus. The conditions seemed perfect for travelling.

As they passed through the gates, Godwin glanced back and made fleeting eye contact with Edgar. He also looked up one last time at the house that had made such an impression on him, beautiful, unique Thasofolia, with its wondrous atmosphere, its timbers and scent of burning pine; and he looked at Lydia's window, an empty rectangle on the façade of the building. Despite himself, he mourned her in every part of his being.

The sense of loss was overpowering. They progressed silently along the track out of the village, between the fields and down towards the river, a road well known to Godwin. He could smell the trees in the morning air, a sweet and poignant reminder of the fabulous hours he had spent in the surrounding woodland. A portion of his heart would remain in this valley for ever; he comforted himself with the knowledge that no one could alter that; but his departure from it meant that he would wander the map of life for the remainder of his days an incomplete person.

As the morning continued, and they left the bowl of fertile farmland to penetrate the mountains along the pass, Godwin struggled to hide his rising sense of alarm. There could be savagery awaiting them. Who were these men that would so shortly be upon them, and how much trust could he place in Edgar's word? He knew so little. Brigand was not a word he had used much before these past weeks. It belonged with 'corsair' and 'buccaneer' in the vocabulary of childhood romances: dashing figures bristling with pistols, depicted in books he had read as a boy.

There was about an hour still to go, an hour that he wished would be interminable, and as they progressed along the precipitous path that skirted the river gorge his heart quickened with dread. Pierrepont was urging his animal forward so that he could ride alongside Godwin and pour out his troubles; but there was hardly room on the path, and the horse was reluctant to break its habit of treading the familiar route in single file.

'Damn thing,' muttered Pierrepont, kicking his heels into its flank, 'go on, sir, go on.' He eventually managed to come alongside. 'It pains me to leave, Tudor,' he said, 'though I know it is appropriate. I believe my heart is broken. How peculiar that Straker should still not raise the subject of my wife. Do you think he means to?'

Godwin's thoughts were elsewhere as he scanned the sharp flanks of the ravine through which they now travelled. There was precious little time left. 'I do not know,' he said. 'I doubt it. There is little reason to talk further on the matter.'

'You must have been very persuasive. Not only has he spared me the ignominy of having to explain myself, but he appears not to have bothered Mr Brooke with the news. I really am so very much in your debt.'

'Not at all.'

'And yet I cannot look him straight in the eye. I see from the way he regards me that his opinion of me and my behaviour is decidedly low. Do you not think?'

'I do not know. You should let the matter rest.'

'And then I think of Lydia and the happiness that might have been ours. Shattered though my life now is, I cannot but resolve to overcome this difficulty and return one day, a free man, guiltless, open-hearted. Do you believe she might recall our former tenderness?'

'How should I know?' Godwin's palms were sweating.

'You know her reasonably well,' continued Pierrepont, his gaze fixed to the horse's mane in front of him, 'you are qualified to pass an opinion, and I would value your judgement. You have already done so much for me. I do not ask you to give me a false prediction of my chances.'

A sudden movement of stones from the steep rocky slope to the right alerted Godwin's attention with a jolt. A few boulders tumbled some yards down towards them, stopping of their own accord near the bottom, so that nothing more than a barrowful of dust and gravel fell into the track.

'It was just a rock fall,' said Pierrepont, noting the flash of alarm on Godwin's face. Behind them, the Prince's servant moved alongside his master on the inside of the track, to shield him in case of any further displacements. Straker travelled silently behind Lady Wishart, and Panayiotis, who brought up the rear, wiped a wrist back and forth beneath his nose to calm an itch. None of them, aside from Godwin, seemed unusually perturbed. The two gendarmes, at the fore, in front of Mr and Mrs Farkas, barely noticed the rock fall and were hooting with laughter at a shared joke.

Pierrepont now opened his mouth to say something further, but was interrupted. There was the crack of gunshot and a rock to the left of the path exploded in a mass of fragments, one of which flew up and hit a gendarme's horse, making it rear and throw him from the saddle. The others halted on the spot, their eyes glazed with shock. Another two shots rang out, echoing across the ravine, and the other gendarme got off his horse, pulled a pistol and began to scan the higher ground, shielding his eyes from the sun.

'Stay exactly where you are!' yelled Straker. 'Just hold your hands above your heads.' Everyone obeyed this command, except the German manservant, who was off his horse and attempting to pull the Prince to the ground. 'Stop him!' shouted Straker. 'Stop him, or they'll shoot!' Prince Leopold protested to his servant to no avail, and it was only after another shot exploded at the older man's feet that he turned to face the rocky uphill slope with his hands held high. The two gendarmes were now bent low, both sporting drawn pistols and waving ineffectually at the frozen travellers to move back. A voice yelled down from the direction of the shots, attracting all eyes to the higher ground on the right.

'Do not move! Do not move!'

'For God's sake do as he says!' reiterated Straker. But before any further signal was delivered by the hidden assailant, the travellers were addressed again, and more gently, from much closer to hand. Four men now stood to their left, having appeared from nowhere while every head was turned the other way. Each of them had a pistol trained at the party, one for each of the gendarmes, the other two shared between the remainder. They were held like that for the moment, hands raised, fingers quivering with fear, while the fifth assailant scrambled down the slope to their right, rifle in hand. His companions kept their aim, eyes darting from one traveller to the next, gripping their pistols with both hands, fingers pressed against the triggers.

'Don't shoot. Please don't shoot,' came the voice of Farkas transposed to a flute-like pitch by fear. His wife shot him a look before returning her gaze to the nearest gunman, a heavy, bearded young man of about her own age with large dark eyes and the face of a child's toy bear.

From around a corner immediately in front of them there now appeared a sixth figure, a man with long hair and a moustache who wore a felt cape and hide leggings strapped around his calves. He walked towards them, thumbs tucked into his waistband, so that his elbows protruded, spreading a swathe of pleated linen sleeve like the wings of a snowy owl. He stopped in the middle of the track to observe the party, one by one, biting at his lip. He then nodded at one of his companions, an older man with a hard face, who now approached the gendarmes and pointed his pistol directly at the nearest one's face. He growled a command, and both gendarmes dropped their weapons and spread themselves out, face down, on the ground.

'Will none of us do anything?' said Prince Leopold from his saddle. 'Are we to sit here while these men are murdered?'

'I beg Your Highness to remain silent,' said Straker quietly. The brigand leader approached the helpless guards and acknowledged their compliance with a nod. One of the other brigands now came to his chief's side and began to speak in English. His accent was strong but clearly intelligible.

'I speak for my *capetanios*,' said the man, 'who is called Demetrios Lambros, and who wishes to greet you and assure you that it is not our intention to cause you any harm. We are men of business. The ladies will shortly be released and returned to Athens. The servants, who are of no value to us, will be held safely for a while until our plan is complete. The other foreign gentlemen will be kept under guard until our terms are met. Until then, the *capetanios* asks you kindly to obey all of his requests.' Demetrios then added something quietly to the man, who nodded and translated, 'It is our unfortunate duty to warn you of our serious intentions. If our demands are not met, if we are attacked, if there is any attempt at rescue, or if anyone tries to escape, we will be forced to kill you all.' The brutality of the final words was so much in contrast to his almost gallant style that several of the captives drew breath sharply and Lady Wishart let out a subdued moan of despair. The abductors now demanded that the five captive men dismount, while Demetrios and his translator (a man he addressed as Pandelis) held a quiet discussion with the two guards.

Pierrepont found himself standing next to Godwin, both of them now resting their hands on their heads while the brigands searched their clothes for valuables and hidden weapons. The ladies, spared the manual searching, were stripped of purses and jewellery.

'Did they have no intention of protecting us?' said Pierrepont quietly, looking towards the gendarmes who were now standing up and in conference with Demetrios. One of them seemed almost to smile at something Demetrios said, and nodded in agreement, as if conceding a well-argued point. 'They seem to know the ruffian. One might think they were in collusion.'

'It is for the best,' said Straker behind them, overhearing. 'If they had decided to fight it would have been ill for us. These men want only money. If they can avoid shooting, they will. But if compelled to fight they will have no hesitation in putting an end to us. Our best and only course is to do exactly as he says.'

The older brigand, who at this point stood near Straker, now turned on him. 'Pssht!' he aspirated violently in the Englishman's face, spraying him with saliva. Straker neither flinched nor blinked, but held the man's fiery gaze until he turned towards the ladies' horses. The five captives were now bunched together and guarded by the younger, heavier brigand, known as Theodoros, while the others collected around the women. From the midst of the group Mrs Farkas looked silently back at her husband, who had been speechless since dismounting, paralysed and wide-eyed, trembling. As if sensing the penetration of her gaze, he looked across the few yards that stood between them and saw that her expression was peculiarly fearless, incongruously so, thought Godwin, for one who was habitually nervous and shrank from intercourse of any kind. And yet it was not courage or resolve that characterized the look she gave her husband in their last few moments together. It appeared to be more a look of gratification, of triumph almost. Her lord and overseer had been stripped of authority and pinned, cowering, to the spot, where she could observe his quailing from the surer ground of her own equanimity.

Lady Wishart was approached by another of the brigands, the one Godwin had heard addressed as Petros, who pulled the stopper from a hide flask and held it out to her. She refused the offer with a nervous shake of the head.

The moment had come for the ladies to make their way, apparently along the main pass through the mountains towards Páparis, accompanied by the same two-man guard, who, to the captives' astonishment, had now been returned their pistols. Their instructions were to go straight to the home of Mr Solouzos, as previously planned, where they should report the incident and arrange for a telegraph to be sent to the Minister of War in Athens. The brigands' demands would shortly be forthcoming.

They were allowed a moment to say whatever farewells were appropriate before the group was split. The Prince's servant, free at last to perform his duties, dismounted and went down on one knee before his master (to the amusement of the oldest brigand, who let out a laugh and spat on the ground), imploring him urgently in German. The Prince laid a hand kindly on the older man's head but appeared to decline whatever private entreaty was being put, and it was only after the servant reiterated his plea, with a forcefulness that in ordinary life might have been considered impertinent, that one of the brigands came forward and hauled him to his feet. Still the man would not be silenced, and berated the Prince from afar, his feet dragging helplessly though the rubble of the track as he was pulled away.

Godwin turned to Lady Wishart, who had remained on her horse, and offered her his hand. She clasped it tight with her gloved fingers. He became aware for the first time that Demetrios was watching him closely from where he stood, some way off, and noticed that he had begun to walk over to him. 'Tell Sir Thomas to do everything that they ask. For God's sake,' he said.

'Of course,' she replied.

'And have him telegraph my father.'

She nodded. 'I will pray with every breath.'

Godwin smiled and squeezed her hand. 'We will meet again. In better times,' he said as she was led away. Demetrios was now by his side, and Godwin turned to face him. They were about the same height and same age. No words were spoken, but Demetrios raised his chin and cocked his head slightly to one side, as if assessing the new acquaintance's calibre and reliability. Godwin could smell garlic and an unwashed body as his captor leant forward to inspect the sides of his face, first one and then the other. Apparently satisfied, a corner of his mouth turned up into a half-smile. It was a face and an expression Godwin recognized, and after a moment the memory of his first evening at Thasofolia returned to him, when he had burst in on the private meeting in Edgar Brooke's study. Demetrios had been there.

The servants and the remaining riderless horses, accompanied by a brigand called Adonis, disappeared downhill, northwards around a rocky promontory. The five remaining captives were now left with an equivalent number of brigands, bereft of their luggage and their mounts.

'Panayiotis tells me he will somehow get word to Mr

Brooke before sundown,' said Straker to Godwin as the two smaller groups departed from them in opposite directions.

'What possible good will that do us?' said Godwin.

'It might. Brooke has influence on the island. If these men are local, he may know some of them. Or their relatives.'

'Brooke could not be associated with brigands.'

'You have much to learn about this country,' said Straker. 'Every man of influence has an association with brigands.'

These words made Godwin wonder whether Straker suspected something, but he was able to hide his apprehension at a call from Demetrios ordering them forward along the pass.

They held to the trail for just a hundred yards before cutting eastwards off the track along a goat path through a small dell, and from there picked their way beside a little brook for about an hour, by which time they were well hidden from the main route, and Demetrios called a halt. He bade them all be seated and then spoke through his translator. His voice was quiet and his manner courteous as he explained the hazards and difficulties they would face together. They were made to feel not so much like prisoners as joint participants in an enterprise they would all – brigands and captives – prefer to have done with sooner rather than later. They would stop now briefly, he said, as the oldest brigand, known as Christos, handed round some bread and cheese, and eat what they could, because from this moment there would be no resting. It was essential that they put as much distance as possible between them and the scene of the abduction. They could rest again at seven, but would be travelling for most of the night ahead.

'What are your demands?' asked Pierrepont. The other brigands looked up at him from their food, and then across to Pandelis to hear his translation. Demetrios paused for a moment and then continued in the same reasonable tone. They were demanding a sum of five hundred thousand drachmas for the release of each of the four gentlemen, a

total of two million drachmas, in addition to an unconditional royal amnesty for all six members of the band.
Only when both sets of demands had been met would they
be released.

'Close to sixty-five thousand pounds,' said Straker quietly
to Godwin. 'A princely sum, to be sure. They must know
whom they have caught.'

'*Do any of you villains know a word of German?*' Prince
Leopold asked the brigands suddenly, in his own language,
and looked at their blank faces for a moment before turning
to Straker. '*They are ignorant. You know a little German?*'

'*Indeed.*'

'*This sum is nothing. It will take no more than a stroke of the
pen to ensure my release.*'

'*But there is the matter of the amnesty.*'

'*Surely that won't be a problem. The King is one of us. He will
grant it instantly.*'

'*The King does not have such powers under the new
Constitution. It must be the government's decision. And amnesties
for brigandage are not legal.*'

'*Cannot the law be changed?*'

'*I doubt it.*'

'*Does Greece want an invasion from England and Germany?
When Athens hears who has been captured the whole matter will
be resolved swiftly.*'

Pierrepont interrupted the German discussion to address
Pandelis. 'Wait a moment. You say there will be a demand for
the release of four gentlemen. But there are five of us. What
is to happen to the fifth?'

Pandelis translated the question, and Demetrios sat still
for a moment, observing the questioner. He then turned to
Pandelis and spoke to him quietly, out of earshot, and in a
local dialect that would be impossible for the foreigners to
comprehend.

'*Is this the one?*'

'*The pervert. Yes.*'

324

'He's scared.'

'He has reason to be.'

'The one to his right. That's our man.'

'Are you going to speak to him?'

'Not yet. Let him sweat with the others. Then he'll do his job properly.'

All the while this dialogue was taking place, Christos, the older, rough-faced brigand, sat aside from the others working on his pistol with a cloth and a small phial of oil. It was a magnificent weapon, fabulously engraved with gleaming metalwork, its wood blackened with age and use.

Demetrios now spoke to Pierrepont through Pandelis. One of them was to be the bearer of their terms to Athens, he said, and would return with the reply.

'Which of us is it to be?' asked Pierrepont. 'Will you choose the one with the least ability to raise such a ransom?'

'The *capetanios* says that he has not yet decided,' came Pandelis' reply. Godwin looked down and took a mouthful of bread. He cast a glance at Farkas sitting beside him, apparently in a daze, his food untouched.

'Go on, have some,' he said to him. 'You will need the sustenance.' Farkas slowly turned his face to look at Godwin but his eyes did not seem to focus; they wandered beyond, to the landscape behind Godwin's head, and then in a wide, slow arc back to where they had previously rested.

They had sat for barely ten minutes when Demetrios ordered them forward, now splitting the party in two, which Godwin suspected was a tactic to confuse anyone who might attempt to follow their trail. Godwin, Pierrepont and Straker were accompanied by Demetrios, Pandelis and Christos. Prince Leopold and Farkas departed from them in a more easterly direction with Petros, the gentle-faced member of the band and the heavy-set younger brigand, Theodoros. The route was almost entirely uphill and pathless, and they had to find their way between gorse thickets, sometimes forcing themselves through walls of brambles. Before long Godwin's thighs ached with the strain, and the repeated impression of sharp rocks under his soles began to bruise. Countless spherical burrs had attached themselves to the bottoms of his trousers, and the prick of ground holly was an incessant irritation to his ankles. They progressed in single file. Theodoros brought up the rear of the group, and would sweep a branch across the trail to obliterate all trace of their passage.

Pierrepont, immediately behind Godwin, spoke up between panting. 'You must understand, Tudor, that a ransom of that size placed upon my head will spell certain doom for me. Neither I, nor my family in its entirety, would be able to raise even a small portion of it.'

'Do not be too concerned yet. The leader seems a reasonable man. As soon as he realizes your limitations he will adjust his demand accordingly. I am sure of it.'

'Do you not think I should be selected to go to Athens? In view of my comparative poverty, and familiarity with the country?'

'I predict that decision will be made without reference to our points of view.'

'Yes, of course,' said Pierrepont, and continued in silence. Godwin was gagged by the circumstances but presumed Pierrepont would be released imminently. Edgar would see to it.

Straker, heavier and less agile than the others, was suffering with the strain. 'We will have to cross the water at some point,' he mentioned quietly to Godwin, 'and that will not be without risks. The Pyroxenian channel is notorious for its treacherous tidal currents.'

'You think they intend to take us over to the mainland?' asked Godwin.

'Unquestionably they must, in order to communicate effectively with Athens. They will be compelled to station us near to if not within the borders of Attica.'

'Will that not be walking into the lion's mouth?'

'I think not. The closer we are to Athens, the more control the government and the Legation will have in order to prevent the spontaneous use of force by hot-headed local militia. It is neither in the brigands' nor our own interests for there to be attempts at armed rescue.'

In contrast to the Englishmen, the three brigands – even Christos, who looked over fifty – were agile, light-footed and seemingly unaffected by the relentless gradient of the route. Their waists were narrow, their physiques lean and wiry, and they sprang like goats from rock to rock. It occurred fleetingly to Godwin that if this situation were, in the last resort, to be resolved in a contest of man against man, the five Europeans, for all their influence, wealth and learning, would not stand a chance against men as fit and strong as these.

When at last they reached the summit of the hill, Demetrios raised a hand for the party to stop. It was now that Christos cupped his leathery hands around his mouth and began a series of high-pitched animal calls. Moments later, from far off, came a single matching call, the sound of which seemed to satisfy the brigands, and Demetrios started them quietly on their route once more.

The going became rather easier as they held the level high ground for a while before descending to a valley. As the afternoon drew on, the light began to diminish, and by the time they reached the river-bed dusk had settled in. They finally came to a halt just at the point when they could barely see more than a few yards ahead of them. They had arrived at a small clearing where a log hut was set back from the river, its roof tiled with rough wooden slats, and with a little fire alight outside. Five horses were tied to a tree nearby. The Englishmen and their captors went into the hut and found that the other party, with Prince Leopold and Farkas, was already assembled there and had begun to eat supper, a fact that caused some joking and laughter amongst the brigands. The Prince glanced at Godwin and nodded a greeting. Farkas, who had refused his food again, did not look up. The new arrivals sat down on the ground beside the others, barely finding space to squeeze into the building and pull down its goatskin flap. Moments later another man appeared at the entrance with bread, cheese and olives, which he distributed among the newcomers. They sat and ate in silence.

Demetrios had his knees up and spread apart. He took a swig of grape juice, swallowed his mouthful, looked across at Farkas and smiled.

'Hey, it's not so bad, friend,' he said. 'Why do you look so sad? We'll soon have this over.'

'He doesn't speak Greek,' said Petros.

'You don't speak Greek? Prick. Is this what we fought the Turks for? To spawn a nation of pricks who prefer foreign money to their own country? You really can't even speak Greek?'

'When the game is rolling we should start with that one,' said Christos. 'I already hate him. I volunteer to do the job.'

'Not so fast,' said Demetrios, smiling. 'We'll stay with the plan.'

Prince Leopold without warning spat out the contents of his mouth and turned to look sharply at Demetrios. 'I have had enough,' he said. He looked towards Pandelis. 'Ask your master if he knows who I am.'

Demetrios was looking at him calmly, his arms resting on his knees as he chewed bread and olives. He nodded a reply to the Prince, and removed an olive stone from between his lips. Then he called something to the man outside the hut, who returned a moment later carrying a hunk of salted meat. Demetrios gestured for Leopold to take it. This was a boon for the Prince alone, Pandelis translated on Demetrios' behalf. He must have the meat, which the rest of them would be denied, out of respect for his royal status.

'I do not want your filthy meat,' snapped the Prince. 'I demand that you release me. And these gentlemen. And if you desire to keep your heads I advise you to obey me.'

Demetrios drank another mouthful and muttered something to Pandelis.

'My *capetanios* regrets your discomfort and wishes you every respect, but says that we are in Greece, and he is Greek, and a Greek bows to no foreigner.'

'And tell the fucker that if he pisses me off I'll get Christos to cut his prick off,' Demetrios added. Christos grunted a laugh and nodded.

'And he asks that you will do everything you can to remain calm,' concluded Pandelis. Leopold spouted a furious run of expletives in German before falling silent and finishing his food.

Demetrios looked around the small room at his fellow brigands.

'Well, the boy knows how to talk dirty. At least they teach their kings something.'

They all laughed, and Demetrios then settled them down and began to talk quietly in the same unintelligible dialect he had employed earlier in the day. Godwin looked across the floor at Straker, a formidable linguist, who sat quite still, eyes cast down. His repeated blinking showed the intensity of his concentration as he tried to interpret the drift of their talk. Later, when the captives were ushered outside and led towards the waiting horses, Straker had a quiet word with Godwin.

'They have it all worked out. It was nigh on impossible to understand, but it would appear our route takes us across a succession of fiefdoms according to a precise time plan. Several names were mentioned, individuals I presume who hold influence in the areas we are to traverse, who have lent their assistance. Few dare refuse men of this sort for fear of reprisals in the future. I should say we are safe enough while on the island. It may not be so easy on the mainland.'

'It would seem we are to continue on horseback. Thank God for that, at least,' said Godwin.

'One part of their conversation perplexes me, however,'

said Straker, lowering his voice and turning slightly away from the nearest brigand. 'I have the impression somebody else is involved in this plan. It may be a larger conspiracy than we suspect.'

'You have just said that several may have been enlisted.'

'No, I do not mean that. It is someone more vital to the plan. Someone who stands to benefit. Perhaps the principal beneficiary and inspiration.'

Godwin hid the sweep of alarm that flooded across his abdomen. 'Who? Have you any notion?'

'They did not mention a name.' He lowered his voice to a whisper. 'They refer to him instead as the *koumbaros*.'

'The what?'

'*Koumbaros*. It is a term employed to denote one's spiritual kin. Such as a chief groomsman at a wedding. Not a relation by blood, but by emotional affinity. In some ways it carries greater obligations for a Greek than ties of brotherhood and family.'

'And who is this person?'

'That I cannot ascertain. But it is clearly somebody upon whom the leader here has placed great reliance.'

'Another member of the gang.'

'More than that, I believe.' Their conversation came to an end as Demetrios walked towards them and gestured for them to mount their horses. It was very dark in the valley now, and Godwin felt the prick of minute raindrops on his skin. Straker moved without delay towards a horse but Godwin dallied for a moment, taking advantage of the gloom to allow Demetrios the opportunity to approach him and register a private understanding between them, wordlessly, if needs be. The chief brigand now stood next to him, bending down to adjust one of the straps on his leggings, and then slung his woven *tagari* bag over his shoulder. When he looked up and saw Godwin still standing there, his expression changed to one of impatience, and he flipped open his palms as if to question the reason for the unnecessary delay. Godwin was shocked at his apparent annoyance and the absence of the smallest hint of recognition; the terrible possibility then occurred to him that Edgar might have failed to inform Demetrios about the change of plan, perhaps deliberately; or the brigands might have decided to take the matter into their own hands. As they began to move off in single file, he turned this appalling thought over. With Godwin dead, the conspirators' lives would be safer and their plans simpler. The close shroud of night, the cold air and the increasingly heavy fall of rain intensified his sudden sense of vulnerability.

The brigands were continuing on foot, each holding the reins of a horse. They showed not the least sign of tiredness, despite the dark, the changing weather and the effects of the long day's travelling, and they moved across the uncertain terrain with as much fleet-footed energy as they had hours earlier in the full light of day.

Godwin glanced at Christos who walked beside him. The short sabre sheathed in his waistband had a wide blade and a comfortable leather handle. The possibilities for the use of such a weapon were unspeakably frightening. It was against a backdrop of fear, cross-reasoning and suppressed impatience that Godwin now worked to fight off his tiredness. He considered yelling forward to Straker, to betray the plot in case he left it too late and was silenced before he could take action. But he stopped himself. The surest way to precipitate the shedding of blood at this stage would be to threaten the brigands with failure.

As the night drew on the rain set in, and its dull patter on the ground and foliage masked the sound of their passing. The brigands wrapped themselves in heavy felt capotes, but the captives had nothing more to protect them than the clothes they had been wearing when abducted. The wet drenched them through to the skin, and at one point Pierrepont asked if he could walk for a while rather than ride, to warm himself up. Farkas could not keep awake, and twice

331

slid off his saddle into the mud, until the brigands prevented it by lashing him prostrate to the horse's back, his arms tied tight in an embrace around its neck.

All sense of time was lost to Godwin. Submerged in tiredness, shivering and soaking, he focused only on the small area that surrounded him, as if embryonically contained. He felt incongruously secure within his imagined bubble, as though moving through a narrow tunnel beyond whose boundaries the world was for the moment both unknown and irrelevant. He could feel the bulky square of his journal, safe and dry next to his undershirt. No-one had objected to his keeping it, thank God. It offered a grain of homely comfort, reminding him that there might come a time when he could read and reflect on all this.

His thoughts were eventually numbed into stillness, his fears anaesthetized, though his eyes remained open and he kept a continual awareness of passing through space. Thus it was that he knew they were descending, though he had not the smallest idea for how long; the narrow tunnel around him pointed down, and as the gradient continued he felt his pelvis tilted rearwards and the rhythmic jolt of the horse's hind muscles resisting the slope.

When one of the brigands called a halt and the horses came to a stop, he was conscious of their arrival at the waterfront, and knew that the time had come to cross over to the mainland. The brigands, as alert as ever, moved quickly to usher their hostages into the two waiting boats. There were other shadowy figures present, different people, taking charge of the horses, whispering urgently, glancing at the captives, passing packages, embracing, pointing. Godwin looked out into the blackness across the water in the direction of their gestures, and in the far distance, well over to their right, was aware of a torch flame.

Once they were in the boats, the brigands rowed urgently, steering leftwards, seemingly away from the waiting flare. It was a tactic Godwin soon realized was designed to counter the effects of the cross-current, a local hazard of infamous repute, which flowed from the left with ever greater strength as they progressed into the channel. It took the straining might of four oarsmen to keep the vessel on course and steady, struggling against the flow. The water lapped and splattered at the sides of the boat in defiance of their efforts. At one point the power of the current overwhelmed them, and Godwin's boat, ripped from the control of the oarsmen, began to spin as it was swept into the blackness by unseen eddies and rapids. There was much yelling and heaving as they fought to bring themselves back on course, which they succeeded in accomplishing at last, though both boats came to rest on the far shore at least half a mile beyond their intended staging post.

The brigands pulled the boats ashore and led their captives over the barren, rough ground of the mainland coast until they reached the flaming torch, which was manned by the sixth member of their band, Adonis, the one who had accompanied Panayiotis and the prince's servant from the scene of the abduction. He must have delivered his prisoners to their holding place and then hurried on by the main route, through Páparis, over the bridge and southwards along the far coast, in order to have reached this point, their pre-arranged rendezvous. The torch was hastily doused as the brigands warmly greeted the small, quick-eyed Adonis before they began to head uphill and inland on foot without further delay.

As the eastern sky began to show the faintest sign of paling they arrived at a hamlet of five cottages, one of which the Europeans were now asked to enter. A fire was burning in the hearth and a man was waiting for them. His eyes were frightened and his movements quick as he prepared bread and dried figs, first for the captives and then for each of the brigands. Demetrios was in high spirits, and joined hands with his colleagues one by one in celebration of having come so far without obstruction.

After having eaten and drunk, the hostages were invited to

remove their clothes so that they could be dried by the fire in the short time available. It was an offer accepted by all except Prince Leopold, who refused to acknowledge Pandelis' question but sat silent and motionless before the hearth, knees drawn up in front of him. The others shared out between them a number of woollen rugs and skins, under which they now lay, body pressed to naked body for warmth, and attempted to sleep while the brigands sat together drinking coffee and whispering their plans for the next day.

It seemed no more than minutes before Godwin felt a hand roughly shaking his shoulder and looked up to see the ruthless face of Christos over him; the brigand's finger was pressed to his lips in deadly warning to remain silent. Godwin was being beckoned to an adjoining room. His clothes, still damp, were in a creased pile next to his head, and he carried them with him as he got up from the fireside, his hands shaking uncontrollably with combined fear and cold. His chances were pretty much even, he thought in that instant moment of assessment. What awaited him in the next room, while the others slept here unawares, was either a reprieve or execution.

Chapter 30

Two days later, Athens awoke to a pleasant morning, pleasant by any standards for the time of year. As the dawn sun rose above the Hymettus skyline it panned clear and golden across the marble pediments of the Parthenon, and by degrees cut shafts of brilliance through the dusty air of the city's new avenues below. But for Sir Thomas Wishart, who was behind his desk by seven-thirty, the fair weather, for once, brought neither warmth nor comfort. In fact, he had just chastised the Legation housekeeper for not having lit the fires early enough this morning; his office was chilly, which only added to his vexation. Indeed he was more vexed than he had been since assuming his position as British Minister in the Greek capital. He sat quite still with his elbows on his desk, as he heard the ubiquitous grind and clamour of the city's builders beginning their day's work. The fingertips of his hands were delicately arched and formed a cage in front of his nose, behind which his face was hidden. His eyes were firmly closed and his lips tight. This whole galling matter would be a test of his mettle, he knew. And to think that it might so easily not have happened at all. The next few years might have rolled on peaceably enough, the Foreign Secretary would have recalled him shortly to a life of comfortable retirement; a summons from the palace would have come and a peerage or something better would have been inevitable. It might yet go that way if a disaster could be forestalled, if this unnecessary, infuriating incident could be put to rest quickly and effectively. One thing was certain:

he would be judged by his handling of the events that were about to unroll, and if matters were to escalate out of his control, his reputation might be blackened beyond redemption.

There was a knock on the door and his secretary came in to announce the arrival of the first of his two expected visitors. It was Mr Tudor. Sir Thomas awoke from his unpleasant reverie into the even less pleasant immediacy of the forthcoming encounter, but hid his discomfiture and instructed that the visitor be allowed through at once. And so it begins, he thought in his final moment of solitary reflection. It would have been better if the wretches had released the Prince instead, but Mr Tudor was preferable to one of the others. If everything were to go wrong, the fewer recognizable family names involved in a disaster the better.

The first he had known about the abduction had been the previous morning, when news came through on a telegraph from Mr Solouzos in Páparis that Prince Leopold's party had been ambushed by brigands, but that Lady Wishart and Mrs Farkas were unharmed and would be returning to Piraeus by ship today. They would be back in Athens before nightfall. A further message from Solouzos had advised him that appalling consequences might ensue if any action were taken before the brigands' precise demands were articulated, and for that they must wait until contacted by a messenger. Such contact had been made before dawn this morning in the form of a note delivered to Sir Thomas' home from the Hotel d'Angleterre, and scribbled by none other than Mr Tudor, who had been released by the brigands for that very purpose. Tudor had apparently travelled for two days and a night without a stop, eventually arriving long after midnight at his hotel, whereupon he had washed, changed and rested for a moment before sending his note to say that he bore with him the brigands' terms and that Sir Thomas should send for the War Minister to be in attendance when these terms were presented.

Godwin now entered the room, the same room where he had last stood alongside Fortinbras Pierrepont a few weeks earlier to receive Sir Thomas' advice about travelling in Greece.

How little had changed in the appearance of the room or its occupant, thought Godwin, and yet how much had occurred to affect the way he would henceforth regard the rather stunted man who now stood up as he entered. Despite Godwin's own British citizenship, there was no sense of comfort or security for him in this displaced slice of Westminster officialdom. In his heart he was impatient to return to the captives as soon as possible. He felt cheated not to be sharing every minute of hardship and danger with them, and he wondered why that should be. It certainly wasn't heroism that made him want to get back. Perhaps it was guilt, because he had been released while the others remained in fear of their lives. Perhaps the experience of shared danger had revealed to him a depth of comradeship he had never previously known. Or perhaps it all stemmed, link by link, from his irredeemable loss, his departure from Thasofolia. How drab this world was in comparison to that inhabited by Edgar Brooke, how bereft of enchantment. The fugitive band of captors and captives belonged somehow to that other place, and they represented his last link to it. And, above all, his last link to her. He was still Edgar's man and representative, the one on whom the fortunes of Thasofolia and the Brooke clan rested.

Sir Thomas now shook him by the hand and muttered his regrets and hopes for a quick solution.

'Have you heard news of Lady Wishart?' were Godwin's first words.

'She is safe. Thank you. And returning to Athens with Mrs Farkas. The hostages were unharmed when you left them?'

'They were well enough. Sleeping, actually. Though the conditions are uncommonly harsh, I believe they will remain unharmed for as long as their captors can be sure of no intervention. The brigands' demands must immediately be met. They will not hesitate to take extreme action should it become apparent to them that their enterprise might fail.'

Sir Thomas frowned. 'If it were my decision alone I would see to it that the matter was sorted peacefully without delay. But I fear the Greek government will not comply. And we have yet to inform London. I cannot say it is the English way to obey the commands of peasant bandits. Especially peasant bandits who are holding a relative of our own Queen.'

'If you do other than obey them, sir,' responded Godwin calmly, inclining his head and fixing Sir Thomas with a look that left no room for contradiction, 'they will execute that relative of our Queen. Allow me to emphasize this certainty now and I shall not have to repeat it at a later stage.'

Sir Thomas blinked and pursed his lips. 'I understand,' he said. 'Although whatever decisions I make will be governed by the response of the Foreign Secretary. And he has yet to hear the demands, as have I. You have them with you, I presume?'

Godwin explained that he had been told to deliver the letter to none other than Kostas Paleologos, the Minister of War, but that he could summarize them briefly. The brigands demanded that he return to their new base, nearer the capital, with an official response by sunset on Thursday – tomorrow – and assuming everything went according to their design, they would send him back to Athens on Friday with details of how the exchange of money, amnesty documents and prisoners was to be effected. It was their hope to conclude matters by Sunday.

Sir Thomas paused for a moment in thought before speaking. 'The sums are high indeed but not impossible to realize,' he said. 'We will telegraph the Foreign Secretary who in turn will see to it that the families of the prisoners are alerted.' He rose to his feet and began to pace the room. 'But it is the matter of the amnesty that will incur more serious obstructions. In

King Otho's day such things were commonplace, and that is perhaps why there was so much lawlessness. No-one, least of all the present Prime Minister, who is holding on to his position by a thread, wishes a return to the dark old days. The granting of amnesties under the new Constitution is no longer considered a royal prerogative. We may have to propose an alternative.' He continued on his circuit as noises from beyond the door indicated that the other visitor had arrived.

A knock on the door now preceded the entry of a short stout man, who pushed past the secretary and stalked into the room without waiting for an invitation. His clothes were tight fitting, buttoned to straining point, probably cut in the days before he had reached such rotundity, and his neck was wedged tight in its stiff collar, as if splinted, which meant that he had to turn from the waist in order to face whomever he chose to address. And at this moment that person was Sir Thomas, whom he eyed fiercely before conceding a greeting in heavily accented French. His voice was gruff and frosted.

'Good morning, Minister,' replied Sir Thomas, also in French. Even if Kostas Paleologos spoke some English, it was well known that he was too defiantly patriotic to flatter foreigners with the use of their own mother tongue. 'Allow me to introduce to you Mr Tudor, who has recently arrived in Athens having been released by the brigands. He has brought with him a letter for you from them.'

Paleologos cocked Godwin a furious glance and held out a hand, not in offer of greeting but as a demand that he submit the document without more ado. As he snatched the envelope and began to rip it open, he said, again in French, 'The Prime Minister wishes me to inform you that this is a problem for Greece, and that it will be handled by the Greek people, without the assistance of outsiders.'

Sir Thomas answered without smiling, 'And on behalf of Her Majesty we should like to thank you for your assurance. We have no doubt that there will be a speedy conclusion to the whole unfortunate incident.'

'These shepherd scum must not be allowed to hold our nation to ransom. We do not want your warships. The days of your Lord Palmerston are history.'

'I assure you,' replied Wishart, 'that Mr Gladstone has much admiration and personal affection for your great nation. I do not believe he will approve the sending of British troops.'

'The Prime Minister wishes me to say that Greece's other allies will not tolerate a British show of force. Especially our Russian friends,' said Paleologos, removing a fat index finger from the torn envelope and wagging it in front of Sir Thomas' waistcoat. He now cast down his eyes and squinted at the coarsely written Greek text of the letter. It took him just moments to read, and he all but spat his response, a vicious expression of disgust that made Godwin's heart sink.

'Five hundred thousand for each prisoner. And a pardon! Are they mad? Not one of them will finish this with a head on his neck, I swear it.' Godwin darted a look at Sir Thomas who was blinking repeatedly but staring at the floor. Paleologos was clearly not of a mind to be contradicted. 'Do they think we will allow ourselves to be laughed at by the whole world? Wait until their blood is flowing into the sewer and then see who will be laughing!'

Still Wishart did not respond, and so Godwin spoke up, calmly, imbuing his tone with as much deference as his patience would allow. 'Sir, with respect, I believe the sums of money demanded can be met. The families of the prisoners will prefer to part with such sums rather than endanger the lives of their loved ones.'

Paleologos twisted his torso in the direction of Godwin and glared daggers at him for his impertinence. 'And then what? No-one will be safe in Greece again! Brigands will be everywhere! Like before.'

Godwin remained coldly unemotional. 'Sir, these prisoners will be dead before the first shot of your assault is fired. One hint of an attack and it will all be over. Prince Leopold

340

as well. What will the world think of Greece then?'

'Mr Tudor, allow me,' interrupted Sir Thomas, placing a hand between them and then turning to smile at Paleologos. 'Minister, now that we have the demands, let us return the matter to our respective governments before we say anything further. There will be a resolution to which we shall all be in agreement, I am quite sure of that.'

Paleologos grunted an incomprehensible word and shook off his anger with a wobble of the jowls, like a dog drying itself after clambering from a river. 'You will not expect us to break our own laws.'

'How could we ever contemplate such a notion?' said Sir Thomas.

'The amnesty is out of the question.'

'We have every confidence in the Greek government.'

Godwin held his tongue, and Paleologos' mood subsided, now that his point had been plainly made. He took a seat, crossed his legs and began to discuss the basic practicalities of the crisis, asking Godwin to approximate the location, describe the condition of the hostages and the supplies available to them. The change in his manner was pronounced; he now seemed interested, helpful and almost affable, listening carefully to all of Godwin's replies and making useful suggestions of his own. Above all, he stressed, while the negotiations were proceeding, the captives must be made to feel safe and measures should be taken to ease their hardship. He felt sure, he said, heaving round his torso to address Sir Thomas, that this was one area in which the English could contribute most usefully to the situation. Wishart did not respond to the patronizing tone of this remark, but smiled and nodded, adding that he would see to it at once that Mr Tudor returned to the captives laden with supplies.

Their conversation came to an end an hour after it had begun, with Mr Paleologos shaking Godwin warmly by the hand, expressing his hope that he would not judge Greece and Greeks by the actions of a handful of peasants. He added that his government's formal response would be presented to him at six o'clock the following morning, here at the Legation, but that for obvious reasons, details of how the Prime Minister intended to proceed must remain confidential.

Satisfied that national pride had remained untarnished, and that he had achieved an effective articulation of his position, the War Minister now took hat and coat and withdrew from their presence, his short legs strutting purposefully towards the carriage that awaited him on the street outside, where a small crowd had begun to gather.

'Word is out,' commented Sir Thomas, looking out of the window at his departing visitor and noticing the onlookers. 'By tomorrow morning the newspapers will have nothing else to report. This will become a political battleground for the opposing parties. It is no wonder the little man was so adamant. He and his leader might be out of a job before the month is through.'

Godwin spoke quietly. 'I take it I can have your assurance that the Greek government will not be permitted to authorize an attack?'

Wishart sighed and turned to face him, but avoided looking him in the eye. 'We can express our opinions in the strongest terms, but short of invading the country with our own army we cannot enforce them. This is a delicate matter. Four great powers are competing for the friendship of the Greek government. British political influence in this corner of the world depends on our retaining that friendship. If these men,' he gestured vaguely in the direction of the Acropolis, 'especially the Prime Minister, feel they are being bullied into a situation that will bring about their own political doom, they will respond like cornered dogs and bite the nearest person to find a way out.'

'Telegraph the Foreign Secretary,' said Godwin. 'Telegraph my father, anyone who might extend their influence to Mr Gladstone.'

Sir Thomas replied that he would send straight to the palace in Athens and request an audience immediately. King George, he said, could also claim family relationship to Prince Leopold, and although considered something of a joke by the more hardened and veteran members of the Athens establishment, his voice was sure to be heard in the debate. They could count on him for support.

Shortly after, Godwin found himself out on the pavement again, the sun now streaming into Stadion Street from the direction of Constitution Square. Several people in the crowd outside began to shout questions at him, which spurred him quickly on up the street towards his hotel. To his dismay, another crowd had assembled at the d'Angleterre, and he had to push his way into the lobby. Heads turned to watch his progress towards the grand staircase, but he managed to reach his room without further interception, and collapsed on the bed.

One thought, above all others, hung above him as he drifted into an unsettled sleep: something had gone wrong with the plan. Either Edgar had failed to pass the message to the brigands, or Demetrios had taken matters into his own hands. Either way, the implications were the same: Fortinbras Pierrepont had not been released, and if anything were now to happen to him, the blame would rest squarely on the shoulders of Godwin Tudor; for having compelled him to remove himself from Thasofolia – and from Lydia.

Chapter 31

The guards at the Attic border post of Sikamino looked with silent curiosity at the caravan that was approaching from the Athens road. They had spotted it some way off as it emerged into view around the edge of Mount Parnitha, and over the hour or so that it drew near, they began to see more clearly who was coming – about twenty uniformed and mounted soldiers, a single man in black in their midst, and a small mule-cart at the rear. It was quite an event in the guards' otherwise mundane spell of duty, something to lighten the dreariness of this rather barren, rocky and windswept outreach of Attica. Earlier that same morning a dispatch rider had arrived to warn them that an official party would be arriving later in the day. There would be a foreign gentleman in the group who should be permitted to pass through the border without impediment. Furthermore, there would be men arriving from the other side of the boundary who were to accompany the foreigner into the province of Boeotia. No attempt should be made to intercept, detain or question these men, unless commanded to do so by the captain of the mounted militia. This was by order of the highest authority in the land, the guards were told.

It was a dull, cold afternoon, and Godwin had a woollen blanket wrapped around his shoulders. The ten-hour ride from Athens had been a silent, solemn affair. They had departed before dawn, and Sir Thomas Wishart, joined by an official party of Greek government representatives, had been at the Legation to see him off. Aside from the militia, he was

344

accompanied by a cart carrying supplies: food, fresh clothes, blankets and wine. There was also an amount of money sent by Sir Thomas to the brigands as a token of good faith. But the essential item that he carried with him in his pocket, the narrow envelope with its single sheet, so eagerly awaited by both captors and captives in their place of hiding, contained news less heart-warming and cheery than anything packed on the cart.

Godwin had spent the long journey to this point trying to predict which of several possible reactions Demetrios might have to the War Minister's response. Much would depend on the manner of the Minister's wording, and of that he had no inkling. If his rejection of the terms was phrased with as much anger as his initial response the previous morning, it might provoke a fatal fit of pique on the part of the brigand, and they might all be doomed. Sir Thomas had warned him to ameliorate any potentially impulsive reaction with an assurance from the British Foreign Secretary personally that the money would shortly be raised and that Wishart himself would see to its delivery. The approach must be co-operative rather than combative.

The border guards boiled up their coffee-pots when they estimated the party would be with them in about ten minutes, and Godwin accepted a cup of the dark, grainy fluid thankfully, easing himself back on a chair to relax after so long in the saddle; but he barely had time to finish it before he spotted, across the plain about half a mile into Boeotia, a solitary horseman waiting. He got up to leave without delay, aware that there was no time to waste, and keen that in every respect he must be seen by the brigands to be entirely compliant with their terms. He took leave of the troop captain, and, holding on to the cart-mule with an extended rein, trotted across the frontier to where his man stood waiting. He had little doubt there would be others hidden behind rocks or bushes, their rifles at the ready in case of betrayal, but was surprised in the event that only one other joined them, coming up alongside a mile or so beyond the rendezvous. His two escorts were the brothers, Petros and Theodoros Lekas, and as soon as sufficient distance had been covered, the younger, Theodoros, broad-chested, with a thick mop of dark curls, greeted Godwin warmly, slapping him on the back and smiling, as if reunited with an old comrade. His older brother seemed no less amiable but had a quieter, less demonstrative way of showing it. Godwin felt pleased to see them, although he could not ignore the peculiarity of his predicament: locked in an embrace with an unwashed peasant who might yet prove to be his executioner.

The journey to their encampment – a collection of shepherds' huts on a hillside some fifteen miles north-west of the frontier post – was shorter than Godwin had been expecting, and they arrived before the last of the daylight subsided. The brigand party had moved considerably nearer Athens since he had left them, as Straker had predicted. They were clearly confident of a degree of acquiescence on the part of the Greek government and believed there would be no rescue attempt.

As Godwin rode up to the huts, Pierrepont appeared running towards him, arms outstretched, followed by Straker. Prince Leopold stood behind them, in shirt-sleeves, hands on hips, an expression of eager enquiry on his face. Dishevelled and stripped of his usual spruce dignity, he looked younger, more athletic and lively, like the boy he was. He and Straker showed a stubbly growth of beard, though the fair-haired Pierrepont had no more than the merest adolescent sprinkling under his nose. Of Farkas there was no sign. Godwin thought the hostages looked healthy and relaxed, though drawn, and they seemed to be enjoying relative freedom of movement, a fact which spoke of trust and mutual under-standing between them and the brigands, something that had presumably evolved in the time they had spent together since Godwin's departure. Demetrios now emerged from one of the huts and came towards him, smiling broadly, while Christos and Adonis turned their attention to the laden cart, pulling at its ropes and examining the parcels.

Demetrios opened his palms and turned to his fellow brigands, grinning.

'*What did I say? These Englishmen. They may be poofs but when they say they'll do something you can be sure it'll be done.*' He slapped his hands together and called Pandelis over to translate.

'Have you got the letter?' he asked through Pandelis.

'I have brought money,' replied Godwin eagerly, reaching to his saddle-bags. 'Not the ransom yet, but a gift of good-will. From Sir Thomas Wishart.'

'*How kind. Only now does he acknowledge the friendship we have had all these years!*' The other brigands burst out laughing. '*And so. The letter?*'

'Sir Thomas also wishes to convey his assurance that you will not be harmed. You will be free and safe for the moment to move without fear of intervention.'

'For the moment?' There was a flicker of seriousness in Demetrios' eyes and Godwin cursed his own choice of words.

'Well that's marvellous!' said Pierrepont.

'*Hey look at this,*' called Christos from beside the cart. '*Salted beef. Fresh chicken. Wine. The koumbaros was right. These men we've caught are kings.*'

'The letter,' repeated Demetrios.

Godwin continued to fiddle with the straps of his saddle-bags. 'And the best news is that Sir Thomas has telegraphed London. All the money you demand is being raised. He will see to its realization in Athens personally.'

'Tudor, you are a miracle,' said Pierrepont. 'Who is paying my share?'

'It does not matter for the moment, does it?' muttered Godwin.

Demetrios walked up to him now, until his face was within inches of Godwin's. His breath smelt like an old stable. Pandelis was at his heel.

'I want the letter. The government's answer,' he said, the smile fading on his lips.

Godwin looked him in the eye and hesitated a fraction. 'Of course,' he replied, and fumbled in his pocket to retrieve the document. Straker, sensing his alarm, moved quietly in and stood by his side.

'The ladies?' he asked quietly.

'Safely home. Tell Mr Farkas.' Straker did not immediately go but watched as Godwin found the letter.

Behind him, Prince Leopold was helping to unpack the cart and had discovered something that was causing him and Theodoros much hilarity. Neither spoke the other's language and they were irreconcilably divided by culture and society, but the two men had found common ground in humour and were bent double with laughter.

Godwin passed the letter. 'It is from Mr Paleologos,' he explained to Pandelis. 'And he is not of a conciliatory disposition though there is no doubt that he wishes to avoid confrontation. I mean to say, his tone may sound harsher than his intentions.' Pandelis was translating this as Demetrios ripped open the envelope. He stared at the Greek script on the paper for a moment with a blank expression and then passed it over to Pandelis to read out.

'*Hey capetanio,*' called Theodoros, clutching his stomach and gasping for breath, '*they've sent us one of those little toilet tents, like the ones the bishop uses when he—*' he resumed laughing and could barely get the words out, '*with a thing for—*' He put a hand on the Prince's shoulder who in his turn took up giggling again and they both doubled over once more.

Pandelis read out the letter quietly while Demetrios listened, his face like stone. As soon as the short statement was concluded, he snatched the letter from Pandelis' hand and walked towards the nearest hut.

Godwin turned urgently to Pandelis. 'Tell him all will be well. The government would be expected to make this sort of statement at first.' Pandelis did not answer but turned to watch his chief.

'*Into the hut!*' Demetrios called to his men, and pointing to Theodoros snapped, '*Pull yourself together and group the prisoners. I want them rounded up in the next hut. Load your gun and stay there with them until I say otherwise.*'

'What is happening?' asked Godwin with a flood of dread. Pandelis shrugged his shoulders and followed Demetrios into the hut. Theodoros recovered from his laughter and walked away from the Prince, shaking his head. The captives looked at each other and allowed themselves to be herded into the second hut, where they joined Farkas, who was lying curled up against a wall. They sat down on animal fleeces that were laid out in a semicircle around the small hearth, and Godwin gave them a hurried account of what had happened in Athens.

'The newspapers are already calling for a military assault,' he said quietly. 'The Prime Minister's hand is forced. Public opinion can only be restrained at present by the government's plain assurance that the brigands' terms have been rejected.'

'And how much time does Sir Thomas think he can hold out against a rescue attempt?' asked Straker.

'He hopes I shall return tomorrow night with positive news from the brigands. News that will stall the government or instigate a compromise.'

'That is a small hope,' said Prince Leopold, stoking the fire with a stick. 'These brigands are brave men, soldiers. They would rather die than compromise.'

'The King is profoundly affected by it all,' said Godwin. 'He swears there will be no military intervention and has promised to raise the ransom money from his own treasury, if necessary.'

'He exceeds his powers,' said Straker grimly. 'A noble response, perhaps, but he shows his immaturity.'

Pierrepont was attempting to lift Farkas off the ground so

that he could sit up and participate. He managed to get him up and slid a blanket around his back. Farkas could not conceal the shaking of his hands, and his eyes stared sightlessly into the hardened mud of the ground before him.

There was a sound from outside and the door opened. Theodoros stood aside to allow through Demetrios and Pandelis. The captain's face was deadly serious as he stood in silence to observe them, chewing on the inside of his lip. Farkas glanced up at Demetrios, and his expression at last came to life, animated by panic. Demetrios closed his eyes for a moment without saying anything, then turned to Pandelis, nodded, and withdrew.

'My *capetanios* wishes to say that you should now eat and rest,' Pandelis said. At this Farkas let out a muffled cry of relief and his head sank forward. 'This food has come for you, and you will eat well. And then you must sleep. We shall be leaving this place during the night.' The other brigands now entered, carrying in armfuls of the provisions and bottles from the cart, and squeezed down on the ground beside their captives to share out the fresh food.

Petros, habitually even-tempered and thoughtful, was sitting next to Farkas, and glanced over at him several times, uncomfortable with what he saw. The petrified hostage was sitting motionless in front of his untouched plate of food. Petros tutted and leant over to help feed him piece by piece. He wedged the food into little packages with his thick, dirt-graven digits, and passed them to the industrialist's mouth with encouraging, gentle words, gradually persuading him to open his lips and take some. By the end of the meal, Farkas' stupor seemed to have eased somewhat, and he turned silently to look at the man who had fed him so patiently, but no words passed between them. Pierrepont watched the brigand's gesture and spoke to him in Greek.

'*You are a kind man,*' he said, but Petros neither replied nor looked up from his food. Pierrepont was of course unaware of Petros Lekas' legendary reputation amongst brigands for

350

brutality. He had earned himself the nickname 'gentleman butcher' for his peculiar combination of compassion and ruthlessness.

Although the tension of their situation had risen since the announcement of the government's official response, the prisoners were buoyed by the wine and fell asleep shortly after their evening meal. Godwin, overwhelmed by a sense of responsibility, stayed awake longer than the others, and wrote quietly in his journal where he lay curled, while Christos, who had been assigned first watch, sat cross-legged nearby, working by candlelight with a thick needle and thread to repair the soles of his shoes. All the brigands kept a set of basic cobbler's tools in the folds of their clothes and knew something of the craft. For a man whose life was spent in flight across the rugged landscape of Greece, a broken pair of shoes could spell death as surely as the barrel of his enemy's gun.

All too soon they were roused from their slumber and set once more upon the trail, now without horses; but the weather was clear and the moon illuminated the difficult terrain. A single mule was led behind them, loaded with as much of the newly arrived provisions as could be fitted on; the rest was left in the huts as a gift for the shepherds when they returned. No explanation was given as to what fate or destination they were bound for, but Straker discovered, after a quick word with Petros, that the distance would not be too great and a higher degree of comfort awaited them.

For the moment, then, it seemed to Godwin that Demetrios was prepared to stand-off the government and see how matters developed. He seemed too intelligent a leader, thankfully, to be overcome with panic at this early stage. Godwin had no doubt that in the last resort Demetrios would precipitate a tragedy rather than face defeat or capture, but it was clear it would not be an option undertaken lightly. Demetrios possessed pride in abundance, but he was also practical and resourceful, and both these qualities gave the hostages reason to hope that their survival would be his foremost concern until every possibility for a successful outcome had been attempted and exhausted.

Having argued himself into accepting this thread of hope, Godwin continued with a lighter heart across the rocky scrubland, picking his way between boulders and brambles as they gradually began to make for higher ground. He was fairly sure that they were heading south, which would take them towards the west of Athens, near to the route he had first travelled when journeying out to Thasofolia.

He noticed that Christos always placed himself at the head of their line. Although older and heavily built, Christos was sure-footed, with sharp eyes that scanned the blackness of their surroundings, like an owl that could see things invisible to other creatures, detect its prey and outmanoeuvre danger. Godwin was walking next to Pandelis, and quietly asked him about the old brigand.

'No other man alive has taken as much lead in his body as Christos,' replied Pandelis. 'All those guns shooting at him, the feel of the wounds. It makes a man hard. And yes, he has sent more men to the next world than the village butcher has gutted chickens. But inside he is pure. I have seen him weep at a wedding. That is the way with a real man. His skin must be like steel, to take the shots. But his soul is always preparing for God.'

They had been walking for around three hours and there was still no sign of an imminent dawn, when the brigands called a halt. After an exchange of bird calls across a shallow blackened valley, they were joined by Adonis, who had left their previous encampment at dusk and gone ahead in advance to check all was well. Whatever news he now delivered to his colleagues initiated an urgent whispered conference. Demetrios was clearly perplexed at what he heard and at one point spat on the ground and threw his hand up in the air. The others fell silent at this expression of anger, until he began whispering again. This continued for a while until Straker got up and approached where they were sitting. He sat down beside them and began to talk in Greek. Godwin expected to see him repelled, but was surprised at how they accepted him into their circle and listened to various contributions he made, nodding, and apparently heeding. A while later, Straker returned to Godwin to tell him what he had learnt.

'We're heading for a small village called Skourta, on the far side of the hill over there.' He gestured. 'This fellow has just come back and said that troops were there last night asking questions about us. The villagers were terrified, of course. They'd been warned a couple of days ago that we were on our way there, but knew too well what the brigands would do to them if they let the cat out of the bag to the authorities. And so they said nothing and the troops made an example of them by taking whatever they could carry. Money, livestock, dowries. The savings of a lifetime. These rural militia are really no better than brigands themselves. Sometimes worse. Many of them are former convicts or bandits. The village is in a terrible mess. Poor people. Caught between the hammer and the anvil.'

'Have the troops been sent to attack us?'

'Possibly. Or, at best, just to keep a watch out, so they know where we are if the negotiations break down.'

'How do they know we are in the area?'

'They probably don't. But that means there must be hundreds of them, scouring all the villages of Attica. It will surely not help our cause.'

'What does Demetrios intend to do?'

'I'm not sure. He's furious. That one with the mean face, that Christos, advocates pursuing the troops and making an example of them. I've no doubt he could do it very effectively. But Demetrios has more sense, thank God. I think he'll lie low and try to persuade whoever sent them to call them off. Whatever happens, the prospect for us is even less secure than it was. I believe it is imperative that you return to

Athens with a new negotiating position as soon as possible.'

'You think Demetrios might compromise on the amnesty?'

'I don't know. But I doubt you will have to wait long to find out.'

Within the hour they were skirting the hill and approaching Skourta, just as the sky began to pale in the east. It was a village of about twenty houses, strung out along a track that led steeply up and around a hill, on the top of which, positioned for its prominence rather than its accessibility to the small community of herdsmen's families, was a small church – a single whitewashed room with a bell on its roof. A small cluster of people with anxious faces had come out to watch their arrival. They were wrapped in sheepskins and they huddled together like penned animals.

There was a goat *mandri* along the side of the road which the brigand party passed before reaching the first house, and both captives and captors stared at it in silence as they walked. Within its roughly constructed wooden fence were the bodies of a dozen or so goats. They lay in their own blood that had spread and soaked into the earth, so that in the half-light they looked as though they rested on randomly shaped vermilion carpets. Their throats had been cut. Adonis tutted ruefully as they left the sight behind them, while Demetrios, with a tense jaw and fierce eyes, led the way to the largest house, little more than an elongated hut, from which they could now hear the quiet wailing of a woman.

A slight, moustached man, whose face was engraved with the pains and anxieties of a lifetime, met them at the door of the building. He did not seem surprised at their arrival, and after acknowledging their presence on his threshold, neither greeted nor made eye contact with them as they filed into his house. His wife, a small, thick-waisted matron, looked over her shoulder as they came in, stifling her sobs as she prepared a broth.

Two small window apertures had their shutters locked so that it was as dark in there as if it had been night outside. The new arrivals settled themselves as close to the hearth as they could squeeze, while their host put a fresh log on the embers. Breakfast was egg-lemon soup with rice, served on tin plates without a spoon, and they lapped it by the light of the fire and candles.

Demetrios now came in and began a lengthy and rather formal statement, spoken in a quiet voice and directed at the desolate owners of the house. Their faces looked at him with surprise. Straker, sitting next to Godwin whispered a translation.

'He says he will repay all the damage,' whispered Straker. 'He's going to give them the gold you brought from Sir Thomas, to compensate for the destruction done by the troops. He's thanking them for their loyalty.'

'A kind gesture,' replied Godwin.

'And shrewd. If he means to keep us here for a while he needs to be convinced of their reliability. Which means either terrorizing them or bribing them. He stands to gain more by the latter because it will make them stand fast against his enemies. If he were to—'

As if overhearing Straker's commentary, Demetrios now turned his attention to the two Englishmen and looked straight at them. The air froze. Straker halted mid-sentence, his mouth open. No matter how reasonable the brigand chief seemed, there was a coldness in those dark eyes that left the recipient of his stares in no doubt of its ever-present danger. Straker closed his mouth and looked to the ground.

'You—' Demetrios pointed at Godwin – 'come with me.' It was the first English he had spoken, and his accent was heavy. He also pointed at Pierrepont. 'And you.'

'Me?' said Pierrepont, the surprise and slight alarm of his expression edged with the possibility of hope. Pandelis, prompted by Demetrios, then announced to the remaining three hostages that they should take the opportunity to compose a short letter each, which would be delivered to the British Minister. They were handed paper and pencil to share.

Pierrepont got up and came alongside Godwin as they stooped to pass through the low doorway and muttered, 'Am I to return to Athens with you, do you think? Perhaps they have discovered at last how little value I represent.'

'I don't know. Say nothing.'

The two of them were led by Pandelis and Demetrios along the track to the next house, some fifty yards beyond, and ushered indoors. It was empty apart from a single wooden chair, and cold as the air outside. The shutters were open, but neither fire nor candle burned within. Behind the solitary chair Christos stood rather formally, feet together and chin raised. In one hand he held a small leather case that fitted into the palm of his hand, the sort used for bottles of ink when travelling; and in the other he had a towel, some strips of cloth like bandages, and a length of rope. A bucket full of water sat next to him on the dirt floor. He looked up as they came in, and Demetrios spoke quietly to him.

'*When did he get here?*'

'*He's been waiting a while. Outside the back door.*'

'*Is everything ready?*' Christos nodded. Demetrios now pointed at Pierrepont and directed him wordlessly to sit on the chair. Pierrepont half smiled, pointed to himself questioningly, looked towards Godwin, and then back to Demetrios before obeying. Christos leant forward, took his arms, placed them behind the chair, and began to tie him up with the rope.

'What are you doing?' Pierrepont asked, and then repeated the question in Greek, the second time more urgently. 'Tudor, tell them. What are they doing to me?' Godwin looked at Demetrios, but he was facing away, his expression implacable. Just then, the other door of the house, diametrically opposite the one they had come through, opened and a third man entered. Godwin caught his breath. It was Panayiotis.

'You?' blurted out Pierrepont. 'What are you doing here? Tudor! Ask him.'

356

Godwin turned to Pandelis. 'Tell us what is happening. Why is Panayiotis here?' he demanded. But neither Pandelis nor any of the others took notice of the question. As soon as Christos had finished securing Pierrepont to the chair, Panayiotis came and stood in front of him, legs apart. He stared at the seated Englishman with contempt for a moment before raking up the slime of his throat and spitting at him full in the face. Pierrepont let out a cry and flinched back, almost destabilizing the chair, so that Christos had to put out his hands to steady it. Pierrepont looked up at Panayiotis again, and a change came over his expression as he suddenly understood what this was about.

'I did not harm her,' he said, a quaver in his voice. 'I swear it.' He turned his livid face around to where Pandelis stood. 'Tell him I meant his sister no harm and did her no harm. I was a fool, yes, but it was finished before it even happened.' He looked across to Godwin, blind fear distorting his features. 'Tudor, stop them, you've got to do something.' Demetrios drew a pistol and pointed it directly at Godwin's face, freezing him to the spot. Behind the chair, Christos now ceremoniously drew his *giatagan*, a short sabre with a thick, curved blade. He passed the weapon over Pierrepont's head to Panayiotis, who took hold of it, savouring his grip on its leather handle.

'For God's sake, Pandelis, tell him to stop it!' yelled Godwin. 'This will not help your cause!'

Panayiotis now looked over to Demetrios, who nodded, and he edged forwards over the chair, so that his legs were splayed either side of Pierrepont's thighs. While Christos gripped the chair from behind, Panayiotis held his victim's head by the hair and roughly pulled it back, exposing the full width of his throat to the air. Pierrepont struggled like an animal to free himself but was powerless in the hands of the muscular Greek.

'This will teach you to keep your hands to yourself,' he said in Greek, and with his left thumb and index finger gripped

Pierrepont's nose tight, pulling it upwards, stretching it by the roots. He bent low and positioned the blade. 'There's not a woman in the world who'll take you after this. You're lucky I don't hack your balls off.'

It was over in a matter of seconds, and Pierrepont, who had passed out from the pain, sat with his head to one side, bleeding profusely. Christos held open the leather case and Panayiotis placed the nose inside it before hurrying out of the hut by the same door he had entered. A moment later Godwin could hear the sound of hoofs galloping away. Pandelis now hurried over to where Pierrepont sat unconscious and, taking the towel and bandages from Christos, began to dress the wound. Christos trained his hard and mocking stare on Godwin for a moment, as if to say that he was fortunate to have escaped this time but might not be so lucky next, and then kicked over the bucket, diluting and spreading the blood to the furthest reaches of the floor.

Godwin, who had been speechless with horror, now turned on Demetrios. 'How can you allow such a thing?' he cried. 'This man was supposed to have been released at the start. Do you think this is going to make them offer you the amnesty? Do you think that by showing you are a butcher of men they are going to pardon you and let you roam free and lawless wherever you please? If you think that, you're a fool!' Pandelis did not translate the outburst, but continued to apply his bandages, wrapping them, in a cross shape, around Pierrepont's head, leaving his eyes and ears exposed.

Demetrios now took the leather case and handed it to Godwin with a few words, which he spoke in a sincere, controlled voice, no more animated than if he were describing to him the route of their day's march. His measured tone and manner exacerbated Godwin's anger. 'This man was supposed to go free,' Godwin said, keeping his voice low so that his words were almost spat. 'That was the plan, that was my condition. He shouldn't be here at all. Mister—' He was silenced on the instant by Demetrios' forefinger, which was whipped out and held in the air between them, menacingly. The brigand's eyes were hard and direct, mortally threatening. It was enough to persuade Godwin that he should say no more. His business complete, Demetrios now departed the hut, leaving Pandelis to translate his earlier statement as he worked on the slumped head.

'My *capetanios* says you must take this box to the Minister, who clearly does not realize how serious we are. And if you do not return with better news, you will be carrying something heavier on your next journey back to Athens.'

Theodoros appeared at the door, filling its frame and blocking out all the light. He looked from the figure of Pierrepont to Godwin, whom he had come to collect. All trace of his usual amiability had vanished from the puppyish features, and with a silent and sideways gesture of the head he indicated to Godwin that it was time to depart.

Chapter 32

Petros Solouzos and Lydia Brooke faced each other silently over their cups of tea in the drawing room at Thasofolia. In the absence of her aunt, Lydia had been compelled to entertain Mr Solouzos until her father returned to the house from the village, an event expected imminently. Her frock was of the darkest blue, a colour that set off the gold of her hair to dazzling effect and distracted the eye from the singular pallor of her skin. She had eaten almost nothing these past few days and slept little.

'You must be very shocked by all this, my dear,' said Solouzos.

Lydia turned her tired face to the window and said nothing. She was being difficult, Solouzos thought. But, then again, she was grown up now and he could no longer condescend to her in the way adults do to children. He could no longer expect her unconditional enthusiasm, her curtsies, coy smiles and kisses. It was her privilege to withdraw a notch if she chose, to contain her feelings and shade her demeanour. 'Of course, everything is being done,' he continued. 'I have been in communication with Athens. We hope for a quick release.' Lydia still did not answer, but smiled into the emptiness. 'And so, my dear, how are you spending your days as we wait for developments in this horrible affair?'

'I am tending to poor Hermann.'

'To whom?'

'He had seemed to be improving, and we were convinced

of his recovery, but his condition has suddenly declined
most dreadfully.'

'Whose condition?'

'Why, Hermann's. Our guest who had the terrible accident.
He has lost a foot. And lies upstairs. His cut now appears
badly infected. I really should return to him as soon as I can.
And will, when I am relieved by my father.'

Solouzos had not the slightest idea who or what she was
talking about, but saw this as an opportunity to release her
from what was clearly a burdensome duty. 'My dear, do not
let me keep you. You have more pressing business to attend
to, and I am perfectly able to wait alone.' Lydia's face bright-
ened a little and offering her thanks she rose and left the
room without another word.

Solouzos also had more important matters to consider. In
a moment he would be confronted with Edgar, his oldest
friend, and would have to put into motion the stratagem that
was being forced upon him by a power too great to ignore;
he would put to Edgar a proposal that in the saying would
unhatch a podful of deceit and treachery. Pressing the point
might squeeze the juice out of a lifetime's mutual trust, and
leave their friendship shattered. But it was not his fault, he
assured himself. Edgar had kept secrets, acted on his own,
and had conspired – although Solouzos did not yet know the
extent to which he might be involved, and he prayed it was
not as he feared.

He did not have to wait long. Edgar strode into the room
from the direction of the hall shortly after Lydia's departure,
and beckoned his old friend to join him in the study. The
sight of his strong handsome smile dissolved Solouzos' misgivings, and they stood in silence facing each other in the
study, their conflicts of interest dwarfed by a spontaneous,
but unspoken, flood of reciprocal warmth and admiration.
Solouzos was deeply moved and had to tense his lips to prevent too strong a show of emotion. There was still business
to complete, though he now felt they would begin from a

threshold of mutual understanding. They both took their seats.

'Above all,' Solouzos began, 'you must know that I will never judge your actions harshly. I know you too well to think you would undertake anything without good reason. Heaven knows, we've both had to bend the rules from time to time over the years.' He had hoped this generous and conciliatory opening might bring a smile of appreciation to Edgar's lips, but he was wrong. His friend nodded slowly behind the desk and held his gaze. 'And because you can rest assured of my understanding and loyalty,' Solouzos continued, 'I know that the two of us will be instrumental in bringing this ugly business to a speedy conclusion. There is a way that all our interests can survive, and of course the mechanics of our approach will go no further than these walls.'

Edgar placed a finger to the side of his mouth, in thought. 'You think there is something we can do together, you and I, to help in this matter?' he asked.

'It is the only solution. The government will not and cannot allow an amnesty. It also cannot appear to bow to British pressure, and at the same time it is in great fear of the opposition party, whose demand for an armed response to the emergency is gaining popular support. The Minister for the Interior has asked me to intervene in order to find a solution. I believe that influence can be brought upon the brigands to accept a guarded escort into exile, on the strict proviso that they never return to Greece, thereby allowing them freedom and their money, but sparing the government the ignominy of having to grant an amnesty.'

Edgar kept his gaze and spoke quietly. 'I did not know that you were so closely involved.'

Solouzos crossed his legs uncomfortably. The stale scent that always accompanied him had drifted to the corners of the room. 'Well, it's clear to me,' he said, 'that they have enlisted my assistance principally because of my close acquaintanceship with you.'

'And why on earth should I enter the government's calculations?' said Edgar.

Solouzos blinked, his smile frozen. 'Because of your association with the brigand leader, Demetrios Lambros, of course. The Prime Minister himself has asked that you intercede on the government's behalf, under my nominal authority, as a direct means of negotiating with Demetrios. You have the opportunity to save the situation and your own interests.'

'Interests?' replied Edgar without a pause, 'I fail to understand. You speak as if I have some interest in the abduction. I scarcely believe this to be your meaning?'

'The government does not know that you have. Your assistance is merely requested because of your eminent qualifications.' He now looked down and spoke in a low voice. 'No other persons but I know of the several visits Demetrios has made to this house in recent weeks.'

Edgar made not the slightest movement. 'Demetrios is my godson and now lives in the vicinity. It is not unusual for me to receive him at my house. I have many godchildren because of my position here. It does not mean that I am responsible for their every action.'

'I have heard a rumour – and this is information given to me alone, let me emphasize – that you have – how shall I say? – lent your approval to the enactment of something. Something big.'

'I had always known you to be immune to vicious rumours. Especially with regard to your friends.'

Solouzos uncrossed his legs, leant forward and sank his bushy eyebrows on to the tips of his fingers. For a moment he sat there, speechless. 'So, you deny foreknowledge of this situation?' he asked.

Edgar let out the puff of a laugh. 'Have you lost your senses?' he said. 'What reason do you think I might have to involve myself in such a conspiracy?'

Solouzos looked straight at him. 'I do not know,' he

conceded quietly, closing his eyes. 'I had assumed it was for the money.' He felt his words emerge like writhing demons, defiling the air between them. Edgar said nothing, and his silence enhanced the poison that Solouzos felt spreading across the peaceful terrain of their friendship.

'Then you will not work with me to find a way out?' he asked softly.

When Edgar answered, his tone was practical. 'I had heard that Mr Tudor is speaking for the brigands. You should co-ordinate a strategy with him. You must know that my political position is too delicate for me to become involved. I must stand aside both from government and opposition interests. The prisoners were my guests but I can no more be held responsible for what has occurred than I can allow my position to become destabilized by taking an active political role in its solution. It is widely known that I have deplored Demetrios' lawlessness for many years. As have you.' Here he paused for Solouzos to digest the import of this last remark in silence. They both knew how invaluable the brigand and his methods had been in the old days. No-one had benefited more than Solouzos. 'I shall write a personal letter to my godson, if you think it will help, expressing my disappointment, and will advise that he compromise his demands, but any further action I regret I will not be able to undertake.'

'If there is a massacre,' Solouzos said, 'you must be aware that there will be a thorough investigation. The whole of Europe would demand it.'

'And so should I,' interrupted Edgar.

'They will not rest until every stone has been upturned. The perpetrators and their sponsors will be found, and the reprisals will be terrible.'

'We would expect nothing less.' Solouzos felt the years of closeness shrivel in an instant and turn to weightless dust, like a silk sheet dropped on flames. The deed had been done. They had shown their colours and taken their stands.

Solouzos looked up. 'I am sorry, old friend,' he said. Edgar stood and escorted him silently to the door.

'I too am sorry,' Edgar said at last, and smiled, a final, parting gesture of reconciliation. 'Let us meet again in better times. When this matter has passed to history.'

Solouzos looked at him and nodded. He then went to leave, but stopped himself and turned back to face Edgar, who still stood in the doorframe. It might be years before the wound of this encounter healed, if ever, and there was something he needed to say, something that had sat on his conscience for a quarter of a century, and even grown with time, like a tumour whose malignity fed off the ignorance of the one most affected by it.

'Edgar, do you think much about Eliza nowadays?'

Edgar's eyes narrowed almost imperceptibly. 'No. I do not.'

'Have you stopped loving her?'

'She is no more. I cannot love what is not.'

Solouzos looked to the ground and thought about the comment. Then he looked up at Edgar. 'I have loved her since I first set eyes on her. And I love her still. And there is not a breath I take that does not end with her name on my lips.' Edgar neither moved nor spoke. 'Do you resent me for this?'

'What would resentment serve?' said Edgar.

'Nothing. Nothing,' said Solouzos, and turned to depart.

'Petros,' called Edgar from the door and Solouzos looked back. 'It might be that you possess what I have lost. I would not deprive you of it, however painful its keeping may prove to you. It is peculiar, but I had not realized until this moment how great and complete my loss has become.'

'You mean how much you miss her? How empty your life is without her?'

'Not at all,' replied Edgar. 'Quite the opposite. I said my loss is complete. Now I clearly recognize it. Complete, I say. She is become for me a thing with no existence or bearing. And so, nothing.'

Solouzos shook his head, and with a sudden rush of feeling said, 'At times your rationalizing makes you seem less than human. Unless it is all an act; and that somewhere inside you there is still a heart beating.'

'The beats of my heart cannot pause to dwell on detritus.'

Solouzos said no more, but turned and walked towards the hall.

Chapter 33

When the news broke that the English gentleman had returned in the night from the brigands and was once again resident in Constitution Square, the Hotel d'Angleterre was besieged by crowds even before dawn broke. Foreign tourists, now too fearful of bandits to leave the capital, mingled freely with all types of Greeks in the crush, anxious for news of developments. A smattering of hawkers skirted the crowd, sensing opportunities for trade, newspapermen hustled the hotel door staff, protesters yelled their opinions on what must be done, and scuffles erupted between over-eager onlookers competing for the best view. Even the rear door of the hotel, which had provided Godwin privacy when setting out for Pyroxenia weeks earlier, was not immune. Nevertheless, it was from here that he finally emerged, at seven o'clock, and a passage was cleared through the throng with the assistance of an armed guard. Mounted cavalrymen escorted his carriage the short distance down to the British Legation, and there dismounted to join a detachment of police already assembled around the entrance. The crowd here was kept at bay, and by degrees during the course of the morning a section of Stadion Street was closed to all traffic and pedestrians.

Inside the Legation a large number of officials had gathered. There was barely space for them in the room and they buffeted one another, their manners and goodwill strained by the crush and their attempts to hear what was being said. Sir Thomas, with Godwin at his side, had his translator read out the contents of the brigands' new letter, replete with its insulting rhetoric – which was traditional in such circumstances, the Minister explained, and must not blur the essentials of the missive. He then drew their attention to the notes scribbled by the captives. All three repeated the same message in different terms: armed attack must be prevented at all costs; their lives were now in great danger; the diplomatic might of all Europe should be sought to persuade the Greek government to concede to the brigands' demands without delay. It was at the point when the final letter had been laid on the desk that Godwin produced the small leather case from his pocket and warned the assembled company – legation staff, War Minister Paleologos, the King's aide-de-camp, the Prime Minister's private secretary and a host of civil servants of varying rank – that it was his sad duty to reveal to them evidence of the brigands' barbarism and determination in this matter. As the case opened, all necks strained forward to look at what it held, and at the sight of it recoiled, a subdued murmur of shock passing across the room.

'I take it this is not—' began Sir Thomas.

'It was Mr Pierrepont,' said Godwin, and thought he could detect the smallest sign of relief on some of the faces present. Had Prince Leopold been the victim, their task would have been considerably more complicated. Nevertheless, this gesture on the part of the brigands was the trigger Sir Thomas required to take action, though the pain it caused him was apparent to all by his expression as he rose to his feet. Her Majesty's government, he explained, would not tolerate the murder or mutilation of British citizens. He was therefore instructed to inform the King and Prime Minister of Greece that the Foreign Secretary in London had authorized the sending of two British gunboats to Piraeus in order to assist the Greek government. The craft were already at sea, having departed from Malta two days previously on a precautionary mission to the eastern Mediterranean.

He attempted to continue, but the statement to this point was enough to cause an uproar in the room, as several of the Greeks began speaking at once. Translators' words were lost in the cacophony of different languages, and Sir Thomas' voice, a thin reed of monotonous calm, could barely pierce the texture of the confusion. Did he now advocate military intervention? they asked. Did he defy their request that Britain withhold a show of force? Was he wresting control of the situation out of the hands of a democratically elected Greek legislature? Sir Thomas had his hands raised in an attempt to restore order to the proceedings, and eventually subdued their voices, if not the anger in their eyes. He answered that no, far from desiring the matter to be resolved through force, the arrival of the British ships should be seen as an act of assistance, to help the Athens government reach a decision that would satisfy the British requirement to protect its own citizens. Another outcry followed this remark. Hands waving papers were held aloft, vying for attention, heavily jowled men shook their heads in disgust, and one or two were already putting on their coats to leave in protest.

'Do you threaten us?' asked Paleologos, his face twisted with fury. 'You expect us to obey England?'

'We do not seek obedience, Minister,' replied Sir Thomas. 'My government wishes only to demonstrate its support for a reasonable solution to the problem.'

Paleologos let out a cry of anger in Greek and wheeled his hand in a sudden and dramatic arc through the air, like a conductor at the symphony's climax. It was a signal for his party to show their disgust by departing, and after a moment of noisy shuffling, jostling and squeezing through the door, every Greek had left the room.

'From this time,' called Paleologos, pointing savagely in the direction of Godwin, as a tall servant helped with his coat, 'from this time we will no longer negotiate with this man. You have my warning not to interfere further. The arrival of your navy will be seen as an act of aggression

against Greece. From this time we send our own representative to negotiate.' And with that the man stormed out of the
room, oblivious to the servant's attempts to hand him his
umbrella.

Godwin was leaning against a wall with his arms crossed.
Once the door closed behind the last of them, he
commented, 'I hardly feel that your announcement, sir,
helped to improve our situation.' Sir Thomas looked at him
tersely.

'You are not in a position to judge, Mr Tudor,' he replied.
'What you see and hear in this country is not always a
reflection of the true situation. I might have guessed
Paleologos would respond in a manner somewhat like
that. And yet only yesterday I met the Prime Minister himself
and informed him how we must be seen to react if the
brigands' threat of violence were increased. He understood
and calmly accepted the situation. Furthermore he gave me
his assurance that no military rescue attempt would be
undertaken. And this concession I take to be a triumph for
our cause.'

Godwin stood straight. This was a new development.
'Indeed. If it is true. In which case, why authorize the
gunboats?'

'So that the brigands can be offered exile and freedom by
a party other than the incumbent government.' Godwin
looked at him, awaiting further explanation. 'Do you not
see?' continued Sir Thomas. 'Mr Gladstone will not countenance enforcing the Greeks to grant an amnesty in
contradiction of their own law. The dispatch of our ships
will, in a sense, demonstrate how seriously we regard the
situation, but, more than that, it will serve a very practical
purpose. We will land a detachment of marines, spirit the
villains off shore and be outside Greek waters in a matter of
hours, before the populace, the opposition politicians or the
newspapers have noticed. And even if the story were to come
to light, the loss of face in allowing the British a small hand

370

in the proceedings would be nothing in comparison to the prestige gained by the government's having achieved the prisoners' release without having succumbed to the humiliation of granting an amnesty. It would be a victory for them and the perfect solution for us.'

'And it requires the co-operation, in advance, of both the government and the brigands.'

'The Prime Minister has offered his. It is for you to obtain the same commitment from the brigands.'

'It is indeed an excellent plan,' said Godwin. 'But if it has all been agreed as you say, why then did the Minister seem so genuinely enraged? I cannot believe he had prior knowledge of your arrangement with the Prime Minister.'

Sir Thomas sighed and returned to his chair. He confessed that he, too, was disappointed at Paleologos' explosion. He had expected some show of resistance, for formality's sake, but not such a visceral response. It was more than theatrical. Either Paleologos, for some reason, had not been informed of the proposal (and such deception was not uncommon, even between fellow members of the same cabinet, in the slippery waters of Greek politics), or, God forbid it, the Prime Minister had changed his mind without informing the Legation. However, in the absence of any official notification of a change, Godwin must now return without delay to deliver a personal message from Sir Thomas Wishart, acting on behalf of Great Britain and Her Majesty the Queen.

'What message?' asked Godwin.

'I shall write it immediately. It will give the brigands the complete and unconditional assurance of the British and Greek governments that they will not be attacked.'

Godwin stood and stared at Sir Thomas for a moment. 'Is it not perhaps an overstatement to make such a promise?' he asked. 'Especially after what we have witnessed this morning? If the brigands' hopes are raised too high their fury will descend with even greater force should they have reason to suspect a betrayal.'

'Good heavens, man, we must make the most of this opportunity,' replied Sir Thomas, his face brightening. 'Since you were here last I myself have met the director of the Ionian Bank to give my personal guarantee so that the requisite sums in gold can be drawn here in Athens. The preparation of this money is already under way. I hope that when you next return here – with the brigands' assent – we shall be able to send you back with news that our ship, complete with the ransom money and a guarantee of safe-conduct from Greece, will be docked at Páparis, awaiting the brigands.'

'And if they do not agree to the terms?'

Sir Thomas pursed his lips and stretched for a sheet of writing paper. 'If they refuse this very reasonable and generous offer, they must be prepared to accept the consequences.'

'An assault?'

'All of Europe will see that we did everything that could have been done.'

'And is that all that matters? What about your written assurance? What about the lives of the men?'

Sir Thomas made no further comment, but put pen to paper and began his letter of guarantee on behalf of Greece and Britain, a letter that in time would achieve immense notoriety, would become etched into the history of the modern Greek nation and the annals of British diplomacy, and indeed would become synonymous with the name of Wishart, the single relic of his career, for which his life's work and term of office in Athens would be remembered. A century later that same sheet of paper would be rediscovered in an Athenian government archive and would find its way into a glass cabinet in the National Historical Museum, which, by coincidence, stood on Stadion Street, close to the site where the letter had originally been composed. Had Sir Thomas known, in that moment of flushed, almost triumphant recklessness, that his memory would be upheld for all time by this sheet and this sheet alone, that thousands of curious tourists and schoolchildren would peruse it in its display case, and that it was probably the only sheet of British Legation headed notepaper to survive from his era, he might have taken greater care with his handwriting and prose. As it was, he completed the note in a matter of seconds, not without a certain bravura, so that his hand-writing seemed a little more cavalier than usual, as if it belonged to a man more bold and headstrong than he was in reality. By this too he would later be judged, so that future generations would perceive him a shade inaccurately, and would miscalculate, or choose to neglect, the true nature of the cautious, often indecisive and bureaucratically inclined English Minister who took upon himself responsibility for the hostage party, that morning, towards the end of November in 1869.

Chapter 34

Petros Solouzos left Thasofolia on the valley road bound for Páparis, a route he had ridden so many times in the past, in all weathers and different circumstances, but never before with such a heavy heart. He could not ignore or brush off the sense of impending calamity. But his depressing reverie was interrupted by the sound of hoofs approaching from behind. He was not far from the spot where the travellers had fallen captive, and a flash of anxiety went through him as he turned in the saddle to see who might be coming. There were certainly some in these parts who would count themselves his enemies; and word had probably got out that he had been enlisted by the government against the brigands. There could be any number of local worthies who would resent him for this. He cursed himself for having elected to travel here alone at such a time. Why had he not listened to his wife's warnings?

The sound of galloping rumbled through the gorge but he still could not see anything: a protruding rockface blocked the view. Could it be that Edgar himself planned some mischief? Panic gripped him. He would not know until the assailant was upon him. He fumbled in his saddle-bag to find his pistol, unloaded though it was. And then the rider came into view. Within seconds he was by his side, smiling and extending a hand. It was Daniel Brooke. He greeted Solouzos warmly and asked if he could ride with him for a short way.

He wanted to talk, away from the prying eyes of his family

and village gossips. Nobody ever told him anything, he complained. What was the news of the abduction, and was there any way he himself could get involved or be of use to the hostages? He knew that Prince Leopold would do the same for him without hesitation; only a coward would neglect such a duty. And there was Mr Straker, he added, a gentleman whom he held in the highest regard, and who had offered to represent him in Athens.

'He has sympathy for my situation and an interest in my future. He may prove a significant ally; and, besides, he is an old friend of Mr Tudor, for whom we all have the greatest respect. I would like to assist him if I can.'

'Mr Straker approves the German mining proposal,' said Solouzos, 'and is therefore in opposition to your father. Does he seek to encourage a division in your family?'

'You know about his opinions?'

'Of course,' replied Solouzos, smiling. 'There is little in the affairs of this island that escapes my notice. You must know that. You recall our former discussion on the matter of the mines?'

'I recall that you are opposed to the plan. And that you would not have me contradict my father's will in the matter.'

'Well, I may have news for you on that. Things have changed a little.'

'Indeed?' said Daniel, and dug in his heels to bring his horse up alongside Solouzos, even though it meant riding precipitously close to the edge of the track. 'You mean you have come round to the idea?'

'Let us say merely that I am considering it as a possibility.'

'That is splendid news! I feared my father's pigheadedness was going to ruin your future as well as my own. But now perhaps you and I can work together, with the help of Mr Straker.'

'Whatever I feel about your father's ideas, you are not justified in using such language. I won't hear it,' said Solouzos, and he raised a reproving finger.

'But I am so frustrated. He and I differ in every opinion. Why has he done so little to help in this matter of the abduction?'

Out of loyalty and because he was an old family friend, Solouzos attempted to explain and defend Edgar's perspective; but it was uncomfortable territory, given the circumstances of the earlier meeting.

As he spoke his reasonable words and turned his phrases to cast Edgar in as moderate a light as the truth would allow, he began to wonder privately. To what devastation was Edgar driving himself, what lonely oblivion? It might be that his years of solitary self-reliance had taken their toll on his mind and that he was pushing himself into a stronghold of impenetrable isolation. He seemed to be turning allies into enemies, alienating his family, and repelling the goodwill of those around him. Perhaps he had chosen this rogue beast destiny as a way of destroying himself, a means to vent his loathing of the world and his own person. It was a passion long bottled and fermented. Edgar's passion was not obvious to strangers, but it fuelled the man and was fundamental to his being – buried, volcanic and igneous. It was somehow appropriate, Solouzos thought, that it should be a vein of lignite that was discovered deep beneath the ground owned by Edgar Brooke. A rich, smouldering fuel of vast potential to ignite. And it was similarly appropriate that so private and opaque a person should refuse to have this magnificent resource brought out into the light of day. It was the property of none to dig up, but belonged to the landmass beneath which nature had concealed it, the mountains, meadows and forests. None should feed or draw its benefits but those to which it was symbiotically bound, the mosses and wild flowers, the prickly shrubs and the impenetrable brambles, the hibernating mammals, preying birds and insects, all those elements that contributed to the rugged wilderness of the Greek landscape. To unearth what lay within, with shaft and drill, would be an act of defilement, something that would strip the place of nobility and bring ignominy to those who perpetrated the deed. And so it was with Edgar himself. Though he could not find logic to explain the way he felt, Solouzos was suddenly overwhelmed with shame and a sense of mourning for that rugged man and his fiery heart, the friend he might just have lost.

But the reality of his present position returned to him, displacing nostalgic ruminations. He fell silent and his face hardened as an idea presented itself, an idea brutal in contrast to the gentle reflections it had replaced. He spoke to Daniel now with a new tone of voice, and the change made the younger man look up at him.

'However, I confess that I, too, had hoped your father might be of more help. You may not have heard, but the government has appointed me to negotiate a settlement with Demetrios. In your father's absence, and bearing in mind the responsibilities you wish to assume on the island, would you consider lending me your own assistance? That is, if you feel qualified and resolved to bear the consequences. It could, of course, be a great opportunity to establish your reputation in Athens. As well as a means of helping your friends.'

At that moment both men were distracted by a shriek that came from somewhere higher up the valley ahead of them. It was a clear, high sound with a haunting edge, and it echoed through the rocky gorge so that they heard it three times, in a diminishing sequence. A moment later they saw a huge eagle fly out from behind a rock, quite close, wings spread, with a rodent twisting in its claws.

'So?' said Solouzos. 'Would you be ready for this?'

They pulled up their horses. The question was answered by the expression on Daniel's face before he even said a word.

'Now that you have proposed it,' he replied, 'I will be able to think of nothing else.'

They rode on together into the gorge for some few miles. From the eagle's perspective they were just two small figures alone in the grandeur of the landscape, meandering their delicate course along the little road. Daniel had known the brigand Demetrios for as long as he could remember, and although some years separated them he regarded his awesome spiritual relative as something of an elder brother – of the type who goes to sea but returns every now and then to the warmth of the family hearth with secrets in his smile and the tinkle of gold in his pocket. It could be just the personal link that Solouzos required. He listened approvingly as Daniel rambled on. Fate had dealt him an unexpectedly fortunate hand.

And yet, despite both men's satisfaction with the outcome of their encounter, neither one of them slept well that night. It was not anxiety about what lay ahead, or preoccupation with the finer details of their plan that kept them awake in their beds. It was a sense of transgression and culpability. Neither was aware of the other's lonely thoughts through the long dark hours, but they were united in shame, of the type that made them want to hide their heads beneath their pillows, like rats crawling under a stone to avoid the gaze of a predator.

Edgar Brooke, meanwhile, was also awake in his bedroom, and at work by the light of a candle. It was a large room but almost empty, containing just a single narrow bed, a small table and an upright chair. It could have been the room of an ascetic, an individual who had lost interest in everything that did not fulfil a necessary function in his daily living. One solitary object of decoration remained. A portrait. It hung on the far wall, and appeared almost as a blemish against the virgin faultlessness of the whitewash all around. It was of a woman, dark, with sensuous lips, spirited eyes and a hint of a smile. She was in the bloom of health and youth, bursting with vitality, and seemed only to be pausing briefly to allow the viewer a quick look before she would be off, full of purpose, with the breeze and sun in her hair.

Edgar removed his jacket and wedged his pince-nez on to his nose. He went over to the portrait, looked at it for a moment and removed it from the wall. His face did not betray a trace of feeling, and he went about his job with the matter-of-fact adeptness of a carpenter at the start of a day's work. With the use of various tools, he surgically detached the canvas from its wooden stretcher, laid it on his simple table and began to attend to it with a pair of scissors. In a matter of minutes he had cut the canvas into thin, regular strips, and these he proceeded to snip horizontally, so that by the time his job was complete the painting had been reduced to scores of small and perfect squares, which he gathered into the palms of both hands and dropped into the fire. There they fizzed and bubbled as the flames consumed them.

The task complete, he dusted down his hands on his trousers and turned his attention to the pressing business of the letter. If he could finish it tonight it could be in Demetrios' hands by the following afternoon. Panayiotis would see to it.

*

The next day, all five members of the Brooke family assembled on the lowest terrace of the garden, at the point where the outer perimeter fence of Thasofolia met the adjacent field that led, in turn, down to the plane trees and the river. It was a dark and cloudy afternoon, colder than it had been, and misty. While they stood in a line, heads bowed, Percival broke the pattern by glancing up and grimacing at the sky, assessing its prospects. They had come together to bury the body of Hermann Kopfling who had died the previous evening, smiling, while looking into Lydia's face and holding her hand. Edgar had insisted they bury the body immediately, rather than attempt to take it to Athens or contact the boy's relatives, and no one dared contradict him. He said a few words at the side of the grave and sang a verse of an old Celtic lament. It was a short ceremony, and when it was done, the family returned promptly to the house to shelter from the rain that had begun to spit quite persistently. The hole where Hermann's shrouded corpse lay was filled with soil, and a light breeze brought some golden plane leaves from the river-bank to settle there.

Chapter 35

By the time Godwin returned to the village of Skourta, having travelled through most of the night with a guide to get there, it was nearly forty-eight hours since he had last seen the hostages; and there was a noticeable difference in their condition. Aside from complaints about lice in their matted hair and beards, aside from the state of their clothes, their broken fingernails and scuffed shoes, they now showed signs of nervous shock that had not formerly been obvious. Up to the time they had arrived at the village they had of course been anxious about their fate, but there had still been a strong sense of hope, an overriding feeling that all would be resolved, that despite their hunger, discomfort and quiet fear, they would not have to endure anything worse than they had experienced to that moment. There had also been a degree of excitement, occasionally comedy, in the air, and an acknowledgement that they were part of an adventure which in later years would provide them with endless possibilities for exotic tale spinning. But these fragments of novelty and fascination came to an abrupt end that first morning in Skourta, when the captives sat in horror as they heard Pierrepont's cries for mercy and screams of pain. All sentiments of camaraderie with their captors were dispelled. The handful of men who had for a few days been their courteous, playful, even reluctant, warders were now, as they had appeared to be at the start, a bunch of cut-throats, full of envious loathing for them and their wealth. Pierrepont's life would never be the same again, if he even survived, which was far from certain. And the temperature of their predicament had risen to a dangerous new level.

Some of the brigands were also nervous. It showed in the way they flinched at unexpected sounds from the hills around, the way they tossed on their mats at night, and left meals unfinished; it showed in the loose movements of their bowels, the stench of their excrement, the deepened lines on their foreheads, and the hunted bleakness of their dark-circled eyes. Conversation was sparse. Tempers were short. And everyone was beginning to curse Godwin for taking so long to get back.

When he did arrive, the villagers halted whatever they were doing to take stock of him, eyeing him with suspicion, as though his having seen them and their compliance with the brigands might stand against them at some later stage; and they turned from him as soon as their instinctive curiosity allowed, and disappeared from sight.

The Prince greeted him with a mixture of joy, resentment and something like hunger. He was agitated, and held Godwin by the shoulders, almost shaking him to get the news out more quickly. When Theodoros intervened to calm him, placing a hand on his arm, Leopold flung it off and advanced on the young brigand aggressively. Straker stepped forward between them to prevent a scene, after which the Prince turned away and retreated, staring thunderously at the ground. As soon as Straker had heard the barest outline of news from Godwin – that a solution of sorts was in the offing and there was reason to be moderately reassured – he held back, and said he was content to talk in detail later. Pierrepont, he mentioned, had not spoken a word since the mutilation. It was probably because of the pain: the muscles of his jaw, palate and tongue had been severed from the cartilage and tissue of the nose, and the effort involved in swallowing or speaking would have been unbearable. They had all been kept awake at night by the poor fellow's groans, and he had several times wet his trousers because they could not get him outside to urinate. It was good that Godwin had arrived with fresh clothes, because the house was beginning to smell of dried piss.

Farkas seemed unchanged, except for his heavier beard, an unusually thick growth. He remained as if in a waking coma, his ability to express himself anaesthetized. If fear was his affliction, it had withdrawn to some hidden and desolate wasteland in his psyche and had no means of venting itself in the material world. Godwin had brought a letter for him from his wife, which sat unopened, resting against his knee on the ground in front of him.

The letter from Sir Thomas he delivered straight to Demetrios and the effect of it, after Pandelis had read it out in translation, was immediate and beneficial. He smiled and put an arm around Godwin's shoulders.

'This is better than last time,' Pandelis translated on Demetrios' behalf. 'They do not grant us what we ask, but they give us an assurance of safety. If it were sent by the government in Athens alone, my *capetanios* says he would put it in the fire. But from the English – that is a different matter. The whole world knows that the English keep their word. They will raise their own flag above the Parthenon before they allow you people to be killed. They have seen sense at last.' Demetrios added something else, gesturing to his nose and causing the other brigands to laugh, but Pandelis thought better than to translate it.

Godwin now asked to be allowed to rest. He had slept hardly at all in the last few days, and he ached all over from the continuous riding. Demetrios nodded his assent, and Godwin fell asleep on a skin in front of the hearth, next to the still form of Pierrepont. He was aware, during the course of the next few hours, of people arriving and leaving, agitated whispers, hard rain hitting the roof tiles, broken murmurs of agony from the man beside him, and, finally, the smell of something hot and steaming near to his head. At last, a metallic clang made him look up with a start and he saw above him a woman stirring a cauldron on the fire.

The atmosphere in the hut was now close and vaporous. Everyone had come in to escape the rain and had settled themselves in groups, talking quietly, or sitting dozily in shared silence. Various pots bubbled over the hearth, the fire blazed healthily, and the shutters were closed, so that despite being early afternoon it was already dark inside and the candles were lit.

Pierrepont was sitting up on a stool nearby, having his dressing changed. He was looking straight at Godwin as the bandages were unwrapped from around his head, and the darkened stain of his blood in the cloth became wider with every layer removed. At last the bandages came away and the horrible extent of his disfigurement was plain to see. The flesh around where his nose had been was purple, engorged and swollen. The wound itself, no longer weeping, but crusted with congealed blood, was almost black in the candlelight, though circled with a belt of yellow fatty matter that protruded from underneath the sliced skin. It was hardly a face at all, and certainly not recognizable. Pierrepont, in his new identity, was still looking at Godwin as Adonis stepped aside to retrieve a fresh dressing. His mutilated features spoke clearly though no words were said. Godwin held his gaze, refusing to allow himself a show of horror or distaste, and yet pity or sympathy also seemed inappropriate, and so he just held the look, for quite a long time, while the new bandage was applied, and the courage required for him to keep from turning away was greater than anything yet demanded of him since the beginning of this whole affair.

Farkas seemed to have come round a little, as Straker pointed out to Godwin with a nudge and a nod, and was sitting on the other side of the room playing a card game with Petros. Though he said nothing at all, and his face betrayed no expression, he seemed to have got the hang of the rules and was laying down his cards to the apparent satisfaction and continued encouragement of the brigand beside him.

'The distraction will do him the world of good,' said Straker, edging closer in. 'Petros seems to have taken him under his wing. Feels sorry for the fellow.'

'Prince Leopold appears to be unsettled,' said Godwin.

'He has been more than that. Yesterday he tried to attack Demetrios. Thank God it was not Christos. Demetrios seems to regard our condition with some understanding. He was in good spirits and chose to overlook the incident. But that Christos – if he has ever tasted the milk of human kindness he has long since forgotten its flavour. I confess it is the thought of his blade that keeps me from sleeping at night.'

Demetrios was sitting cross-legged on the far side of the room with Christos, Adonis and Pandelis. They were leaning inwards around a single flickering candle, their half-lit faces resembling Caravaggio's gnarled peasant apostles, and discussing something in subdued voices. Godwin told Straker everything that had happened in Athens, but could not help glancing occasionally across at the brigand conference. He wondered if his friends' fate hung in the balance of this dialogue.

'I agree with Sir Thomas,' said Straker, 'that freedom and passage into exile for the brigands aboard an English vessel may be our best hope, but I fear the Greek government may not be so amenable.'

'That is also my concern,' said Godwin. 'The newspapers declare that opposition politicians have secretly communicated with the brigands to encourage their demand for an amnesty. Their intention is apparently to compel the government into calling an emergency session in the chamber of deputies.'

'And thereby gain a fresh opportunity to drive them from office,' said Straker, smiling sardonically. 'Yes, that is a credible notion and one that would not be uncharacteristic of Athenian politics. It might explain the messengers coming and going. There was one here while you slept.' Godwin looked briefly across at Demetrios again. He was talking

385

slowly, deliberately, as if explaining very basic and clear truths, and in his hand was a sheet of paper, a letter, though from this distance and in the half-light he could not begin to see what was written upon it. If it were the official offer from Athens, the brigands' response to it appeared calm and measured. All might be well, Godwin hoped.

While Godwin watched from across the room, Demetrios looked carefully at his three friends in turn, fixing each of them with his dark eyes. Christos was once again at work on the metalwork of his pistols, rubbing with a cloth in small circular movements. He had a steel jar in front of his crossed legs and dipped the fabric occasionally into it with a pointed index finger.

'It is no use pretending everything is the same as it was when we started this business,' said Demetrios. 'We thought the English would make them do as we ask and we were wrong. It hurts to say, but now I've said it. We are practical men, not kids. The question is: what now? It is more than likely that we will not get the amnesty, though the money awaits us. Are we prepared to compromise? The *koumbaros*, here, is clear. He writes that he has heard Deputy Solouzos is on his way with an offer from the government. This and the English assurance are enough to get us away from the whole business quickly and safely with our money.'

Adonis wagged his head from side to side. 'But exile? Would you leave Greece, *capetanio*?'

'It is easier for me,' Demetrios replied. 'I have already given my word to leave the island. If I leave Pyroxenia, what else is there for me in Greece?'

'You're leaving?' said Adonis. 'You didn't tell us that. Why?'

'It was part of the deal. You didn't think we got clean off the island without a bit of bartering, did you? The *koumbaros* handled it all. It cost. Money and promises.'

Christos now spoke, without looking up from his work. 'We don't get the amnesty. But does your *koumbaros* still get his king-sized share of the money? Don't we deserve a bit more to compensate?'

'We stick to the same sums,' said Demetrios emphatically.

Christos shrugged, apparently accepting the point. 'They can banish me,' he said. 'I'll be back within the week. That's my way. I'm an outlaw.'

'Of course, that is an option,' said Demetrios. 'But then it'll be every man for himself. Pandeli? You're very quiet. What do you think? Obviously, we would make a condition that our wives and children are safely conducted to wherever we decide to go.'

Pandelis paused for a moment before replying, and then nodded, his lower lip pronounced, as if having resigned himself. 'The *koumbaros* says it is our best course,' he said. 'That's good enough for me.'

'So,' concluded Demetrios. 'The four of us are in favour of accepting Solouzos' offer when it comes? Good. We'll talk to the brothers later. Theodoros will be fine. Petros – I'm not so sure. He has a big family and a lot of animals.'

The four of them were ruminating on this when Christos spoke up, raising his pistol to the candle and wincing down the barrel to inspect some detail. His voice was deep and gravelled. 'Let Petros go now, if he wants. It's not too late. The five of us can handle this without him.'

'What still perplexes me,' Straker was saying, and he pulled his knees up under his chin, 'is Mr Brooke's apparent reluctance to be involved in the negotiations. Have you heard reason why?'

'No,' replied Godwin.

'Has he not sent word offering his services?'

'To my knowledge his name has not been mentioned.'

'Sir Thomas, I know, has little faith in him. Perhaps the government feels the same way. But I am surprised that he has not attempted himself to communicate with us. He would surely be in a position to influence events.' Straker fell silent, a look of intense concentration fixed in his slightly bulbous and bloodshot eyes. Godwin thought fast. He knew he would have to say something or seriously jeopardize his credibility in the future. Pierrepont would soon be talking and would reveal the identity of the man who had mutilated him. Godwin did not believe that Edgar could have condoned the act or even known about it, but the worst conclusions would be drawn by the other captives, particularly Straker, unless the situation were defused in advance. 'He must believe it to be in his best interests to stay out of the affair,' continued Straker, 'though it is not an honourable choice. The Prince was his guest.'

'It is a political business,' said Godwin. 'I have gathered that much from my visits to Athens. And Mr Brooke treads a fine line in matters political. He may be compelled to inaction. A wrong move might cost him his property. You know how his enemies would capitalize on the smallest error.'

'That is true.'

While they were talking, Theodoros was attempting to feed Pierrepont. It was a laborious business and required a deal of patience, as tiny spoonful after tiny spoonful of some sweetened liquid had to be teased between his inflamed lips.

'However, I think you should know,' continued Godwin, 'that a member of Mr Brooke's staff did come here on the morning I left two days ago.' Straker looked up, as if struck by a bolt.

'Here? For what purpose?'

'I am sorry to say it was the worst purpose. It was he who carried out the crime against Mr Pierrepont.'

'What? Why did you not tell me before?'

'I have barely had the opportunity.'

'But it has the strongest bearing on our position. Who was it?'

'Panayiotis.'

'He is in league with the brigands? Does that mean Mr Brooke has some connection as well?'

'No,' replied Godwin, trying to moderate his tone, 'I think not. At least, there is no evidence to suggest that. This was a private matter. Between the two men.' He went on quietly to explain that the mutilation, while convenient for Demetrios, was perpetrated as an act of family revenge.

'Nevertheless,' said Straker, after digesting the story's import, 'it reveals a line of connection between Brooke, through a member of his household staff, to Demetrios. There need be no political meddling if Brooke can merely press upon this boy to communicate some message to the brigands. He chooses not to.'

'Perhaps he does not even know of Panayiotis' involvement.'

'But when you told Sir Thomas, did he not telegraph the Nomarch in Páparis and have word sent to Thasofolia?'

'I did not mention the matter to Sir Thomas.'

'Good heavens, Tudor, are you seeking to protect Brooke? Can he have woven such a spell over you as to make you negligent of your duty?'

'Do not excite yourself, John. You are under much strain, but allow me to speak.' Godwin felt a rush of heat as he thought how to proceed, all the while under Straker's unblinking stare. 'I fail to see how Mr Brooke can use his position to help. Placing pressure on the brigands will only increase our danger. Surely you can see that this situation is only to be resolved through the raising of the ransom and the matter of the amnesty, and that is entirely a political matter. The identity of the outlaws and their connections with other parties are incidental and nothing more. Let us not complicate matters further or the negotiations might risk being stalled.'

His words seemed to satisfy Straker for the present. 'I'm sorry if I appear irritable,' Straker said. 'And I hope you are proved right.' His forehead sank to his knees. 'There is nothing for us to do now except await the government's formal offer.'

*

That evening, as it continued to rain outside, and after their meal was finished, they were all sitting in the house, for want of anything better to do. Christos began to sing some of his *tragoudia*. He did not have a beautiful voice, in fact it was little more than tuned speech, rough and deep, with an emphatic vibrato that made his whole head shake as the phrases tailed off; but there was an approximate metre and melody, and the ruggedness of the man added poignancy to his rendition. He sang a tale of love and brigands in times gone by. Occasionally the line of the tune would twine upwards and away in a more elaborate turn of phrase; the old brigand's eyes would close and his face would show the pain of expression before sinking back with resignation to the established melody.

Demetrios came over to sit with Godwin and Pandelis. He wanted to talk, and indicated that Pandelis should translate. All the while, by the light of the fire, the others listened to Christos or dozed, their thoughts far away. Godwin put down his pen and closed his journal.

'You think we are evil men. Especially what we did to your friend,' said Demetrios quietly, his voice and Pandelis' translation like a soft accompaniment to the background song.

'Does it matter what I think?' said Godwin. 'It makes little difference to your intentions.' He was leaning against the wall, head resting back, and looking up at the ceiling through half-closed eyes. He had been drinking steadily from a jug of wine and felt the call of sleep.

'No, it does not matter. But you might think differently of me if we had met in more pleasant circumstances.'

'How different everything would be if we could choose circumstances,' replied Godwin.

Demetrios smiled. 'Our lives, yours and mine, will take us in such different directions. Where will you and I be in

390

twenty years, and in whose company? If God spares us.'

'Never mind about God,' replied Godwin, also smiling. 'There are others rather nearer who have the power to spare. Or otherwise.'

Demetrios enjoyed the humour and nodded. 'You are too intelligent to think that I threaten a man's life for enjoyment,' he said.

Godwin was tired and a little drunk. His head tilted sideways and he looked at Demetrios. 'There are plenty of ways to do business without having to kill people.'

'What do you know? You know nothing,' said Demetrios. There was neither mockery, resentment nor condescension in his tone. It was as if he were making a factual observation. Godwin closed his eyes for a moment and reflected on the words. 'I have a young wife,' continued Demetrios. 'I have my life before me. I do not play this death game for pleasure.'

Godwin now raised his hand. 'Wait,' he said, eyes closed and eyebrows knotted. 'The simple truth is this: I could no more kill an innocent man than eat my own arm. Whereas you, if compelled, could accomplish the deed with relative ease. And have done on numerous occasions, I do not doubt. Don't expect me to absolve you of your sins.'

Demetrios was smiling again. 'Once more, I say: you know nothing.' He looked around the room, grinning, before returning his gaze to Godwin. 'You live in a world of books, ideas—' he gestured with his hand to imply a litany of useless ephemera. 'You do not remember the animal inside you.' He pointed at Christos. 'The man he sings the song about, Petros Ziskos, he was a king of men. Like a great bear. A master of all animals. My grandfather knew him. His whole life was a long test of manliness, until there was no one left to challenge him. When he died, at the hands of the police and the courts, and when they took his head from his body, he suffered no loss of honour, because these men and their ways were beneath him. Amongst his own kind he was unchallenged to the end. But he did not become king without brutality. There are many stories.' He clasped his chin and scratched his upper lip through his moustache for a moment. 'Once, a promised ransom never came and Ziskos was forced to leave two young twin sisters at the side of the road with their throats slit. He sent a message to the parents expressing his sorrow but explaining that he could not accept failure. He did what had to be done. To keep order. And honour. That was a real man.'

Godwin was staring into space and raised his eyebrows. 'The sort of man they sing songs about,' he said quietly.

'And you?' asked Demetrios, nudging him cheerily in the ribs. 'Where do you keep your fire? Is there a woman somewhere?'

Godwin's eyes were blank, still, distant. 'A woman,' he repeated.

'Someone who holds your heart in her little hand,' said Demetrios.

Godwin came to and drew a deep breath. 'Yes, there is a woman. And she holds my heart indeed.'

'Good!' said Demetrios, and slapped Godwin on the knee. 'And does the squeeze of her pretty little hand bring you agony and joy in equal measure?'

'I would say that is probably the truth.'

Demetrios was delighted. 'You are more of a man than I thought. This woman will be waiting for you. She thinks of you even now, as she prepares for her bed. Do not worry, my friend. It will not be long until you are back in her arms.'

Christos' song came to a gruelling conclusion and the singer fell silent, face raised to heaven, his eyes closed in mournful reminiscence. Some of the assembled men, including the Prince, had fallen asleep. Straker sat hunched, arms over his knees. Farkas leant back against a wall, lost in his own world, a dried tear on his cheek.

Godwin thought of Lydia and wondered if she knew or cared about the pain of his heart. Would there ever be a time or place for him to sit alongside her and reflect on these tempestuous events? Could he imagine her face smiling at the memory of them, as one does distant childood follies? The thought of such pleasant intimacy seemed so very remote, as did the prospect of one day returning to the standards of normal living. The time might come again when he would laugh out loud, and rejoice in the company of friends, but at present such ordinary pleasures seemed part of an unattainable paradise. He lay down on the sheepskins, pulling a coarse woollen blanket up over his chin and around his ear. Beyond the doors of the house Attica was being swept by the wet, cold and wind. Here within, though insulated, a subtler chill had hold of him. He felt it bite at his bones. Innocent contentment was denied him and might never again be more than a poignant memory, like one of Christos' songs, or one of the photographs he had left to curl and rot in the box at Thasofolia. The end of this affair was close, he felt sure; but the consequences would remain like a scar for ever.

The winter raged and they all lay squeezed in that refuge for warmth and comfort. Pierrepont had just that moment pissed himself again, and Theodoros was tugging at his trousers, trying to get them off his slumped form. Godwin watched from where he lay on his side, aware that he should be helping but longing to pass into sleep, to ease himself away from the realization that he had joined the company of the damned.

Chapter 36

When Godwin received the summons, the following day just before lunchtime, to meet Demetrios in the neighbouring house, he assumed this would be the moment when the brigand's final decision and answer to the powers in Athens would be communicated to him; and it followed from this that he also assumed he would shortly be on his way back to the city with positive news, so that, as he rose to leave the room where he had been contained with the other hostages, he bade them all farewell with encouraging words. They had been informed that a messenger had earlier arrived on government business, and Godwin was in little doubt that this was the formal proposition for the brigands' safe-conduct into exile, as outlined to him by Sir Thomas Wishart. He left his friends, therefore, with the assurance that Demetrios' response to the new offer would be positive, and that their release was imminent.

He went over to Pierrepont and took one of his hands in both of his. It hung limply in his clasp, like cold meat.

'I am so sorry, Fortinbras,' said Godwin. 'We will see that justice is obtained for this terrible crime.'

Pierrepont looked straight at him and parted his lips. 'Justice?' he said, and the pain of speaking made him flinch. 'I cannot be helped by justice.' They were the first words he had uttered with the voice that was to be his from this time on, thick and muffled, with blurred consonants and inexact vowels.

'I will see to it myself that you receive all the help that can be provided,' replied Godwin, before turning aside, unable to sustain the demands of those bloodshot, staring eyes any longer. Pandelis was waiting for him by the door.

The rain had stopped, but it was dull outside. Pandelis, stone-faced and silent, led the way up the slight rise to the neighbouring house. He opened the door and ushered Godwin over the threshold, remaining outside himself, to one side of the entrance like a sentry. Demetrios was not in the room, but two men were standing by the table and they looked straight at him as he came in. It was Solouzos and Daniel Brooke.

'What is happening?' cried Godwin, utterly taken aback. His surprise at seeing them, combined with a sudden rush of calculation as to what their presence here might imply, made his thoughts reel for a moment and he could find nothing more to say.

Solouzos did not greet him. His former congeniality was absent and he spoke with solemn urgency. 'We do not have much time, Mr Tudor. I am glad to see that you are well. The others are in a satisfactory condition?'

'Yes. Apart from Mr Pierrepont. He suffers horribly.' Godwin looked towards Daniel. 'What are you doing here?'

'We are here in a last attempt to find a solution to this terrible business,' said Solouzos. 'All may now depend on the degree of faith placed in you by the brigands. Do you have their trust?'

Godwin, having been sedentary and silent for most of the past twenty-four hours, bored, waiting and ponderous, was disoriented by the shock of the meeting and the feverishness of Solouzos' manner. 'Have you come on your father's authority?' he asked Daniel.

'I require no authority save my own,' was his reply, though the high pitch of his voice betrayed more uncertainty than his words implied. Solouzos intervened by stepping forward and putting out a hand in front of Daniel.

'Daniel is here to help me in the negotiations,' he said. 'And I am here to represent the Minister of War, Mr Paleologos. We have a proposal, but I fear it has fallen foul of your captor. He was expecting quite another offer, one which I gather has been voiced by your Legation on the basis of nothing more than an informal discussion. Sir Thomas Wishart was exceeding his authority in extending such an offer. And in the matter of his assuring the brigands of their immunity from attack. I cannot pretend that this morning's developments bode well for the hostages.'

Godwin was still looking at Daniel. The secure grounding on which he had assumed, for better or worse, the conspiracy to be constructed now seemed uncertain, its possibilities alarmingly extensive, perhaps out of control. 'But does your father know of your involvement in all this?' he insisted. 'Has he approved your coming?'

'Communication between the government and the English Legation,' continued Solouzos, deflecting the question from Daniel, 'appears to have broken down altogether. The Prime Minister is of the opinion that a crime committed by Greeks should be a matter for the Greek courts and no one else.'

Godwin now turned his attention to Solouzos. 'And what has Mr Brooke to say on the matter?'

'Mr Brooke, for his own reasons, wishes to distance himself from the affair. He believes his position to be too delicate. Daniel is acting on his own initiative.'

'Father has done nothing to help,' said Daniel. 'He has neither consulted me nor deigned even to speak to me about the incident.'

'And so you have taken matters into your own hands?' Godwin asked. 'In defiance of your father, perhaps in the hope of outmanoeuvring him and taking control of the family's representation?'

'Can you blame me?' answered Daniel. 'He has excluded me all these years, and now he would prefer to see these men die than risk his own standing.'

Godwin looked around the room. 'No, I cannot and do not blame you,' he said quietly.

'We have no time for this,' interjected Solouzos. 'Our being here has nothing to do with the Brooke family or its interests. Daniel has come because he has known Demetrios all his life and thought he might yet have some influence on his decision. As might you.'

'What is your proposal?' asked Godwin.

Solouzos took a deep breath and gathered himself. 'Mr Paleologos has insisted that an amnesty is illegal and cannot be enacted,' he said. 'However, a pardon, a royal pardon, is possible.'

'What is the difference?'

'It is technical. A pardon would have to follow from a conviction, which in itself must result from a formal trial. By the thirty-ninth article of the eighteen sixty four Constitution a pardon without trial is expressly forbidden. However, if the brigands were to release the prisoners, allow themselves to be taken to Athens under military escort and stand trial, they have the assurance of Mr Paleologos that a royal pardon will be granted. It will be nothing more than a formality.'

'And the ransom money?'

'That, too, will be granted, but on foreign soil, or aboard an English vessel off the coast of Greece, out of sight of the nation. It is a good offer, do you not agree?'

'But Demetrios, you say, thinks not.'

'He does not trust politicians. He says he will agree to the trial and conviction only if it is carried out without him or the other brigands having to attend in person. Or, alternatively, he will agree to the establishment of a temporary court here in this village, but again, on condition that the hostages will remain in the hands of the brigands, at gunpoint, until a pardon has been officially granted. Of course, neither of these provisions will be acceptable to the government.'

'What on earth do you imagine I can do?' asked Godwin.

Solouzos leant forward over the table, resting his weight on his fists. A dusting of scurfy scalp flakes clung to the circumference of his black collar. He spoke with quiet intensity. 'Assure Demetrios of the government's good faith. It is our last hope. He does not know yet, but I have been informed that a rejection of these terms will result in the mobilization of two hundred troops within twenty-four hours. They are already deployed not far from here. By this time tomorrow the village will be surrounded and a tragedy will ensue. He appears to hold you in high regard. He admires the integrity of the English and has heard something of your family's standing in England. An assurance from you might change his mind.'

Godwin looked from Solouzos to Daniel. 'What do I know of the government's good faith? For all I know it may be a trap.'

Solouzos looked directly at him from beneath his frowning, overgrown eyebrows. 'It is for you to decide if that is a matter for consideration. The brigands were risking their lives when they embarked on this plan. That was their gamble. The important issue for us is to secure the release of those men, innocent men who never had the privilege of choosing or gambling their fate.'

'You are asking me to deceive them? You believe the government means to withhold the pardon?'

Solouzos' face softened. 'My friend, I do not know. The men of power use me just as they use you. I fulfil my role to the best of my ability in the faith that others will fulfil theirs likewise. I can only hope that right will prevail. There is no other way. If you have an alternative solution, let me hear it.'

Their conversation was brought to an abrupt end by the arrival of Demetrios. He threw open the door and stormed into the room, followed by Christos, Petros, Adonis and Pandelis. Though he said nothing for a while, his eyes burned as he paced around the room. The others waited until he was ready to speak. Eventually he came to a stop, clicked his fingers at Daniel and turned to face Godwin, addressing him in Greek which Daniel translated.

'He wants to know if you have heard the proposal.'

Godwin nodded in reply. Demetrios flung out his hand angrily and said something further.

'He wants to know what you think about it.'

'Tell him I think it sounds a reasonable offer. Not as good as the other perhaps, but still a way out of the situation that could end to the benefit of all.'

'*Demetri, see reason, for heaven's sake,*' said Solouzos in Greek. '*The politicians are under pressure as well. This is a way out that will save them face.*'

'*If I want your fucking opinion, I'll ask for it,*' said Demetrios, whipping round on Solouzos and jabbing a finger at him. He turned to Daniel and indicated Godwin. '*Ask him if his country's Minister in Athens is a man of honour.*'

'I do not know him intimately,' replied Godwin, 'but honourable behaviour would be expected of any man who occupies his position.'

'Then we need not fear attack?' asked Daniel on Demetrios' behalf, 'now that he has given his word in writing?'

'*I have already told you,*' interrupted Solouzos, '*Sir Thomas was not authorized by the government to give that assurance.*'

'*But now that it is given, he and his army will make certain that it is upheld,*' said Demetrios, advancing threateningly on Solouzos.

'*Army?*' replied Solouzos. '*Are you mad? You expect the English to go to war with Greece over this?*'

Godwin cut through their heated interchange speaking in a tired, impassive voice. 'Tell him I believe he can no longer assume immunity from attack.' Daniel did not immediately translate, but looked from Godwin to Solouzos.

'*What did he say?*' asked Demetrios.

'Tell him,' insisted Godwin; Solouzos nodded and Daniel translated. On hearing the warning Demetrios raised his face, punched the air and yelled a string of obscenities. The other brigands present, aside from Christos, hung their heads and looked to the floor. Christos raised his eyebrows.

'*In which case,*' Demetrios said to Daniel, recovering from his outburst, '*you can ask my English friend here why I should believe any assurances any more. I am surrounded by lies and deceit. Ask him if he thinks we will be granted pardons if we submit to the government's demands for a trial.*'

Godwin paused before answering. The door swung open on its hinge to reveal the world beyond, and it looked as though the sun outside was at last trying to break through. A child, a little girl, wandered into view, and, drawn by curiosity, edged towards the threshold to peek at what was going on inside. Christos stepped into the doorframe, filling it completely with his broad figure and blocking her view. She looked up at him and covered her face with her hands, but he went down on his haunches and smiled at her, taking down her hands, patting her curls and telling her softly to go off and play, whereupon she ran out of view.

'Tell him,' Godwin began, aware of the determined stare of Solouzos on the other side of the table, 'tell him that it has to be the *capetanios'* choice.' Daniel translated. 'But tell him also,' continued Godwin with deliberation, 'that my experience of those politicians, which is limited and based more on hearsay than evidence, would lead me to regard any such offer with suspicion.'

'You can't say that,' said Daniel, flabbergasted.

'Tell him!' roared Godwin at the boy.

'*What does he say?*' asked Demetrios. Daniel stalled and turned to Solouzos. Eventually it was Pandelis who spoke, translating word for word what Godwin had said. Solouzos looked at Godwin with resignation and shook his head, sighing.

'*At least we have one honest man here,*' said Demetrios, before resuming his circular course around the room, clutching his chin, his face as dark as a mountain storm.

No-one spoke. Christos, standing near the door, yawned and stretched his arms, as if to rouse and prepare himself after too many days of unnecessary inaction. Daniel watched Demetrios, while Solouzos held his ground, gazing intently at Godwin.

Demetrios finally stopped and turned to Solouzos. *'I don't know why you're still waiting here. You should be on your way.'*

'I am waiting for your answer.'

'Isn't it obvious?' replied Demetrios.

'Be careful, old friend,' said Solouzos. *'I understand how you feel. But they will destroy you. You don't understand how desperate they are. This could bring down the government.'*

'Be gone, coward,' said Demetrios without hesitation. He looked at Solouzos with contempt. *'After all I've done for you, you should know me better than to think me such a weakling. Go and report to your masters. Tell them I piss on their wives. And tell them that unless they are prepared to follow the English Minister's proposal they are signing the death warrants of these men. That is my oath, as a Greek and as a captain of good men.'*

Solouzos closed his eyes and let out a long breath. He reached for his coat. Godwin needed no translation to gather the implication of their short dialogue.

'We have our answer,' Solouzos said to him with a bitter edge to his voice. 'I will report back to Mr Paleologos. I am sorry, Mr Tudor, that you did not think to help the captives by the only means available to us. I pray the Lord that you rest easy with your conscience in that decision.'

'There is yet hope,' replied Godwin. 'When I return to Athens, I will go in person with Sir Thomas to the Prime Minister and plead the case. We will seek the authority of Mr Gladstone by telegraph. Perhaps even a personal message from the Queen asking for the protection of her cousin.' Godwin now turned to Pandelis. 'Ask Demetrios what message he would like me to convey to Sir Thomas Wishart. And to the Prime Minister of England.'

Demetrios was heading for the door when Pandelis put

the question. He stopped at the threshold of the house to give his answer, in a subdued, almost sulky, voice, barely turning his head to look over his shoulder. Godwin did not understand his remark, but could see from the faces of Solouzos and Daniel that its content was ominous. For a moment nobody spoke, and Demetrios left the room, followed by Christos and Petros.

'What did he say?' Godwin asked Pandelis. 'What message does he wish me to convey?' Still Pandelis failed to reply, but looked at Godwin, his mouth slightly ajar. Finally, it was Solouzos who spoke.

'There is no message,' he said.

'What do you mean?' asked Godwin.

'Demetrios said that there is no further room for negotiation. The government has made its offer and he has replied with his own. There the matter must rest.'

'Am I to make no representation on his behalf when I return?'

Solouzos was putting on his coat. 'You will not be returning,' he said.

'What?'

'Demetrios says you are now to join the other captives.'

'Remain here?'

Solouzos sighed again and made for the door. 'He says he wishes to take you to the village church tomorrow. It is a holy day. For the *Panagía*, the Presentation of the Virgin at the temple. There will be feasting and dancing. Demetrios has an insane notion that you should remain for it. Goodbye, Mr Tudor. And good luck.'

'No. Stay a moment,' called Godwin, and Solouzos, already almost outside the door, stopped in his tracks. 'Please,' Godwin appealed to Pandelis in a half-whisper, 'allow me a moment alone with Mr Solouzos.' Pandelis grimaced and exhaled tightly through his teeth. 'I beg you,' continued Godwin. 'There may yet be a way to save us all. You can trust me, you know that you can.' Pandelis shook his head and turned to Adonis, the only other brigand left in the room.

'*What does he ask?*' said Adonis urgently. '*If he's got another idea, let him speak. Demetrios has gone mad. We'll all be killed!*' He turned to Solouzos. '*Tell him, Kyrie. We don't want to die.*'

Pandelis glared at Adonis. '*Just pray to God that I don't tell the capetanios what you've just said.*'

'*All right. I'm sorry,*' said Adonis. '*You know I'll follow Demetrios to the end. But what does the Englishman ask? Whatever he suggests is worth a try.*'

'*To speak alone with Solouzos.*'

Adonis raised his eyes to heaven and held out his hands in disbelief. '*Is that all? Let's go. Leave them for five minutes.*' Pandelis reluctantly nodded his assent and pushed past Solouzos, glancing around gingerly outside before finally closing the door behind him and Adonis.

Godwin paused a moment, looking from Solouzos to Daniel. 'I had hoped to speak to you alone,' he said to Solouzos. 'It is a matter of great delicacy.'

'We have no time for niceties, Mr Tudor. Besides, young Mr Brooke is now my assistant in all matters relating to these negotiations. Whatever you have to say can be said to both of us.'

Godwin turned aside from them and stared into the hearth, at its flameless embers and wisps of wood smoke.

'What I have to say,' he began falteringly, 'will involve me in an act of betrayal, the very idea of which is heinous in the extreme and contravenes everything I hold sacred or honourable.' He knew he had only the briefest of opportunities to make his exposure, if make it he must, but still could not bring himself to begin. He pictured Edgar at Thasofolia: the magnificent, powerful presence of the man who brooded silently in the midst of his family at the head of the dinner table; the contained assurance of the landlord who rode across his beloved, sun-drenched property, lionized by his people, their captain and brother; he pictured

Edgar the visionary, the romantic, the brilliant but perpetually unfulfilled artist, the man of high ideals, tormented by a sense of tragedy, flawed by the shortcomings of his own character and species. For all his monstrous intemperance and egocentric ways, for all his disregard of gentler feeling and common courtesy, Godwin could not help but love him. His faults and coarseness dwindled to insignificance when viewed beside the breadth of his understanding and perspicacity. Men such as this stood tall amongst their peers in life, and etched the landmarks of man's place and rank within creation, for all the rolling years.

The tears tumbled freely down Godwin's cheeks as he recognized that he loved Edgar, loved him indeed, and it was his bitter duty now to bring down this majestic man, to expose him as a villain, without sparing the time to explain the wider perspective; and the result of his treachery would be devastation for him and his family, for generous-hearted Mag, for Percival, entirely innocent and well disposed, for Daniel, bursting with virile exuberance, on the cusp of a golden manhood; and for Lydia, beloved, elusive, incomparable darling Lydia. None would stop to hear Godwin's pleas for understanding, just as he himself had closed his ears to Edgar when first hearing of the conspiracy. Once the poisonous words were spoken his voice would go unheeded, like Cassandra's, a lonely cry in the wilderness, heart-torn and deranged. The carrion birds would gather with glee, and glory in the maceration of the fallen colossus. He could hear their cackles and sense their greedy pecking at the carcass even now.

'Mr Tudor, I must insist you say whatever it is you wish to say,' said Solouzos, his hands quivering in front of him with frustration. 'If there is anything you know that might help, this is the very last moment you will have to reveal it.'

'Yes,' said Godwin, recovering, and turned to face them. He raised his chin, straightened himself and spoke out clearly. 'You mentioned that the Prime Minister is determined to deal with this matter according to the precepts of Greek law, without aid or intervention, because the perpetrators of the crime are Greeks.'

'That is correct.' Godwin glanced at Daniel who was looking at him intently, a thickening frown forming across his forehead.

'And do you believe he might be more inclined to accept the solution proposed by Sir Thomas – the solution which Demetrios and the brigands evidently consider acceptable – if he were to discover that the principal perpetrator, the engineer and sole manipulator of this entire affair, is not Greek at all?'

'Not Greek, you say?'

'Would it make a difference?' cried Godwin, his charged feeling forcing its way into his voice and making it crack.

'Of course it would make a difference. It could change everything. Do you have evidence of something none of us know?'

'God!' cried Godwin, and covered his face with his palms. The moment had arrived. He must make his exposure.

But before he could speak, the door of the house flew open, slamming into Solouzos who stood close to it. The handle caught him sharply in the soft tissue of his elbow making him scream with pain and reel aside, doubling over and clutching his arm. Christos was there, and beside him Demetrios, staring fiercely across the room at Godwin. He clicked his fingers at Daniel without taking his eyes off the Englishman, and spoke softly.

'*What was he saying*, koumbare?'

'*He was about to tell us something. Something that he said would help, would make the government change their mind and accept the English plan.*'

'*And what is this something?*'

'*He didn't get to say it. You came in. It's something about a foreigner. He says there is a foreigner involved in all this, giving the orders. Is it true, Demetri?*'

'*The raving of a desperate man*,' replied Demetrios, advancing on Godwin until he stood in front of him, face to face, his dark, fiery eyes, just inches away, burning into Godwin's face.

'*If it could help, you should tell us*,' said Daniel. '*It must be something to do with the Prince. Some plot. An enemy of Germany. The French, perhaps.*'

'*It's nothing*,' said Demetrios, without taking his eyes off Godwin. '*Don't listen to him*, koumbare. *He's making up some nonsense to try and save his own skin.*'

'*It didn't sound like that.*'

'*Well that's what it was. If he had anything helpful to suggest don't you think he would have shared it by now? He's had every opportunity. Now be off! The pair of you, go!*' He flicked his wrist at them repeatedly, compelling them to shuffle their way backwards to the exit. Solouzos was rubbing his elbow, still frowning from the numbing pain.

'Mr Tudor,' he called, looking to Godwin beyond Demetrios' shoulder, 'it is not too late. Tell us what you know.'

'*Be gone, I say*,' snapped Demetrios. Solouzos was being forced back towards the door.

'What you have said exactly echoes my own worst fears,' he insisted, straining to catch a glimpse of Godwin, now half obscured by the huge figure of Christos, who stood threateningly before him. 'If you have a name, say it, say it now! Mr Tudor!' But he was bustled out of the building before any reply came; he stumbled on the doorstep, and just recovered his balance, shoes slipping in the muddy ground, before being pushed roughly by Petros in the direction of his waiting horses. The moment had passed.

Left alone with Godwin, Demetrios looked him close in the eye once more.

'*Traitor filth*,' he said. Godwin, not understanding a word, returned his gaze with steely impassivity. '*When the bullets start to fly I'll make sure my first ball finds its way into your treacherous skull.'* With that he spat into Godwin's face and called Christos to take him back to the other house, where he was to wait with his fellow captives until further notice.

Chapter 37

The morning of 21 November broke cold and clear over Attica, and those who were out at dawn to tend their livestock or light the fires of their roasting pits could see, if they spared a moment to look, a trace of frost on the grasses and ground foliage, the first of the winter. One or two would tut despairingly at the thought of the hard weeks ahead. They would cast an anxious look across at their log stacks to see if they had enough firewood to last them through, and wander back indoors, cursing the change of season.

It was going to be a fine day for the festival of the *Panagía*, the Holy Mother, the saint of all saints; and from earliest light the interlocking hills and boulder-strewn panoramas echoed to the ring of church bells, mostly distant tinkles, specks of melancholy, untuned sound, with little in the way of resonance, a far cry from the voluptuous bronze tonnages that shook the cathedral towers of Europe on Sundays, but decoratively appropriate to the aural landscape of this region.

In Skourta, as in almost every village of the land, the scent of roasted lamb and wood smoke mingled and hovered low in the windless air, almost at nose height, a deliciously teasing blanket of promise that grew in pungency as the morning progressed. Children took turns to rotate the skewered beasts on spits above pans of embers, until their little arms tired of the labour, and then others would take on the job, biting their tongues with concentration and watching as the skin browned and contracted around the animal's skull, revealing the teeth and a pair of globular, lidless eyes that slowly cooked in their sockets. Occasionally an adult would intervene to spoon oil, lemon and oregano across the blistered flesh, which would then glisten, bubble and drip fat into the fire, making the coals hiss and giving rise to fabulous fresh vapours. That pervasive smell, familiar to all in Greece as a sign of imminent festivity, had spread to the furthest boundaries of the village by the time they all came out of church, at eleven o'clock, though there were at least three hours of cooking time left before the feast began.

The brigands had been donated their own lamb by an anxious village headman who did not want to put a foot wrong. He had known brigand visitors in the past and remembered the form. As it turned out, Demetrios proved to be rather different from the others, and at first refused the offer, saying that it should be they giving to the village for the inconvenience caused in making their temporary station here; the headman appreciated the sentiment but pressed the lamb on him, also inviting him and his guests to attend the dancing after church.

The village church, which looked down from its position perched among the hillside cluster of homes it served, was little more than a side chapel by the standards of his own country, Godwin thought; and as the comparison flashed through his mind he felt a jab of nostalgic longing for the comforts of an English church, like the one near his home, set in its dell adjacent to the school, with its old mullioned porch, gilded weathervane and smell of polished oak. He despised himself for having so long resented that little building and all it represented. What he would give now to be tucked into one of its safe and tidy pews, listening to the gentle metre of the rector's sermon, while the spinster organist dozed on her stool, and sparrows outside leapt randomly from yew branch to mottled gravestone. He could hear their song and the flutter of their wings in the wintry cemetery even now as he imagined the scene, together with the drone of a hymn just begun indoors, the sound of it muffled by the thick old walls of the church.

Today, the church at Skourta, with its neat little basilica, its humble collection of icons and its single bell up on the roof at the east end, had drawn a sizeable crowd to commemorate the child Virgin's Presentation, considerably more than were resident in the village itself. Herdsmen and homesteaders travelled in with their families from further outposts of the district, together with relatives and *koumbari* from neighbouring villages, invited for the day, many of them curious to see proof for themselves of the rumoured events that had been taking place there. In fact, nearly double the number of visitors had turned up for the festival compared to the previous year, despite Demetrios having enlisted the headman's assistance to keep unwanted sightseers at bay, and having ensured that all routes to the village were carefully monitored by sentries. By nine o'clock the church was full to capacity, though in perpetual movement, with people coming and going, shuffling through, lighting candles, occasionally talking amongst themselves, while the bearded priest droned on, raised his thick fingers into the air as the liturgy demanded, and performed his chanted celebration in a coarse vibrato, his singing not dissimilar to that of Christos. He was decked in a simple chasuble edged with gold and purple (which had clearly belonged to a larger man in the past, and hung loose and lopsided over his white alb), and he went about his business routinely, shuffling to and from the chancel, glancing up from time to time at the congregation, and working his way through the various stages of the ceremony as a farmer might check his animal pens and door bolts before turning in for the night. Although at this moment elevated by dint of the venerable role he fulfilled, the priest was an ordinary Skourta villager born and bred, son of a goatherd, a peasant amongst peasants, and he boasted about the quality of his beehives, olives and grapes with as much conceit as any man in the community.

The hostages stood in a cluster near one wall of the building surrounded by a ring of brigands, some of whom held their heads high with pride as people stared and strained their necks to catch a better glimpse of the extraordinary clutch of foreign gentlemen. The story had got about that there were kings amongst them, and more than once Godwin caught the eye of someone who responded with a meek bow and lowering of the head. But above all they stared at the peculiar man who stood in the middle of the group, half concealed by his friends, the one with the bandages wrapped cross-shaped around his face that barely left space for his eyes and mouth at the edges. Godwin noticed one or two onlookers wince at the sight, knowing, or just guessing, what had occurred.

Straker, who had listened solemnly to Godwin's account of the previous day's events, stood resolutely attentive and silent throughout the church service, exactly as he might have done at Anglican matins. He was seen to close his eyes and lower his head in prayer, as if taking the opportunity of divine intercourse for what might prove to be the last time. Prince Leopold, by contrast, was lost to everything and barely took his eyes off the ground. His pugnacious restlessness of the last few days had evaporated and he now seemed drained of energy, resigned and helpless, perhaps afraid at last.

Farkas had also changed. For days he had appeared to be contained tight within an impenetrable shell, circumscribed and internalized; but now it seemed as though his vacuity had been fractured by a new spirit pushing its way through the shell and leading him out. His eyes were concentrated on the priest, as if his heart burned with some new-found discovery, a secret, an answer that wiped clean the diseased thoughts of a lifetime. He was thinner, scruffy and by now heavily bearded; he looked very different from the man who had travelled out to Greece for the first time just weeks previously. Had it not been for prior knowledge, Godwin might have mistaken him for a simple local worthy come to pay his respects at the church with the others. The immensely wealthy Anglo-Hellene industrialist, who bullied his wife and flaunted his cocksure opinions without restraint, had been lost on that track beside the gorge several days earlier, when he felt the steel of a gun barrel pressed to his temple.

When Demetrios had had enough of the service, he led the party of brigands and captives out of the church, measuring his pace and casting a fierce glance to the left and right as he made his way to the door. Godwin was under no illusion that, for all Demetrios' apparent reasonableness and preference for avoiding violence, he was at heart a brigand just like those of the old school; he had to look the part, to induce fear with his gaze and imply fury in his decisions. If for one moment the threat of terror was lifted or the ghost of weakness detected, his lordship over those who followed him and those who fell in with his plans, including the population of this village, would begin to crumble. And with characters like Christos at his shoulder, blade ever sharp and pistol loaded, such a lapse could prove fatal, no matter how many oaths of loyalty and years of comradeship bound them.

Outside the doors of the church there was a small patch of level ground, about a quarter of an acre in all, just below which, to one side and tucked into the incline of the hill, was the roof of the second house that the brigands had been using. Theodoros was there outside it, tending to the lamb, and he waved up at them as they came out of church. It was on the levelled terrace beside the church that the dancing was to take place, and people now began to assemble, awaiting the start. Two musicians, a drummer and a clarinettist, had already arrived and were seated on a pair of chairs placed there for their benefit. Others stood around or squatted on their haunches waiting for the action to begin.

'Why is that young fellow always so good humoured?' said Straker to Godwin, indicating to Theodoros on the lower ground, who had now begun a little dance step as he turned his spit and hummed a tune. 'At a time like this, when his fate surely hangs in the balance as precariously as our own.'

'Perhaps it is a good sign,' replied Godwin. 'It may be he knows something we do not, something that sets his mind at ease.' Straker answered with a grunt and turned to watch the people arriving for the dance. The men were dressed in their best *fustanellas* pinched tight at the waist, their holiday suits remarkably clean and well presented when compared to their usual daily clothes, and their scarlet caps set jauntily back on the head. Most wore simple ornamental waistcoats, little more than narrow strips of coloured cloth that fell down from either shoulder, though one or two, including the headman, sported embroidered waistcoats and neckerchiefs, together with shining leather pistol holsters at the navel. The women were bedecked in shapeless woollen dresses edged with colourful needlework and richly embroidered collars. Their cotton under-blouses had full, pleated sleeves, which billowed luxuriantly from beneath an upper bodice laced with silver and gold. At the waist, tied below a silver-buckled girdle, was a full-length coloured apron, and their heads were covered with headscarves and veils, silky, lightweight and tasselled, that hung long at the back and were voluptuously elegant when set beside the overall heaviness of the costume.

Godwin noticed quite early on that one particular girl had caught the attention of Mr Farkas. She was no more than eighteen years old, with moon-shaped cheeks and an innocent, questioning frown that slightly dimpled her forehead. Farkas stood slightly to one side of the other hostages and stared at her unashamedly, following her every move as she wandered around the terrace. She paused from time to time to talk to friends, smiled, glanced at the musicians as they experimented with a few rhythms, and eventually settled herself in a small group of similarly attired girls her own age. When the music struck up in earnest, she took the

413

hands of the girls standing on either side of her to form a line in preparation for the first dance. This moment was preluded by a long clarinet figure – a sustained note followed by some extravagant cascading scales and ornaments – after which the drummer took up his accompaniment, an orderly rhythm of paired quick beats followed by two longer ones and then the quick pair repeated with occasional variations for effect.

The girl raised her hands and formed a line with the dancers, and they began a lilting step, a set pattern of little forward and backward motions, with a side-step which gave a gradual movement to the right. At the sight of the girl dancing, Farkas took a pace away from his friends and his mouth fell open. He clutched a cap tightly with both hands in front of his waistcoat as he watched her head bob up and down in time with the music, her feet gliding across the ground, her expression concentrated and unsmiling, like that of all the other dancers. The solemnity of her full-cheeked face, combined with the graceful little step and the wiry coarseness of the music, was indeed picturesque, Godwin thought, but there was something else that had hold of Farkas' heart, some sudden realization or spell, that had perhaps been building these past few days and followed on from whatever enchantment had held his attention inside the church. Others had begun to notice, and Petros, who had spent so much of his time recently coaxing Farkas out of his catatonic stupor, now came and stood beside him and looked at him sideways with a querying smile.

'*What is it?*' he asked with a jerk of the chin, though he knew Farkas spoke almost no Greek. '*You see how beautiful our girls are in Greece? What would your wife think? Eh?*'

Theodoros, who had been relieved of his duties roasting the lamb, now joined them and began his own dance on the spot, arms out, thumbs clicking, his boots pirouetting in the dust with more grace than would be expected of one so heavily built. The clarinettist, standing close by, enjoyed this

414

improvised jig and added a little more flair to his tune, adorning it with twisting decorations, oriental trills and mordents. The main line of dancers, segregated into male and female sections, continued its measured, jogging progression, led at its front by an energetic young man who set the pace and occasionally leapt from the ground, clapping his boots together, slapping his thighs or flinging himself around in the air before resuming the set step and attaching himself to his neighbour by means of a held hand-kerchief. The line of the dance, though labyrinthine, followed an approximate circle, and the arrangement of those participating, within their gender groups, was accord-ing to height, so that the tail end consisted of children, the shortest of whom, at the end of the line, could have been no more than ten years old; and it was this mischievous-faced little girl who had more difficulty than any other in conceal-ing her smiles and enjoyment. The others remained inexpressive, even as the pace of the music changed, and the drummer took his place at the centre of their circle. Their solemnity and the straightforward lilt of their step in the face of the increasingly exuberant antics of the clarinettist and lead dancer, set in relief the rise of tension as the music approached its climax.

Godwin found himself standing next to Demetrios, with Pandelis also close by. It had been twenty-four hours since the incident with Solouzos, and he hoped the captain's blood had cooled enough by now for them to re-establish some kind of rapport. So much would depend on Demetrios' personal inclination if matters came to a head; it was worth a try; anything that might make him pause and reflect before committing the unthinkable, if the worst were to occur; any-thing to ease the atmosphere that existed between them at this moment. Demetrios was looking forwards, concentrat-ing hard – on the dance, Godwin presumed, judging by the direction of his gaze.

'Tell the captain we find this dance interesting,' Godwin

said to Pandelis. 'So very different from our own country, where the men dance in pairs with women, where there is much laughter, and where dancing is seen as a prelude to romance. And yet this has a romance all of its own, different from ours, but very striking.'

Pandelis replied without hesitation. 'Do not bother my *capetanios* with trivialities.' His voice had an edge that Godwin had not previously heard. 'He has more to think about today than dancing.'

'Very well,' said Godwin. 'But please tell him that I am sorry for what happened yesterday. It seemed a desperate moment and I lost myself. I now see the error of my ways.' Pandelis turned to look at him with a sneer.

'You are asking my *capetanios* to forgive you?'

'Yes,' conceded Godwin. 'And assure him that I will never again speak about – that subject. To anyone. He has my word.'

Pandelis puffed into the air with amusement but otherwise remained silent. Still Demetrios stared forwards, his unmoving gaze fixed on a single spot, until his eyes began to widen, as if he had registered something vital and new. And then, without pausing to think, he strode forwards across the terrace, pushed his way through the dancers, breaking the line and causing one of the girls to fall in the dirt. With both hands he grabbed the waistcoat of a man who stood watching on the far side.

'What do you think you're doing here?' he yelled in the fellow's face, as the music faltered to a halt and all heads turned to watch. The girls huddled together like nervous sheep, distancing themselves as much as possible from the scene, and the village headman walked over to see what was going on.

'What's the matter, friend?' asked the headman, whereupon Demetrios whipped round on him.

'This man was supposed to be watching the south road. Anyone might be passing through, for all we know,' he snapped. Adonis now came alongside and stared aggressively at the headman, while Demetrios returned his attention to the errant sentry, shaking him violently and asking again and again what he thought he was doing here. The man stared back wide-eyed into the brigand's face, speechless with terror, his arms hanging apart helplessly. From somewhere in the crowd a woman's voice began to wail. Godwin and the other hostages looked on, puzzled at the drama that was unfolding.

'Friend,' said the headman, placing a hand on Demetrios' arm, 'I think this man's watch was finished. Another should have taken his place. But we will send him back to make certain.'

At this point, Adonis, infuriated at the headman's apparent contradiction of Demetrios and his audacity in seeking to intervene, pushed him backwards with such a jolt that he fell to the ground, whereupon Adonis pulled him up and slapped him harshly around the face, an act that caused many in the crowd to gasp with shock. On seeing this, Demetrios let go of his own man and turned on Adonis.

'What the fuck did you do that for?' he asked, advancing on him.

'We can't put up with that sort of impertinence, *capetanio*,' replied Adonis. 'If they think they can get away with that, next thing they'll be calling in the troops behind our backs.'

'Have you forgotten everything I told you?' Demetrios said, through gritted teeth. He then took hold of Adonis by the collar, and in an act that gave vent to all his pent-up fury and anxiety, swung him around and threw him across the open ground so that Adonis rolled, stumbled and skittled to the far side of the terrace, tearing his clothes and forcing several to step aside before he came to a stop close to the brink above where the lamb was being cooked on its spit.

Christos now stepped forward and clapped his hands at the musicians, encouraging them to start up the tune once more, and Theodoros, whose urge to dance was now uncontainable, shoved his way through to the front of the line, roughly pushed aside the leader and took up position at the head himself, grasping his neighbour's handkerchief, hand aloft, and starting afresh the steady, rhythmic step. The others followed nervously and Demetrios wandered back to the hostages, scowling this way and that at the crowd as he went. The priest, together with a few village elders who were not participating in the dance, leant on sticks at the edge of the crowd and silently watched the brigand captain return to his place.

Farkas, seemingly oblivious to the whole incident, took advantage of the moment and walked towards where his girl was standing, having withdrawn from the dance. She had by now noticed his attentions, and cast her eyes to the ground, blushing. Meanwhile, the clarinettist and drummer had resumed the full-blooded pace of their strain, rapidly finding inspiration and passion after Christos slipped each of them a couple of coins and leant down to whisper something in their ears.

Farkas was deaf to the music, deaf to Theodoros' yelps of joy as he spun in the air and clapped his hands, and deaf to the words of a man who had walked over to stand beside the girl and was now addressing him, asking his business. Afterwards, Godwin remembered quite clearly watching the wealthy manufacturer from Liverpool, who took no notice of the man's questions but held out his hand to the pretty maiden, lowering his head slightly to engage her eyes. It was a poignant and pathetic moment, the action of a man deranged by shock, perhaps, but strangely moving and innocent, nonetheless. It would be the last clear image Godwin formed before the mayhem began, and he would never forget it: Farkas peculiarly rejuvenated, like a youth struck by love for the first time, overwhelmed by the bliss of his imaginings, his whole world and cares suspended, bleached, their substance dissolved. He held out his hand to the girl, and the clarinet twined its curling melody to a deafeningly shrill climax, while the drummer filled the air with cross-rhythms and counter-beats, and Theodoros, heavy, sweating and breathless, leapt from the ground and kicked the toe of his boot high into the air. And that was the moment.

No-one knew exactly where the first shot came from, but its sound ripped through the scene, and before anyone could digest what had happened they saw Theodoros fall like a ship's crate to the ground, limbs quivering, a tremendous hole in his head spouting blood into the red-brown dust even as the crack of the shot still echoed around the hills. The music stopped. Demetrios began yelling orders, and people scattered from the scene, while others crouched to the ground. More shots rang out, dust spat up in clouds, wood splintered and women screamed. One of the dancers was lying motionless, face down, a pool of blood soaking through her white dress around the pelvis. More shots pounded into the little terrace, followed by the hideous squeals of a man calling for his mother. It was Pandelis, hit in the chest and writhing on his back, arms and legs flailing, his eyes popping from his head with pain and shock. A small group of villagers who stood nearby stared at the twisting figure, and backed away, forming a wide circle around him, too horrified to run. Another shot silenced him and they all scattered for cover.

'They're all around us!' shouted Adonis. '*What do we do?*'

'Kill the prisoners!' yelled Christos.

'*No!*' called Demetrios, 'Fall back, take cover. Take them with us. We'll make a run for it!'

'Are you mad?' called Christos. 'Kill them first, then run!' Prince Leopold, as yet unharmed, fell to his knees on the spot, bowed and covered his head with his hands forming the shape of an upright egg on the ground. Christos noticed him, drew his short sabre and began to stride across the terrace. He neither paused to assess the danger nor hurried, but walked at a measured pace, eyes fixed on the Prince, regardless of the flying bullets and frenzy all around. Straker, who had never strayed far from Leopold's side, saw the old brigand's move and positioned himself in front of the Prince, holding out a hand, appealing.

'You can't do it, you mustn't do it,' he said, his voice gentle in the midst of the chaos; then he repeated the words in Greek, his accent immaculate. Petros, meanwhile, had grabbed Farkas and Pierrepont with each hand, and pulled them, half stumbling, over the edge of the terrace, down to where the abandoned lamb was roasting. He scrambled with them around the side of the house, out of range of the shooters, to take stock of the situation. Tears rolled down his face, as breathlessly he began to murmur his brother's name.

Godwin, still above, looked straight at Demetrios, who had his pistol drawn. 'Go!' he yelled at the brigand. 'Lead the way! I am with you!' Demetrios aimed the pistol straight at him and pointed down the route Petros had taken. Godwin ran to the little precipice and slid down, Adonis close on his heels. Demetrios himself returned his attention to Christos.

'Come on, let's go!' he called. But Christos had made his decision and no power on earth could prevent the consequence of it. His arm was raised ready to strike, his eyes ablaze, and before Demetrios could say anything further he brought the blade down on Straker's forearm, which had been raised horizontal in protection of himself and the Prince. The sabre cut straight through, severing the limb entirely. Straker fell to his knees, head bowed. Christos did not hesitate, but rapidly recovered from the first strike and swung the dreadful weapon again, bringing it down with tremendous force in the centre of his skull. And so ended the life of John Straker, scholar, orientalist and diplomat from Northumberland, in that moment of blinding pain and violence, head cloven like a market-stall melon, his last breath exhaled into the ground of a remote Attic village neither he nor anyone in his old farming family had previously known existed.

'All right,' called Demetrios, putting out a hand to Christos.

A shot pelted into the orange tree behind his shoulder, and a sizeable gash was ripped across its trunk. 'All right. You've done it. Now bring the other one. Any hope we have lies in him. Come!' Christos was finally persuaded by a bullet that flew past his arm, tearing his sleeve, grazing his forearm and exploding in the ground at his feet. He put an arm down, lifted Leopold cleanly off the ground, and followed Demetrios over the edge of the terrace to join the others.

As Demetrios gave the order to split into two groups, Adonis glanced back around the corner of the building. He called back to report that hordes of soldiers in blue coats were scrambling down from the high ground above the village.

'Where is Straker?' asked Godwin, 'Where is John Straker?' No-one took any notice of the question.

'It's finished,' said Christos. 'Let's do them here and run. They'll slow us down.'

'Not if we have one each,' replied Demetrios, and quickly he set Petros and Adonis with Farkas and Pierrepont on their way out of the village by the south road, the way that led down to a shallow gully and a stream. There was a maize field there that had not been harvested because the crop had the blight and was being left by the lazy landowner for his goats to graze on. They could take cover in the dead crop and work their way north when the coast was clear. They were to make for the Pyroxenian channel, a mile north of Páparis, the point where they had crossed the water a few days earlier. 'Come,' he called to Christos, 'bring the Prince. We'll work our way over there, by the trees, and get around behind them. They'll never expect that.' And without more ado, the two brigands, along with Godwin and Prince Leopold, broke cover, heading west as fast as they could, scrambling over rocks and prickly shrubs, out towards a plantation of stunted oaks that was half obscured from the village by a slight knoll.

'We're holed up with little cover,' called Christos from the rear as they ran. The bullets had stopped for a moment as the attacking soldiers poured into the village, searching for their quarry. 'We can't get away like this until night. We must either hide and wait or find horses.'

'Just keep on,' Demetrios replied.

Shouts from the village above and behind them, followed by the sound of shots, told them that their pursuers had seen something. Demetrios signalled to the others that they should fall to the ground, and he looked out from behind a smooth rock to see a band of soldiers, led by two men on horseback, heading south out of the village, past the house where they had been cooped up these past few days, and down towards the gully.

'They've seen the others,' said Christos between heavy breaths. 'They're heading that way. This is our chance.'

'Yes,' replied Demetrios. 'We can't do anything for our brothers. God help them. Make sure your guns are loaded.' And they were off again, the brigands grim-faced as they hurdled over the obstacles on the ground, their prisoners terrified, running as they had never run in their lives to keep up.

Further south, on the lower ground, a similar scene was being enacted, but Pierrepont had stumbled and been unable to get up again. Petros and Farkas ran on, and Adonis tried unsuccessfully to pull his prisoner up again. Eventually he left the Englishman lying there, and hurried on behind the other two, but after no more than half a minute he turned his head and saw the detachment of soldiers speeding towards them. There were still several hundred yards of open ground to cross before the maize field, and it was plainly impossible that they could reach it unseen. Adonis stopped and doubled over, out of breath.

'No good!' he called to Petros. 'If we raise our hands and spare the prisoner we might get away with our lives. It's over!'

Petros, too had stopped, but made no reply. Instead, he paused for a moment, looking hard towards the distant landscape, his eyes narrow and blinking; then he went calmly up to Farkas and held out his hand to him. It was a bizarre

422

moment, a tableau of silence in the furious panic of their flight, the veteran brigand eye to eye with the prisoner he had compassionately tended this past week, and shaking hands with him. He even seemed to smile.

'My brother is dead,' he said, 'but it's not your fault. You would have made a good Greek. You know that now, friend.' Farkas looked back at him, not understanding a word, but, recognizing the familiar benign tone, managed a smile in return. Whereupon Petros slipped a hand behind his back, neatly drew the pistol that was tucked into his belt there, and fired it into Farkas' forehead. Farkas careered backwards, his arms flung out and a portion of his skull blown clean off, before there was even time for the smile to fade on his lips.

'It is better for you like this,' said Petros, walking up to the body and looking at its face, 'reborn and dead within the hour. No time to taste the ugliness of the world.'

Adonis now turned to face his pursuers, raising his hands high in the air, while Petros Lekas, known to his peers as 'the gentleman butcher', the quiet, philosophical one, the one who appeared to have a soft touch but had shown himself so many times capable of savagery beyond the repertoire of most brigands, let fall his pistol and sank to the ground, head hanging, to spend his last moment of freedom in mourning for his dead brother. Half a minute later the soldiers were upon him.

None of this had been witnessed by Demetrios' group, which now made good ground, so far unnoticed, towards the scant cover offered by the trees. Godwin had not seen Straker fall and assumed that he had managed to slip away in the mayhem and was perhaps even now safely under guard. Until this moment he himself had thought of nothing except avoiding stray fire and making plain to Demetrios that he was there with him, in with the brigands, that he was on their side despite the attempts of others to rescue him. It was a peculiar notion but instinctive, one he did not entirely manufacture. In spite of everything that had happened, he

423

felt subtly bound to Demetrios, both the man and what he represented: the alliance with Edgar, the visionary plot to re-establish Thasofolia's fortunes. Theodoros had gone down, but surely Godwin would not be blamed for that. The soldiers' intervention was as unwelcome to him as it was to the brigands; they were a band at one in their flight; would not Demetrios see it like that, despite the warped logic? But as they ran towards the woods, and the possibility that they might indeed escape became a reality, Godwin's rush of twisted loyalty suffered a collapse, and he felt his bowels turn. They were still running for their lives. The Prince, athletic and fleet-footed, kept looking back over his shoulder, mouth open and eyes wild, as if fleeing from the monster of his childhood nightmares. Godwin, less quick, was now further burdened by a sudden change of heart. Of course his chances of living through this had been narrowed, irretrievably; if the rescue mission were to fail he believed it more than likely he would be executed before nightfall, either in retribution for fallen brigands, or as a demonstration of punishment, or for simple practical reasons. If the brigands were to hold on to one last hope, it would be in the person of Prince Leopold, and no entreaties from Godwin or whimsical appeals to the gentler and more romantic sides of their nature would prevent them dispatching him without ceremony on the spot. For the first time, now that they had reached the leafless oaks, the idea occurred to him that he should take some action to stall their flight.

He thought about turning around and running back, yelling for help and risking the aim of Christos' cherished pistol. But such an obvious betrayal would endanger the Prince's chances even if he succeeded in saving his own life. There was no time to devise a plan, and so he feigned a stumble, falling to the ground with a cry. Perhaps they would just leave him there to save time; pausing to kill him would waste valuable seconds.

'The bastard's down!' yelled Christos.

'I'll deal with him,' said Demetrios, 'you go on with that one', and he turned back to Godwin while the other two sped past him into the woods. 'So,' he said, dropping to one knee and pulling a dagger from his belt, 'this is where it ends for you. I would have preferred to use the gun, but I may need the lead for others.' His voice was calm, and though he poured sweat from the effort of running, he went about his task with measured efficiency, laying aside the dagger on the ground for a moment and ripping down the collar of Godwin's shirt to one side of the throat, to expose a breadth of naked neck. Godwin was inflamed by a sudden desperate terror and fury; he began to writhe wildly under the brigand's grip, yelling at him as he struggled, his face flushed, the veins and ligaments of his neck engorged with the strain. 'It's all right,' said Demetrios quietly, using his knees and hands expertly to control Godwin's movements, 'it will soon be over. Don't die in torment like this.' Neutralized and powerless, Godwin felt for a moment that he could do nothing but yield, as he might to a doctor. He was pinned. He could not understand Demetrios' gentle advice but the implication was clear, and he was right. It was pointless to resist. 'That's it,' Demetrios breathed into his face, 'leave this world at peace with yourself, my friend.'

But Godwin would not give up the fight, and as Demetrios removed a hand for one passing instant to retrieve his weapon, Godwin's fingers gripped around a sharp-edged stone to the side of him on the ground. He brought it up to Demetrios' face with all the force he could muster; it caught him on the orbital bone above his right eye. The violence and shock of the blow threw the brigand off balance and for a moment he fell back, grasping his head with both hands as a stream of blood began to pour from the wound. Just at that point there was the sound of gunshot and shouting voices a little way ahead of them. And then Christos' voice rang out.

'Demetri! We're trapped! They've cut us off.' Demetrios

425

turned and looked to see what was happening, and Godwin quickly wriggled from under him. Ahead of them he could see a line of soldiers advancing into the wood on the far side, led by two men on horseback.

'Kill the Prince!' called Demetrios. 'Do it now!' Christos needed little persuasion, and pulled his old pistol from its holster. Prince Leopold was sprinting forward towards the approaching horsemen, yelling unintelligibly, Christos at his heels, still close enough to get an easy shot. He raised the pistol, took aim, closing one hardened eye and staring the length of the barrel, and pulled the trigger. Both Demetrios and Godwin froze on the spot as they watched, and were still standing seconds later when no sound came, no smoke, no gunshot. Christos lowered his pistol and stared at it in his hand, apparently confused.

'What's wrong with the damn thing?' he shouted, but then without warning the pistol fired, misfired, its barrel exploding in his hand, letting off a spray of steel shrapnel, some of which caught Christos in the face, causing him to reel back and clutch his eyes. His fingers were black and mangled, and he let drop the remains of the pistol he had been polishing so patiently these past few days.

From ahead one of the horsemen was shouting. 'Not that one! It's the other one, he's the leader. But don't kill him. Whatever you do, don't kill him.'

'My God,' murmured Demetrios as he stood facing the advancing pair, and drew his pistol. He seemed to have forgotten Godwin for the moment. 'It's Daniel!'

Godwin heard the name and looked up at the men on horseback who now were riding at full gallop towards them, straight past the standing, impotent figure of Christos. One of them was a uniformed soldier; the other, steady in the saddle over the uneven ground, and holding on to his reins with one hand as he overtook his comrade, was Daniel Brooke. From beyond, a round of shots signalled the end of Christos. The soldiers had caught up with him, and by the

426

time Godwin looked across, the old brigand was on his knees. It took several more rounds to bring him down, and he fell at last face first on to the rocky ground. Two soldiers stopped to kick over his body and search him, while the remainder ran forward, following the riders.

The two horsemen pulled up in front of Demetrios, who stared at them defiantly, pistol in hand, blood still pouring from his eyebrow. Daniel let go of his reins and held up both hands to show he was unarmed. He indicated for the soldier not to draw his gun.

'So, *koumbare*,' Demetrios said calmly to Daniel. 'Why do you tell them not to shoot? Have you not brought them to me? Perhaps you should kiss me now, like Judas did in the old book.'

'Let your weapon go, Demetri,' said Daniel. 'If you tell them who's behind all this they will spare your life.'

'And what good would that do?'

'They don't care about you. They want to know who gives your orders. They may even let you go. It's not too late to strike a deal.'

Demetrios laughed. 'Another deal?' he said.

'This time it's different,' said Daniel. 'They have assured me. And there is no other option.'

'There you are wrong, little brother,' replied Demetrios. 'There is one other option.' The words were barely uttered when he raised his pistol and pointed it directly at Daniel. This time the shot rang clear and true. Daniel took the blow full in the chest with a cry and fell back in his saddle, hanging over the horse's tail by the stirrups. The animal reared up in fright and turned wildly on the spot. The mounted soldier needed all his strength and skill to try and control his own horse, which shied and tossed its head, while Demetrios moved fast to reload his gun. Daniel was being flung from side to side, suspended like a limp toy, his outstretched arms brushing the dirt by the horse's stamping hoofs. Eventually his feet slipped free of the stirrups and he fell to the ground as the horse bolted away. Demetrios looked up. The soldiers were approaching, but he had nearly accomplished his task and had already discarded the loading rod as he turned around to face Godwin. But the soldiers had arrived at their stand and taken their aim. Before he had the chance to find his target he was struck from behind by three separate rounds almost simultaneously. He staggered forwards to Godwin, hands apart, the pistol falling harmlessly to the ground. Two more shots were fired, the impact of which pushed him further towards Godwin, his feet staggering, legs caving at the knees, barely able to take the weight of his body. Another laboured step and he arrived face to face with his prisoner, resting both hands on his shoulders to stop himself falling. 'The Lord has abandoned me,' he whispered, staring into the Englishman's eyes as the life left his body; and then he slumped forwards, leaving Godwin to bear the burden of him in an embrace. It was over.

By the time Godwin let the body of Demetrios slip through his arms to the ground, Prince Leopold had returned to the scene, surrounded by a circle of soldiers. He went straight to where Daniel lay spread-eagled, and knelt down to check his neck for a pulse. When Godwin arrived at his side the Prince looked up at him. His face was smeared with dust and sweat.

'We are saved,' he said, his voice incongruously blank and unemotional. He turned his face back to Daniel. 'We are saved and he is dead.'

*

The Prince and Godwin were placed on horses for the ride back up to Skourta, a journey that took them less than ten minutes, which was peculiar, Godwin thought, because shortly before, their flight across the same ground, at perhaps four times the speed, had seemed to last for at least half an hour. The same herd of goats that had raised their heads from the grass to watch them running away from the village earlier, now looked up again to observe their return.

All the while the smell of cooking lamb still hung in the air.

By the time they arrived at the level terrace, the two captured brigands, Petros and Adonis, were standing outside the church, tied, shackled, and surrounded by a group of soldiers who taunted them and blew cigarette smoke in their faces, not far from the lined-up bodies of Theodoros, Pandelis, Farkas and Straker. Adonis hung his head and blinked at the ground, but Petros stood tall and stared into the distance with a frown, consumed in thought. The other two brigand casualties, Christos and Demetrios, whose corpses had been slung over the back of a horse for the walk up to the village, were now pulled off and placed in line with their associates. Daniel was being carried up on the shoulder of a burly soldier who was obviously feeling the strain of his burden as he reached the church. He let fall the body with hearty relief when he arrived at the line of corpses; one or two of his friends gave him a cheer as he shed his load, to which he gave a mock bow. Daniel fell to the ground in a heap, face down and knees bent, so that his rump stuck in the air and his shirt rode up, exposing the bare skin of his back. One of the soldiers seemed to crack a joke about this, but the burly one who had carried him up was too tired to straighten the body out, and waved a hand dismissively as he walked away.

Pierrepont was also there, his bandages filthy, a small patch of blood seeping through at the cross, indicating that his wound had begun to weep once more, but otherwise unhurt. When he saw the other party arrive he walked forward and held Godwin in a tight embrace, saying nothing at all but shaking with emotion. He remained like that for some while until Godwin prised himself away, having noticed the Prince standing over the body of Straker. He walked over in order to stand beside him, passing through groups of soldiers – and there were many of them – who were sitting around relaxing near the bodies, smoking and laughing. They carried on like this, occasionally throwing a

429

cigarette stub in the face of one of the brigands, while Godwin and the Prince stood, hands joined and speechless, looking down at the jumbled mess of clothes and skewed limbs that was their dead friends. Near to them, lying in the dust but undamaged, was Godwin's journal. It had earlier fallen from the folds of his clothes.

*

No-one in years to come was to sing songs about the passing of Demetrios Lambros, last of the swashbuckling brigand captains. His name would be remembered only as the perpetrator of the Skourta murders, a mean-minded, uncouth torturer and ruffian, a leftover from bygone times, who had no place amongst Greeks of the modern state. And normality soon returned to the village that had played host to the bizarre drama, just as smoothness returns to a tree trunk that has grown around and enveloped a line of barbed wire. Many years later, after the motorway had been built across the wilds of Boeotia, and everything that had once been a village had grown into a town, the occasional carload of tourists would deviate from the National Road, perhaps to find a picturesque route to the Peloponnese, avoiding the urban choke of Athens. Sometimes, as they drove through, those who carried guidebooks with them might spend a moment glancing out of their car window when they passed the sign saying 'Skourta' by the side of the road, and would indulge their imagination in picturing the dramatic events that had taken place there. But there was nothing to indicate that the road along which they sped, about half a mile to the east of the village, was constructed over what had once been that stunted oak plantation, and that it crossed the very spot where the veteran brigand Christos had fallen, finally brought down with a chest full of lead. Very occasionally someone would stop for a coffee or a Coke at the village café, and might ask one of the old men tossing beads there if he knew where exactly the celebrated murders had taken place. And such tourists would always leave the village with a feeling of privileged knowledge, for there was rarely an occasion when a local person was not able to relate the incident back to some member of his own clan, someone he distinctly remembered, a great-uncle perhaps, who, in his turn, as a boy, had heard an eyewitness account from some long-gone and forgotten village resident, someone who had been there, had heard the shrill turn of the clarinettist's tune that morning of the *Panagía* in November 1869, and could recall, as if it were yesterday, the hunted expressions on the faces of those five foreign gentlemen as they stood huddled together in the church, awaiting their fate; those they had called kings.

Chapter 38

Petros Solouzos returned to Skourta the morning after the killings, which was later than he had hoped. He had been delayed by dramatic events closer to home, in Páparis. The rider who brought him the ghastly news from Skourta had barely arrived when word reached Solouzos that a British gunboat had unexpectedly docked at the port. The captain of the vessel had sent a message to the Deputy warning of his intention to deploy a detachment of twenty armed British marines on the island, and wished to assure the local authorities that this was not to be interpreted as an act of hostility towards either Greece or Greek citizens. Their destination, the captain explained, was a place called Thasofolia, and their business was with one Mr Brooke, an Englishman and a resident of that village. Solouzos had managed to delay the disembarkation until necessary protocol had been accomplished, by telegraph, with Athens. Once this had been achieved, and the British troops sent on their way (taking with them the messenger from Skourta), Solouzos was free at last to depart for the scene of the massacre.

On his arrival, he found the village all but deserted. The soldiers had returned to Athens the previous evening, together with their captives, the two surviving foreigners and a collection of corpses. Two foreigners? Solouzos asked, dreading some awful new twist in the story. Surely there had been three. No, the village headman replied. One of them, the Englishman without the bandages, had left quite promptly after the showdown. He had commandeered two horses and insisted on taking with him the body of the young man who had been shot from his horse.

'Did no one try to stop him?' raged Solouzos. 'What do you think this is? Some petty quarrel about a herd of goats?'

At this, the headman's face turned to stone and he walked up to look Solouzos in the eye.

'Shame on you. After what we have endured. Where were you when the bullets were flying? Eh?'

'That foreign gentleman is an important witness. He knows something. He should be under guard.'

'I'd like to have seen you try and stop him. He's not running away. He's just taking the boy home. And a couple of our men have gone with him to help and make sure nothing goes wrong.'

'The government will—'

'To hell with your government,' spat the headman and turned his back on Solouzos. 'Just leave him be. He'll come back as soon as he's finished his business.'

Godwin and his entourage had already slipped through Páparis before dawn and, by the time Solouzos was having this encounter, were on their way towards the mountain pass that led to Thasofolia. The landscape over which they journeyed, now familiar to the silent and brooding Englishman, had lost both its menace and its beauty. As they descended out of the gorge and reached the fertile river basin, Godwin procured a small cart from a group of itinerant shepherds who were encamped near to the road. Daniel's body, which had been sewn into a hessian shroud and strapped across the back of a mule, was now transferred to the cart, and lay flat for the final stage of its journey home. News of the Skourta killings had reached the village with the British marines the previous evening, and word of the body's imminent return had been delivered by a rider galloping ahead of Godwin's party earlier in the day. And so, as they rode into Thasofolia, the entire population of the village was

433

there to watch, silent, apart from the mournful moans of the women.

They passed into the courtyard of the Brookes' house and the gates clattered shut behind them. Mag was there to receive them. She handled the situation in her usual practical and capable way, and after instructing the servants to take Daniel's body to be dressed, she greeted Godwin and led him into the house. Her short, shapeless grey hair would not lie straight today, but stuck out slightly on one side as if rebelling against her assumption that, just because she held no interest in personal vanity, it should meekly comply with the flat and drab style demanded of it. The asymmetry of it, in that moment as she stood before Godwin, lent her habitually austere face a degree of vulnerability that endeared her to him.

'Edgar has fled to the mountain,' she said. 'Panayiotis is being held and questioned about his involvement in the crime, and, because of his association with us, Edgar has been implicated. It is all nonsense, but Edgar knows only too well how his enemies could exploit the situation and do terrible mischief, and so he has decided to leave. For a while.'

'What if they find him?' asked Godwin.

'Elias Lambros is sending search parties. He is compelled to do no less. But even if they knew where he was hidden they would not touch him. A party of British soldiers is also here, to assist in the search.'

Godwin was taken aback at this. 'What on earth are British soldiers doing here? What are their orders?'

Mag raised her eyes. 'Now that it's all over, they say they came here to escort Edgar to Athens so that he and they together could work out some sort of solution to the crisis.'

'Against his own will, if necessary?'

'Perhaps. Or perhaps there's more at stake here than we all suspect.'

'What do you mean?'

'It is not my place to ask, Mr Tudor,' said Mag flatly. 'I am

434

a mere woman and excluded from discussions that touch on power and money. All I know is that Edgar has not been seen to be co-operative in recent years. Things did seem to be coming to a head. There's little doubt in my mind that Sir Thomas Wishart intended to remove Edgar to Athens in order to exert pressure of some sort.'

'To make him change his stance on some particular issue.'

'Perhaps.'

'And the abduction of the hostages gave Sir Thomas the opportunity to take action against Mr Brooke? The whole incident might therefore have been to Sir Thomas' advantage.'

'Or to the advantage of whoever's case Sir Thomas has chosen to represent. I don't know. One can do no more than speculate.'

It took a while for the implications of Mag's notion to set in, and Godwin pondered it silently before looking up at her again. 'And Panayiotis?' he asked.

'He will be taken to Athens. He won't stand a chance. But he'd sooner die than say anything against Edgar. Poor Panayiotis. He will bear the brunt of the courts' anger.'

'But he was not one of the abductors. His involvement was a matter of family honour. No matter how appalling his deed, he did not intend to murder innocent men.'

'It doesn't matter. It will be better for the newspapers to pin the blame on him rather than on a dead brigand who can't be seen to suffer. Or his peasant minions. The politicians will make a show of it, and obscure their own mishandling by satisfying a hungry public's desire for retribution. Panayiotis' head will be hung out for all to see.'

Godwin looked to the ground. 'I was near to Daniel when he died. He fell like a hero. Prince Leopold will tell the world that he died attempting to save our lives.'

'That is small comfort,' said Mag, sighing, 'though it will no doubt help Edgar's case. He sacrificed his son.'

'No,' Godwin replied, 'Daniel risked and sacrificed his own

life. It was noble and it was reckless, but it was not accomplished on behalf of Edgar. Daniel alone should bear the credit for his courage.'

'And who's to question the matter,' said Mag quickly, 'now that the boy is dead? If his death helps Edgar to prove his innocence in all this, then let it be so. We have suffered enough.' Godwin conceded the point in silence, and a change came over Mag's face. 'Enough of this,' she said gently. 'We can talk later. There is something more pressing for you at present.'

For all his hardships of the past days, Godwin felt a shiver at Mag's words. 'More pressing?'

'She knows of your arrival,' Mag said gently. 'She waits for you. In the drawing room.' Godwin hesitated before nodding, and turned to leave. 'Do not express your surprise too sharply when you see her,' said Mag before he reached the door.

'Surprise?'

'You will find her changed. There is nothing we can do to console her. Perhaps it is not even consolation she seeks. She is so very private at times.'

A few minutes later Godwin was in the drawing room, standing with the door shut behind him, and she was there, sitting low on a stool by the fire, fanning it, as she had been just weeks before when he beheld her for the first time. So little time ago. This should have resembled that earlier moment, but did so only in the way that a garden in winter bears slight relation to the same place in June. The very air in the room had changed its hue, and a chill evening light flooded in from the french windows, casting pale dullness where once there had been golden warmth. He approached, but she did not turn to look back. He could see that her hair was shorter, that it had been coarsely shorn and barely reached her neck.

'Please don't say anything about Daniel,' she said, pre-empting him.

'All right.'

'You will stay for his burial, I trust. We shall do it to-morrow. At the pool, I think. He would have liked that.'

'Of course.'

Lydia now turned to face him. Her cheeks were sunken, blotched and scratched, and her eyes ringed with darkness. No-one could have cut her beautiful hair like that, Godwin thought. She must have inflicted this on herself.

'My dear girl,' he said, and walked towards her, but she jerked back around as if stung, and returned her attention to the fire.

'Did anyone tell you about Hermann?' she asked quickly.

'Yes.'

'So much to happen at the same time.'

'So much, indeed.'

'It makes you wonder if life can ever be the same again. Or if it's worth trying to make it the same. We make so many mistakes. Everything we do is a mistake.'

'There is always a reason. And, given time, we grow to understand.'

At this, Lydia let out a muted cry but immediately stifled it with a hand at her mouth. Godwin approached and laid his fingers on her shoulder. She tensed at the feel of his touch, covering her face with both palms, but did not pull away.

'Let me help you,' he said softly.

'It's all my fault. Again.' Her voice was cracking and her shoulders heaved.

He moved towards her. 'How can it be? Why do you say such a thing?'

'Why can't I be different?'

'Because the world and all our lives would be poorer if you were,' said Godwin, and placed his other hand on her other shoulder.

She buried her face still deeper in her palms. 'Why don't you hate me?' she said, rocking backwards and forwards. 'You should. They should all hate me. And instead—'

'And instead I love you,' he answered, interrupting her crying. He waited for her to respond, but she neither spoke nor moved. 'I loved you from the moment I first saw you. And I will always love you. Nothing can ever happen to shake my love for you. Darling Lydia.' He knelt down and drew close to her face, so that he could smell the familiar herby scent of her skin. 'Come away with me,' he whispered, close to her cheek. 'Tomorrow. After the burial. Away from this place, away from this country. Let me take you home to England.' Still there was silence, and Lydia remained bent double, motionless, face wrapped in her palms. 'Nothing you have done can affect my love,' continued Godwin. 'It's all—' he searched for the words – 'this place, your life here, your family. Come with me to England and I swear to make you the happiest woman alive. We will build your life anew. There will be no more misunderstanding when we are away from here, no more misfortune.' He had said enough, and now stayed silent, waiting for her to recover, still holding her by the shoulders.

Eventually, she took a deep breath, as if coming up from under water. She drew her hands back across her forehead, pushed her fingers through to the roots of her hair and scratched at her scalp impatiently, before resting her chin on her hands, facing the fire.

'That morning. At the pool,' she said. 'When we last saw each other—'

'There was a reason for that, too,' Godwin said softly. 'Do not punish yourself.'

'No. You do not understand.'

'I think I do. Let it be.'

'I will not let it be,' she said a shade tersely, and Godwin let go of her shoulders. She pulled out a wet handkerchief from her sleeve and blew her nose. 'What you do not understand,' she continued, 'was that it was important for Daniel to feel close to me. To feel closer than anyone else.'

'What do you mean?'

'He needed me. He's always needed me and I kept pushing him away. Father said that I should do something. And he was right.'

'Said that you should do what?'

'That I should make Daniel feel special. That I had been putting him down and that he didn't feel like a proper man, and that he loved me, loved us all, and felt as if no one valued him.'

'Your father told you that you should – that you should do what you did that day, by the pool?'

'No. Not that. He just warned me that Daniel's spirits were low, and that there was a danger he might leave us. Or do something awful. Daniel always thought I allowed others close to me but never him. And he always thought Father was neglecting him.'

'But why,' asked Godwin, 'why did you choose to do – to do what you did? In my presence?'

'You see? I said you wouldn't understand.'

'But why?' insisted Godwin.

'I didn't choose. It just happened.' She turned on him, her eyes flashing impatiently. 'It sprang out of a game, almost. We've always played games. Isn't that what children do? Except we forgot we weren't children for a moment. And so it just became confused. And I wanted to be close to him again. And then Daniel seemed intent on something, too, something else, a different kind of game, maybe, and I didn't stop him, because I was confused, I don't know.' She covered her face again and seemed to be about to start crying, but recovered and raised her chin. 'I don't know,' she repeated more firmly. 'Several things. And nothing in particular. It just happened. And wouldn't have happened again. I think Daniel was desperately ashamed. It made everything worse, you see. He loathed himself all the more. And I think that's why he got himself killed. And that's why I think it's my fault. Everything that happens is my fault.'

'It's not true, Lydia,' replied Godwin, but she seemed lost

to his words. 'I was there when he fell,' he went on. 'And I saw him the day before, as well. He was trying to help. He wanted to save the Prince's life, and mine, and the others'.'

Lydia was staring at the wall, and for the first time seemed almost to smile. Encouraged, Godwin took her hand and held it tightly. She turned to look at him, now with a definite, though slight and pained, smile. Godwin smiled back at her.

'Thank you for trying to comfort me,' she said, with a hint of the old captivating warmth in her eyes, 'and I know that you will find it in you to forgive me for what happened. For that I am grateful. *So* grateful.' Squeezing his hand, her face was a picture of sincere empathy and Godwin's hopes soared. Perhaps the wind was changing, he thought, perhaps there was a chance she might now emerge from the depths; and he would be there, hand outstretched, to draw her safely home. But she turned away from him again towards the wall and her smile faded. 'You do not, and you will not, ever, understand,' she murmured. 'Father will. He is the only one now.' And she let slip his hand. After a pause, she rose to her feet and walked slowly away. Godwin turned on his knee to watch her and spoke before she reached the door. He could not let it finish like this.

'Lydia!' he said. 'Am I to have an answer?'

She looked at him curiously. 'An answer? To what?'

'Do you accept me?'

Her eyebrows were slightly knitted. 'Accept you? How?' He had poured out his heart, had laid his life before her, and she had not even seemed to notice.

'Will you come home with me?'

'I misunderstand you. This is my home.'

'And will always remain so? No matter what?'

She looked confused, almost injured. 'Of course. How could it be otherwise? Father is here.'

'It would never be my intention to cut you off from your father. He will surely also return to England now. After everything that has happened.'

'Never.'

'I have property. Wealth. You would be comfortable,' he said, his voice rising. 'I can also provide for your family to a degree.'

'Father will never leave.'

'You cannot see what this place is doing to you. Where it will end.'

'This is my home,' she repeated, her eyes fixed on a spot somewhere behind his shoulder, as if in a trance. There was distance between them, Godwin reminded himself, and she probably could not focus properly.

'Lydia.' He approached her, softening his tone. 'I ask again, will you come with me?'

Her face suddenly crumpled and tears filled her eyes. 'I do not understand your raving!' she cried.

'It is you who—' he began in hot blood, but raised his fist to his mouth to stop any further words emerging. 'Forgive me. I – I have not slept and – I am not myself. I did not mean—'

'I do forgive you! But I do not understand what else you want from me! Please allow me to leave.'

'Of course,' said Godwin. He stayed where he knelt and lowered his eyes. To reiterate his plea now would be a mockery; and she was close to hysteria. 'Do not let me detain you,' he said quietly, looking at the floor, and was aware of her departure only by the click of the door behind her.

It was dull and damp by the pool. The funeral had a rather military atmosphere because of the marines, who made up the majority of those present. They stood tall in their scarlet uniforms, raised their rifles and fired a salute over the grave. The noise and echo were deafening. Mag, Lydia and Percival huddled close together to shelter from the spitting rain under a single umbrella, and perhaps to offer one another comfort. The village priest was there, as well as Barba Stamos, Elias Lambros, and a few members of the household staff. A

441

message had been received from Solouzos saying that he would not be able to get there until the evening and so they had better proceed without him, as the following morning he would be compelled to return promptly to Páparis, along with Mr Tudor and the detachment of marines; and thence to Athens.

The simple pine coffin was lowered into the ground to the accompaniment of a chanted prayer from the priest and the swinging of an ornate censer. Clouds of delicious incense wafted across the still air and drifted over the surface of the pool's dark waters. Godwin looked up to the distant rim of the bowl above and wondered if Edgar lay concealed in the bushes, observing the ritual. He had always scorned priestcraft. What memories of the boy would the bullish landowner now take with him to his own grave, whenever and wherever that awaited him?

When the ceremony was complete, the marines marched slowly away, one of them, at the fore, playing a ballad melody on a silver whistle. The other mourners, too, moved on, though Godwin lingered, hoping that Lydia might stay for a while to talk. But she looked up at him, smiled faintly and then walked with the others towards where the horses were tethered. Godwin hurried over to walk the last few paces by her side. She took his arm and he held his umbrella over her head.

'I almost wish you could have made one of your exposures of that ceremony,' she said. 'I doubt this place has seen the like of it before. And I hope will never again.'

'There would not have been sufficient light,' said Godwin quietly as he walked. He neglected to remind her that the camera was smashed.

'Daniel would have loved to know the soldiers were there. He rather would have liked to be a British soldier. He had a weakness for uniforms. He was so vain, you know.' She smiled at the ground.

Their feet crunched through the damp ferns.

'Lydia,' said Godwin softly, after a suitable pause, and came to a stop. 'I leave tomorrow.'

'And I will mourn your departure, Mr Tudor,' she said without hesitation, looking up and straight into his eyes. There was the faintest flicker of defiance in her look, something that might have passed unnoticed to anyone else, but to Godwin, so keenly tuned to her moods, it spelled an absolute and final resolve. Although he had thought about little else since their encounter in the drawing room the previous evening, and had searched all night for a thread of hope to lighten his despair, he now knew with complete certainty that it was over, and that it would be futile to attempt to change her mind. At last it dawned on him that she had probably never viewed him as a lover. He, like Pierrepont, and perhaps others, had entertained a fantasy all along. And she was offering him the chance to depart with a dignified friendship intact. 'We will all mourn your departure,' she added, further depersonalizing her expression of feeling. 'I am sure Father would like to have seen you again. Perhaps you will return in happier times.'

At these last words, Godwin felt a great weariness. He nodded and let his head slump. 'Perhaps,' he said, and did not intervene as Lydia was called to take her horse. He followed a few paces behind the party as they made their way back to the house. The clouds darkened across the already dark gorge, and the rain began to fall more heavily. An absolute gloom descended on the great bowl of farmland and the surrounding hills of Thasofolia. None felt its weight more crushingly than the young Englishman, whose life had been changed by the rare enchantment of this place and who was now preparing to leave it for ever.

Chapter 39

HMS *Endeavour* was anchored a mile or so from the port of Piraeus when Sir Thomas Wishart arrived adjacent to it on a small coastal steamer and was whistled aboard by the ship's crew. He had purportedly come to visit and bid farewell to the surviving hostages of the incident at Skourta, now that several days had passed during which they had recovered in the safety and privacy of a British military vessel. The decision had been made to keep the former captives away from Athens, despite their request to attend a funeral service for their fallen friends at St Paul's Anglican church, because of the publicity that their story had generated. Feelings in the capital were running high; the Legation building was continuously besieged by the curious and furious alike, and it was all the police could do to prevent the parliament building itself being stormed. Sir Thomas' contention, made publicly and printed in several newspapers, that the Skourta incident, although tragic in many ways, had not been an absolute disaster and should now be laid to rest, had first been received with shock and then universally vilified. The English envoy had since become the subject of widespread vituperation and there were reports that placards had been sighted in the city calling for Wishart's blood. The Prime Minister himself had to move around his capital under cover of dark for fear of public mobbing, while the opposition, taking full advantage of the government's apparent miscalculation, had its daggers drawn and was preparing for the kill.

Notwithstanding this emotionally charged response – Sir Thomas remarked to his wife that morning as they finished their breakfast tea – he failed to see why everyone chose to emphasize the negative side of things; after all, the crisis had been brought to a close, the Prince had been saved, and those brigands unfortunate enough to have survived would swiftly be brought to justice and guillotined. Some good would yet come of it; brigandage might at last become a thing of the past. Surely, after a suitable period of time, everyone's feelings would subside and they would all see sense. Lady Wishart had said nothing in reply, but let fall her teacup and left the dining room.

Godwin was already waiting in the captain's quarters when Sir Thomas was ushered in. He shook hands but could not bring himself to return the Minister's faltering smile. Whether or not Sir Thomas had a suspicion of Godwin's state of mind was not immediately obvious, as he deposited his case, removed his coat and, in the absence of any conversational encouragement, filled time with a babble of pleasantries. It was clear that he had nothing of substance to say but was performing an uncomfortable duty in accordance with what was expected of him. But Godwin had no time for the Minister's stream of inconsequential blather. He wanted rid of him, and would shortly have it so, but not before he had completed his own agenda. There was still an issue outstanding in this affair, and it was his business to have it aired.

'His Majesty King George graced our church with his presence yesterday,' said Sir Thomas, 'which we all thought was a very kind gesture, and one I'm sure the families of the deceased will appreciate, when they hear of it. The entire street from Constitution Square down to St Paul's was a dense mass of people come to show their respect, and all silent, for once. Of course, it was only a service of memorial. The bodies are to be returned to England. They join you aboard this vessel, as you have probably heard. There will be an appropriate ceremony at the port tomorrow, and as soon as they're safely stowed in the hold you should be able to set off. I'm sure you cannot wait.'

'Did Mr Brooke attend the service?' asked Godwin.

'Mr Brooke? No. He will doubtless assist in our investigation in due course. What an appalling tragedy for the Brooke family! Such a fine boy.'

'Mr Brooke has still made no communication with you?'

'None,' said Sir Thomas, hurriedly following his remark with, 'however, I do have a telegraph message from your father. Very brief, I fear, but I'm sure it will bring you some comfort.'

'My father be damned!' said Godwin forcefully, and stared at Sir Thomas. 'I care neither for my father nor for myself at this time. I wish only to atone to some extent for the deaths of three innocent men. And on that score I have something to tell you. Something I should have told you before.'

'Whatever can you mean?'

'Regarding the murders. Information that I have no doubt will irrevocably tarnish my reputation, if not implicate me as an accessory to the abduction. I welcome such an implication. And I willingly stoop to bear the burden of its responsibility.'

'Now come, sir, you have undergone a most terrible experience.' Godwin was breathing heavily, his lips trembling and tears spilling from his eyelids as Wishart went on, 'Your distress is natural and understandable, and to have been so close to such atrocities, but pray do not—'

'Edgar Brooke conceived the plan,' Godwin blurted out, 'the entire enterprise was his, the brigands were enlisted by him and the terms for the prisoners' surrender devised by him and him alone.' It was out. Godwin closed his eyes and breathed long and deep. Sir Thomas stared at him for a moment and then looked away.

'You are deluded,' he said quietly.

'No delusion,' replied Godwin, smiling through tears. The

relief was exquisite. 'Mr Brooke told me himself of the conspiracy before it was enacted and I agreed not to reveal his secret so long as he allowed me to accompany the hostages and work as intermediary in the negotiations; and for that decision I shall spend my days in penance.'

'This is some nonsense cooked up by the Greek government. I have already heard rumour of it in Athens. The Prime Minister seeks to avoid blame and therefore puts it upon some other. The man's son was killed, for heaven's sake!'

'It is the truth.'

Sir Thomas, who had been pacing somewhat uncomfortably near the door of the cabin, now put his arms behind his back and strode purposefully across the floor to Godwin. His expression was deadly serious, and his manner suddenly authoritative and senior. His voice when he spoke was cool but viperous, a quality that made Godwin recognize there was more to this man than he had previously thought; his job in this extraordinary country had a dark side to it, something that had occasional need of secrecy and ruthlessness, something that demanded more intelligence than he had previously credited Sir Thomas with possessing, but it was a devious, labyrinthine brand of intelligence.

Wishart held out his index finger. 'Now you listen to me, and listen well. There have been some mistakes these past few days, but what's done is done. Her Majesty's government is clear that nothing further could have been achieved, short of taking hostile military action on Greek soil. The Prime Minister of Greece avoided such a confrontation, but narrowly, and for specific reasons. There are issues connected with this matter that far outweigh the significance of three men's lives, and you, for all your arrogance and speculation, have glimpsed but the smallest detail of them. The Foreign Secretary wishes me to make it abundantly clear to the Greek nation that no further abuse of Britain, British interests or British subjects will be tolerated in connection with this incident. Much has been conceded, but a line has now been drawn. You will do your nation no service by interfering. There will be no accusations, no talk of a conspiracy. Do I make myself clear on the subject, Mr Tudor?'

'You make yourself perfectly clear, sir, though I should be guilty of mendacity were I to remain silent on the true facts of the situation, and you should find yourself answerable for an even greater crime than the one for which you are already culpable through your woeful mismanagement of the crisis.'

'My answerability is my affair. I am answerable only to Her Majesty's appointed government. As for your preoccupation with personal guilt and conscience, I fear that the sensibility of artistic young men is of little concern to the workings of international relations and economics.'

'And why all this deception?' asked Godwin.

'There is no deception,' replied Sir Thomas. 'I seek only to stifle unnecessary rumours.'

'Tell me who stands to benefit if Edgar Brooke goes unpunished.'

'I do not know what you mean.'

'Is it the mining proposal? Do you intend to use your hold over Mr Brooke to ensure he no longer stands in the way of the German developers and their lignite mines? Is that your intention? To gag him for the remainder of his life and force his compliance in matters that have potential to impede smooth relations between the British and Greek governments?'

'Would you have impediments? Would you risk injuring a relationship that could alter the entire balance of power in the eastern Mediterranean? Have you no idea how close Greece is to an alliance with Russia, at the expense of England? Do you not know what that would mean for the future of the Balkans? Mr Tudor, you are a young man and little experienced in these matters. The whimsical ideas of a heavy-drinking and unstable landowner in a remote corner of Greece are no basis upon which to create obstacles in international politics where there need be none, no matter whether he be a British citizen or not.'

Godwin shook his head. 'You allowed the attack on Skourta to go ahead because you wanted it so, am I not right?'

'Now you talk like a madman.'

'You and the Greek government in tandem. What a performance you put on in the negotiations! It was all an act for the benefit of spectators, was it not? You probably knew from the start of Mr Brooke's involvement, and that is why you took no action to include him in the negotiations. John Straker was right, I now see, to raise the question. You wanted it all to go wrong at Skourta.'

'You are to be pitied for entertaining such a notion.'

'It was imperative that the plot should fail, so that you would be able to compel Mr Brooke into submission. Neither you nor the Greeks ever had it in mind to offer the ransom or the amnesty. But did you not see that people would get killed? Were you so blind? You may have achieved your ends, but there is blood on your hands, sir. You are not only unprincipled, you are a deceiver, and an incompetent deceiver at that. Shame on you!'

There was silence between them. Sir Thomas eventually sighed and turned away. 'I will attribute your ravings to the ordeal from which you have so recently been released,' he said, reaching for his coat. 'You have a long journey home, Mr Tudor. I strongly advise you to spend the time in reflection. Should you decide to promulgate your absurd exposure on your return to England, you will at best be in receipt of public pity. If you persist, that pity may change to ridicule, and from there it would be but a short step to invoke the law against your pronouncements. Thereon, I fear, the path for you would prove to be less amusing. I think that I speak on behalf of the Prime Minister, the Foreign Secretary and all Her Majesty's elected representatives when I counsel you to forget the accusations you have just placed. I shall regard your comments as the offspring of heightened passions, and shall therefore keep them to myself. For that you should, and I am sure one day will, be most grateful. Goodbye, Mr Tudor.' Sir Thomas held out a hand, but Godwin made no move to return the gesture; and so the Minister turned on his heel, with a slight cough, and went towards the door. 'I shall now pay my respects to Prince Leopold and Mr Pierrepont,' he said from the doorway. 'Am I to convey any message from you to Lady Wishart?' And the look in his eyes as he made this final remark convinced Godwin of a shrewdness in Sir Thomas of which he had formerly been ignorant. But he made no reply and turned to face the window.

PART FOUR

Chapter 40

From the final entry in Godwin Tudor's journal:

Since I know now that she will never be mine, and that in all likelihood I shall never again rest my eyes upon her face, I must be of a mind to persuade myself of the folly of that former infatuation, and to examine the reasons for its emergence, thereby to heal the wound. In this endeavour I find myself divided into two persons. The mechanical Mr Tudor, possessed of an ability to tabulate and classify, embarks on the task with vigour. Jacket thrown aside, a tune on his lips, he assembles the causes and justifications for the absurd enchantment into a neat row, like so many toy tin soldiers paraded for execution, and proceeds to dispatch them one by one with neat precision and logic. The creative Mr Tudor, however, is deaf to such surgical reasoning. He can apprehend his folly but not comprehend it, and is therefore immune to argument. For him, language, formula and discourse break like eggshells against a castle's walls.

The human spirit is as resistant to regulation as grand nature herself. Therefore it is perhaps appropriate that I should look to nature for an example, to demonstrate the manner in which she dissolves the impediments to her hegemony. It would appear that she employs the flow of her very lifeblood, a thing which we call 'time'. As the years and changing climes pass by, there comes an inexorable crumbling of even the highest defences, together with the gradual softening overgrowth of dense new foliage. It is thus

*that the ancient castles, towers and ruins of Pyroxenia have
met their doom.*

*And if I abandon myself to such a destiny, what will be
left in my heart? A wild place, perhaps, that defies
habitation, like the wilderness which Mr Brooke perceives as
he views the mountains that press upon the frontiers of his
bountiful farmland.*

*Perhaps that is my destiny: to allow the well-tended
garden of my mind to give way to an untamed
wilderness.*

*

In the closing pages of the journal Godwin recorded little
else in the way of clues to his emotional state, and the
account of his return home revealed none of the vivid
descriptions and insights that made the rest of his account
lend itself so well to an imaginative reconstruction.
Pierrepont's spirits began to rise a little and Prince Leopold
became very quiet and contemplative. The last page, headed
Marseilles, 30 November 1869, contained nothing more than
the time of their arrival in the port. Godwin's desire to write
further had run dry. Perhaps too much had been knocked
out of him: his sense of wonder, his innocence. Perhaps he
finally submitted to total cynicism as he felt the shackles of
society and convention reforge themselves around him.
Perhaps he was too preoccupied with thinking about why he
had been spirited out of Greece in such a hurry. Or perhaps
the return to ordinary life, from which he had deviated, after
all, only recently, acted to isolate his memories of Greece,
entombing them, so that the whole brief episode took on an
unreal shape – something that he could neither revisit nor
touch upon without exposing himself to dark chasms of
grief. Whatever the reason, a satisfactory resolution to the
tale eluded his descendants, one of whom, after chancing
upon the journal nearly a century and a half later, decided
that the matter could not be allowed to rest.

*

Eleftherios Venizelos Airport, Athens, present day

The marble-lined arrivals hall was uncomfortably muggy for the queue of long-suffering customers at the car hire desk; and the staff handling all the paperwork seemed more interested in bickering with each other in rattled Greek than dealing with their frustrated clientele on the other side of the counter. When his turn came at last, Ben scooped up the keys to a Mercedes four-wheel-drive that he had pre-booked online in London, slipped the sunglasses from his forehead down to the bridge of his nose, and walked briskly out of the terminal building, pulling his neat wheeled bag by its telescopic handle behind him. He checked his watch: nearly midday. He was on a mission, didn't have long here, and certainly had no time to waste.

Ben Tudor looked affluent and dapper as he hurried through the noise and bustle outside, past stacks of parked trolleys and groups of dazed, lizard-necked youths with backpacks. Ben always dressed well and certainly would not compromise his standards for the so-called discomforts of air travel. In fact he always found flying rather restful: an opportunity to have himself pampered in Business Class, take a nap perhaps, or tie up some loose ends on his laptop.

Having claimed his gleaming hire car, familiarized himself with the dashboard, the aircon and the left-hand drive, Ben gingerly began to weave his way through the circuitous filter roads and flyovers that fed traffic to and from Athens' new international airport. He had come to Greece in order to retrace his ancestor's steps, and in consideration of this was immediately struck, of course, by the speed and ease of his access to what had formerly been the hinterland of Europe, the frontier of boundless adventure and exoticism. No lengthy sea voyage of acclimatization, no rites of passage, no life-threatening hazards, no fabulous novelties; and, therefore, of course, not much excitement, either. But, on the positive side, there was the convenience. This was to be a two-day flying visit, a folly – his wife had teased – slotted in between a spell of pressing work, family and social commitments. This morning he had snatched some breakfast at a petrol station on the M4 near Slough, and now, with lunchtime approaching, looked forward to a snack at a picturesque *souvlaki* taverna in the middle of Athens – if the traffic wasn't too awful. The 'City Centre' signs were in English, as they seemed to be the world over, which was helpful, and the congestion was no worse than he expected, so his progress towards the heart of the capital looked to be on schedule. Yes, thought Ben, reflecting on the spun-out, eloquent, but sometimes rather pained descriptions of his ancestor's journey: there was something to be said for modern travel.

But much of the enchantment of former times had vanished. Around the site of the airport, where old Godwin would have expected, and found, ravishingly novel land-scapes, people and ways of living, Ben Tudor now saw stretches of hillside devoured by housing developments; at the spot where Godwin would have stood, half a day's ride from his hotel, to contemplate Attica's panoramas, his great-great-grandson now strained his neck to catch a glimpse, behind advertisement hoardings, of anything between and beyond the concrete. Angry hooting from cars behind reminded him that he should concentrate on moving for-ward when the lights changed rather than waste valuable seconds looking at the view. He could see that the new air-port was spelling devastation for vast tracts of Attica, formerly golden, sweeping plains and gentle mountainsides rising through the mist. Now, the olive and fruit trees of Hymettus were being cleared by JCBs, while truckloads of rubble and hardcore poured in to ground the footings for a new and massive south-east urban spread. Athens was on the rise once again.

Re-reading his great-great-grandfather's journal over lunch in the Plaka a little later, Ben Tudor was particularly interested in the personality dichotomy that Godwin was trying to summarize in that last entry. Here and elsewhere in the ancient volume his ancestor was struggling to enunciate something about himself as a way of explaining a kind of conflict within. There were many references, implicit and explicit, to his character being strangely divided. At times, as in that rather wistful final passage, the division was between the artist and the scientist (the 'creative' versus the 'mechanical' Mr Tudor). Sometimes it was the *ingénue*, the innocent believer, versus the cynic – faithless and godless. And at others – most tellingly – it was the rational, level-headed intellectual versus the disturbed victim of so-called inner demons. Godwin was clearly a man subject to profound swings of mood and capable of dark psychological meanderings.

Ben had seen some old photographic portraits of Godwin in a family album, taken in late middle age; a fine, lean, serious face. He had died young by modern standards, aged fifty-something, and rather a black sheep in the family's history. He had never found suitable employment and was apparently rarely content to stay at home for long, preferring to take to the road, painting watercolours and writing poems. None of his photographs had survived, and had it not been for the journal there would have been no record of Godwin having undertaken this sort of work. The best that could be said for the errant ancestor was that he must have been a romantic, but this was overshadowed by his impossible unreliability as a husband and father. And then there was the great enigma of his long, probably psycho-somatic, childhood illness. A modern shrink would have had a field day with him.

The joy of the tale's rediscovery had fallen to an unusually appropriate beneficiary, as fate would have it. Having reached the gateway to middle age and achieved a level of wealth that allowed for relative freedom, Ben thought that he had earned the privilege to indulge his nostalgic and romantic inclinations. These had recently been fuelled by the unexpected deaths of both his parents, an event that compelled him to sieve through roomfuls of inherited paraphernalia; in the midst of which he had discovered the rather battered cloth-bound journal, wedged tightly into the lower drawer of a monstrous Victorian roll-top desk. The text, handwritten in purple ink, was unimaginably neat and regular by modern standards. *Godwin Tudor* announced the opening page, and, opposite, a first entry dated *20 September 1869*. Ben turned to the first page. So much text crammed on to the small, browning leaf. A laboured, thin handwriting that spoke of a long-lost culture where people had time to spare, where writing was a considered a well-tempered craft, not the scribbled slapdash affair it is today. Those pages, dense, geometrically perfect and free of error, came from a world where orderly prose was a discipline cultivated by men and women of refinement, the sign of a schooled mind.

Ben had begun to read, and from that moment was locked to his chair, tuned to the peculiarity of the outdated script, which at first made slow and difficult reading, as if he were having to translate it spontaneously from a variant of his own language; but as he progressed the process became more fluent, until he was engrossed, as swamped by its stylistic idiosyncrasy as by the temper of the voice behind it. He felt the narrative struggling within a confined arena, circumscribed by the spirit of the age, but the further he read, the more he became aware of a bigger canvas hiding between the lines of immaculate and erudite prose. He began to delve into the complex truth behind the characters and actions so sparingly alluded to; began to enrich the tale in his own mind, finding hidden nuance, colour and feeling. And he lost himself in a Victorian journey, became a bystander in the extraordinary romance that unfolded, in no less a way than if he had been present at the time, there in Greece, a silent but proper member of the house party, attending the dinners, accompanying the travellers on horseback.

The temptation for Ben to compare his every encounter and experience in the modern city of Athens with those of his ancestor was, of course, overpowering. There was no way of measuring how much Godwin would have been mystified by the trappings of present-day Greece. He had been an intelligent man, a Victorian at that, who believed in progress and would have predicted a degree of transformation in the future, based on ever greater scientific and spiritual revelations. He would also have expected the world to have shrunk, the experience of travel to have become less stimulating, and the diversity of culture less pronounced, as remoter corners of the world were more regularly frequented by those who toured for leisure, like himself. This had already become an issue in his lifetime, and was frequently mentioned by travel diarists; but nothing could have prepared him for the pace and extremity of the transformation.

Traffic in multiple lanes now choked the streets that Godwin had walked, and car horns provided an incessant cacophony of protest. Vehicles, abandoned by frustrated drivers unable to find parking slots, rested up on kerbs, often blocking the pavement, while battalions of motorbikes wove their way at speed between jammed cars and past fashionable boutiques. Their riders were mostly peacocking young men with dark glasses and flowing curls, who flagrantly flouted the helmet law and barely stopped to avoid the thousands of pedestrians – rather a chic lot, all in all – picking their way across the roaring boulevards and narrow back streets: girls in cling-tight tops with plunging bosom lines and glitzy accessories, middle-aged peroxide blondes dripping gold and fur, elderly matrons with worried faces and arthritic joints, still wearing traditional black.

Ben did not linger in the city, despite the thrill of being able to retrace his ancestor's steps from the shadow of the former royal palace, down Ermou (known to Godwin as Hermes Street) and on to the old town, with its little alleys, sunken churches and market shops; fascinated though he was to measure in his own pace the distance Godwin regularly trod between Constitution Square and the then English Legation in Stadiou (Stadion Street); to stand at the hub of the vast, throbbing city and contemplate the changes. But he stayed in Athens for just one night; long enough to drink in the atmosphere and feed his nostalgia. Long enough also to study his road map and plan out the next morning's drive to Pyroxenia.

It was simple enough. Straight out of town through the suburb of Kifissia and on to the principal northbound trunk road. This was now a motorway, and, for all Ben knew, the very route mapped by Pierrepont's company, for which Fortinbras himself performed several surveys before having to leave Greece, his job unfinished. The motorway would lead most of the way to Páparis, where a new bridge crossed over to Pyroxenia, bypassing the town centre. After this there was a winding road over the mountain to Thasofolia. Ben found the village on his map, and the sight of its name made his heart jolt. He estimated that the journey would take somewhere between two and three hours – a far cry from the three-day mule trek Godwin had endured at the mercy of the elements.

He left central Athens early, to avoid the worst of the traffic, but it still took nearly an hour to be clear of the city, and the suburban development continued all the way along the main route, even as it wove past Mount Parnitha, well beyond Athens, in fact not so far from Skourta. The roadside boasted an endless succession of industrial estates, marble dealerships, new churches, concrete works and farm machinery outlets, interspersed with brazen, aggressive hoardings full of exclamation marks, giant-sized pictures of winking salesmen, pouting girls, sizzling burgers, on and on until Ben began no longer to notice. He could see a landscape beyond all the buildings: a hard, rocky, scrubby landscape with few trees, and he imagined this to be the very terrain crossed by Godwin and his unfortunate fellow captives as they fled, often by night, under the eye of the brigands. But the desolate loneliness of the atmosphere they must have felt was now gone.

A large blue sign on the right indicated the slip road for Páparis, and after a short drive down towards the channel Ben crossed the new suspension bridge and descended to the landmass of Pyroxenia. Páparis, the one-time Venetian jewel, with its medieval alleys, battlements, palm trees and minarets, no longer existed. Blocks of flats, crowned with aerials and satellite dishes, now spread for miles inland, with little or no sign of the older settlement that may have existed. But once beyond the inevitable string of industry that had eaten into the countryside around the modern town, he at last began to get a sense of the magic Godwin had encountered on this route.

It was still only half-past nine, and Ben was already crossing the mountain pass between thick pine forests, and would surely be at the gates of Thasofolia, if it still existed, within the hour. The weather had turned fine, and as he rolled down his window a flood of pine scent poured into the car, that rich, sticky odour to which his ancestor repeatedly referred. Nothing about Greece until this point had borne resemblance to Godwin's impassioned descriptions, but here at last was a familiar world.

The realization that the route had begun to descend, and that the road was now cut into the side of a gorge, falling away on the right to a deep river gully, informed him that he might be near the spot where the travellers had been accosted by Demetrios' crew. Once through the gorge, the steepness on either side began to level, and the road turned to the left around a prominent headland into a flat river basin, with fields spreading on either side; the river itself was lined with gigantic plane trees. Ben knew exactly where he had arrived at, and scanned the level landscape ahead for the little rise that would mark the exact site of Thasofolia.

It was only then that he noticed. In retrospect, he thought he should have guessed. The diary had intimated what had been about to happen, but because the consequences had not been witnessed by Godwin, he had neglected to consider that it might actually have occurred. The shock of it forced him to stop the car. The best that could be said was that the forest higher up remained untouched, where it lay out of reach, majestic and precipitous. Further down, where the slopes and gullies were within practical reach of exploitation, the landscape had been disembowelled, levelled, terraced and gashed. The perfect horseshoe of mountains that Godwin rapturously described was now misshapen with craters, a moonscape of open-pit mines and pyramids of slag belched up from the depths of the earth; and as far as the eye could see were the criss-cross scars of roads cut into the hillsides. In some parts the forest had disappeared altogether; in others lone plantations swayed, isolated in the midst of the devastation. Edgar's fears had materialized.

And now Ben came to the road sign announcing the village, a tatty, dusty sign, dented on one side where someone had taken a pot-shot with a rifle. Much of what had been fields and farmland was now houses, and he could not immediately see the knoll at the heart of the village because the view was obscured by tenement blocks. But as he reached the middle of the town, passed a couple of petrol stations, a bank, a large new church, a paved square and a high street full of shops, he could see the road in front rising up and bending to the right, and, at the crest of the hill, a collection of dark, mature cypress and cedar trees towering above everything. His heart leapt. Suddenly he was nervous about moving any further. There was a building hidden beneath the trees, eaves, a glimpse of tiles, a wooden balcony. And then he was there, in front of a gateway. He stopped the car, the engine still running.

Two modern steel gates were open, to one side of which, fixed to an old stone gatepost, was a large hand-painted sign. The letters were orange, Latin rather than Greek, the script hand-painted and florid. *Kurisumala Ashram.* There was the courtyard, with the two long buildings stretching down either side, attached to the main house. This must be Thasofolia, Ben realized. It could be nothing else. It was exactly as his great-great-grandfather had described it, though perhaps less grand. Somewhere in his reading of the account, perhaps because of the very British gentility of those who peopled the scenes, Ben had allowed himself to picture it as more substantial; but in reality, though large, it was a simple construction, rendered, whitewashed and shuttered, with long balconies and old-fashioned half-cylinder Byzantine roof tiles.

He pulled into the courtyard and parked at the side. A tall bearded man was there, dressed in a red sweater with baggy orange trousers, doing some open-air carpentry. He wore glasses and had an intelligent look about him as he glanced at Ben, blinking rather over-emphatically.

'May I help you?' The man's voice was gentle, lightly shaded and American.

'I'm looking for a member of the Brooke family,' Ben blurted without thinking. 'Is there anyone here?' He cursed himself for asking such an idiotic question. Of course the Brookes could no longer be here. The name would have died out when Daniel fell at Skourta.

'I don't know if she's about,' the man answered without hesitating, in his singsong San Francisco accent, and looked up around the courtyard. He spotted a woman walking along the first-floor covered walkway that ran the length of the building to the left-hand side. She too was dressed in red, and her heavy unharnessed breasts swayed from side to side beneath her sweater as she walked. 'Sita! Have you seen Lydia anywhere?' the man called.

'Not recently,' came an equivalently mellifluous American

voice from the woman. 'She was with Amatan earlier. She may be in the vegetable garden. I know she wanted to do some seeding today.'

'I'm sorry,' the man said, returning his attention to Ben like a shopkeeper who has to tell his favourite customer that he's run out of stock, 'we don't know where Lydia is right now. But you're welcome to go wait in the house till she shows up. Make yourself comfortable in the Hall of Joy over there.' He pointed towards the front door. 'Would you like some orange blossom tea?' Ben could barely reply. The thrill of being there, combined with the shock of hearing the one name that he most associated with the place though least expected to encounter, was almost too much. 'Have you come far?' asked the man.

'From Athens. And from London yesterday.'

The man smiled and nodded knowingly. 'You sure will need to equalize, then. Go take a rest and I'll bring some tea and cake. My name's Ramana.' Ben offered a hand, but Ramana placed both palms together and made a little bow of greeting. 'Please remember to take off your shoes before going indoors,' he said and walked slowly over to the side-building, swinging his arms.

'Excuse me,' Ben called over to him. 'Is this house still called Thasofolia?'

The man smiled back and waggled his palm in the air indecisively. 'Sometimes, I guess. More by the local people, that kinda thing. It's a pretty name, but things have moved on, know what I mean?'

And so Ben got out of his car, walked across the yard and went into the front hall of Thasofolia, as Godwin Tudor had done nearly a century and a half before.

There were no hunting trophies hanging from the walls. Indeed, there was nothing on the walls at all except a gigantic photographic portrait of an Indian holy man, smiling beneficently down on those who came in, his forehead striped with three horizontal yellow lines. A pretty design of flower petals had been arranged around a candle on the floor at the foot of the portrait, and incense burned in several places. The huge baronial hearth that used to blaze a welcome to all who arrived had gone; the walls were bare and whitewashed, and there was no furniture, just comfortable mats around the edge. In the centre was a circular indoor pond, with water lily leaves coating its surface. Ben sat down on one of the mats, more than content to wait and allow his imagination to take flight.

'Hello. Can I help you?' It was a woman's voice, an English voice. Ben turned to look at her. She was perhaps in her early fifties, with a handsome, practical face, a face that belonged to someone who had long since fathomed and dismissed the nonsense of glamour. 'Have you come from Babaji's ashram?' she asked.

'No. I've come from England,' Ben answered. 'Are you Lydia Brooke?'

'Yes.'

'Named after the former Lydia Brooke, I presume?'

She smiled and frowned simultaneously. 'Well, actually, yes, as it happens. How do you know about that? Have we met?'

'No. My name is Ben Tudor. I think my ancestor may have been a friend of your ancestors.'

She came forward into the room and shook his hand as he began briefly to tell the story of Godwin's diary.

'Tudor?' she said, trying to recall something. 'Yes, I think I have heard about him. Mr Tudor. It definitely rings a bell.' She was interested and invited Ben to her office, through a door at the far side of the hall. He could not help noticing the old plane-timber panelling as he passed, with its patterns of knots and flecks that looked like faces, and he imagined all that had taken place here. Lydia led him down a corridor to another room with large windows that looked over the surrounding countryside. Ben wondered to himself if this office could have been Edgar's study, where he would sit and look across his property to ease the weight of his problems.

'Edgar Brooke,' she said, walking round behind her desk. 'He was old Lydia's father. My – hang on a minute,' she counted fingers, 'my great-great-great-grandfather. Quite a character. Bit of a rogue. Rather tragic in the end. He's the one we have to thank for the bloody mess out there.' She gestured to the distant scarred landscape. 'He sold the mining rights in eighteen seventy. In his defence, I suppose he might never have guessed it would be this bad.'

'No,' Ben could not stop himself from interrupting. 'With all respect, that's more untrue than I can say. Edgar would have done anything to prevent the mining. He stopped at nothing in the attempt.'

Lydia looked at him quizzically, intrigued at his presuming to correct her. 'Well,' she said, 'I'd like to hear more. He certainly looks like a rogue. Liked to see himself as a bit of a Lord Byron.' She indicated a wall behind his back. 'There he is. Dressed up like a Christmas turkey.'

Ben turned and saw an oil portrait of a young man in a turban of scarlet silk, sporting a jewelled finger; and there in the background was the horse, the Negro servant and the Parthenon, just as Godwin had described each of them. It was eerie to see the painting, and Ben felt his skin tingle.

'That's not Edgar,' he said quietly, looking into Percival's eyes. 'It's his twin brother. Percival. This used to hang above the mantelpiece in the dining room.'

'Percival?' she replied with the faintest wisp of outrage. 'I'm sure you must be mistaken. Everyone has always known this as Edgar. It's been reproduced in magazines. It must be Edgar. Percival was rather a withdrawn, shady person, I think. No-one seems to have much to say about him, though he is buried here.'

Ben sighed. Percival had been almost written out of the family history. 'He had a mental handicap. And loved music. We have lots to talk about,' he said. Just at that moment the door opened and Ramana entered with a tray.

'Oh, hey, Shanti,' he said, blinking emphatically as before, 'I heard voices and thought you must be here. This is for our visitor.' The cup steamed with a light scent and the cake looked delicious.

'Shanti?' Ben asked after the man had departed.

'Some of them call me that. It was a given name. Once upon a time I belonged to a community of these guys. Followers of Shri Mahesh Nityananda, otherwise known as Babaji. But that's all history. I've moved on.' She smiled. 'This lot come from the ashram in Santa Barbara, California. They pay a good rent and that keeps the place on its feet. Company for me, too.' She told Ben how she kept a wing of the house, where she lived with her mother, but that the rest of the place was given over to the ashram. There were benefits: her tenants were quiet, industrious, helpful and on the whole intelligent. The downsides were a claustro-phobically monastic atmosphere, a police state of spiritual correctness, and the irritatingly immature addiction to silly red clothes. 'But I'm grateful to them. We need all the help we can get. Especially since the mines closed down.'

'Closed down?'

'Yes. The whole hideous enterprise ground to a halt at last about a year ago. They'd been losing money for years. And so they packed up, left their bloody mess and shipped out. Lorries, workers, the lot. It's much quieter now, I can tell you, and half the village is deserted.'

Ben looked out of the window. 'So, it's all over.'

'And we've made it our mission to replant the trees. Babaji talks about the benefits of forests in his many rambling books – thank God! – and so all this lot are well committed to it. They've got reforestation grants from the EEC, stuff from the World Bank, Greenpeace, this and that wildlife fund, you name it. And hordes of volunteers from Nityananda's ashrams all over the world. That's what I thought you were.'

'I'll plant the odd tree with pleasure,' Ben said, 'but would much appreciate a little wander round. Just to indulge my nostalgia for the past.'

She said he was welcome to help himself to the house, so long as he didn't intrude on any meditation or silent space groups. There was a little family cemetery down near the river, if he was interested, and plenty of old pictures hanging on the walls. She had a lot to do today, but invited him to stay overnight as her guest, saying they could talk further at supper. Her mother, apparently, knew a lot about the family's history and would be very intrigued to meet him.

'One thing I've been wanting to know,' Ben said as she was leaving. 'My great-great-grandfather refers several times to a very special place on the estate. Some kind of circular pool, surrounded by cliffs. Do you know it?'

'Well, yes,' she replied. 'It's always been known as Daniel's Pool. Daniel was Edgar's son. He was murdered by brigands, poor fellow. They buried him beside the pool. It is a very special place still, and mercifully unspoilt. You've got a four-wheel-drive, haven't you? You can drive there.'

The family cemetery was reached by a path that went out through a gate on the lowest of three lawn terraces, perhaps near where Hermann had hidden to watch the light in Lydia's bedroom window. The flagstoned path led from the garden through a small meadow of longer grass, where a flock of sheep were grazing, downhill to a ring of cypress trees encircled by a five-foot wall. A single wrought iron gate breached the wall and led into the glade, where the grave-stones were distributed in a circle. Ben felt his stomach move as he realized he was standing in the company of the actual persons he had read about, the main players in Godwin's drama. The gravestones were simple, rectangular, barely two feet off the ground, each bearing nothing more than a name and a set of dates. Within seconds he had spotted them all, but walked to each in turn, savouring the intimacy. Rebecca Brooke, Edgar's mother, was here, as was her delicate child, Alithea, who had died young; and Edward, infant son of the

Howards, the neighbours who were murdered in their beds. Then he stood before a line of them, each name as familiar to him as that of a friend. First, Magdalene Brooke, 23 August 1818 – 1 October 1884. Then Hermann Koptling, died 17 November 1869. Percival Brooke, 2 February 1821 – 19 February 1876. And then there was Edgar Brooke, 2 February 1821 – 21 November 1906. He had lived long; thirty-seven more years to the day, coincidentally, after Skourta. Perhaps it was the pain of anniversary memories that stopped his old heart in the end, Ben wondered, at the turf before his feet and thought of the big man who lay there. This time yesterday Ben had barely left England; and now he stood beside Edgar Brooke.

Ben then turned to his right, almost paralysed by the magnitude of feeling that awaited as he reluctantly raised his eyes to admit the name inscribed on the next stone. Here she was, simply laid there, next to her father. Lydia Brooke, 5 June 1853 – 9 January 1951. Ben was stunned by the dates and had to read them again and again. She had lived to be ninety-seven; lived to hear of the Korean War, the Berlin airlift, lived to see pictures of nuclear explosions. How small a fragment of her long life was occupied in the company of Godwin Tudor, how insignificant a speck. Perhaps, in her young heart and wisdom, she had secretly known this would be so; perhaps she had known that the years were still just beginning for her, that her life had barely emerged from its rosy dawn glow.

Chastened by sombre reflections of this sort, Ben made his way to his car in the courtyard and drove off to find the pool. Lydia's directions took him along a road away from the village, which after a couple of miles branched off on to a rough track eastward through the woods. The trees here had not been felled, there was no sign of any mining work, and once he had got away from the tarmac road, travelling deeper into the forest and splashing through muddy potholes, he caught the flavour of an environment little disturbed since former times. Rays of sunlight penetrated the densely interwoven fir branches like theatrical spotlights, illuminating patches of the pine-needle and bracken bed beneath. The ground on either side then began to steepen into cliffs, until there was little more than a small fissure of light in the landmass that hung above, and he had to turn on the headlights to see the track clearly. This must be near where Eliza Brooke had fallen to her death, he recalled.

Ben came to it as a man returns to the house where he spent idyllic playful days as a child: full of reverence, warmth and melancholy longing. It was every bit as breathtaking as he had imagined, but the words with which he was later to describe it would have been phoney approximations had he not himself come here; had he not experienced that silent sanctity like a personal benediction breathed into his face; had he not felt the shallow ripples of ice-cold water over his bare toes as he tentatively trod across Lydia's sunken stepping-stones to the rock; had he not laid his palms against the rough lichen on the rockface and followed the course of a mineralized drip falling from the heights to the black calm of the water all around; had he not lain down in the carpet of ferns and wild flowers, and gazed at the circle of blue sky above, from which that frenzied young Englishman had looked down in despair at his beloved in the company of another man. Ben's pilgrimage was now complete. A resolution to the tale still eluded him, but his appetite for union with his forebear, for a sense of immersion in the atmosphere Godwin had imbibed, was satisfied.

Chapter 41

Lydia Brooke's two-storey private wing on the north side of the house formed a small promontory that overlooked the top garden terrace. Ben had thought he had a fairly good idea of the house's layout from Godwin's descriptions, but could not marry up this particular extension with anything he had read about. His suspicion was that it had been converted out of Mag's office and the old kitchen pantries, together with some of the upstairs staff accommodation.

He was greeted at the door by a diminutive old lady, so short that he wondered for a moment if she belonged to a lost species from the world of Tolkien, with long white plaits and a voluminous shawl. Every tiny finger of her hands bore a ring of curious and contrasting design, and her ears drooped under the weight of pendulous earrings.

'Mr Tudor!' she exclaimed, grasping his extended hand warmly in both of hers, 'Ben, isn't it? Ben Tudor, you darling boy. You're so welcome, come in, come in.'

Lydia called from somewhere inside. 'Ben. This is my mother, Elsa.' There was a smell of garlic browning in a pan.

'Is this it?' said Elsa, spotting the thick folder under his arm. 'Is this Godwin's diary? Blessed fathers! It's all so exciting.'

'You know of Godwin?' Ben asked, slightly flabbergasted.

'Of course I know about Godwin. Old Lydia sometimes mentioned him, you know.' She smiled almost coyly. 'I think there was a little bit of something there, don't you? Wasn't Godwin a little bit in love with her?'

471

'Well, yes, perhaps. Certainly, in fact,' Ben answered, barely able to contain the rush of questions that suddenly had to be asked. 'So you actually knew Lydia? The same Lydia? Edgar's daughter?'

'There's so much to tell you,' she said, leading him by the hand into the apartment with her jewelled fingers, 'it's all so exciting. I've got two things to show you, and they're both so thrilling, I don't know which to bring out first. But don't let's spoil the pleasure. Come and have a gin and a nice little chat. Over here by the fire.' And, slightly bent like a benign witch, she led him towards a fireplace and two comfortable armchairs.

'I'm not one of the family,' Elsa said, pouring the drinks, 'I married in. But I seem to have ended up knowing more than anyone else.' She allowed herself a little giggle. 'Why don't I tell you a bit about the early days?'

Old Lydia had apparently had a son – no husband was mentioned, and Ben wasn't bold enough to ask – but the son, abandoned in early adulthood by his wife (who could not abide life at Thasofolia), had died here in his late twenties of typhoid, leaving a daughter of his own. This girl, named Magdalene, was brought up by Lydia, eventually married an Italian diplomat stationed in Athens, and died giving birth to her only child, in Berne, in 1934. The child, a boy called Daniel, survived, and was sent back to Greece to the care of his ageing great-grandmother. He was the apple of the old lady's eye, and she spoiled him terribly.

'That was his problem, I think,' said Elsa, a shadow flitting across her jovial face for a moment. 'The rest of his life was such a let-down. Of course, they had to go back to England during the war while all sorts of terrible things were going on here. First the Italians, who set fire to the house, then the Germans, then, of course, the civil war, with communists running all over the place shooting people. They came back here in the end, but poor Daniel wasn't cut from the right cloth to make an estate manager. Far from it, he really rather went off the rails. He was so lovable and charming and intelligent, but so completely unreliable. I met him at the Ramakrishna mission in California, and that's where we got married. By then he was called Raja.

'We decided to come and live here with the old lady, who had single-handedly put Thasofolia back on its feet. Well, with the help of the villagers. They all loved her so much, they would have done anything for her. Having us both here in those last years was such a joy for Lydia, lovely old thing that she was. And then I got pregnant, but old Lydia died just before our baby was born. And both Raja and I were convinced that her spirit had travelled to the body of our child. Just between you and me,' and here she leant forward conspiratorially, 'my Master *told* me it was so.' She took a sip of gin and spoke up again. 'It must have been. The dear old thing couldn't bear to leave Thasofolia and so took another body and came back straight away. So, after our daughter was born, we called her Lydia.' Here her voice faltered and rose in pitch. 'And then Raja just took off and left us. He hardly got to know little Lydia at all. He wrote very beautiful poetry, you see. But I was left here on my own with the baby. I never knew where he'd gone. Until I got a message from someone in Delhi one day, ooh, it was not until 1969, eighteen years after he'd gone, around Christmas time, telling me he'd been found dead on the summit of Arunachala, a holy mountain in the south of India. He'd just died there.' Huge tears sprang spontaneously to her eyes and plopped down on to her cheeks. But she wiped them away with a smile. 'He was a lovely man, and had the clearest wavelength to the Masters of anyone I've ever met, but he was quite mad at the same time. The Brookes are an eccentric family, as you've probably discovered. They haven't had much luck in marriage and domestic life. Bad family karma, I suspect.'

'And Lydia – old Lydia – used to mention my ancestor, you say?' Ben asked.

'Yes indeed,' said Elsa, cheering up again and patting him on the knee. 'She had a photograph. She treasured it very greatly and hung it on the wall beside her desk. She would call it *Mr Tudor's exposure*, because I believe Godwin had taken the photograph himself, and she always only knew him as Mr Tudor. Very quaint, don't you think?'

'Do you still have the photograph?'

'Of course I have the photograph. It's one of the two things I've got here to show you. It really is most beautiful.' She carried on her singsong prelude to the photograph's quality and prettiness as she stretched a hand down into the shadows beside her chair to find what she was looking for.

'Can I help you?' Ben asked, barely able to tolerate the suspense.

'No, no, just wait a moment.' She slipped on a pair of half-lens glasses that hung around her neck on a long string, and hunted around on the ground with her hand, all the while muttering. 'Now which one is it? Don't look, now, I don't want to spoil the surprise of the next thing. Is this it? Yes, here we are. Very lovely. Such a beautiful girl she was. Your grandfather must have had very good reasons for not sweeping her off her feet there and then. But I suppose she was not the dustpan-and-brush sort, to be swept up.'

Ben did not bother to correct her two-generational slip of relationship between himself and Godwin. For her, having known Lydia personally and heard first hand about the old days, the gap was of less consequence. And now with a beaming face she handed Ben a large oak frame, its front turned teasingly away, so that he received it by its old brown string, which was hardened into an inverted V from having hung for so many years by the same hook. As Ben turned it round, holding his breath, he noticed some patches of mildew on the inside of the glass, blemishes emphasized by the angled light but diminishing from view as he laid it on his lap. And then he looked at the exposure and beheld the girl on the rock. She was surrounded by the pool's water, a light mist hanging above its surface. Her face, youth and loveliness were indescribable, hauntingly matched by the dreamy setting. The various greys and textures were both mysterious and vividly sharp, bringing to mind Pre-Raphaelite exactitude blended with the enchanted atmosphere of a Julia Margaret Cameron. Ben looked into the girl's expression, her slightly open mouth and large, appealing, short-sighted eyes.

He became aware, in the distance, of an ethereal sound of chanting; but it was nothing more celestial than the ashram residents, who had begun their evening devotion. And here was the lovely Lydia Brooke, as seen and adored by his great-great-grandfather in an instant, still and spellbound, that morning by the pool. Her looks were delicious enough to cause Ben a stab of pain because he would never have the opportunity to see her in the real world. The absolute impossibility of that privilege was momentarily infuriating.

'Sunset puja,' said Lydia, coming in with a pair of steaming platters. 'It won't go on for long. Oh, so you've seen the photograph. Mother says she still looked a bit like that in her nineties, didn't she, Ma?'

'Exactly like that,' said Elsa. 'It was in the eyes. All the men loved her. And she had plenty of lovers, you know.' She chuckled. 'But she didn't let any of them stay for long. She never forgot your grandfather. But I don't think they ever became lovers, in the proper sense, did they?'

'I don't think so,' replied Ben.

'She was so strong,' Elsa continued, 'a wonderful, energetic, original person, and she always got her way. No-one could deny her anything. And so clever. As a young woman she lived here alone with her father. And her little boy, of course. Poor old Edgar. He was a broken man after his son was killed. He did very little for the rest of his life. In fact, this was Edgar's chair.' She patted the broad wooden arms of the reclining chair in which she sat. 'He spent his dotage in this, as I shall probably spend mine.' She chuckled again. 'During the summer Lydia would put him in front of the open french windows with a blanket on his lap, and he would just sit there all day looking out across the woods and hills, dreaming about who-knows-what.'

Ben dwelt for a moment on the image. The great, bullish Edgar Brooke broken by circumstances, shrunken, impotent and ancient, left to ponder his melancholy thoughts for hours in the warm Hellenic breeze, staring out – perhaps half blind – across the property he cherished so dearly.

'Who ran the estate?' Ben asked. 'The farms, the timber business?'

'Well, Lydia did. But it all began to wind down when the mines got under way. Most of the farmers needed little persuasion to pack up and go and work in the mines, where they could make more money. Everything changed so quickly. Nowadays we don't farm at all. Except our own vegetables from the kitchen garden, and we sell any surplus at a village market once a week, but what with the new supermarket a couple of miles down the road, no one's very interested in them any more. All rather sad, really.'

They began to eat. It was delicious, vegetarian and spicy. The chanting had stopped, and out of the window Ben saw a small troop of red-clothed people emerging on to the lawn, walking and talking quietly together in little groups, many of them barefoot. Lydia explained that there was a rule of silence for the community after nine o'clock and that this last hour was specially set aside in the daily timetable for social intercourse.

Elsa looked a little vexed as she negotiated a roasted pepper that slid around the plate refusing to give way to her fork, and finally picked it up with her fingers.

'Tell me,' Ben said to her, 'I'm longing to hear. What did Lydia have to say about Godwin?'

The warmth returned to Elsa's face. 'Just happy references. The way one talks about a childhood romance, the person who always has a special place in one's heart. She had many regrets as well. And burdens of her own.' Here a slight knot darkened Elsa's jovial brow. 'There was a dark side to Lydia, you see. She was wonderful, positive and full of golden energy, don't mistake me; but I have known dark Masters in my time, and I recognized one residing in her somewhere.' For a moment Elsa sat in silence and stared wide-eyed at the fire. The dancing flames were reflected in the silver of her rings.

'My understanding was that Godwin had hoped to marry her,' Ben added, 'and that they parted on less than happy terms.'

'Ah.' She aspirated the word on a long breath and turned to smile at him, pulling the shawl around her shoulders for warmth. She was every inch the woodland enchantress. 'There you are mistaken, dear child,' she said softly, 'and I have something new to reveal to you.' Ben did not answer, but leant forward, completely entranced by her wide, unblinking eyes. 'They parted very properly. And contentedly, too.'

'But,' Ben faltered, 'but it says clearly in the diary that – I mean – was he telling a lie when he—?' he stopped as Elsa shook her head, eyes closed and smiling. Lydia had moved around behind her mother's chair and was leaning over it, also smiling.

'He came back,' said Elsa. 'Mr Tudor came back to Thasofolia.'

'Came back? When?'

'In eighteen ninety-five. Just before he died, I believe. In other words, twenty-six years after his first visit.'

'What?' Ben said quietly, gazing into the old woman's face. 'Are you sure? He was married then. With a son of his own.'

'A grown-up son. Lydia's boy was also grown up. All I know,' and her voice fell to a whisper, 'and I know it as a fact, is that he came here to pay his last respects to Lydia and Edgar. Because he knew he was dying.'

'And—' Ben could hardly think what to say, 'and what happened?'

477

'He stayed for a fortnight or so, and talked with them, went for the occasional walk, when his strength allowed, did some painting on the lawn, chatted about old times, settled old regrets. He needed to heal himself within. I think he probably had cancer, don't you? He came and laid his troubled spirit to rest.'

'And Lydia told you of this visit?'

'She did. And there's more.'

'Go on, Mother,' said Lydia from behind her, 'don't keep him waiting any longer, poor chap.'

'Very well,' said Elsa. 'Here's the other thing I wanted to show you.' She leant down again to the side of her chair and retrieved another picture frame. 'Lydia had this propped on the wall next to her bed. It's by Edgar. He was an awfully good artist, you know.'

She handed it to Ben, and for the second time that evening he sat in silence as he looked through a window into the past. It was a watercolour, quite sketchily done, but with a striking sense of place and atmosphere; the colours were bright, the light golden – late afternoon in the sun. It was rather a peculiar composition, neither portrait nor land-scape, but trapped between the two. It showed a pair of figures, a middle-aged man and woman, sitting together on a garden bench, surrounded by plants in full bloom, with a carpet of brilliant green lawn at their feet and a backdrop of mountains and forest. Ben could tell instantly that the man was Godwin; though the detail of his features was not especially distinct, the character of his face and posture were spot on. He had less hair than in any of the photographs in the family album, and was leaner. She, of course, must be Lydia – older than in the photograph Ben had just seen, and wearing a rather heavy pair of spectacles, but still recogniz-able. They were immaculately dressed, sitting back relaxed, and occupied independently of each other: she reading a book and he turned slightly away, looking to some distant horizon. It was a moment of utter contentment and simplicity, where conversation was absent and unnecessary because the union of these two people was complete in silence; they were at peace, with time to spare, their burdens buried, their misunderstandings shrivelled to nothingness.

'Turn it over,' said Elsa. There was a sheet of paper stuck to the back, and on it was written, in a thin, regular hand:

17 September 1895. Lydia Brooke in the company of her friend, Godwin Tudor Esquire, on the occasion of his return to Thasofolia, an event that has brought comfort to the old man who herewith lays his faithful brush to rest.

Edgar Brooke.

They did not say anything for some while. Ben remained looking at the painting, transported by the peculiar blend of happiness and melancholy that it evoked. Elsa was motionless and deep in thought, smiling in the direction of the hearth; and Lydia stared open-eyed into space, still leaning over the chair, rolling the stem of her empty wine glass back and forth between thumb and forefinger. This was their silent memorial to those who had been in this place in former times, to their drama and its passions, now calmed to nothingness. Elsa was the first to speak. She was gathering her resources to rise and make her way to bed.

'It is a great blessing,' she said. 'Tonight we have been granted the privilege of placing the final piece in a jigsaw that has taken almost a hundred and forty years to complete. The Lord Maitreya and his divine brotherhood of Masters devise their plans for us with beauty and perfect symmetry. How blessed we are! May it ever be thus. Peace be with you darlings,' she concluded and hobbled towards the door, her joints stiff from sitting too long.

Chapter 42

Lydia and Ben stayed up very late. They left their ancestors and talked long, by candlelight, about the problems facing her as she tried to make ends meet and keep what remained of the estate intact. It was a lonely task.

When it was time to go to bed, Ben passed her the diary. She noticed his hesitancy as he handed it over and reassured him that she would look after it.

'It's not that,' Ben said. 'It's just that I think I should warn you.'

'Warn me? About what?'

'About something you're going to discover when you read it. Unless you know already, of course. But I doubt you do. It's to do with Edgar. And the incident at Skourta.'

'The murders? The brigands and the bungled rescue attempt.'

'Yes,' he said, 'but has Edgar's involvement in the planning of the incident ever come to light?'

'I think he had to go and appear at an inquiry after some rumour or other came up. It's all well documented. The chief brigand was one of his workers, or something. Isn't that right? But he was completely cleared and the matter was never raised again. God! He lost his own son.'

'I know,' Ben said. 'But I'm afraid the truth was rather different. Edgar was involved. It's all in the diary.'

'What?' She narrowed her eyes at him and took the book, turning to go. 'How absolutely gripping. I'm sure I won't sleep a wink.'

His bedroom, opposite Lydia's, had an appropriately antique and rustic flavour, with old pieces of furniture, high timber ceilings, wooden floorboards, and coarse-woven local fabrics for curtains. A redundant fireplace in the corner spoke of bygone times and a radiator close to the bed now took the chill from the air. A window was slightly open, and looking out of it Ben could see the black outline of distant mountains against the clear sky. He lay in bed awake for some while, enjoying the utter silence, and then began to drift off to sleep.

It was after three o'clock when he first became aware of the crying, and for a moment the sound and atmosphere of it dovetailed into the narrative of his dream, some mutant off-shoot projected from the experiences of Godwin in this same house. A woman's voice quietly weeping, a lonely woman, injured in her heart. And then he woke fully, switched on the bedside light and came to his senses. It was Lydia. Ben wondered for a moment if he should go and knock on her door to see if everything was all right, but thought better of the idea, and put out his light again.

When he came down in the morning, the sun was stream-ing in from the lawn and Lydia was eating fruit and yoghurt in the kitchen. She greeted Ben with a fresh smile, and offered him a bowl. She looked well, rested and full of pep. It was difficult to believe she had been up half the night crying.

'Did you read it?' Ben eventually asked, as he ate his break-fast, she having so far not volunteered the information.

'From cover to cover,' she replied, walking to the cupboard to retrieve a pair of coffee cups.

'I'm going to rewrite the story as a novel. It will mean using a fair bit of imaginative reconstruction, but the bones of the tale are there. And they're strong bones. I know where Godwin was coming from. Would you approve?'

'It's a great story. Would make a lovely film.' She came to the table and sat opposite him. 'There is just one matter, though. Something you'll need to know before your story is complete. Godwin didn't even know it. At least not when he wrote the diary.'

'And you're going to tell me now?' Ben asked, smiling, thrilled once again by the anticipation of a new twist to this tale.

She got up to make the coffee. There was a smart chrome cappuccino machine on the side. 'I found certain parts of the diary difficult to read,' she said. 'Just so moving. Deeply, deeply poignant.'

'I can imagine,' Ben replied. 'It must be a shock to discover that business about Edgar and the brigands. I can understand how the whole thing left him broken. But he was lucky in a sense. Never to have been properly rumbled.'

'No, you misunderstand me,' she said, turning back, a full, frothy cup in each hand. 'I found all that fascinating, and not altogether surprising.'

'Oh?' Ben said, cocking an eyebrow. 'So what was the difficult bit?'

'Did you hear me crying?'

'Yes.'

'I'm sorry if it woke you up.'

'I'm sorry I couldn't help.'

'There's nothing you could have done. It wasn't comfort I needed. I wasn't crying out of sorrow: I was just so moved. It was a reconciliation. You see, there haven't been many of us in the Brooke family over the years. A lot of only children and premature deaths. So when I find out all about a very close relative, a direct ancestor, one that I knew nothing about before, it's really very important and moving.'

Ben was a little flummoxed. 'You mean Edgar?'

'No, no,' she waved her hand. 'We knew about him. No, I mean my great-great-grandfather.' Ben looked blank. 'The father of Lydia's baby.'

Ben hesitated. 'But he's not mentioned in the diary,' he said.

'Oh, but he is,' she replied. 'Lydia gave birth in August eighteen seventy. Think about it. Count your months.'

'You mean to say,' Ben stumbled, 'it was Godwin?'

'No, not Godwin. That never happened, no. It was another.'

'Not – not Pierrepont?'

'Don't be ridiculous!' She was playing with the foam on top of her cappuccino, turning it over and over with her teaspoon. 'We never knew much about the father of that little boy. Only that he had come here briefly and died before the baby was born. We've always imagined him as a dashing, handsome, terribly romantic young man. He would have to have been to net Lydia. As it turns out, the only true things we knew about him were his name, because his gravestone is here, the fact that he was German, and that he was a classics scholar. Godwin's diary has introduced him as a real person at last. I am descended from Hermann Kopfling, you see.'

The revelation left Ben speechless.

'And so, you see, when I read last night of the gauche, rather pathetic little boy, with a hanging lip and red hot cheeks, I had to readjust more than a century of family mythology. And how very much more human and real that poor boy is than the swaggering student prince character we've allowed to haunt our ancestry all these years. Poor Hermann! So in love. So weak, wounded, hopeless. But, at the same time, a man who sacrificed everything for love. He would have happily frozen to death out in that garden as long as it meant he could be near his beloved. That must have done it for Lydia. That utter abandonment to passion.'

'And all that time Godwin was blind to what was going on,' Ben said. His appetite for breakfast had evaporated. Despite the passage of years, he was inexplicably troubled by the news. The girl in the old photograph looked at him appealingly from where she had been left the previous night, propped up on a chair next to the kitchen table. His eyes met hers. Perhaps he felt a trace of resentment towards her on his ancestor's behalf; that Godwin had loved so hopelessly, that he had offered himself so completely, even at the time when she was carrying another man's child. Ben felt the breeze of old Lydia's breath glance across his face. This was the closest he had come to her, and for a moment he thought he could sense the strange spell that had had them all bewitched. He looked at her ravishing face. Perhaps she was stealing his heart even now from beyond the grave, as skilfully as she had done to others when she still breathed the fresh mountain air. For all the years, Ben could feel her sting, though faint and somewhat sweetened by distance. The secrets of her heart, those explanations never given, the words she left unsaid, that tore men's hearts.

Ben took a group photo in the yard before leaving, using his neat little Sony digital, and then a couple more, promising to e-mail them the following day when he got back to his computer in London. Godwin would have liked that. How distant were the days of his black-out tent and the single sensitized plate, wet with carcinogenic chemicals. Perhaps it was those precious bottled substances that had poisoned his body as he laboured away in the stifling darkness, and led to his untimely death.

As Ben finally drove away from the gates of Thasofolia, and turned to glance one last time at the crowd of red-clothed people who were waving him off, with Elsa and Lydia standing in the middle, he could not hide from the smiling gaze of Godwin Tudor who beamed down on him from some celestial plane. Laughing at his own absurdity, Ben actually shifted in his seat and turned his head this way and that, as one does to avoid an invasive piece of foliage tickling the neck, all the while telling his persistent ancestor out loud to leave him be and get himself back to paradise. Old Godwin was pleased; they were all pleased, it seemed, Ben could almost see them – Edgar, Mag, Solouzos,

Panayiotis, Lambros – all those witnesses from the past, assembled *en masse* to see him off.

But, as he wound his way over the mountain pass, through those fateful gorges and across the rugged, boulder strewn peaks, his euphoria subsided into quiet contentment and he realized that it was he, of course, who was pleased in their place; he who had tickled himself with a desire for consummate finality, he who had come to Greece on a whim, to spin the thread a little further and tease out a resolution. Those characters he sensed so intimately – friends, as he now saw them – smiling and applauding him from their etheric dwelling-place in the sky, were nothing more than the projection of his own thoughts, creations of his imaginings, the personification of his own wish-fulfilment. But that was OK. Ben could live with that. It did not detract from what had happened to them. And it did not take away from the pleasant satisfaction of seeing their story's completion.

*

Ben flew out of Athens airport later the same day. It was only after he was settled in his seat, after they had taken to the sky, the seat-belt sign had pinged off and he had a plastic-cupped soft drink in the moulded circle of his fold-down table that he turned his attention to the buff-coloured A4 envelope Elsa had given him as he said goodbye. It was a gift, she had whispered in his ear with a kiss, something for him to pass on to his children, in the hope that it might induce them to come back to Thasofolia, and their children after them, as Ben himself had come, with blessings in his wake. He now looked inside and saw that it contained another envelope, much smaller and browned with age. The address on it was written in the hand that had now become so familiar to Ben, the same immaculately neat, sloping letters, though somewhat more shaky, less well formed. It was a letter from him to her.

Moreton Hall
Hindhead
Surrey

12th April 1896

My dearest Lydia

I do not wish to disturb your thoughts with sad tidings, and yet to do otherwise than write to you at this time with an honest heart would give cause for you to reproach me in years to come, years when you will live and breathe the warm air while I rest beneath the turf, and the very thought of such reproach grieves my heavy heart as it prepares to beat its last. For I am fading, and henceforth you will not hear word of this frail shell whom once you graced with friendship, except, perhaps, through another's report or distant memory.

Whether our encounter in this life has brought me more joy than pain is a question that once I asked myself, but now see as a thing of no concern. My love for you is not to be judged by degrees of pleasure. It is not of the world of matter, to be placed on the scale or weighed in the balance. Our flesh, the deeds we commit and the things we create may be subject to the measure, but not a love like this. Joy and pain are but the distant resonance, while my love for you is the present song; they are but the patterns of dust caught on the edge of the morning light, while my love is the blazing sun that illuminates them. My love abides, my love existed before we met, and my love will continue as the centuries roll by, when we and our story are shades forgotten. But my love must perforce now return to its cave, to its sleeping state, whence it emerged that morning long ago by the water's edge, when our eyes met and the spirit took wing.

And so farewell in this life, most beautiful of beings, song of my soul, my sunlight, my love. Do not judge me by the deeds of my body, which is frail, finite and blemished. Remember me instead as the soul of all that you cherish, for that I truly aspire to be, and I shall live and shine with you perpetually, in an everlasting embrace.

Your devoted friend
Godwin Tudor

THE END

Author's Note

This book sprang out of my profound affection for Greece, cultivated over years of close familiarity. I have always had a particular love for the inland countryside there – often neglected by modern visitors – and share this passion with travellers and artists from former eras, especially the nineteenth century. It is this particular period of Greece's exotic and turbulent history that has consistently held a fascination for me.

Three themes connected to this period – each of which underpins the structure of this novel – are outlined below.

1. *Greece – a traveller's destination, then and now*

Zorba the Greek has a lot to answer for. The modern-day perception of Greece as a holiday destination where tanned, island-hopping tourists can encounter exuberant moustached rogues, where they can meander idly down sea-fronts peppered with picturesque cafés, where they can watch the sun set against whitewashed windmills to the tinkling accompaniment of bouzoukis, has overridden almost every other image of the country in popular thinking. In the nineteenth century, of course, Western European attitudes towards Greece were very different. There was little or no interest in beaches, lying undressed in the sun or nibbling tomato and feta salads at seaside tavernas. Instead, Greece was seen as a destination for scholars and intrepid Romantics. Having been under Turkish rule for so long, Greece was thought to possess a flavour of the Levant, brimming with spice, colour and adventure. The poetry and exploits of Byron (together with other artistic wild cards) had persuaded many of Greece's potential for voluptuous romance, while it also still offered an enticingly dangerous *frisson*. It was a frontier state, at the fringe of civilization, and the risk of mishap was part of the attraction. There was a genuine danger of brigands, as exemplified by the celebrated Dilessi murders of eighteen seventy, and in several published travellers' diaries of the time there is an almost self-conscious expectation that a real brush with rural savagery might be waiting on the other side of every rocky headland. Many of the accounts are breathlessly romanticized and exaggerated. They aspired to tap the popularity of Edmond About's much-loved eighteen fifty six novel about a brigand kidnapping, *Le Roi des montagnes*. Perilous mountains, raging rivers and gloomy forests were more akin to the spirit of the times than the sun-soaked seascapes so popular today. The rugged wildness of Greece's interior landscape was far more fascinating to the nineteenth-century traveller.

But, above all, the pre-eminence of classicism – then the cornerstone of western learning – ensured that all nineteenth- century visitors, whether scholarly or just curious – would spend a major portion of their time in Greece investigating, satisfying and recording their impressions of the ancient ruins. The journal, the notebook and the sketchbook were their essential companions. Armed with their Murray guidebooks and their classical texts, these were the package tourists of the day, into whose ranks Godwin Tudor rather reluctantly fits, espousing himself, much to his father's dismay, to 'the gentlemanly pursuit of knowledge'.

2. *Greece and power politics*

The particular timing of this story is important, not just because of the budding tourist industry, but because Greece was a flashpoint of Great Power politics at the time. Its independence from Turkey, sealed in eighteen thirty two, was an internationally momentous event, but particularly significant for Britain because it marked the establishment of a close ally at the gateway to the Orient – this in the face of an imminent collapse of Turkey's Ottoman Empire and the regional instability that would inevitably derive therefrom. Cultural divisions in the area (Muslim vs. Christian, Slav vs. Latin, Orthodox vs. Roman Catholic) were to become the issues thrashed out in the Balkans over the next half-century. Greece, because of its massive coastline and ports, its strategic proximity to Turkey and its special place in the hearts of all educated westerners, was central in territorial negotiations between the major powers, particularly Britain, France and Russia. Greece and Britain had been firm allies – politically, dynastically and culturally – since Independence, but the new nation's hunger to establish a powerful defence against Turkey and to wreak vengeance after centuries of oppression, was, by the late eighteen sixties, inclining her politicians to side with whichever Great Power supported her grandiose ambitions. The spectre of Russian influence in the region was terrifying indeed for Gladstone's government in London. Godwin Tudor's inadvertent involvement in an episode that threatened to tip the balance of Greece's allegiance is illustrative of just how fragile Britain's stake in the Eastern Mediterranean had become.

3. *Images of God, nature and man – the confusion of a young Victorian*

Godwin's theological doubts, combined with his interest in science, are allied to his naturally liberal inclinations, and this was something that became increasingly prevalent amongst educated Victorians as the late nineteenth century progressed. Many found themselves in contradiction with the iron edicts of traditional Anglicanism, especially if those edicts could not keep pace with almost daily scientific discoveries regarding the origin of life, the constituents of matter and the structure of the universe. Those who demanded theological re-evaluation and a fresh perspective on the ultimate Godhead sometimes espoused themselves to the fashion for supernatural enquiry (seances and ghost watching); others looked to secularist societies and flirted with social liberalism. Godwin can be seen as belonging to this enquiring, politically and philosophically progressive sector, but he is hampered by his resolutely Establishment family background. This personal dilemma finds expression at Thasofolia because Edgar Brooke, in a sense, replaces his father, sharing and articulating Godwin's own visionary aspirations, and thus becomes something of a role model for the young Englishman – in a way that Sir Harold Tudor, for all his stern efficiency, had failed to embody. Having consciously defied his father's intractable values, Godwin is doubly wounded by having to betray Edgar's trust.

GENTLEMEN & PLAYERS
Joanne Harris

'WILDLY ENTERTAINING . . . A LITERARY GOBSTOPPER
WITH AN ANISEED HEART'
Independent on Sunday

At St Oswald's, an old and long-established boys'
grammar school in the north of England, a new year has
just begun. For the staff and boys of the School, a wind of
unwelcome change is blowing. Suits, paperwork and
Information Technology rule the world; and Roy Straitley,
Latin master, eccentric, and veteran of St Oswald's, is finally –
reluctantly – contemplating retirement. But beneath the little
rivalries, petty disputes and everyday crises of the school, a
darker undercurrent stirs. And a bitter grudge, hidden and
carefully nurtured for thirteen years, is about to erupt.

'CONSTANTLY SURPRISING AND WICKEDLY FUN'
The Washington Post

' A CLEVER STORY OF OBSESSION AND REVENGE...MS
HARRIS HAS SCORED ANOTHER SUCCESS'
Sunday Telegraph

9780552770026

BLACK SWAN

RANDOM ACTS OF HEROIC LOVE
Danny Scheinmann

'TENDER AND INSIGHTFUL'
Observer

1992: Leo Deakin wakes in a mysterious South American
hospital. His girlfriend Eleni is dead. Dazed and bruised,
Leo's only certainty is that he is somehow responsible for
her death. Sapped of all passion and drive, he feels his
life is over. But Leo is about to discover something that
will change his fate for ever.

1917: Moritz Daniecki has survived fighting in the Great
War. But at what cost? Abandoned in the Siberian wilderness,
he is determined to return to his beloved Lotte, the memory
of whose single kiss has sustained him throughout the war.
What lies before him is a terrifying journey over the
Russian Steppes. If he ever makes it,
will she still be waiting?

9780552774222

BLACK SWAN

THE BOOK THIEF
Markus Zusak

'A NOVEL OF BREATH-TAKING SCOPE, MASTERFULLY TOLD'
Guardian

HERE IS A SMALL FACT

YOU ARE GOING TO DIE

1939. Nazi Germany. The country is holding its breath. Death
has never been busier.

Liesel, a nine-year-old girl, is living with a foster family
on Himmel Street. Her parents have been taken away
to a concentration camp. Liesel steals books. This is her
story and the story of the inhabitants of her street
when the bombs begin to fall.

SOME IMPORTANT INFORMATION
THIS NOVEL IS NARRATED BY DEATH

It's a small story, about:

a girl

an accordionist

some fanatical Germans

a Jewish fist fighter

and quite a lot of thievery.

ANOTHER THING YOU SHOULD KNOW DEATH
WILL VISIT THE BOOK THIEF THREE TIMES

'BRILLIANT AND HUGELY AMBITIOUS'
New York Times

'EXTRAORDINARY, RESONANT, BEAUTIFUL AND ANGRY'
Sunday Telegraph

9780552773898

BLACK SWAN

THE CRIMSON PORTRAIT
Jody Shields

'ANYONE WHO LOVED SEBASTIAN FAULKS'
BIRDSONG WILL ENJOY THIS'
Marie Claire

Spring 1915. On a sprawling country estate not far
from London a young woman mourns her husband,
fallen on a distant battlefield . . .

The eerie stillness in which she grieves is shattered as
her home is transformed into a bustling military hospital.
Disturbed by the intrusion of the suffering soldiers, the
increasingly fragile widow finds unexpected solace in the
company of a wounded officer whose mutilated face,
concealed by bandages, she cannot see. And then their
affair takes an unexpected turn. Fate presents the woman
with an opportunity: to remake her lover – with the
unwitting help of a visionary surgeon and a woman
artist – in the image of her lost husband . . .

Inspired by the extraordinary collaboration between
surgeons and artists in the treatment of the wounded
during the First World War, *The Crimson Portrait* is a
compelling read – as stylish and darkly erotic as Jody
Shields' bestselling début *The Fig Eater*.

'AS FULL OF EMOTIONAL DETAIL
AS THE ENGLISH PATIENT'
Los Angeles Times

'COMPELLING . . . EXQUISITELY WRITTEN . . .
WITHOUT A FALSE LINE'
Washington Post

'DARK AND ATMOSPHERIC . . . WONDERFULLY
DESCRIPTIVE AND POETIC'
USA Today

9780552999762

BLACK SWAN